AMERICAN
FICTION

AMERICAN FICTION
VOLUME 13

the best unpublished stories by new
and emerging writers

Bruce Pratt, Editor
Michael White, Finalist Judge

Cover and interior design by John Wander

The publication of *American Fiction* Volume 13 is made possible by the generous support of The McKnight Foundation, the Dawson Family Endowment, the Lake Region Arts Council, Northern Lights Library Network, and other generous contributors to New Rivers Press.

For copyright permission, please contact Frederick T. Courtright at 570-839-7477 or permdude@eclipse.net.

New Rivers Press is a nonprofit literary press associated with Minnesota State University Moorhead.

Alan Davis, Co-Director and Senior Editor
Suzzanne Kelley, Co-Director and Managing Editor
Wayne Gudmundson, Consultant
Allen Sheets, Art Director
Thom Tammaro, Poetry Editor
Kevin Carollo, MVP Poetry Coordinator

Publishing Interns:
David Binkard, Katelin Hansen, Jan Hough, Kjersti Maday, Richard N. Natale, Emily Nelson, Joe Schneider, Daniel A. Shudlick, Lauren Stanislawski, Michele F. Valenti

The *American Fiction* Volume 13 Book Team:
Danya Adair, Katelin Hansen, Kelly Nerby

Printed in the USA
New Rivers Press books are distributed by Consortium Book Sales and Distribution.

New Rivers Press
c/o MSUM
1104 7th Avenue South
Moorhead, MN 56563
www.newriverspress.com

CONTENTS

Preface
Bruce Pratt
Introduction
Michael White

HAND PICKED

Winter Burial *19*
John Zdrazil
1st Prize

Hearts like Lemons in Fists of Dew *31*
Dallas Woodburn
2nd Prize

Ollie's Back *49*
Lynn Sloan
3rd Prize

What to Take in Case of Fire *65*
Lee Hope
Honorable Mention

LIFE CHANGES

Glass Frog *85*
Jill Birdsall

Cages *95*
Steven Ostrowski

You Call Me Ugly? *109*
Yanshuo Zhang

Brush Strokes *121*
Madeline Wise

WIDE OPEN

The Human Nature *137*
Marguerite Del Giudice

Everything Shining *143*
Leigh Camacho Rourks

Green Hills *157*
Terry Ruud

High Life *171*
Timothy Zila

A Blind Horse *183*
Robin Mullet

FINDING HOME

Circus *191*
Julia Lichtblau

The Story of Cha Cha McGee *207*
Beth Mayer

Things You Know But Would Rather Not *227*
Patricia Ann McNair

The Polish Girl *245*
Molly Power

SPIRITUAL CLOSURE

Falling Through Chairs.. *261*
Carol Cooley
The Father *275*
Mathieu Cailler
The Hand of God *289*
Libby Cudmore

CONTRIBUTORS
ABOUT NEW RIVERS PRESS

PREFACE
BRUCE PRATT

This is my inaugural year as editor of this anthology. After two years as an assistant editor, and mindful of the diligence of my predecessors, I challenged myself to read every submission, including those that our screeners had not recommended. I finished or read well into each story, before assigning it to either the "no" or "maybe" file.

After my first readings, there were roughly sixty stories in the "maybe" file. I set those aside for a few weeks, so that when I began my final readings I would rediscover what it was about them that engaged me. I thought often during this process of Eavan Boland's paraphrase of William Trevor's sage advice to writers: "Sometimes when you are stuck with a story put it away as a writer until you can pick it back up as a reader." This wisdom, I discovered, works for editors, too.

Each time I decided that a story was not right for our anthology, I was pestered by the ineluctable reality that my own prejudices, despite my best efforts to the contrary, had informed that decision. Time and time again I was drawn to Russell Bank's introduction to the 2004 edition of Frank O'Connor's *The Lonely Voice*, where he wrote: "For one thing, the short story is the most recent invented literary form and is still, clearly, in the process of being invented." Therein lies the rub. There is no clear definition of what constitutes a short story — it is an evolving form — and many of this year's submissions reflected that reality.

I was also aware that all of us who submit to literary publications and contests have a story of an oft-rejected piece that found its rightful place in a respected journal or won a prize. That will be the case for many of the stories I did not send on to the finalist judge.

The criteria I used in making my final decisions were simple:

The piece had to read and feel like a self-contained story. Many submissions, especially the longer ones, read like the first chapter or chapters of a novel, and lacked the quick character revelations and reader engagement that are the lynchpins of great short fiction.

I did not select stories set, for no apparent reason, in a foreign country, whose prose was peppered with italicized words in European or Asian tongues, or were laced with lengthy depictions of setting, and read like travelogue rather than fiction. Hemingway's "Hills like White Elephants" succeeds not because it is set in Spain, but because the reader becomes invested in the characters, just as *The Quiet American* is not a novel about Southeast Asia, but rather a book that probes human frailties in the shadow of war and political intrigue.

I eschewed stories that relied on vocabulary or histrionic language alone to sustain them. Elegant and vibrant prose, rich nuanced language that mines and extols the vast pandemonium and possibilities of the English language, intrigue and excite me, but only when they compliment and complement the story.

I rejected those stories that read like outlines for screenplays — not because they were experimental or visual in nature — but because their expository prose read like stage directions.

Finally, I chose the stories I felt were populated with engaging characters in compelling situations, resisted predictable endings but were not so vague or abrupt as to seem unfinished. In short, stories that even after I'd read them several times, left me thinking.

Our finalist judge, Michael C. White, once told a group of MFA students, "You'll know you're a writer when you've collected enough rejections to sink a small boat." I have saved every rejection slip and letter I have received and I am getting there, because, as is the case with most writers, that collection dwarfs my acceptance file. Tasked with making such yes or no decisions myself, I have developed an ever-greater respect for editors and screeners. It's the kind of work that keeps you awake at night.

It was an honor to read so many excellent submissions, and a humbling, agonizing experience to decide which would be included in the anthology. I cannot imagine the difficulty the judge had in reaching his final decisions on prizes and honorable mentions.

Bruce Pratt

INTRODUCTION
MICHAEL WHITE

2013 American Fiction Awards

First Place: "Winter Burial," John Zdrazil
Second Place: "Hearts like Lemons in Fists of Dew," Dallas Woodburn
Third Place: "Ollie's Back," Lynn Sloan
Honorable Mention: "What to Take in Case of Fire," Lee Hope

As with any fiction contest, the winning entries speak as much if not more about the judge — his or her literary biases, blind spots, tendencies, and preferences — than they do about the quality of the stories themselves. To speak of absolute qualities or the inherent strengths residing in the stories themselves is artificial. Contests are all about what sorts of things — style, content, and theme — that the judge likes or dislikes or thinks is important or unimportant. This isn't to say that all of the stories in this collection, and in particular, the wonderful stories that I've chosen don't have brilliance in them. They do, and often in abundance. But the brilliance they have is just the sort that dazzles me, the judge. Another judge would, and with legitimacy, probably have picked other stories. So before I state which stories I selected and why, I should tell you the sorts of stories that do dazzle me.

First, I like stories that actually *tell me a story*. That may seem to be obvious or simplistic, but having read and judged tens of thousands of supposed stories over the years, that's not always the case. Many stories are not stories at all; rather they are clever stages for which to showcase the writer's linguistic talent, audacity, sense of irony, complex philosophy, political ideology, or his homage to his favorite author. Of course, any good story will highlight all of the preceding things, but the notion of "story" — that complex movement of character in conflict over time — for me, should come first, and everything must be subordinate to that. And I am not, of course, talking about simple plot — that is, what happens and when. Story, on the other hand, includes plot but it also includes the crucial elements of character, conflict, pacing, language, and movement (especially of character). When I finish a story, as Raymond Carver once alluded to, I like to be able to retain it in my memory, so that I could retell its story outline to a friend and to have that person say, "Ah, that's really interesting." Second, I love prose — original or modest, quirky or conventional, Joycean or Hemingwayesque — but as with the other fictional elements the prose should not be a separate "show," a dazzling pyrotechnical display of skill. It should give nuance to character, make situation and setting more important, or deepen my knowledge or appreciation of the inner workings of the story. Prose that gets in the way and tries to highlight itself is like being on a date with a woman who won't stop looking at herself in the mirror. It becomes distracting. Third, I like characters for whom I can feel something — admiration is good, but so, too, is curiosity, empathy, interest in, or even animosity toward. What I don't want to feel is simply pity, and when I read a story that plays just on my pity or, equally, my revulsion for a character, then I feel the writer is somehow trying to manipulate me. Fourth, I like narrators that I can identify with, even if they are nothing like me. Narrators that I can learn from or want to get to know. Finally, and in some ways most importantly, in a story I want something to matter — to the characters in the story and thus to me. Too many authors don't want to take the risk of having their stories, and their characters' stories, "mean" something, to be of significance. There is this sense that meaning and significance aren't hip and are to be eschewed at all costs. I love irony and subtlety, but irony and subtlety have to be balanced with something that is really and truly desired and felt and wanted in the story. Not moral certainty, but emotional striving by characters. They want something dearly and by wanting it, we the reader want it, too. Having thus laid out the sort of stories I tend to like, I must admit every really good story will deviate from some or most of the above "requirements," but they will do something so stunningly beautiful, so original, or so compelling that they change my mind and win me over completely in spite of myself.

Now, having listed my own personal biases, let me say that the three stories I selected have some or all of my requirements for a great story. The story I chose for First Prize, "Winter Burial," was the most quiet but also the most self-confident of all those I read. In a few simple pages it assuredly created a world, a man who had suffered loss, and a voice that I wanted to continue to hear long after the ending. The story, which had obvious affinities to the TV series *Six Feet Under*, nonetheless was original and powerful and unrelentingly honest. The feelings that the undertaker had for his workers and for his dead friend were both nuanced and overwhelming. He won my empathy because he never asked for it. His voice was pure and powerful. The same could be said for my Second Prize selection, "Hearts like Lemons in Fists of Dew." In this story a woman returns to her childhood home after having been gone for some time. Her father is dying, and her mother tries to think of what life will be like after he passes. The narrator not only lives in this present moment but in the past with the disappearance of a beloved childhood friend. Coming home ignites both past and present in the narrator, and the author skillfully weaves both stories through memory and through the delightful use of the metaphor of fog, which tends to place the mystery of past and present in a shroud. Finally, in the Third Prize story, "Ollie's Back," the author breaks almost all of my stated requirements for a good story. However, it succeeds, and wonderfully so, by making what's going on in the characters' lives important to them. The main character, and his now imprisoned lover, had a dream of starting a restaurant. The dream is so vivid and real and compelling — as is the food: "Pee Dee chicken bog, chainey briar, and peach pie with my Aunt Ida's caramel sauce" — that you can literally taste the characters' passions and obsessions and goals for their future. While the passions are perhaps small, they are nonetheless real and vivid and important for Ollie and his friends. These three works, in their various ways, made me appreciate what "story" is and why I read — to enter into the meaningful lives of others and to partake of their stories.

Michael White

HAND PICKED

WINTER BURIAL

JOHN ZDRAZIL

I had been trying for a couple of hours to make Dwayne's face and hands look right when my secretary knocked on the prep room door. "I turned the chapel lights off and locked the front door," she said, without stepping inside. "Are you all right?"

"Would you take a look, please?" She walked in and stood next to me, taking her time. "He looks gray," was what I said, but it was more than that.

She assured me he looked peaceful, like she always does when we get a difficult case. "And if he was here... I mean, if he was *here*, he'd tell you to quit fussing and call you names that I will not repeat. He'd say to take off those silly gloves and grab your ice fishing gear and head for the lake." She stood a moment longer beside me, then stepped out of the room, which suddenly felt colder. I was about to explain for the umpteenth time that I owned no ice fishing gear when it hit me again that Dwayne, a sheet covering him from the waist down, would never listen to that excuse again.

Reappearing in the doorway, she held my coat by the collar, like a cat, shaking it at me like Dwayne used to do and bellowing in his tone of voice, "There's nothing more to be done here, Undertaker!" Her face held Dwayne's let's-get-you-out-of-here stare for a moment, then it softened to the look I've seen her give people wandering around the funeral home during visitations, looking for a Kleenex box or something to hold them up.

"Phones are transferred to the answering service. You really should go home..." She hung my coat on the open door. "Or somewhere."

Dwayne's right hand covered his left, his right thumb tucked in the crook between his left thumb and forefinger. *You and your clients both dress alike and hold your hands the same way*, he used to tease. *The only difference being that you're vertical.* I covered his cold hands with a gloved one of mine; my heart had been imploding all day, chamber by chamber. I would bury him — his body — the day after next. I heard the back door open and shut, heard her try the knob.

I gingerly tried to close the left side of Dwayne's lips, the remnant of a gap where an emergency room tube had been. It gave the impression that Death had set the hook and reeled him in. "You know I don't have any ice fishing gear," I sighed.

•   •   •

Ellen would be home late. She's volunteering at the community theater this week, ushering, working concessions, cleaning up backstage after each performance. Since fall, she's taken on a Brownie troop, signed up for a couple of Community Education classes, and I think she's even helping an altar guild at another church, different than the one where we sit next to each other most Sundays. *Anything to keep busy*, I overheard her tell a friend on the phone, loudly enough so I could hear.

I've been working late as much as possible. Things at the funeral home have never been so close to being in compliance. Things at the house are orderly;

neither of us is there much, and when we are, one of us is always keeping things tidy.

• • •

I pulled the sheet up to Dwayne's neck, went downstairs to the selection room and again ran a cloth over his casket. I drove the hearse through the C-store's car wash, picked up a mini-pizza and a pack of cheap cigars, then headed for the graveyard where Runeberg Lutheran used to stand.

I figured that Butch, my gravedigger, would be thawing the gravesite. The frost line has been murder this year, he's said. All this freezing and thawing and freezing and thawing has driven it a foot deeper than usual. Not like when the ground freezes once, hard, and snow insulates it. I suppose I could have gone out to Dwayne's fish house, which sat empty on the lake. But I figured it'd be better to stand around Butch's fire.

• • •

When I first started working in this town, five years before I bought the funeral home, almost every service from November until February ended at church. Then we'd drive the casket out to the small building in the back of one of the bigger cemeteries in the county, where we'd store it until burial in the spring. One April I buried twenty-five.

During arrangements these days, I gently push winter burials. It may cost an additional hundred dollars to have a winter grave dug, but it's better than driving past those rickety things they call mausoleums, thinking that the body of someone you love is in a place that's less secure or dignified than most people's garden sheds. The families sit in the funeral home's lounge, their loved one's body just yards away behind a locked door, a roomful of caskets one floor below. I want to tell them, *It's best just to get it over with*. What I say is *Peace of mind and Closure.*

I actually prayed that Dwayne's family would agree to winter burial. If they were hesitant, I would've offered to pay the extra myself. I couldn't endure the thought of abandoning Dwayne out there until the ground warmed. I even hate to leave his body alone in the funeral home overnight. I've slept on the chapel couch before, sometimes hoping Ellen would ask me the next morning where I'd been.

The irony is, I really hate standing out in the cold for committal services. But it's preferable to stashing good caskets in those little buildings, better than having to wonder what the ground's going to be like come spring. Our town cemetery is practically a slough: schedule burials too early in March, the graves fill with snowmelt. I've called the vault men when we're heading their way, so they can pull a pump out of the hole. I don't want any family to see a vault practically floating when we arrive. We've had to use dummy set-ups just off the graveyard road, so the family doesn't see the swimming pool they're committing their loved ones to. I tell them about *Soft ground around the grave* and *Cemetery liability.* With a winter burial, the ground is stable, at least.

●　●　●

I pulled onto the gravel leading to the graveyard, which sat on a hill surrounded in the summers by a faithful rotation of wheat, soybeans, and corn. Butch's fire illuminated the area, making it look like Runeberg Lutheran was burning for a fourth time. A full moon hung low, its yellow baby fat slowing its rise above the January earth. To thaw the ground, Butch hauls out scrap lumber and dry logs the night before he digs, then piles them and sets them on fire inside a three-foot high frame he's made out of roofing metal and a couple of old stock tanks. He'll stay out at a gravesite long enough for the wood to settle, for maximum ground coverage, then he'll stoke the fire again and cover it with another piece of metal. Before he goes to the shop the following morning, he'll stoke it again. The fire itself doesn't heat the ground, the coals do, he says. Dwayne and I used to join him on nights like tonight.

I drove through the cemetery gates — "18" in wrought-iron script on the left post, "73" on the right, the year of the first burial. The flames were jumping high enough for Butch to hide behind. Usually, just as I open the door, Butch yells, *Gerald!* — never pronouncing the G like a J — *How the hell are ya?* at a volume I always tell him could wake the dead, to which he hollers, *None that I've ever covered up!* It's the same volume his uncle used on the rare occasion I'd have to get on his case for not having a grave dug up to his normally high standards.

I inherited Butch's uncle and a half-dozen other gravediggers from the guy I bought out; Butch's uncle was the only dependable one. The rest were untrustworthy: They'd nick gravestones with their equipment or not heed the boundary flags cemetery sextons would plant for them. Three of them dug graves for specific church cemeteries because a long-suffering wife hoped that even superficial involvement with the church was better than nothing. Too many pastors and church councils overpaid those skill-less, unmotivated louses and didn't regret it enough to let them go.

The day I fired Fosston, the gravedigger at this very cemetery, a widow stepped forward to pull a flower from the casket spray. Despite the vault company's best efforts to cover for his drunken backhoe work, the edge nearly gave way. The vault man had to pull Fosston away from his bottle in order to get the lowering device ready before the church service ended. I made what apologies and offers I could to the rattled widow and her fuming children, hoping to stay out of court. I watched Fosston stumble out of the church kitchen door after finishing off the funeral lunch leftovers. After he'd filled in that grave, I told him what happened and assured him the vault company could back every word I'd said; I doubled his check and swore he'd never get a call from me again.

Butch didn't say anything until I was fireside. "How the hell are you holding up?" he asked, the steam from his breath disappearing as it hit the heat from the flames.

"Not bad." I forced a chuckle. I hadn't been able to finish the pizza on the drive out; I offered it to him.

Normally, he'd make fun of me for something like that; he started to say something, then pulled up short. There was an awkward silence, like when a family is seated for arrangements and I see this pleading look in their eyes, as if maybe I have good news, that maybe there had been a misunderstanding.

"When's the last time this place had a church on it?"

The Runeberg Cemetery was like most in the countryside, having survived a series of churches burned down and rebuilt alongside it until there weren't enough parishioners to fight what lightning or bad wiring did every twenty-odd years. "Eighty-one. Six years after I got here." I stared into the fire. "You want a smoke?"

The memory brought a smile to his stubbled face. "Ninth-grade-a-rillos?"

"Yeah," I laughed. "Kiddy Smokes." Dwayne called them Trainers.

● ● ●

One summer, after the funeral home was mine, my brother sent Dave, his fifteen-year-old, to spend a month with Ellen and me. The kid was on the fringes of trouble at that time, and I think his parents hoped that a few weeks of polishing caskets and learning how to wash cars while wearing a suit might do something for him.

My brother never said as much, but I wonder if he thought the experience would convince Ellen and me against considering having kids. Despite the relative calm in our household at that time, that decision had already been made.

The second day the kid was here I confiscated fifteen packs of cheap, sugary cigars he'd shoplifted and stashed in his suitcase. Instead of throwing them away, Butch and I and Dwayne smoked them graveside all summer, after Butch was done digging. We always made sure that Butch had enough change for a couple bottles of whatever obnoxious flavor of schnapps was on clearance at the municipal. That was a great summer: The funeral home was busy, the bugs weren't bad until August, and I got to spend many sunsets with two good friends.

When Dave came, Ellen and I hadn't been fighting for a few months, but while he was here, that peace deteriorated. Cycles of quiet and volatility have been the hallmark of our married life, with each subsequent descent from relative tranquility more painful and divisive than its predecessor. I hoped, for Dave's sake, that there might be some relief in knowing that our fighting wasn't about him. Left to his own devices on the evenings I didn't need help, he quickly found the wrong crowd in this small town and left here none the better.

About the only things in the funeral business in which Dave took any interest were the shelves that held the boxes of unclaimed cremated remains. I found him staring at them one day as I was passing by the closet where they were stored. "What are these?" he asked. I watched water well up in his eyes during my explanation. Later that day, I overheard him talking to the secretary, about how they had gotten there, why family members hadn't picked them up. I stood outside the office, knowing I had interrupted a deep discussion: She had stopped typing and turned her chair to face him.

The next couple of days we had no calls, and I found him at the closet again, first arranging the containers by date of death, then alphabetically. After he went back home, I found them neatly organized by the age the person was at the time of death. He had hand-written a catalogue of them by name, date of death, and position on the shelves. He had dated the bottom of the page and signed his name.

I gave Butch a smoke, which he stuck in his mouth and pretended to try to light by sticking his face into the flames. He's always known how to get a laugh out of us. He then pulled a glowing twig out of the fire and offered it to me.

"This new section of the cemetery," Butch puffed, "will be easy to come in on with the hearse. Not a lot of stones you hafta walk around or lift over." Butch is twenty years my junior, but his accent makes him sound like an old-timer from the Swedish Lutheran Church.

Sometimes I close my eyes when he's talking, just to listen to his brogue, its rises and falls gentle as the farmland in the north end of my territory. In the older sections of a cemetery, the stones are either those old-style white plates or they're huge. Granite's gotten so expensive in the last fifteen years, not many can afford stones bigger than a 30 x 24 x 6. Dwayne's grave was virtually in the prairie.

"He was pretty young, wasn't he?"

"Fifty-seven."

"Hadn't bought plots?"

"Until today. We'd talked about where he wanted to be buried, way back. His family were among the original members here. But he didn't see any rush, and I wasn't going to force the issue."

"Probably didn't want to think about it."

I nodded, not wanting to think about it either.

"That Dwayne was a pretty good friend, wasn't he?"

Even after a bump or two, Butch had a politeness about him none of the other area gravediggers could've mustered with a year of charm school. He's what I call a rough gentleman.

"I'm going to miss him."

Butch pulled a bottle from his coat pocket and handed it to me. Brandy. "Good stuff," he said. "For you." He realized how bad this was. I took three swigs before handing it back.

When my marriage started to get ugly, the friends who had been ours began dividing themselves; Ellen walked away with the majority. Someday, I suppose, lawyers will divide up what remains between us.

Dwayne was one of the few friends who stayed with me. He's rolled with the difficulties of being friends of the small town mortician — with my own idiosyncrasies, as well. If we'd planned to go fishing and then I got a call, he'd wait around until I was done, and then we'd take off. *Fishing for an hour is better than not fishing at all*, he'd say as I was washing up. If a family stopped in at 4:58 and wanted to prearrange services or check on a military marker that hadn't been delivered, he'd wait for me at the bar before ordering.

When the heart attack took him, the list of people I call friends was practically cut in half. Now there's just Butch, really. There may be others, but none I can really count on.

● ● ●

Butch took a swallow, then another before handing me the bottle, reminding me that Dwayne had said, *Make sure mine is deep. I don't want any hillbilly Frankenstein from the southwest part of the county trying anything funny with my corpse.* It was one of the few dead jokes I ever laughed at.

The *was*es of my life blew through my mind. I inched toward the fire, attempting to keep out a cold inside me that no parka could deter.

"Funeral's at ten?"

"Ten."

"So, you'll be out here eleven-thirty?"

"Depends on how long Pastor Dale goes."

"I talked to the boss, told him you'd probably want this one filled in immediately. I'll be at the funeral, then I'll just stay out here."

● ● ●

When I was just out of school, I worked for a funeral director with an uncanny sense about people. During arrangements, I used to watch him read families, and then he'd suggest something to them — little things, like corsages or hymns or ways to word the obituary. Without fail, the family members would ' say something like, *I was wondering about that.* Butch, in his coarse way, had me figured out. My voice cracked as I thanked him.

"Vault guy'll be ready by eleven?"

"At the latest."

"You want me to duck out of the service early, come out here — just in case?"

I shook my head. "They're always…" I had to take a breath. "I'm not going back to church after the committal; I'll be here until it's over."

"Dwayne's wife ask you to pallbear?" The bottle was half empty, and my ears were starting to feel warm.

"She asked, but I told her I'd better not."

● ● ●

I was a casketbearer at Butch's uncle's funeral. I even seated myself in the pew with the others, instead of sorting sympathy cards and lining up vehicles. I don't think I've sat through an entire funeral service since. Butch had dug the grave using his uncle's backhoe, but told me he'd fill it using nothing but a shovel. After the crowd left the cemetery, I took off my jacket and helped. Only after we had packed as much as we could did he fire up the backhoe and tamp down the gash.

The only other time we've ever used shovels was when a family asked if they could fill in the grave themselves. While I was thinking about getting sued and potential disaster and someone having a nervous breakdown graveside, I was saying *I think we can arrange that, but allow me to speak to the man who digs the graves and the vault company and, of course, the cemetery.* My hands were shaking as they drove away from the funeral home, and all the calm I faked during arrangements escaped in a tantrum I threw in front of Butch at the graveyard. His eldest daughter was in the truck as he was scoping out the grave, even before the sexton marked it for him. After I'd flown off the handle about the bind the family had put me in and said things that should never be said in the presence of children, I profusely apologized to both of them. After blubbering my way through that, I handed his girl a twenty so she could take her mom and dad and sister out for ice cream sometime. Butch accepted my apology, assuring me that the family's request would be no problem — that he'd bring extra shovels, that he'd take care of it.

After the committal, as I watched the family fill the grave, I noticed that there were no heavy clunks as the dirt hit. Butch was standing by his truck, and I wandered toward him. As I was going to comment on what I wasn't hearing, I saw a homemade sieve made of door screen resting on a pile of rocks and pebbles weighing down the back end of his truck. I could tell he'd just made the sieve, because the one-by-twos which composed its frame were not weathered or aged: That's the kind of man Butch is.

• • •

After talking about the frostline and the summer of cigars, I said, "I don't think Ellen is going to take off work for the funeral." Butch's cough sounded fake, and he continued to stare at the fire, trying to glance at his watch without making it obvious.

After a thick silence, Butch asked if I wouldn't mind staying at the grave for awhile. One of his daughters had a basketball game in town. He had read me again.

"You should see her, Gerald," he explained, pronouncing the G properly, "she's all elbows out there — a gangly seventh grader with no dribbling ability whatsoever." He laughed. "Grew so damn fast that she doesn't know what to do with all that *length*. I should get there before the third quarter, because that's when she usually fouls out. Defensive specialist, you know." I said I could stick around.

He gave me a pair of work gloves so I could shake down the logs and get the coal bed established. "Fill it with logs, then, and the lid on top, if you would, please." I nodded, and he handed me the bottle. Before he walked to his truck, I think he said something about stopping in at the visitation before coming back out to dig. He might have asked a question, too, but I didn't catch it.

When Butch pulled onto the gravel road, the flames were just below the rim of the frame, and I thought I heard Dwayne's voice telling me, *It'd be best just to get it over with.*

HEARTS LIKE LEMONS IN FISTS OF DEW
DALLAS WOODBURN

June in Ventura is a gloomy month. The fog creeps in from the ocean and stretches its fingers inland, settling in the creases of the hills, the spaces between office buildings, the narrow yards of houses. Cars maneuver slowly down Foothill Road, their headlights switched on even in the middle of the afternoon. The fog seeps down Main Street, covering the shops and restaurants so only the heads of the palm trees and the arching buttresses of the movie theater stretch above it, peering over the fog like tall people peer over a crowd. At Poinsettia Elementary School, in these last days before summer, recess becomes a giant game of hide-and-seek, children slinking through the fog-covered soccer fields, refusing to come back inside when the bell rings. The fog sinks down over the lemon orchards like a thick blanket, catching in the branches of trees and wrapping the small, unripened lemons in fists of dew.

A heavy midmorning lethargy persists throughout the day. But at night, the fog lifts, and people go outside in their backyards and driveways to gaze at the stars in the crisp, clear sky. At bedtime, anticipation flutters across the city.

AMERICAN FICTION

People close their eyes, hoping to wake up and find morning sunshine, warmth, summer.

Michelle returns to Ventura on a foggy day. She'd forgotten how, in the fog, even the most familiar streets seem cloaked in secrets. The entire town feels quiet, under siege.

She turns into the driveway of her house — her parents' house, the house she grew up in — and cuts the engine. The blinds are slanted closed, all the way closed, even in the upstairs bedroom windows. The rosebushes have been recently pruned, beaten back to thorny stumps, and the mulberry tree that Michelle and Rae climbed as children has been uprooted. "Diseased," Michelle's mother told her over the phone. Michelle tried to prepare herself for its absence, but she is shaken to see the tree gone. Even the stump has been removed, and the spot where it used to be is now patched over with sod. Without the mulberry tree, her parents' house looks naked, vulnerable. Like a ship that has battened down the hatches, floating unanchored in a roiling sea of fog.

● ● ●

When Michelle was fifteen, Rae's family moved away. Michelle sobbed in the bathroom, her cheek pressed against the cool tile. Her mother came in with freshly laundered towels and found her lying there.

"Honey, oh baby," her mother said, coaxing Michelle off the floor and onto her bed, stroking her hair.

"I loved her," Michelle sobbed. "I loved her so much."

"I know you did."

"No, I mean I *loved* her, Mom. I still am in love with her."

Her mother smoothed Michelle's hair away from her forehead. "Oh, honey. You don't know what love is. This is called grieving."

"She was my soulmate," Michelle said.

"Dr. Stevenson says it's normal for you to feel this way." Her mother reached over and plucked a tissue from the box on the nightstand. "Shelly, listen to me. It's going to be okay," she said. "You're a strong girl. You're going to be okay. Someday this will all feel like a long time ago."

• • •

Michelle climbs out of her car and stretches. The fog is so thick that Rae's old house across the street is just a shadow, like the beginnings of an idea before it is fully formed.

On summer mornings like this, she and Rae would escape into the fog after breakfast and race down the block, across El Dorado Street and into the lemon orchard. Their favorite tree was an old, gnarled beauty seven rows up, far enough from El Dorado that traffic noise didn't reach them. The lemon orchard was their place, their Shell and Rae Hideaway, and on foggy days its mystery was amplified, its solitude more pronounced. On foggy days, anything could happen.

Rae disappeared on a foggy day.

• • •

"In here," Michelle's mother calls from the depths of the house. Michelle shuts the front door behind her and abandons her duffel bag in the entryway. With all the blinds shut, the living room is dim, but a light blazes from the kitchen. She finds her mother elbows-deep in a bowl of ground meat. She smiles at Michelle and wipes a strand of hair across her forehead with the inside of her wrist.

"Well, if it isn't my world traveler," she says. Michelle moves in to hug her, but her mother steps back, studying her daughter's face. "Look at you," she announces after a few moments. "You look great."

"Thanks, Mom. You too."

"You look healthy. I'm glad. I'm always worried you'll come back all bones. Supposed to be the food in England's terrible."

"It's not so bad," Michelle says.

"Well, I hope you're not too cultured for your mom's meatloaf, because that's what I'm making tonight."

"No, that sounds great."

"Your father requested it. And used to be you loved my meatloaf."

"I still do." Michelle smiles, but the skin on her face feels tight. "Nothing beats your cooking, Mom."

"That's what a mother likes to hear." She washes her hands in the kitchen sink and flicks them dry. Michelle glances around the kitchen. It looks the same: paisley patterned wallpaper, ceramic sunflower cookie jar, hand-painted plates displayed above the breakfast nook. But it seems smaller than the kitchen of her childhood. Across the room, still proudly taped to the refrigerator door, is the rainbow of ribbons Michelle won in youth track meets.

Her mother holds out her arms. "Come give me a hug."

Michelle is a good three inches taller than her mother, and she hunches around her like a shell, as if shielding her from something dangerous. Her mother's hair smells the same, a faint whiff of coconut shampoo and the hot metal of her straightening iron. After only a few moments, her mother disengages herself and turns back to the bowl of bloody meat. "Gotta get this in the oven," she says. Then, her tone casual, "Your father's upstairs, if you want to say hi."

• • •

That summer, Rae's face smiled from MISSING posters throughout the city. Michelle taped the posters to lampposts and slipped them under windshield wipers and stuffed them into mailboxes. *If I give her photograph to every single person in Ventura, then she will come home and everything will be okay.*

But Rae stayed missing.

Authorities combed the lemon orchard, but found nothing. Not a charm from her bracelet. Not a pink shoelace. Not a single strand of her dark hair.

A suspect was never named.

A funeral was never held.

That winter, Rae's family moved away. Michelle never set foot in the orchard again.

•　•　•

When Michelle's parents bought this house, it was a new house in a new housing development. Michelle was just over a year old. She doesn't remember living anywhere else, doesn't remember the fresh-paint, new-carpet smell of the big empty rooms. She has seen pictures, snapped on a disposable camera, of the house when it was brand new — vulnerable flowerbeds, the mulberry tree just a sapling, braced with wooden stakes. Michelle cannot remember the tree as anything less than magnificent, its leafy branches stretching towards the sky, perfect for climbing. She wonders, if the tree were still there, if it would seem smaller too.

Rae's family moved in across the street when Michelle was three. One of her earliest memories is sitting in a little red wagon with Rae, being pulled along the sidewalk by Rae's older brother, Jonathan. Rae had shiny dark hair and a moon-shaped birthmark on her right knee. She wore a silver charm bracelet and bright pink tennis shoes. She liked holding Michelle's hand, and her hands were always cool and dry. Even as they grew older, even as they stopped holding their parents' hands to cross the street, Rae would still grab Michelle's hand when she was excited. As if she were trying to transfer emotion from her palm to Michelle's.

As kids, they shared every shivery detail of their lives. Rae's distrust of the ice-cream man. Michelle's dream of drowning. Rae's love of lime-green

Skittles. Michelle's fear of snails. They were born one year and one month apart, and Michelle often daydreamed that Rae was her sister, and that she, Michelle, had been given to her parents because Rae's family already had Jonathan and Rae, and Michelle's parents didn't have anyone. Michelle's hair sprang up in tufted golden curls, and her compact frame was the opposite of Rae's willowy height. But they had the same sun-freckled shoulders, and Michelle liked to imagine the same blood flowed through their veins.

Until the foggy June Michelle turned fourteen, and suddenly Rae didn't feel like a sister anymore. Inkling feelings, leaking out, expanding. Like an overripe lemon, skin stretched taught with pulp and juice, ready to drop from the tree.

● ● ●

Upstairs in the master bedroom, Michelle's father is propped up with pillows in the king-sized bed, dozing in front of the TV where Anderson Cooper broadcasts live from the Gulf Oil Crisis. The volume is turned down so low that his voice is an unintelligible murmur. Michelle hovers in the doorway. Her father looks much older than his sixty years—painfully frail, his cheeks sunken, a blanket pulled all the way up to his chin. Michelle tries to summon the memory of her father in the green windbreaker and bright yellow baseball cap, tries to reconcile that man with the withered man dozing before her. Despair wells up in her throat. She lets her eyes wander to the glowing TV screen, the images of the wounded ocean bleeding oil.

"A shame, isn't it?" Michelle's father peers at the television. "A damn shame," he repeats, shaking his head.

"The news is always depressing," Michelle says, searching through the layers of blankets for the remote control. "You should be watching something else. Don't they play *M*A*S*H* reruns on one of these channels? Or there's probably a game on somewhere."

"I don't want to watch television," her father says, nodding towards the bedside chair. "I want to talk to my only daughter. You look beautiful. When did you get in?"

Michelle sits, hugging her belly. "Just now. Traffic was horrible on 101."

"But you made it safe. That's what matters. It's good to see you."

"You too, Dad." Michelle can't hold her father's gaze for long, so she reaches for his hand and holds that instead. His hand is a cold potato with shriveled skin. Instinctively, Michelle glances towards the window, but the blinds are shut tight.

• • •

That June day, the day everything changed, Michelle ran upstairs to her room and vomited once more into the toilet. She leaned against the sink, swishing mouthwash around and around her teeth. It stung her gums. She kept swishing. Finally, she spit it out. She spit it out and kept spitting, fiercely, rhythmically. Her eyes squeezed shut, as if in prayer.

"So how's work treating you?" Michelle's father asks.

"Fine," Michelle says. "You know — busy as always." She works for an advertising firm in London.

"Any opportunities for a transfer coming up, you think?"

"Dad, please — "

"I'm just asking. I thought you said you'd think about it."

"I really don't want to get into this now."

Her father draws his hand away from Michelle's and coughs weakly into his fist. He wipes his mouth with a tissue from the nightstand. "I worry about your mother, after all this is over."

"Don't say it like that."

"I'm just telling it like it is. I know your mother. She hates to be alone."

"Mom? She's never struck me that way."

AMERICAN FICTION

"She's more fragile than she lets on. She misses you. London is so far away, Shelly. Why do you have to be so far away?"

"It's not that far. All I have to do is hop on a plane and I'm here."

"There must be great advertising jobs in Los Angeles."

"I like London. I'm happy there."

Her father's hand clenches and unclenches a fold of blanket. "I don't know what we did wrong. You couldn't wait to put an entire continent and an ocean between us."

"Dad, it's not like that." Michelle reaches for his hand again. "I'll think about it, okay?"

On the TV screen, a young man smiles to show his gleaming white teeth, free of coffee stains, and holds up a new brand of toothpaste. The commercials are always louder than the TV programs, and the toothpaste jingle fills the darkened room like a gust of wind. Michelle wants to crawl into the commercial and live there. She would marry the smiling man and floss every day and spend the rest of her life under safe fluorescent lighting.

"I should let you rest," Michelle says, releasing her father's hand and standing up. "I'll come get you when dinner's ready."

Her father opens his mouth as if to say something, but then only nods and lets his head fall back against the pillows.

• • •

Michelle began running track shortly after Rae's family moved away. She ran the mile and the two-mile. She developed a habit of vomiting after races. Her coach said she pushed herself too hard.

Michelle's father attended all her track meets. He was a firm believer in positive reinforcement and parental support, vowing to be different than his own parents, who had never attended a single one of his boyhood tennis matches or football games.

Michelle's mother defended her in-laws. "They had five kids to worry about. We only have Michelle."

Still, there were a lot of track meets, and her father did not miss a single one. He'd settle himself in the top row of the rickety wooden bleachers, wearing his green windbreaker and bright yellow baseball cap, giving Michelle a thumbs up as she nervously jogged to the starting line before a race. There was something fierce and protective in her father's devotion to her track meets, as if he was trying to ward off ever-lurking danger, control what was uncontrollable. *If I cheer on my daughter at every single track meet, I will be a good father and she will turn out okay.* Driving home after the meets, Michelle's father would put on his *Best of James Taylor* CD. Sometimes Michelle felt like talking about the race, and her father turned the volume down. Other times Michelle gazed out the window, silent and spent, and the only voice in the car was James's crooning.

"I would always glance at the stands, hoping to see my parents," Michelle's father confessed once at the dinner table. "It would have been great to see them there. To know they were proud of me."

"Of course they were proud of you," Michelle's mother said. "It was a different time then. People didn't say 'I love you.' They didn't need to. You just know love."

● ● ●

Afterwards, Michelle vomited into a clutch of leaves while Jonathan looked away. He asked if she was okay. He asked her not to tell anyone.

"I think it'll be best if this is our secret," he said. Michelle nodded, standing up. Her legs felt hollow.

"Rae's not in my room," she said. "I was being honest."

"I'm sure she's at our house then. We probably missed her somehow."

As they left the orchard, the fog was clearing. Michelle searched for the moon, but it was a new moon, only a tiny sliver of light in the darkness.

• • •

"It's not like your father has the flu," Michelle's mother says, wrenching the knife into the meatloaf. She cuts a thick slice, which she spatulas onto a plate. "He's not getting better, honey."

"I know that."

"We eat dinner in the bedroom now. He doesn't have the strength to go up and down those stairs."

Michelle grabs a tumbler from the cupboard above the sink and fills it with water from the tap. The same tumblers from her childhood, made of gauzy blue glass. Rae once called them mermaid cups, as if the ocean had been frozen into dishware, the ideal ocean blue of animated movies and coloring books. Different from the real ocean ten minutes away, closer to brown than blue and flecked with seaweed and tasting bitter, acrid — not the way water was supposed to taste.

"No, dear — use the Britta," her mother scolds. "The tap water isn't good here, remember?"

Michelle pretends not to hear, downing the glass, remembering the sting of ocean water up her nose, the sour vinegar of it in her mouth, spitting it out and spitting again and again and again, trying to dislodge the taste.

• • •

That June evening, Michelle led Jonathan through the orchard, exhilarated anger fizzing inside her, picturing the shock that would fill Rae's face upon seeing her brother in their hideaway. She wanted to see hurt in Rae's eyes. She wanted to show Rae that it didn't matter, none of it — all their whispered confessions, their jokes, their promises — it was all just childhood stuff. Silly games. Pretending.

Michelle didn't know she was going to kiss Jonathan until they reached the old gnarled lemon tree and found it empty. Unease clenched her belly, but she told herself Rae was nearby. The next tree over. Watching.

"It's so dark here," Michelle said. And it was. The trees were shadowy figures with outstretched arms.

"Is this the one?" Jonathan asked, nudging his foot against the lemon tree.

"Yep. This is our hideout."

"Rae?" Jonathan called. "Rae!"

"Rae!" Michelle yelled.

Somewhere in the distance, an owl hooted.

Michelle stepped closer to Jonathan. "It's spooky in here," she said, hugging her arms.

Jonathan looked down at her, and something shifted in his expression. "You scared?" he asked, putting an arm around her. His arm was heavy and his arm-hair prickled Michelle's bare back.

Michelle nodded and bit her lip. She *was* scared, suddenly. She and Rae had never ventured into the orchard after dark. Everything felt heightened. The rustling of the leaves, the shadowed trunks of the trees were like something out of a dream, a fever-dream, disorienting. Like when she conjured a place in her dreams and it was different from the real place.

"Don't be scared," Jonathan said, tightening his arm around her. There was something in his voice that Michelle had never heard there before. She knew what was going to happen and she imagined Rae was hiding nearby, watching. Defiantly, Michelle tilted her face up to his.

It was not what she expected. It was not sweet or gentle. His beard was rough against her face. He pressed her against the tree and Michelle felt her fear expand until it filled her completely.

"What about Rae?" she said. "We should find Rae."

Jonathan grinned at her. "You and I both know why you brought me here, and it wasn't to find Rae. She's upstairs in your room right now." He leaned closer. He smelled of sweat and cigarette smoke. "I could always tell you had a thing for me."

On foggy days, anything could happen.

It was Rae she thought about as he held her to him there, his hands pulling at her hair. She thought of Rae and she felt angry and panicky, like the order of the world had fallen away, and she knew it was her fault. She was the one who had started it all. She had blurred the line between them, and then she had left Rae there alone. Michelle knelt in the dirt of the orchard, at the base of their lemon tree. She kept her eyes closed. She fought the impulse to gag. She offered this as her penance.

Then, the taste of the ocean, bitter and acrid. Jonathan released her and she spit it out and spit again and again and again, trying to dislodge the taste.

● ● ●

"This tastes delicious, Evelyn," Michelle's father says, a napkin tucked under his chin. He used to be a fast eater, sometimes even burning his mouth because of his impatience to fill his stomach. Now his chewing is delicate and painful.

Her mother smiles. "I'm glad you like it, dear."

"Yeah, Mom, this is great," Michelle chimes in, feeling like she missed her cue. "It's good to be home."

Her mother raises an eyebrow. "I'm surprised to hear you call this home."

"Evelyn — "

"What I mean is, I'm glad to hear her say it. I'm *glad* to hear you say it, Michelle. I just thought maybe you'd outgrown this place."

"Well, yeah, I grew up. But this house will always be home."

Michelle catches a glance between her parents and the knowledge hits her. Still, she asks, "What? What was that look?"

"Nothing," her mother says.

"Tell me."

Michelle's father sighs. "We're selling the house, sweetheart."

"When?"

"We had our first meeting with the realtor last week."

"Where will you live?"

"I'll just get a nice little apartment in town," her mother says. "Or a condo. It doesn't make sense to keep this place. It's too big."

Michelle nods and takes a bite of meatloaf. Her mouth is dry. The meatloaf is hard to swallow. She chews and chews. Her father chews; her mother chews. The dim room is filled with their chewing.

● ● ●

That June day, Michelle hadn't wanted to answer the door. She thought it was Rae, wanting to apologize, to explain, to talk. She couldn't handle seeing Rae. Not for a while.

But the knocking persisted, so Michelle undid the latch and yanked the door open. Rae's brother Jonathan stood on the front porch. Behind him, the sun sank blearily through the fog. Jonathan was sixteen, with Rae's dark hair but a thicker build and curling, sarcastic lips. He was growing a beard and it shadowed his jowls in patches.

"Rae's supposed to come home. It's time for dinner," he said.

"She's not here."

"She's not?"

Michelle shrugged. "Sorry. I don't know where she is."

"Bullshit, you two are attached at the hip. I know she's hiding in your room or something. It's her night to do the dishes and I'm not letting her push it off on me again."

"We were hanging out earlier, but then I had to leave. You can search my room if you want. She's not there."

"Well, she hasn't come home," Jonathan said. "It'll be dark soon. You know better than me where she could be."

Michelle and Rae were eight years old when they first ventured into the orchard and claimed the gnarled lemon tree as their hideaway. "I have an idea," Rae had said. "Let's promise never to show this place to anyone. It's our secret." Michelle promised. Rae stole a paring knife from her family's cutlery drawer and they carved their names into the tree trunk.

"I think I know where she is," Michelle told Jonathan. She hollered to her parents that she was going over to Rae's for dinner, then stepped outside and closed the door behind her.

"C'mon, I'll show you."

● ● ●

Michelle kisses her father goodnight and helps her mother with the dishes. She reclines on the living room couch and tries to read, but can't focus. Her mother rifles through stacks of junk mail on the end table.

"Have you seen my reading glasses, Michelle?"

"No. Sorry."

"This is what happens when you get old. You start losing things."

"We all lose things."

"Please don't take that tone with me," her mother says, sighing. "Please don't start."

"I'm sorry, it's just — I can't believe you're selling the house. Is it because of finances? I can send more money if that's the reason — "

"No, it's not. Your father and I are managing just fine. Thank God the firm gave him good health insurance."

"Then why are you selling it?"

"Like I said before, it's too big. Too big and too empty."

"Maybe if you opened the blinds it wouldn't feel like such a morgue in here."

"And look out the window at what? The fog? You can hardly see across the yard. It makes you father anxious, and I don't much care for it either."

"C'mon, Mom. I know how much you love this house."

"Love changes. Now I just want a fresh start, away from all these memories."

"You say that like you hate it here."

"Michelle, listen to yourself. It's not fair for you to act like you suddenly care about this place."

"This is my home too."

"You've visited three times in eight years. The only reason I could get you home now is because of your father."

Michelle stands up, feeling claustrophobic. "I've missed it here, actually." She crosses the room and takes a jacket from the hall closet.

"Where are you going?" her mother asks.

"Just out for a short walk."

"It's dark out. Be careful."

"I will," Michelle says, stepping outside into the night.

● ● ●

Michelle knew as soon as Rae pulled away. She wasn't smiling. Shame lurked in her eyes. She untangled her hand from Michelle's and wiped her mouth, the charms on her bracelet clinking softly against each other. Neither of them spoke. Michelle's hands shook as she swung herself down from the tree. Leaves littered the ground. She ran.

Rae called after her, tears in her voice, "You're my best friend!"

Michelle kept running.

● ● ●

It is a clear night, cool and quiet. Michelle breathes deeply. She heads out in the opposite direction from the orchard, but soon doubles back, feeling drawn towards the darkened trees.

She counts seven rows up and plunges in, heart racing, the dirt packed hard under her feet. The trees do seem smaller, the gaps between their branches wider than she remembers. Or maybe there is more moonlight tonight. Once, she stumbles over a root, but she catches herself before she falls.

She slows down, examining each tree, knowing she is close.

For the first time in years, she tries to summon Rae's face. She can picture her dark hair, she can hear her laugh, but her features have become a blur.

The trees all look the same. Michelle thought some part of her would *know* when she found their tree, but now she's not so sure. It's been twelve years. The tree was old. Maybe it died. Maybe it was yanked out and a new tree was planted where it used to be.

Michelle hoists herself up onto a branch. She sits there for a long time, swinging her legs in the dark. She expected Rae to be everywhere in this orchard, but this orchard is not their orchard anymore. This tree is not their tree. Or maybe it is. She has no way of knowing.

Rae's lips were chapped. Her tongue tasted of bubblegum toothpaste.

When Michelle returns home, her mother is still awake, reading a magazine in the deep-seated armchair that used to be her father's favorite sitting place. Her small frame is swallowed up by the overstuffed cushions. The house looms around her, dark and cavernous.

"Mom," Michelle says, switching on another lamp. "Remember that day, a long time ago, when I told you I was in love with Rae?"

That June day, Rae and Michelle perched side-by-side on a branch of their lemon tree. The fog curled around them. Rae's hair glistened darkly in the shadows. Her bare shoulder leaned against Michelle's, a warm steady weight. Their legs dangled, their thighs touched. The moon-shaped birthmark on Rae's knee winked up at Michelle, as if it knew her secret.

Rae whistled a few notes. "Is that how the song goes?"

"What song?"

"That one we heard on the radio. I can't remember the words."

"I don't know," Michelle said.

Rae whistled the notes again. Her voice sounded loud in the stillness of the orchard. Then, abruptly, she stopped, turning to Michelle with wide eyes.

"Did you hear that?" she whispered.

"What?"

"I swear I just heard a footstep."

"I didn't hear anything."

"Someone's out there," Rae said. She nestled her body closer to Michelle's. Beneath them, the tree branch shifted. A lemon fell and thumped softly on the ground.

"There," Rae said. "What was that?"

Michelle laughed. "It was a lemon. You're such a dork."

"I think someone's out there." Rae reached for Michelle's hand.

The dark leaves whispered to each other. The fog pressed close.

Michelle met Rae's eyes. She leaned in, lips parted, knowing that nothing would ever be the same.

OLLIE'S BACK
LYNN SLOAN

**@ollies_back. It's eatin' time. Low country cookin'. Dipped
oysters, quail&more. Respond for time&place.**

Ollie peered from his kitchen, where Sol and Angel stirred and sliced, into his
living room, still unable to believe that his third-floor ghetto apartment had
morphed into what Simone called a pop-up restaurant. Her idea, her money,
and Ollie's chance to climb out of the hole he'd fallen into. Angel had painted
ninja skateboarders busting through the long cracked wall and Ollie had
bought mismatched tables and chairs from the Goodwill and spray-painted
them black. The place rocked, maybe. What Ollie knew about cool came from
Donnie. Cool, or pathetic? Shiny flatware, water glasses to be filled, vases
with purple calla lilies. Calla lilies, who was Ollie fooling?

At the wholesale florist, he'd heard Donnie whisper *the purple* even though
he hadn't heard Donnie's actual voice in four years. At Dabney & Oliver's, the
place the two of them had built from nothing into the best food restaurant in

Providence and all of Rhode Island, Donnie ran the front of the house and Ollie ran the back. (Dabney was Donnie's I'm-not-Portuguese nom de restaurant.) Donnie knew how to pick flowers. He had style. Donnie was the fucking king of style.

Ollie heard the deep fryer sizzle: Sol on the porch outside the kitchen's back door, starting the oysters. Steamed cowpea shoots, corn dodgers, quail breast with cheesy grits, and preserved fig cobbler would follow cousin Nettye's batter-dipped oysters for opening night. No choices, no substitutions, don't tell me about your food allergies. BYOB. He checked his cell phone. Time to light the candles. He adjusted a calla lily.

Sweet, stuttering boy, take it easy. Ollie pressed the heels of his palms together as if that might drive out that voice. He did not want Donnie in his head, not tonight, not ever.

His phone buzzed. Simone. "Look out the window."

Below, a crowd blocked the sidewalk and the steps. The dry cleaner was closed, praise the Lord, and the neighbors wouldn't complain — Ollie had fed most of them trial runs of tonight's menu — but if the cops took an interest, opening night would be closing night.

"Where…you?" Anxiety brought Ollie's stutter on bad.

"Burgershake," Simone's name for the dive on the corner.

"How'm I…supposed…How'm I going…to handle?" Dealing with diners had been Donnie's job. Ollie touched his collarbone where the crucifix Donnie had given him used to rest.

Simone sighed. "I'll come up."

Simone was supposed to be his silent partner. With her shoe-polish black hair and her bulldog jaw, she looked fierce. Back in the day when she was a Friday night Table Two regular at D & O's, Donnie had said she was a clean-hands lawyer, even thought it looked like she wore NFL shoulder pads under her expensive suits. Ollie didn't doubt she could control a crowd.

Grateful, Ollie turned toward the kitchen and shouted at the twins,

"*De volada!*"

Minutes later, Simone appeared at the back door and sidestepped through the kitchen into the living room. "I'll buzz them in and get them seated."

Three months ago she'd shown up at Loni's Grill, the twenty-four-hour dump where Ollie had landed after bouncing down the Zagat's scale. "What happened to you?" she'd asked. He was so overjoyed to see someone from the good D & O days, he'd said, "Hard times," instead of *what the hell do you think?*

When the cops thundered into D & O's kitchen, Ollie had cried out for Donnie, but in the hours and days that followed, he learned that Donnie had been dealing cocaine out of a storage locker by the harbor. That and all that it implied about Donnie having a secret life ate through Ollie and he told the cops the truth. He knew nothing. *Can't be. Yes, partners...but Donnie...he handled...business side. Don't know...about...storage locker. Don't know. Don't know.* When they understood that Ollie was as stupid as he said he was, they let him go. At every place he'd gone after that, he'd failed, like Donnie had said he would. *You need me, sweet boy.*

A few nights later Simone was waiting in her black Lexus at the end of his shift. "Get in."

She missed Dabney & Oliver's, best restaurant in Rhode Island, no, all of New England, hadn't had a decent meal since, yammered on about what Ollie could do with a good cut of lamb, his meat pies, the heavy Anglo food that had been D & O's specialty. Asked if he'd seen Donnie. Ollie shook his head. "Let not thy tongue give voice to thy thoughts," as Pappy used to say. Donnie had led the way out of Monck's Corner up the Atlantic coast to this too-big, Yankee city. They were both eighteen and a pair of hicks. Ollie had trusted Donnie, had trusted everything to Donnie, who was serving four to fifteen for Class 1 Felony possession of cocaine. And D & O was history. Simone went on and on about how there was no decent place to eat within a hundred miles. By this time they were sitting in the square watching early-shift workers trudge toward the office towers. What kind of restaurant would he have if he could pick? She had some money to park. She missed hanging out at Dabney & Oliver's. She'd kind of like to own a restaurant, not that she knew the first thing. She kept circling back until he was tired and cold and wanted to go home. She asked what new angle he thought would succeed here in Providence, where the upscale options were limited to lobster and food that kept forever in a barrel.

He said, "Low country," and here he was running a kitchen again, preparing twenty-six four-course meals out of his 7 x 10 foot kitchen with a four-burner stove, an electric deep fryer on the back porch, and the help of Sol and Angel, the twins from downstairs, while Simone ushered in groups of twos and fours and pointed to where they should sit. Ollie nudged aside Sol and lowered the flame under the grits.

When Simone popped in, she said, "Show time," grabbed a corn dodger, and disappeared, Angel hurried out to open the wine bottles that most groups had brought with them. Ollie plated the oysters, and Sol helped Angel carry them out.

The week of rehearsals had paid off. A few snags, but okay. The sweat and hurry in the tight kitchen felt good — the sizzling, the steam, the heat, the back and forth with the boys. A few times he glanced up expecting to see Donnie smile at him from the dining room, then remembered the betrayal and pulled himself back by focusing on the one and only thing he could do well: abracadabra the raw harvest of fields, forests, and sea into food that pleased. By dessert everyone was shoving bills into his apron pocket. Into the twins' too. The buzz almost lifted him off his feet. He was back. He was really back. He could do it on his own.

When the last of the diners had left, Simone reappeared from his bedroom, told him to leave the cleanup to the twins. Time to count. He carried in two shot glasses and brandy. She divided the cash, mostly hundreds, into stacks.

"Cash at...door. You are...good." He filled her glass, less for him, his hand shaking. In the kitchen he'd felt so sure, but now the lights were up and the cracks showed. Angel's painted ninja's looked like what you'd see in the alley. Why would people come twice to this dump?

"The yahoo with the Rolex couldn't believe I turned him away." Simone pushed her glass forward for a refill.

"How...many...?"

"Turned away? Four parties of four. I said next time they'd come in first." She patted the stack of money. "$2,700. Pure gold."

"And." He reached into his apron pocket for his tips.

Simone thumbed the bills like a pro. "A total of $3,940. Not bad for our first night."

Ollie teased out four hundreds to pay Sol and Angel, along with a couple extra twenties. "We're a...success?"

Simone clinked his glass. "Say it again."

Hiding his thankfulness and disbelief, he paid the twins and returned to see that Simone had unbuttoned the waistband of her suit skirt and the brandy level had dropped an inch. She was settling in, but he was exhausted and wanted her gone. He said, "You want, I'll pay Vin." Vin was their purveyor. "For next weekend, I'm thinking cheese straws, terrapin soup" — he never stumbled talking about menus or food — "Pee Dee chicken bog, chainey briar, and peach pie with my Aunt Ida's caramel sauce." Though he had doubted there would be a second weekend, he had planned a menu. "Terrapin, chainey briar won't come cheap, but Vin says...he can get it."

"You're making this, aren't you?" She laid her heavy paw on his, meaning she'd pay Vin, then pulled out some bills for Ollie's walking around money. Eighty-twenty partners. He was lucky to get 20 percent. After the cops closed D & O's and seized every asset they could lay their hands on, all Ollie had left was his reputation as the chef who'd eluded the law and let his partner take the rap. Donnie was beloved. Donnie could screw everyone and still persuade the angels on high that he was blameless. For her 80 percent Simone had fronted every dime from the Goodwill furniture to the rice shipped from Charleston, plus she covered Ollie's rent and all, and bought a used truck for him to run supplies. Vin wouldn't deliver in this shitty neighborhood.

"Pee Dee chicken bog?" she asked.

"Chicken and rice. Pee Dee's where it comes from."

"Chainey briar?" She reached for the brandy, which was empty.

"Vines, vine tips." He could smell the piney woods and taste the tang.

Simone nodded as if he'd sought her approval. "That's fine. Any more of this tucked away?" She tapped her glass against his.

"Nope." Eighty percent didn't give her the right to be over-the-top galling. "I'm tired, Simone." He wondered again where she lived. All he had was her office address, near the statehouse, and her cell number. He'd barely known her in the D & O days.

She inhaled a lungful. "I'll be by on Wednesday. We'll talk details about next weekend." She scooped the cash into her purse and stood, not bothering to button her skirt, and leaned over to kiss his shaved head. The touch of her lips made him think of eel.

"To a great partnership."

@ollies_back. By demand. Fri/Sat nites. Drumfish. Duck. Grandma Orton's donuts w/bourbon sauce & more. Respond for tm&place.

Six weeks in, Ollie's Back was a success. No cop hassles — Simone must have paid them off — no neighbors' complaints — Ollie fed the building and half the block — and they had worked out their routine. Simone waved in each party, palmed their cash in her left hand, pointed with her right to a table, and Ollie pulled out the chairs. When the front room filled, he guided the next groups to his former bedroom. Turning his bedroom into another dining space had been Simone's idea: a bedroom he used six hours a day or eighteen more seats and four grand more per weekend? His air mattress and one box of clothes hid behind a black curtain; everything else was in the basement. He needed no other home than Ollie's Back.

He signaled to Simone, Table Eight. No more. She let in the pair with the matching cowboy boots and shrugged at the disappointed who remained on the landing.

"Corkage?" Table Four called. "Here, here." "Us too."

Angel dashed around with a corkscrew. Ollie angled toward the kitchen. Time to plate the duck breast.

A ham-faced guy he'd seen before grabbed his hand. "Great idea. Love this place." Across the room, Simone raised an approving eyebrow.

One beat later, a sinkhole opened inside Ollie. The guy was one of the big-tippers Donnie used to bring into the kitchen for a chef chat. If Ollie stammered too bad, Donnie would cover for him. Ollie touched his collarbone, wishing he could carve out all memory of those days.

"You . . . found us," he managed to get out. From the kitchen came the smell of butter going from golden to caramel. His tongue curled around the pearl of flavor, pulling him back. "If you want to eat . . ." He turned toward the kitchen.

"Bet you miss Dabney."

Ollie pretended not to hear.

• • •

Sweet boy. The first time Donnie called him that he'd been so scared.

Monck's Corner Community College. He and Donnie had been held back after their culinary arts class. Chef Cecil something-or-other told them to scrub down the stainless steel tables again because Donnie had whispered during the demonstration. Aiming two fingers at Donnie, then Ollie, Chef Cecil Fat Ass retreated to his office on the other side of the glass wall as Donnie shot him the bird. Ollie, furious at Donnie for getting them in trouble, turned on the radio — gospel music wailed — then grabbed some rags and a spray bottle. He didn't want to get kicked out. This class was his ticket out of washing dishes at LuRain's Cafeteria.

Donnie's breath warmed the back of his neck. In the office, Chef Cecil was hunched over the phone.

Ollie placed his hands on the table, stiffening. "I've got to finish this and get to LuRain's."

"Sweet boy. This class is for shit." Donnie reached around Ollie and shoved aside the rags. "I've got a plan. You and me."

A plan. A thrill snaked down from his throat to his groin. *A plan.* It sounded like a song the way Donnie said it. Ollie pressed his hands onto the table to steady himself as he looked around at the dinged metal cabinets, the leaky fridges, the row of donated ranges missing knobs, trying to imagine the wide-open future that he'd prayed for, without any real hope. He wasn't smart, he stuttered, he had no money, and no idea of how to get where he wanted to go, but Donnie Cardosa with the twisted smile and tight jeans, Donnie Cardosa, the coolest guy in class, had a plan and that plan included him.

"Sweet boy, let's go."

• • •

In the living room, the ham-faced guy's laugh pierced the din. Ollie turned to the small plates spread out on the board over the sink, the staging area — returning dishes would go in tubs on the porch — where Sol had arranged the sliced duck diagonally over sprigs of cress. Heart knocking — would Donnie never be gone from his mind? — Ollie turned off the flame under the butter and drizzled Peppadew sauce over the smoked duck, Sol following with sea salt flakes. The fragrance of sweet/sour layered over the scent of smoked and singed bird eased Ollie's dismay. Angel positioned the second staging board above the first, and they kept going. Forty-six of everything, which should be beyond the capabilities of this kitchen, but they were pulling it off, week after week. This Ollie could do. In a kitchen he could hang on and skate through whatever came his way.

Simone grinned from the door. "Smells good."

"We're coming through," Ollie said, snatching the bandana off Sol's head as the twins marched into the dining room, their arms bearing small plates. The back screen door slammed behind her.

After the first course, Angel hustled plates and Sol stayed by Ollie in the kitchen. Heat on, off, ladle, cut, scoop, slice, trim, arrange, dab drips in a close-quarter dance.

At the end of the night, the dishes washed and the kitchen cleaned, Sol and Angel took the extra food downstairs, and Ollie stared out his front window, too tired to eat his duck sandwich. Burgershake was dark. Inside the Lovely Coin Laundry, a couple of women leaned against the window. A police cruiser paused and kept going. This had been his view for the past four years. Donnie, who'd been with him everywhere, had never seen it. This apartment, this view belonged to Ollie alone.

A knock at the back door. Simone. "As promised." She held up a bottle of homebrew. "What are you doing in the dark?" She flipped the switch, sailed through the kitchen into the front room, sat opposite his uneaten sandwich, took a bite, and opened her purse. Inside was a wad of bills wrapped in a rubber band.

"Tonight we brought in just shy of five K — some bozos overpaid — plus whatever's in your pocket."

Hiding his annoyance — the sandwich, her attitude, her coming back at all — he retrieved the cash he'd tucked behind the fuse box.

"Bring some glasses," she called.

As she counted, he poured her homebrew. It smelled like Amarguinha, that too sweet Portuguese liqueur. He sipped. Almond coated his tongue. It was Amarguinha, and it was Donnie's recipe, Donnie's one lousy recipe. A trail burned down his throat. What was Simone doing with this? Had Donnie given it to her before he went to prison? Why would he? And it had none of the sediment or cloudiness of five-year-old homebrew. Or had he given Simone the one recipe that he'd promised but never given to Ollie? She was only a fucking female diner.

"Altogether 6,350 bucks," she said. "Here's three for Sol and three for Angel, and more for you." She slid forward three stacks, her black eyes unblinking. She was waiting, he could tell, for him to ask about the Amarguinha.

He concentrated, forming each syllable. "This morning Vin grumbled about payment."

"I'll take care of Vin." She eyed Ollie. "He asked about you."

He. She meant Donnie.

"He's concerned about you."

The pressure in his chest swelled to nearly unbearable. A heart attack? Sweet Jesus, not at thirty-four. He was skinny. He'd quit smoking. He turned to the window, sipping air, fighting the pain. Outside the Lovely Coin Laundry, the hooker with the pink wig leaned on a parking meter.

"Listen," Simone said. "I want what's best for both of you."

Inside his chest he felt crackling, like a slow-motion fist going through glass. "Tell him I'm...fine." What the hell was going on? "Let's stick to business. You and I...we...have been doing...fine."

She refilled her glass. "We don't get a big allotment of friends in this life, Ollie."

"Oh fucking...please."

"Think twice before you burn them."

"Burn? Donnie burned me. Did he give a shit? Did he give a shit about what we had? Did he come to me and say..." He shook his head, still unable to believe what Donnie had done. Donnie had abandoned him. "I could have gone...to...jail, and I didn't know a fucking thing. He's concerned? He...hung...me...out to dry. If they'd...I could have gone down too."

"Could have, would have, should have: Donnie feels the same." She gazed around the room, like some goddamn mama queen of the universe. "The past is behind you. He's practically your brother. A brother, Ollie. You forgive a brother. Go see him."

Brother? Is that what Donnie had told her? Ollie stared past her at Angel's ninjas.

She pushed up from the table. "We'll talk about this later."

Later didn't come the next week. Ollie refused to think about Donnie. He planned meals. He worked out at the gym, where Sol sneaked him in. The weather turned hot. The electricity in his apartment couldn't handle AC, so Simone arranged permits for "family picnics" in different city parks each weekend. Friday and Saturday mornings Ollie set up the grill at dawn, left Sol to tend the hog or whatever — sometimes they ran an extension cord for the deep fryer, too — and returned around six o'clock with Angel, the prepared sides, and the dishes, flatware, everything they needed. Simone no longer came, a relief. She sent Rod, the guy who sent out the tweets, to string up lights, control the gate, help serve, and at the end of the evening settle with the twins. She controlled the money. Ollie saw her once a week, on Sunday mornings, when she came by with his cut and they'd talk about what had gone on. Rod was her eyes and ears.

She mentioned Donnie now and then, but she didn't push. As the summer went on, she dropped her Donnie talk altogether, content, he guessed, because business was good, very good, more than they could handle. Rod limited the crowd by texting the location an hour before to the first sixty who'd reserved spots. Twelve grand plus tips, sometimes sixteen per weekend. She said they needed a permanent space. Ollie'd been afraid to hope for this. A real restaurant. He'd get back most of what he'd lost. Most. A realtor friend of hers took them around to look at what was available.

AMERICAN FICTION

@ollies_back. Hog w/ all the trimmin's.
Respond for tm&plc. #RI foodies.

On the second Sunday in August, Ollie sat by his living room window working out his shrimp order for next weekend — fifteen years in the business and he was no better at math than he'd been in sixth grade — when Simone sashayed in with a bag of *malasadas* from Silva's, Donnie's old favorite. Ollie tensed but tried to hide it.

"Took some of these up to Donnie last week. 'Course they weren't hot like this by the time I got there." She plopped the grease-stained sack on his papers.

"Why are you on about this?"

She pushed aside his papers and sat. "He's up for a probation hearing at the end of the year."

So soon? Ollie ignored the pastry she shoved at him.

"They need to know that he has a job waiting."

"He has a job?" His stomach pitched. That's what this was about.

"I'll write the letter. You'll sign it."

"Ollie's Back isn't legal." As if she didn't know. "No license, no tax number, no payroll and all that shit." Like a jackass, he ticked off each point on his fingers.

"I nailed a lease on the place by the pier."

First she hits him low with Donnie; then she comes in high with the place he liked best, although he thought he'd hidden this fact. Then, like a goddamn prizefighter, she comes in low again by not even consulting him.

She smiled her got-ya-by-the-balls smile.

He touched the spot where his crucifix had been. "When do we begin?"

"Lease starts next week. Things go right, we open September 20. Maybe October 1." She reached for another pastry. "Aren't you happy?"

He refilled her coffee cup. "Location's great. But that place...needs work." If she could sign the lease, she could sign the goddamn letter. "The rent?"

"Don't worry about it." She licked sugar from her fleshy lips.

"When are you going to…going to bring me in…on the business side?" He should have pushed earlier. He'd drifted, like always. And how much of the money she'd socked away was earmarked as his, if any?

"Don't worry."

He stopped himself from slant-eyeing the kosher saltbox in the kitchen where he kept his money. Salted away. Jackass. "I need to know more."

"Need? We're going to *need* more than Sol and Angel to get going."

"Why don't you sign the letter?" he said.

"I don't sign. Clean hands, remember?" She stood, waggling her hands, and nodded at his calculations. "How about dirty duck instead of shrimp?"

Dirty duck was Cajun, not low country. "Ooo-kay." Swallowing his fury, he wrote on his notepad. "Dirty duck it is. And okra and tomatoes, collards to go with the duck, hog, as usual, and banana pudding." He tore out the page and handed it to her for Rod's Wednesday tweet.

From his window, he watched her drive away. This whole thing was a set-up for Donnie, right from the beginning. Ollie stood and kicked his chair. The night Simone had showed up at Loni's, the oh-so-surprised way she'd eyeballed him should have told him she'd come looking. If she'd told him upfront that Donnie was coming back, he would have stayed at Loni's. They knew that. But they expected him to be so shit-faced happy running his own house again that he'd cave. To make one hundred percent sure, Simone waited to push until they were at the get-serious real estate stage. They were a team. But why?

His head hurt from thinking. He paced from his front window to the kitchen. He had seen nothing between them back at D & O's. Not a gesture. No sign of special understanding. No wrinkle in the air between them.

He couldn't think. He needed to cook, needed to cook big. From his saltbox he pulled out $7,700. Plenty. He knocked on Sol and Angel's mother's door. Angel opened, his mother behind him.

"I want to throw . . . a party, a blast-out . . . a big . . . dinner. Nothing to do . . . with business. Neighbors only. Tuesday night." Angel looked puzzled. "*Martes.* Right, two nights from now." Could he take over the backyard, set up the grill, tables, the works? Mom crossed her arms. Sol appeared. They were in.

"Spread the word. Free meal. Six o'clock."

Early the next morning, he took seven hundred bucks and drove into the country to buy produce and eggs from a truck farm he'd used back in the D & O days — he didn't need Vin telling Simone — and he bought a hog retail.

Shrimp and grits, keep it simple, hog, collards, blackberry pudding. No Rod tweet.

In the morning, after carting tables, chairs, dishes, and flatware, down to the yard, he sent Angel with cash to buy the shrimp. By mid-afternoon, as Ollie and Angel cooked the sides upstairs, the scent of roasting hog from Sol's grill floated through the windows. When Sol called up, "*Rapido,*" Ollie stepped onto his back porch. The tiny, retired white couple from above the Lovely Coin Laundry stood by the serving table. He and Angel hustled the food downstairs as the hooker with the pink wig pushed open the gate. She paused, adjusting her gold halter-top while she winked at Ollie, her sly smile was just like Donnie's. That was it. Donnie had led Simone on, and she had fallen. Simone loved Donnie.

Familiar faces flooded in and Ollie hurried to the grill. As he checked the meat that Sol had sliced and sampled the sauce, his brain buzzed with this revelation. It had to be true. Donnie didn't love Simone, that was for sure, he couldn't. He was playing her, like he'd played Ollie.

The Korean guy from the car wash brought a beer-filled cooler and most everyone brought six-packs. Soon the yard was packed. Sol sliced, Ollie dished — not thinking, his nerves sparking, his brain a jumble — and Angel kept things moving. Salsa pulsed from a boom box on the stairs, where the teenagers had carried their food. Smoke, laughter, music. After a while it felt like the juke joints back home. And the folks kept coming. Someone brought out more folding chairs. Moving like he was trying to outrun a freight train, Ollie filled plates. "Bit more of them collards, if you please." "Just a dab of grits." "Not that fatty piece. Yeah, that's good." A blur of eager, smiling faces.

A woman with a couple of toddlers in tow cut in front of Ollie and held out her emptied plate, shaking her head to his offer of more food. She was leaving. What should she do with her plate?

He'd forgotten dish tubs. *You don't think things through, sweet boy. That's why you need me.*

To the woman Ollie said, "Throw it in the Dumpster."

She didn't understand. The plates, all of this stuff except the food belonged to Simone. He grabbed a few fresh plates. "Here, take...these too."

The woman's eyes widened and she backed away, holding her dirty plate. Ollie considered tossing the plates he held over the fence — he would like the racket of plates breaking — but he put them down instead. Donnie was right. He hadn't thought through any of what came next.

"Listen up, you all," he shouted. "Listen, everyone." Someone dialed back the boom box and the crowd quieted. He worked out his words. "We're not washing dishes tonight. So take them and the flatware and throw everything in the Dumpster out there." He jerked his hand toward the alley. "No breaking...please. No...mess. I'm closing down. This is...farewell dinner." A murmur broke out and Sol raised his eyebrows in disbelief.

"So eat till there's nothing left but the burp," Ollie said.

Tomorrow he would pack his knives and head west. Vancouver Island maybe. Coastal. A continent away. In a day or two, Vin would call Simone to say that he hadn't heard from Ollie, and she'd send Rod to check. Sol and Angel would say, "*no comprende.*" Ollie grinned, imagining Simone telling Donnie.

Sol stepped close. "What the fuck you doing? We got something going here, you, me, Angel."

"The grill, fryer...what's upstairs, take...before Boss Lady comes...'round. Start up something somewhere else."

"But why?"

"It's over. That's all."

In that shitty culinary classroom when Donnie kissed his neck, he had been electrified. Sure he would die, he'd lifted his hands to turn and accept what was to come, but before he shifted his weight toward Donnie, he saw on the stainless steel table two skeleton hands, his own sweaty prints, and he watched the fingers narrow into lines and the palms shrink into smudges and then disappear. Now he was back.

WHAT TO TAKE IN CASE OF FIRE
LEE HOPE

(To my brother)

The summer after our Disastrous Move to Michigan, I again revised my list.

1. Stuffed black Baby Bear
2. Two pair designer jeans
3. Make-up kit
4. Two t-shirts, extra large, to hide tiny tits
5. Phone to call girlfriends, who don't exist
6. White Bible with gold script
7. Photographs of me and Dad
(All must fit into one backpack)

Mother, almost forty years old, was nine months pregnant. I had just turned thirteen, too old for Mother to be acting hormonal, especially when I was. We had tantrums galore.

If I talked back, then I was sent to my room. To wait. For hours sometimes. Until my father returned from work when he would shut us in his den for one of his "Discussions" about morals — respect, responsibility, patience, maturity — topics that I had no interest in. He entered into these diatribes under the auspices that I had a voice, when, in fact, no matter how much I argued my point — that Mother had started it, yelled at me, called me names — nevertheless, I was to blame and deserved to be punished.

Guilt. I grew up with that, also from the Missouri Synod Lutheran church that I still attended back then, with its weekly rants about sin, which I committed, like talking back.

"Cecelia, zip your lip." "Cecelia, who do you think you are?" "Cecilia, you smart-alec, you loudmouth, you bitch," Mother yelled. A bitch herself. An inherited trait. Except I was not allowed to raise my voice. Another injustice. I had to backtalk deadpan, bury my yelling within. I remember in my pre-backtalk stage, when I was about six or seven, playing downstairs, when I heard my parents' raised voices in their bedroom overhead, then the house-shaking thump a body makes hitting against a wall. I tiptoed into the paneled kitchen, opened a drawer by the sink, took out a box of safety matches, sat hunkered at the small table and ate my first match tips. A sulfuric waxy aftertaste. Not bad.

That Sunday, at church Mother wore sunglasses under her black feathered hat. With her chignon and in her mink cape, she looked like a glamorous, if heavyset, movie star. My father, who never attended church, wore new purple-blue marks circling one wrist. My mother had big-boned hands. She must have clamped on tight. And she was bigger than he was.

Years later, that summer, when pregnant she grew, of course, bigger yet. The more weight she gained, the more I lost. "You're nothing but skin and bones," she said. At lunch, I ate only one half slice of American cheese and one half slice of white bread. She could not force me to eat more. Our first battle, where I fought back, she had to relent or I'd have spent each mealtime in my room alone. I won that round, although I lost the period I had recently gained. That is, if bleeding is a gain.

"What happened to the nice little girl I used to know?" Mother would ask.

I couldn't answer that. At seven or eight, I had run joyous and free through fields in Wisconsin and caught turtles and frogs in nearby swamps. And when ten or eleven, I'd played dress up with Lisa Lucy, whose mother had a streamer trunk filled with old costumes — velvet robes, golden scepters, jeweled crowns. I was older, so I was the queen, Lisa my servant. I ordered her to call me "Your Majesty," to bow and kiss my invisible ring. Like Mother wanted me to kiss her invisible ring when I was thirteen after our Disastrous Move to Michigan when I'd left behind all my childhood friends.

No matter. I had my lists.

• • •

One day, Mother, bursting to give birth, sat me down at the kitchen table, and served me apple pancakes like back when I was little. Back when she'd take me out to lunch before shopping at Marshall Fields, just the two of us, all dolled up, or drive me to ballet, tennis, or swim lessons. But the pancake turner that she used to flip pancakes was what my father used to spank me, because even when little, I guess, I was bad. "Go to your room and wait." At long last my father would come in and say, "This is for your own good." Pull down my panties, flop me over his lap, and whap me with that metal spatula till my bottom burned. I don't remember my sins.

Sins are something you should forget, if you know what's good for you.

In any case, that summer, Mother, nine months pregnant, served me apple pancakes with real maple syrup and said, "The ultrasound showed it is a boy. Your father did not want another child. But now he does. He always wanted a son."

AMERICAN FICTION

"Since when?"

"Since I was pregnant with you. He wanted you to be a boy so desperately that just before my due date, I drove four hours to Madison to my parents and gave birth to you in that hospital without him. I knew if you were a girl, he'd be too upset for me to bear. Don't tell your father I told you that."

My parents each told me secrets about the other, even back when I was little. And as a little girl, I ate the tips off matches. Though I never struck them. Don't play with fire, Mother said. Instead, even then I made lists of what to take, just in case. At age eight:

1. Pet turtle Elvis tho his back legs rotted off
2. Jeans and hooded sweatshirt
3. White Bible with gold print
4. Poster of Jesus hanging on cross
5. Stuffed black Baby Bear. Leave Mama and Papa Bear behind.
All things must fit into LL Bean backpack.

• • •

I kept revising as I grew. I had a secret notebook with entire lists crossed out. Delete poster of Jesus. Insert *Black Beauty*. Delete sweatshirt. Insert yellow full skirt and chartreuse blouse. I don't know why I thought about fire. Although back in Wisconsin, each fall, my father burned heaps of leaves and let me light the pile. The red-orange-yellow leaves glowed from within. While the aroma of mold and earth curled up gray into the sky, I'd imagine standing in that heap of radiant flames, my body strapped to a stake. Sometimes I'd be burned as a witch, with a whisper huff for breath, though I'd cast a spell to live, or sometimes I'd be a saint so pure that I could walk barefoot on burning coals, or sometimes I was a heroine like Joan of Arc, who rode a white charger into battle and killed in the name of Christ. In my fantasies, fire was not hot.

WHAT TO TAKE IN CASE OF FIRE

Flames did not have tongues because fire could not speak. And flames did not lick. A fire was dry, bone dry. Real tongues that licked were soft and wet, like my dog's.

I had a dog that summer after we moved to Michigan, a Pug named Doug, who my father brought home from the Humane Society, a creature who would need extra protection in case of fire because he was dumb as a stump.

Meanwhile, it grew inside, Mother's infant. "Your father did not want another child," she had said. "Your father thought we were over this stage." *This stage*, meaning me.

I prayed to be worthy to exist at the Missouri Synod Lutheran church, the strictest of sects, and I prayed for forgiveness for talking back. Which I went home and promptly did. Talking back is shorthand for being a bitch.

"You pick up your clothes, or you're grounded," Mother said. She saw things in black or white. She wore a black-feathered hat. Her face was white. I was into grays. I lived in a mist. I demanded my room be repainted in silver cloud.

Toward the end of nine months, Mother was fat. I was fasting. My martyrdom. St. Cecilia burned at the stake.

"Your father always wanted a son," Mother had said over apple pancakes.

One day, when Mother was out, I asked my father if he was glad it was a boy. He shut me in his den and said that in college he had loved a petite woman, a gymnast, but because he was short, had given her up to marry my mother who was big-boned and could give him a big son, an athlete. "Not that I didn't love your mother, of course. Don't tell her I said that."

I grew taller than either of them, but small-boned, fragile, thin. Nothing but skin and bones. Although, while Mother grew bigger yet with her unborn infant, I grew little breasts. I let my hair grow long. I slouched. I wore jeans and huge t-shirts. No boy looked at me even once. Mother said: You'd be pretty if you'd get the hair out of your eyes, if you'd stand up straight, if you didn't talk back, if you weren't selfish, if you'd think of others not just yourself, if you'd smile, if you'd gain weight.

She took off my weight like flesh burned at the stake. Flames do not sizzle, they hiss, like a snake hisses and clings, like the new baby clung to Mother's breast.

"Cecilia, don't hold my baby like that."

"Cecilia, don't ever let my baby cry."

"Cecilia, give me my child!"

"Cecilia, I pity the man who marries you."

Tongues set fires. I was sure of that because one Sunday in church, Pastor Bob read a verse from the Old Testament that said, "For the Lord your God is a consuming fire, a jealous God."

I thought if God can be jealous, why can't I?

The baby was named Matthew, after some saint, though he only sucked and squawked. You could not converse with him. Who was he anyway? Yet Mother doted on Saint Matthew. She nursed "on demand." While none of my demands were met. "I always did like them best when they're babies," I heard her say on the phone to Meredith, one of her new friends.

My father brought home a miniature baseball mitt and talked of little league in a few years.

I played with Doug, my pug. I'd read a newspaper article that said a dog was as smart as a two-year old toddler. Totally accurate. Because Doug could come when called, sit, shake, and fetch. While the tiny angel could only suck, wail, and crap.

And then, after the initial so-called *thrill of birth* wore off, the tensions set in. I'd read that too, in a book on the first years of parenting that Mother had on her night table. I skipped to the chapter, "Problems in the Marriage": "A child can create marital distance, sometimes leading to divorce. Parents must present a united front." Then one night, I heard my mother yell at my father, "If you don't like it here, Kyle, move out."

A threat I had overheard before. She knew that his mother had divorced back when divorce was unfashionable. In his teens, my father had moved out and lived at the YMCA and vowed never to divorce and put his own kids through that.

I sat in my misty gray room when I heard her yell, and I pictured my father saying, "Fine, I'm out of here!" He'd grab his suitcase, come knock on my door and say, "Let's go. Hurry. Pack your things."

I had my list so I would quickly scoop numbers one through ten into my backpack and follow him out to his Buick, not Mother's Audi, and we'd drive off, triumphant, free at last. Except then I'd remember my mother in her black feathered hat taking me for lunch, and the fancy clothes she'd buy me — the red dress, yellow skirt and bright green blouse, black flats, designer jeans — and she'd say, "Don't tell your father," because he'd object to spending so much on my school clothes. Even though I still loved playing dress up. But in my father's Buick, he'd turn to me and say, "It's just you and me now, kid." The two of us speeding down the open highway. That is, until we'd come to a traffic jam, where my father, a Type A who hated to wait, would do a U-turn and head back home.

So I'd wake from daydreams to find myself in my silver gray room on my pearl gray bedspread, light gray carpeting underfoot, dark gray drapes — I'd overdone the gray. But I tended to be dramatic, ever since I'd dressed up in Lisa Lucy's velvet robes and bejeweled crown and ordered her to address me as "Your Enema-ence." I'd been given enemas, prunes, and Ex-Lax, at my grandmother's, my father's mother, who also had wanted my mother to have a boy. That grandmother often made me sit for hours in the corner when I was bad, though I don't remember my sins.

Anyway, that night when I sat on my gray bed in my gray room and overheard my mother yelling again for my father to move out, I opened the secret compartment in my bottom bureau drawer, took out my notebook, and revised my list. This time I included Doug, even though my pug would not fit into my backpack, so I also had to add his Sherpa Bag, which would slow down my exit strategy, but sacrifice is sometimes necessary.

AMERICAN FICTION

• • •

Then came the day when I overheard my father singing to his beloved son. Even now I can hear the tune, my father's raunchy baritone:

The boys they swim in the clear water.

The girls they swim in the scum.

My father sang this ditty to Saint Matthew in his crib. My father did not know I was in the hall. Did my father's father sing it to him? Or did his mother? Surely he must have known that the little mammal in the crib, who was dumber than our pug, could not understand one word of it.

I snuck away down the hall to my gray room, and I wondered about scum, a sticky slimy substance, chartreuse not green, like the yellow-green blouse my mother had bought me. And I vowed to never, no matter if I was in the Amazon or the Everglades or wherever scum was, to swim in it. As a little tomboy I had waded in nearby swamps to catch turtles and tadpoles, but sloshing through that thin greenish slick was different from swimming in sticky scum coating your hair, up your nose, that sulfur stench, like the smell of match tips. Like the matches in the kitchen cabinet in the top drawer. I sometimes slid open that drawer and wondered what would happen if I took out the box, struck a safety match against the sandpaper strip, let the match fall…and purge us of all possessions, like Jesus gave up all he owned and said, "Follow me. Be reborn. Start anew."

It is not as if I suffered abuse. Can't blame it on that. It was more like a daily static, like two sticks rubbing together back and forth, until something combusts.

And as that summer reached an end, the time came for Mother's and my annual shopping trip to splurge on whatever I coveted. "Don't tell your father. It's our secret." I believed in secrets. I believed in splurges.

But during those crucial possible shopping days, Mother's infant colicked. The minisaint shrieked nonstop, even though my parents worshipped him in his crib and came bearing gifts, following their burning star.

It was obvious, even to me, that I was jealous. I prayed in church for forgiveness yet again. But only Pastor Bob was present, and he'd once preached that even bad intentions are sins. So no absolution. Just God and me across the void. No small still voice spoke like in the Old Testament from the burning bush that did not burn. Like in my martyr fantasy, fire was not hot. Ah, to be a martyr, yet feel no pain.

But then Mother announced our school shopping trip might have to wait, while rocking the wailing, scary saint in her arms, rewarding his disobedience.

I said, "You're spoiling the little brat!"

Mother said, "Don't you talk like that to your mother about your brother."

When she referred to herself in the third person, I knew I was in Big Trouble. But I was on a roll. "You're training him to cry."

At that, she stood up, gently laid the little mammal in his crib, swiveled around and said, "Go to your room!"

That old refrain. And now, at long last, I said, "No way!"

She took off after me then — open floor plan — she chased me around the island through the living room, kitchen, dining alcove, around again, I was a gazelle, a thoroughbred, leaping through air. She would never catch up until I slipped on the oriental rug, fell flat on my back, and she leapt on top, outweighed me even after the birth by at least forty pounds, she held my hands down, her big fingers circled my wrists, imprinting bracelets, and she said, "You're crazy!"

"No, you are!"

"No, you are."

"If I am I inherited it from you!"

Yelling into each other's face, me beneath all her weight.

"If I'm crazy," I cried, "so is the Holy Infant you worship. He inherited it too!" Heresy. She raised one fist, then stopped; she had never hit me, no, not once, but words are fire. "May you never have children of your own!" she cursed.

I twisted free. Ran to where? To my room. Right where she wanted me. Locked my door. Straight to my secret hiding place, to my fat notebook, to my many pages of lists...And I heavily revised my latest version.

Delete chartreuse blouse, yellow skirt. Insert Sackcloth?
Delete designer jeans. Insert sweatpants.
Delete black flats. Go Barefoot.
Delete make-up kit. Go Barefaced.
Delete training bras. Go Braless.
Delete white Bible with gold print. Go Godless.
Delete posters. Keep cell phone to call 911.
Delete all photos of Mother and Father. Insert 5 photos of me.
Delete Baby Bear. Insert Doug inside Sherpa bag, zipped.
Get a new fireproof backpack. Asbestos? Illegal now? Some flame retardant stuff like the little saint's pajamas are made of.

● ● ●

As if that could save him.

That night when my father came home, he took me into his den and spoke of Responsibility and Obedience and Humility, and of a "Higher Moral Imperative," as if he were a minister instead of a real estate broker.

"A Higher Imperative?" I asked. "What's that?"

"There are values that are immutable."

As if I knew what immutable meant. "For example?"

He shook his head, quickly said, "Like the fact that fornication is a sin."

"What's fornication?" I asked. I had a good idea, but I wanted him to say it.

He sighed. "Sex without marriage."

What did that have to do with this? I thought of all the sex scenes in movies and on TV and said, "Everybody's a fornicator."

He shook his head, lit a cigar, tapped his small short fingers on his big dull desk. He always tried to take a reasonable tone in our Discussions, as if his logic could persuade me. I remembered my mother said in one of our "secret chats" that my father was an atheist. So I asked, "By Higher Imperative, do you mean God?"

He fell silent.

"Ah ha!" I said.

He had as good as confessed his own lack of belief. His Higher Imperative was invented by him. Plus, I'd got him to shut up, a major victory. But no matter what I said, our "Discussions" always circled around to how I must be punished. He said, "Your mother told me about your fight. Surely you realize that wrestling your mother to the floor is against all moral scruples. Also calling her, and worse, your innocent brother, *insane*. As a consequence, you will receive no new school clothes this fall. And no shopping trips for the next six months."

Strip me bare at a new school where I had no friends? My father did not grasp who he was dealing with. He had underestimated the opposition. If you're going to punish, do it up, like the Old Testament God: "You unleashed your burning anger, it consumed them like stubble."

I went to my room and deleted my entire list, except for Doug. I inserted:

— *Black shirt*
— *Black tights*
— *Sneak out, take taxi to mall*
— *Shoplift black biker jacket, biker boots*
— *Go punk*
— *Go truant*
— *Flunk*
— *Get into drugs*

AMERICAN FICTION

— Have sex with a dealer
— Get pregnant, no, delete that
— Become a prostitute, shoot up.

Make them see what being really bad was. Make them sorry for their sins.

And that Sunday in church, as if part of some Higher Plan, Pastor Bob read from the book of James, "Even so the tongue is a little member and boasteth great things— Behold how great a matter even a little fire kindleth."

That lit me up inside. Even a little fire could do great things.

●　●　●

After the Birth, each night, I was the last to go to bed. My parents retired early due to the little creature who still did not sleep through until dawn. Even saints have insomnia. One night, I trod down the long hall of the rambling ranch house, deep carpeting silencing my footsteps, past my sleeping parents' room, then past the small nursery, both doors ajar so they could hear each peep. I was dressed in my convict pajamas, wide black and white stripes. I was a prisoner in this house so why not dress the part? Yet I also felt this wondrous calm, like I used to get as a small girl in prayer, before I'd learned of the Higher Imperative, decreed by a dictator.

No moon that night, crickets chirped their usual malaise. I snuck into the kitchen, stood by the drawer where the safety matches lurked, then heard something faint, and looked through windows in the back door into the back porch used for storage—lawn chairs, a second fridge, cardboard boxes leftover from the Disastrous Move, a stack of old newspapers. Inside, it was dark as a womb. Except in a far corner, a dim light wavered from a big packing box. A shadow shifted inside like some giant fetus. I jerked back, locked the door, silently hustled down the hall to my room, slid into bed. Did I doze? After however long I woke to a faint smell like the bonfires in Wisconsin. That primitive mix of earth, wood, and heat, but this with a foul chemical tinge. I stalked silently down the hall, the stench and smoke seeping in from under the door to the back room. I stepped to the door, the glass fogged, touched the handle, singed my fingertips, turned and dashed to my room for my cell, called 911, "Fire," gave the address.

Plenty of time, I told myself, for firemen to quench that infant blaze. For me to save Mother and Father from a little fire.

I knocked on my parents' door, flipped it open. "Let us sleep," my father said.

"Fire!" I called again, more loudly, " Fire!" A special authority in shouting "Fire!" as loudly as you can.

Mother instantly leapt up, big and tough and quick, raced down the hall to the saint's door.

I stood to one side in the hall, a faint flickering in the kitchen by then, what if fire spread to the living room and the carpet lit, was it flame retardant like the saint's pajamas? My mother burst out of the nursery carrying her infant swaddled in blankets, my father catching up, leading out wife and child. Darker gray swirling beneath the back room door and cloaking the stainless appliances. I could see it all from where I still stood at the mouth of the long hall. Through a gray mist, I saw my mother flip open the hall closet door, snag her mink stole, saw my family drop to hands and knees and crawl as a darker gray shroud spread in. Crawling toward the front door, my mother — one-armed, the infant clutched to her breast, shrouded in her mink stole — seemed like a wide furry animal scurrying across the carpet, furling at the edges, though she commanded loudly, "Stay low! Keep down!"

Yet I still stood at my post. Beneath a burnt orange tinge, my mother's deep voice. "Do not take one thing. Get out!" The edges of the doorframe to the back room aflame, fire searching for more to burn, sliding toward the living room, the brash cracklings more intense, the smoke darker, I could not hear or see if my family escaped.

Still, I did not move. I imagined them outside, realizing too late, they'd left me behind, that I was burning up like Joan of Arc. They'd collapse from grief, sob, beat their chests, feel their Responsibility. But what if at the last moment, a fireman dashed in, a big-boned athletic type, who flung me over his shoulder and whisked me out? But then I remembered my list, and the ten items secured in my backpack in my room at the far end of the hall. How had I forgotten? My pack was evidence. Should I go get it? I stood thinking even as the edges of the living room carpeting lit with liquid orange, but suddenly from the front door, my father's deep voice, barely heard over the crackling, "Cecilia, Cecilia, this way! Keep low!" He had come to my rescue. He wanted me to exist. I held my breath, fell to hands and knees, and crawled beneath a black mass, an orange haze, past a fire I could not see or hear or smell, feeling my way along the front wall to my father's gray bare feet.

Once outside on the front step, I stood, breathed deep. My hands held nothing. Nothing. After all those lists. Dressed in black and white convict pajamas. What would the firemen think? Would they find my lists, call it arson?

But no firemen, no sirens. What was taking them so long? The little fire growing bigger, fat and furious. Where was Mother?

I saw them then, my mother and the saint, inside her Audi at the end of the long drive. My father saying, "It's all right now. Cecilia, you're here. We're all safe."

He still didn't get it.

"Get into my car," my father said. "We might have to drive away fast." I climbed in. Just my father and I in his Buick. Him in the driver's seat. Would we hit the open road? He sat very still. The motor dead. Even, with the car windows up, an acrid fecund stench, singed skin, hair, eyebrows.

We sat and watched our dream house burn with a smoldering glow. I reached out and touched my father's shoulder and said, "Don't worry, Dad, it's all insured."

I thought he would turn to me and say, "You woke us, you saved our lives." He would see me as the heroine at last. Daughter Saves Her Family's Lives in

WHAT TO TAKE IN CASE OF FIRE

Late Night Blaze. I'd be interviewed on local radio and TV.

My father shook his head. "My company's going under. Real estate's a bust. I let all the insurance lapse." Hands on the wheel, he bowed his head.

I didn't understand. My father was successful, he was immutable.

I said, "We'll rebuild."

"We've lost everything." Slumped over the wheel, he looked smaller yet, his thin hair ashen, suddenly an old man.

"Don't worry, Daddy, I'll save you."

My father did not react.

Muffled, his mouth pressed into his hands on the wheel, he asked, "Where's Doug?"

"Isn't he with Mother?"

"I shut Doug in the back porch last night," my father said. "He kept waking us up."

And I knew then what the moving shadow was in the dim cardboard womb that I had feared. I had locked the door, sealed off his escape. Doug, too dumb to bark, was ashes. I felt nothing, as I had felt nothing since the fire began, only that cool calm.

Then my father lifted his head and said, "I made a little dog house in one of the empty cartons. Doug howled, so..." He stopped, as if holding back.

"Go ahead, tell me."

And my father confessed, "I made him a bed, lined the carton with newspapers...rigged a light bulb inside the box...plugged the bulb into an extension cord. He must've shoved the papers against the light...or else the cord overheated." He sighed and said, "Don't tell your mother."

I knew I also should confess, should say that I ate match tips, that I'd been burned at the stake, that I often revised my list of What to Take, that I had fervently prayed my brother, not Doug, would sizzle to a crisp. That I had seen a dim light flickering in the back room and did not go in. I should absolve my father of his sin.

But it was as if I heard my mother's voice, *Don't tell your father*.

And then at last, sirens, and two small fire trucks streaked in past our two cars. How long had it been, longer than I'd ever imagined, as men in black, shiny rubber boots and black coats with yellow stripes jumped out and unfurled black hoses, and suddenly out of the black Audi, my big mother appeared, and still clutching the saint to her breasts, still shrouded in her soot-stained mink and her blackened nightgown, she strode strong and straight to the firemen, and in the spit and glare of flames, she pointed to the front door that they should go in, commanding the firemen, as she had commanded me. Mother, a big strong woman, stronger in emergencies. Mother, our savior. Fire her element. I had been upstaged.

But the firemen did not go inside. They trained their gushing hoses on the huge florid house from outside. And I sensed that all would be lost.

My father climbed out of the Buick. I watched him walk to Mother and the infant and wrap his arm around her wide frame, wider with their baby and the mink. She was a head taller. He seemed to have shrunk.

I sat alone in the passenger seat and watched as flames whooshed out of the roof, windows, doors. And I thought again of the burning bush that did not burn, and after that fire, a still, small voice, but no still voice came to me, only the strident crackle, a dull orange glow inside "unleashed with burning anger, consuming like stubble" all we had owned, no evidence — no backpack, no lists — only ashes and Doug's charred thin bones.

A house fire doubles in size every minute, a fireman told us that night.

● ● ●

We stayed at a local Motel 6. All four of us in one prefab room. We wore donated flannel pajamas. The saint slept, oblivious, in a Red Cross crib. I lay alone in one queen-sized bed and pretended to sleep. My parents lay in the other bed, and in the dark, I heard my sleepless father say, softly, so as not to wake me, "Could've been faulty wiring in the backroom. It was an accident." Trying to placate his big wife.

She whispered, "We'll get through this." Strong even in the face of disaster. Had to admire her for that... for a moment, until she said, "And the baby is safe."

He said, "Yes. All of us."

Then Mother asked, "Do you know one thing I already regret?"

"What?" my father asked, hesitant.

"Taking that fur coat." The room infested with a feral furry smoky stench.

I knew then that she did not suspect my father. That his secret was safe... with me. And I knew that my father would never again lecture me in his den.

Beneath the poly bedspread, I secretly smoothed down my pink, floor-length, flannel Red Cross nightgown, as years ago, I'd smoothed down my red velvet robe while playing dress up with Lisa Lucy, back when I'd worn a jeweled crown, and commanded her to bow and to kiss my invisible ring. And to call me Your Majesty.

LIFE CHANGES

GLASS FROG
JILL BIRDSALL

What made my brother believe a glass frog would show up in our small town where we swam, I'll never know. That's just the kind of thinking I was up against that summer. But then who would have thought he'd be right?

It was June and already we wanted water. We turned on the garden hose and squirted each other. We screwed it to a sprinkler that went up and down across the grass. We ran back and forth in our bathing suits (and, when our suits were on the line drying, then in our underwear). When the sprinkler broke we lined an old wheelbarrow with garbage bags, filled this to the top with water. We sat in it like it was a pool.

Only two people we knew in town had pools. Mrs. Dow, who had rheumatoid arthritis, stayed in bed all the time while her kids did everything. One brought her meals, another cleaned the house. They took turns running loads of laundry. Her husband didn't do anything. He was tall and traveled. We saw him once. His eyes were blue, and we were afraid because of what we'd heard about him. We were even more afraid of Mrs. Dow. She came out of her bed wearing a pair of pull-on elastic-waist pants. She walked stiff and slow across the floor.

It looked like she was made of something different than skin and bones, my brother said. Of course he said this right there in the Dow's pool. I gave him my worst look but he motioned for me to go underwater with him by the ladder where he had more to say about how her legs didn't bend, her face was tight and didn't give.

When Mrs. Dow spoke, her voice was the one I'd heard calling from the bedroom, turning down at the end of sentences, exactly opposite of her hair that turned up in a too-happy flip. Nothing was going to work out, that's why. She already knew where everything was heading and it wasn't good.

We only went to the Dows' once. It was a big deal. We were staying for lunch. Mrs. Dow made her way into the kitchen while we swam. Her children sat her at the counter with all she needed to make sandwiches for us — waxed paper, a knife, and a spoon. When she was done, they carried the tray of sandwiches with paper napkins and Kool-Aid outside to the table by the pool. The sandwiches were bologna on white bread with scoops of mayonnaise and Mrs. Dow buttered the bread. My brother opened his and then shut it right away. "Oh my God!" he said, drawing out the word God to be funny. I kicked him under the table and, of course, he had to duck under to rub his leg, making more of a scene.

"Is that what you like?" Mrs. Dow asked. With a stiff jab of the chin, she motioned to my empty plate and the sandwich platter. I took a sandwich. "Do you want something different?" she wanted to know.

I didn't want to try it, but I knew I had to, so I lifted the sandwich to my mouth and bit in. I gagged. I had to swallow because they watched everything. Even when they weren't looking they were watching. It was one of those places where everything is important, especially whether or not you ate a sandwich Mrs. Dow took such effort to make for you. I never ate bologna again.

The pool was in-ground and heated. It was supposed to help Mrs. Dow with her condition. I couldn't imagine her getting into the pool. Mrs. Dow sat with us until we ate our lunch but then she had to go inside the house again.

It was no fun at the Dows' house. We felt guilty for everything. Guilty their life was so hard and ours wasn't. We felt too guilty to enjoy their pool. Guilty to be there because of their pool. And, of course, we were guilty for thinking what we all thought, that Mrs. Dow wasn't really sick but maybe just depressed because of her husband.

The other person who had a pool in our town lived closer to us and was a friend of our mother's. Her name was Mrs. Grebbler and she and her husband had dug their pool themselves for their son Paul who was born with polio. Paul had one leg and a stump and he used braces like crutches to get around. The pool was good for him, our mother said. Like Mrs. Dow's pool, it was therapy. Mrs. Grebbler invited us to her house whenever we wanted. It was an open invitation. She called my mother each morning to see if we would be swimming that day. We went a couple of times each week.

The Grebblers' pool smelled. My brother said it was Paul's leg, because when Paul went in the pool he couldn't use his braces and we saw his stump through the water, and this was the only time we saw him like this. The Dows's pool smelled clean like chlorine, but the Grebblers' smelled dank and the leg was the difference, so my brother said it was the leg that made that smell, a musty underneath-the-surface kind of smell, like the bottom of a pond or a private smell under clothing.

My brother pinched his nose, his fingers like a clothespin, and said, "Ewww!"

I said, "Shhh!" and swatted his hand down from his nose.

"What'd you do that for?" he wanted to know. He was like that, really clueless when it came to knowing the right thing to do when we were out.

"Don't do that!" I said right up to his ear and shot a look in the direction of Paul.

"You don't do *that*," he said back at me.

He meant my swatting his hand. He was hurt.

Like Mrs. Dow, Mrs. Grebbler was stern, but stern in her own way. Not because the world was unfair but because she believed in herself; she had things to teach us. Mrs. Grebbler stood very straight. She recycled before it was fashionable in America. She composted, too. She was from Europe. Every time we swam at her house, Mrs. Grebbler reminded us to stay hydrated. She was worried because Paul had a habit of forgetting and he had blacked out and fallen once due to dehydration. So Mrs. Grebbler said every hour or so she wanted us to take in a couple of mouthfuls of water from the hose. Your body needs water in order to function properly, she told us. Our mother wasn't a big water drinker so this too was foreign to us. But then Mrs. Grebbler didn't speak like our mother spoke either. The tone of her voice was different. Her voice didn't come out fully. She spoke from the back of her throat so it was hard to understand her. But she had a way of laughing a little at the end of things, so even if you weren't sure what it was she'd said, you knew it would be okay. Even when she was telling you to lower yourself into deepwater headfirst you trusted Mrs. Grebbler. You knew she'd never hurt you. Everything she did was for your own good. She always said that.

Mrs. Grebbler's plan was to teach us to swim that summer. She wanted us to know how to handle ourselves in water over our heads. That was her one rule, she said. Actually, she had a lot of rules. But that was the most important. The hardest thing was to dive. We didn't expect to do that, but she encouraged us to try. By the end of summer, she kept saying, you will dive into the deep end and swim one lap across.

We said thank you every day. Thank you to her for having us to her pool and for teaching us to swim. We wanted her to know how much we appreciated what she was doing for us; this is how we said it.

We enjoyed the Grebblers' pool in a way we didn't enjoy the Dows' but still we felt uneasy. The thought of diving into the deep end was one reason, for sure, but there was another. It was the same reason my brother and I stayed close to each other in the low end, the same reason that made us long for the deep end. At the Grebbler's, the low end was Paul's end of the pool.

Paul didn't swim; he just liked to go underwater. Wherever we were, he'd stand next to us, hopping to keep balance. I knew he was there because I recognized the sound of his hopping, just like heavy breathing. Then when we'd least expected it, he'd hold his nose and go straight down. The longest Paul ever stayed under water was 168 seconds. My brother said when we saw bubbles we knew he'd come back up. The water wasn't clear like the Dows'; it was always murky at the Grebblers', so I couldn't see where Paul was exactly. I knew he was close. I wanted to swim away when Paul went under, but I wouldn't move. I stayed very still the whole time because I was afraid what Paul would think when he came up if my brother or I had moved. Sometimes my brother held his breath while Paul was under to see how long he could go. Once he went under too, but when he came up he was more scared than when he waited up above and he said he wouldn't do that again. So we counted and waited it out.

Paul didn't go in the water much. If he were alone with his mother he would have been in the pool all the time, I thought. It was a production when he came in. First he had to take his brace off. The fake leg came off with it, all in one piece, my brother said. I didn't look so I didn't know this for sure. My brother was a big looker, though. I tried to block him, he was so obvious, but he'd kick both of his legs in a scissor and splash to get around me. This made everything worse, so at a certain point I had to give up trying to stop him — the lesser of two evils. My brother was interested in how Paul could walk on one leg to and from the pool. He stared when Paul lifted himself on the ladder then swung himself over and hopped to his braces when he was done. My brother was obvious the way he watched and I reprimanded him at home. But he'd do the same thing all over again the next day. At night when we knocked for each other on the wall separating our rooms, my brother talked to me. He told me he saw it, all of it. He had no shame. No matter how many times I told him not to look, he couldn't help himself.

"I'm curious!" he told me.

"You can say that again."

We could use our regular voices in our house. Our mother was downstairs cleaning so there was no one around to hear.

"He deserves some privacy," I said.

"And who made you his protector?" my brother wanted to know.

"He's a human being like you and me," I told him.

"He looks too," my brother said.

I didn't know what he meant.

"He opens his eyes underwater," my brother said then fell asleep.

When we were in the pool, my brother and I always stayed close to each other in case Paul decided to come in.

Then my brother found the frog. It was hiding in a hole under the fence. He teased it with a stick just because he could. It didn't come out right away but he kept at it.

It was my brother's goal to see a glass frog, one that's transparent so you can see right through to the heart and kidneys and all the working organs. He just had to find one in his lifetime. If it meant traveling to Australia or the Amazon, he'd do it for sure, he said. "Just watch me," he said.

So when he jumped back, his hands up in the air like he'd seen a ghost, and said, "Glass frog!" honestly I didn't think much of it. I definitely didn't believe him. Glass frog. He might as well have cried wolf. But "Look!" he mouthed because his voice had left him; he was so thoroughly shaken.

I wouldn't have believed it if I hadn't seen it, and I really wasn't sure I had seen it when I thought about it after.

The frog hopped away before either of us could get a really good look and I'm the first to admit the mind is a tricky apparatus, one only too happy to play tricks. But afterward my brother insisted, there was no question about it, he said. He saw through it. He could see right through to the other side, he said.

"You really could?" I asked.

He said he saw its heart beating.

"It had a heart?" I asked, but he looked at me like I didn't know anything, and since he's younger than me, I didn't like where this was going, so I agreed to agree and just wait until we went back and hope we could find it again.

We wouldn't go in the pool after that.

"Don't you want to go in the water?" Mrs. Grebbler asked us.

"If you're not going in, we're not going to come any more," our mother said.

I was worried about learning to swim. Each day we didn't go in, we missed a lesson with Mrs. Grebbler. The last pool day of that summer, the day before Labor Day, was the day we were supposed to dive into the deep end and that was coming fast.

We had to find the frog, but I no longer believed it was a glass frog. I couldn't remember seeing through it. My brother insisted it was definitely a glass frog. He could remember it perfectly. He saw its arteries and veins, its lungs and liver. He even recognized its appendix, he told me now. But as more days passed, finding that frog felt impossible.

When we arrived the last day of summer, Paul wasn't in his usual chair. I thought maybe Mrs. Grebbler put it away for the season because she had moved a few other things around and was setting a broom handle, her rescue device, near the diving board for our test. Paul sat on the last step of the patio, his leg straight out, parallel with the lawn. He was playing with something. We were careful to stay out of Mrs. Grebbler's view and out of our mother's too. We didn't want the test and we didn't want to go home. This was our last chance to find that frog, and we wanted to find it, badly, my brother because it was his own personal dream of the hour — glass frog — and me, well, I just needed to prove to myself what was true and what was not.

Because Paul stayed on that step, busy all day with we-didn't-know-what, and we had no luck tracking down my brother's glass frog, curiosity — or distraction, you might say — began to creep in, and we looked Paul's way. My brother thought whatever Paul was doing had to do with the fake leg. I went with him over to the fence where our towels were, using these as an excuse. A bright orange trumpet vine had been trained up the fence, and I led to the corner where the vine grew crooked, its coat thick and knobby. Peering through the vines, we strained our eyes.

"That's my frog," my brother cried out.

"Shhh. No, it's not. Just shhh," I told him.

"Glass frog!" my brother said right in my ear.

It was a frog. That much was certain. And Paul was petting it. With one finger he stroked back and forth on its head, between its eyes right on up its forehead to the back of its neck. He did this enough times that the frog went limp in his hand.

"It's dead!" my brother said.

He might just as well have screamed, "Murderer!"

The frog wasn't dead. "It's just limp," I told my brother.

Paul had it mesmerized. That frog was completely relaxed, so much that Paul could do whatever he wanted, and the frog let him. It was transported by the rhythm of his finger, the finesse of his touch.

"Look what he's doing!" my brother said as if it were something wrong.

"Be quiet!" I begged him.

I didn't want Paul to hear us. He had no idea we were there. He had turned the frog over, rubbing it in a circular motion now. He touched it like there was nothing but the two of them in the world. Rubbing its belly, then switching to stroke its head, and the tiny well at the back of the base of its neck, in this way holding the frog in a trance. If Paul noticed us watching, he'd stop, and I didn't want that. No way. I wanted him to keep on doing what he was doing. I watched Paul's finger go up and down the back of the frog's head and my own head started to nod.

My brother tugged on my towel. I pulled away from him but he began punching at my thigh.

"Stop!" I said. "Just stop!"

But he was serious. He was looking at me like something terrible had happened. And he wouldn't look away.

"What?" I said, changing my tone, because I felt bad for him now. He looked really scared.

"Look!" he said to me, motioned with his chin, the rest of him perhaps too fearful to move.

The sun had shifted, end of day, turned, and shone a light like a spotlight on the patio step: There was no doubt about it. That frog was transparent. I could see clearly now. I looked inside it and like a laser the sun shone straight through to the other side.

"See!" my brother said.

I saw where my brother's eyes had landed. On the heart. It was a wet raw-red like a tonsil. Paul stroked the frog's belly and my own belly flip-flopped the same time as the frog's heart fluttered, first a weak flutter, then a longer drawn-out shudder. I pulled the towel from the fence and wrapped it around my brother and me. I was shivering head to toe and wanted to cover my brother, to shield him from such a thing.

My brother was pointing, though, his finger extended through the trumpet vine and on through the fence causing a stir enough to make Paul look up which is when I saw his eyes, Paul's, and it was like I'd never seen him before. In the past, although I hadn't looked at his leg, not like my brother had, all I'd seen was his leg. And, while for my brother the leg was a curiosity, for me it was an obligation to trust and try to be kind. For both of us, everything about Paul related to his leg. Until that day when I saw Paul was more than his leg. I reached for my brother, not to stop him from anything this time, but to stop everything from him. If we were still, if we were solid, maybe nothing bad happened or would happen. But it had and it did. Paul was dangling my brother's frog over the step.

"No!" my brother cried.

But Paul already dropped it.

I didn't have to look to know that real tears were flowing from my brother's eyes, his dream shattered.

Instead of stopping, everything sped up, our lives how they had always been, only now we were detached from them: our mother rounding up bathing caps and nose plugs, we were next on her list; Mrs. Grebbler tapping her broom handle against the diving board which meant we were going to the deep end for the test.

We always thanked Mrs. Grebbler when we arrived and again several times upon leaving. We never raised our voices at her house. We were quiet and respected her. We didn't run by the pool. We listened when she told us anything. We knew she was doing something nice for us. And it seemed necessary to be extra kind because of Paul. Like Mrs. Dow, Mrs. Grebbler had things hard enough, is the way we looked at it.

So we listened to her instructions when she told us, "Tuck your head under and roll." It was the scariest thing we'd done so far, to roll into nothingness, knowing there'd be a shock of cold to greet us, and the trouble of maneuvering ourselves underwater to the other side. It wasn't just a challenge, it was a terrifying entrance into the deep end. But we didn't say a word. My brother and I listened and did what she said the first time around. We gasped for breath and our noses burned, the water shot right up to our heads, but we said thank you when we came up, thank you to Mrs. Grebbler for being patient and teaching us.

CAGES
STEVEN OSTROWSKI

Connor sat on his porch steps, his messy, black-haired head resting in his hand like a sack of stones. "You again?" he muttered as I walked across the front lawn. Sarcasm. Hadn't seen him since, like, Christmas. Now it was early April, but cold and cloudy. Felt more like February, like it could snow any minute. I was wearing my winter jacket, my hoodie, and a wool cap, but Connor was dressed like it was summer: ratty black t-shirt, faded khaki shorts, flip-flops. With his skinny, pale arms and legs, he looked exposed.

I was in a pissed-off mood and the last thing I wanted was to spend time with my nutcase cousin. What I really wanted to do was write a rap about how pissed off I was. Wanted to find a beat that sounded like a hammer smashing something apart and rhymes that spit pure rage. As I sat down, I checked Connor's eyes to see if he was stoned. If he was, I was out of there. Connor got way too weird when he was stoned, and I didn't need that. But his eyes, which were so brown they were practically black, looked okay.

"What's up?" I said.

"Nothin'."

"School?"

"Sucks."

We watched this frosty drizzle materialize in the air. "Did I tell you, me and Carly broke up?" I didn't look at him.

"She was playing you anyway, dude." He didn't look at me either.

I almost told him to fuck off. Probably should have.

He flicked out a finger and examined a long, dirty fingernail and said, "So what happened? Judy call your mother and ask you to come over and hang with me?"

Connor called his mother "Judy." He'd done that since he was, like, nine. And yeah, she *had* called my mother. Said she was worried about him, that he was "growing more and more distant." Spending all his time alone. My mother begged me to go over and keep him company for a while. "Try to cheer him up, Blaise," she said. Yeah, right. Who's supposed to cheer me up?

"Just felt like coming over," I told him.

"It's your life, dude."

"I know. You want it?"

"Already got one I'm trying to figure out how to get rid of."

Conner was, like, famous for saying things to get a reaction out of you. Before I could tell him to stop talking like an asshole, the front door of the neighbor's house opened and a girl in a wheelchair came rolling out, pushed by an old guy. The girl made this strange, high-pitched wailing sound as she rolled down the porch.

"Who's that?"

"They moved in in January," Connor said. "She's all messed up." But he stood up and headed down the steps. Went straight over and up onto their front porch.

"Hey, Petunia."

"Pa-tri-cia," the girl managed to drawl.

"Not to me, you aren't. Did you come out to look for crows?"

Her head moved this way and that. You could tell she was all excited. But the guy — her dad, I guess — mumbled that it was too cold out and wheeled her right back inside.

"She gets sick easy," Connor told me when he came back.

"That sucks. What was that about crows?"

"She likes them."

"*Crows*? Why crows?"

He shrugged. "Because she's fucked up, dude."

"She's not the only one," I said. "So, why crows and not, like, squirrels or cats?"

He let out this long, annoyed sigh. "Okay, so she was out on the lawn one time and I was talking to her, and this crow, which was all lame and undernourished, kept landing close to her wheelchair and hobbling up to her. She was totally terrified, like it was gonna attack her or something. You should've seen her — it was hysterical — making all these bizarre sounds, her body spazzing out and shit. So finally I told her that when a crow gets close to you, it's good luck. Means something good's gonna happen to you soon. That calmed her down." He sort of laughed and said, "So now she's always looking for fucking crows. Problem is, her head can't keep still and she has shitty eyesight and they're usually too far away for her to see. So she gets all agitated anyway."

I looked around at the trees. Only bird I could spot was a grayish-red, miserable-looking cardinal perched on the limb of a Japanese maple across the street. I said, "Too bad we couldn't catch a crow and bring it to her. Give her some good luck."

Connor's head lifted off his hand.

"No, just kidding, man," I said. "What the hell would she do with it? It would have to be in a cage. And I don't know how you'd even catch one anyway."

Too late. His eyes vanished into the idea of it. "Wait up," he said and went into the house.

As soon as he was gone I checked my cell to see if I'd missed any texts or calls. Carly still texted me almost every day to ask me random questions like what I was doing right that minute, or if I'd written any new raps. I wasn't sure how to come across when I answered her, because even though I was desperate to have her back, I didn't want to *sound* desperate.

No texts or calls. I adjusted the volume to max, just in case.

A second later I heard a grunt and Connor came down the driveway carrying the kind of cage you use to transport your dog or cat in. He held it out in front of him like a giant package. There was a folded up plastic tarp on top of it.

"Let's go."

"You got to be kidding me. We're really doing this? This is stupid."

"Then don't come, dude. I don't give a rat's ass." He headed up the street practically jogging.

"So where do you catch a friggin' crow?" I said when I caught up to him.

"Cemetery."

"Why the cemetery?"

"Because nobody'll see us. Catching crows is probably illegal. Like everything else."

"Gee, I wonder why? What could possibly be wrong with putting a wild bird in a cage?"

He gave me a look like I was the world's biggest moron. "The whole fucking world is a cage, Blaise, in case you haven't noticed. We're just gonna put the crow in a smaller one than it's used to. And just for a couple minutes, so don't get all PETA on me. We'll let it out after Petunia sees it up close. I just want to get a look at her reaction when she sees one up close."

● ● ●

After three blocks, we turned right and walked down a long narrow road with fields on both sides and rows of willow trees that were just beginning to sprout their yellow-green leaves. The willows made the road feel like a tunnel. It wasn't raining hard but the air was raw, the kind of cold drizzle that gets inside your bones. Seeing Connor in his t-shirt and flip-flops made it feel even more miserable.

The All Souls Cemetery was surrounded by a mossy, waist-high stone wall. It had two sections of graves: The new section was closer to the road and the tombstones were shiny and all the same size and shape. The ones in the old section, down near the woods, were crumbly and covered in weeds, and the names and dates were half-eroded.

"If anybody asks," Connor said as we walked through the new section, "tell them to bury me down near the woods. I hate the way all these graves up here are so perfect. Walmart for the dead. I deserve a crooked tombstone, don't you think, Blaise?"

"Yeah, sure, whatever. But shut up, okay? You say too many stupid things. You're, like, the king of stupid remarks."

"Not for long, dude."

"There goes another one."

When we got close to the woods we stopped walking and searched for crows. It was so gloomy and silent and gray I swear if you looked hard enough you could see ghosts swirling around in the air.

"This was a stupid idea," I said.

"Quiet."

A second later, a loud, scratchy caw behind us shredded the quiet. We turned to see this gleaming black crow land in the grass near the first row of the new graves and start pecking at something.

"Thank you," Connor said.

"So," I said, "did you, like, Google how to catch a crow?"

"No, but I might add an entry on Wikipedia tonight. My last contribution to the human race."

"The stupid remarks keep adding up."

"Take one end of the tarp," he said. "We're gonna walk real slow, one step at a time, till we get about ten feet from it. Then we wait, let it think it's safe. Then when I say 'now,' we throw the tarp over it."

"We'll never get that close before it flies away," I said. But we were already creeping up on it. The crow had itself a piece of a hamburger, bun and all. It would peck at the food, then hop away and look around, then hop back and have another peck.

"Burger King or Micky D's?" I whispered.

Connor's eyes were zeroed in. I wasn't even there.

When we got to within fifteen feet of the thing it got suspicious. Spread its big old wings a few times.

Connor gestured to me with his hands to stand still.

Beeeeeeeep. My phone — on full volume, too. The crow's wings opened with a gush, it cawed, and it flew off to the low branch of a tree nearby.

"Fuckin-a, Blaise," Connor spat.

"Sorry, man. I can't help it if I got a text."

"Shut it off, man."

"I didn't think of that, okay?"

"Let me guess. Fuckin' Carly. 'I don't want you anymore but could you wait around for me just in case I change my mind?' Sucker."

"Fuck you, Connor. Like you know anything about having a girlfriend." Probably shouldn't have said that — as far as I knew, Connor never had a girlfriend in his life. No, wait, he had one for a couple weeks when we were freshmen. Went out with this goth/emo chick. She dumped him fast, though. Probably too strange even for her.

I turned my back to him and glanced down to read the text: "Don't ignore me please. I want to stay friends forever." I hated that word: friends. What did it even mean? And I hated myself for doing it, but I typed it anyway: "We are."

Carly texted right back: ☺

I felt like crushing the phone in my hands.

I turned around just in time to see the crow fly back to the hamburger. Connor stood stone-still, holding the open tarp in both of his hands. I looked at him and he looked at me. He tipped his head, like, *don't move*, but I gave him the finger and walked away.

I headed back through the old section and climbed down a slope and went into the woods. There was a little winding stream down there, about twelve feet wide. It was dusky and the drizzle was mixed with tiny ice pellets now and they were ticking against everything, making this really interesting, kind of creepy sound. And the stream had a music to it, too, like a hundred small, ice-covered bells all ringing at the same time. The trees and bushes and stones seemed haunted, full of shadows, covered in dark, spongy moss. Mesmerizing. Took me out of my anger a little. I started breathing more slowly, letting my heartbeat calm down, watching the mist flow out of my nostrils.

I got the thought that maybe I could pull a beat out of the place — not hard like a hammer but something soft and spooky. So I leaned against a tree and tried to concentrate on what I heard: everything ticking, and over the top of it this icy jangle of the stream flowing over stones. It was beautiful. I thought if I could capture that beat, that beautiful, spooky sound, and get the right words to go with it, maybe I could nail something.

As I concentrated, my eyes wandered down the stream. So when I actually saw the girl, twenty or thirty yards away, I didn't really register it. So I blinked and looked harder and, yeah, she was real. She stood at the edge of the water on the other side, staring down into it. She had on this long, old-fashioned dress with a wild pattern that looked like giant green vines with big purple leaves. And Doc Martens on her feet. And a purple hoodie with the hood pulled up over her head so that only her long, thick, kinky black hair poured out from under it. Her face was almost hidden by all the hair.

She looked up at me. Then, after about five seconds, she lifted her arm and gave me a small wave.

I waved back, but, I mean, *totally* awkward.

So I dropped my head and went back to trying to listen to the beat, but now it was hard to concentrate. When I stole another peek at her she started walking toward me, still on the other side of the stream. She stopped directly across from me. Her skin was the color of coffee with cream in it. Which is how Carly used to drink her coffee.

Carly.

"Hey," the girl said. First thing I really noticed, besides the wild hair exploding out from under her hood like stuffing coming out of a pillow, were her eyes. She had huge, almond-shaped eyes, like a leopard's.

"Hey."

"I know you."

"You do?"

"Math class. Freshman year. Ms. Donaldson. You probably don't remember me. I looked different then."

"I kind of do. So, like, what are you doing here?"

She took a small step, lifted her leg and dipped the tip of her boot into the stream. She reminded me of a ballet dancer, you know, delicate and precise — except for the shoes. "I come down here to visit my brother," she said. "All the time, actually."

I remembered. Her brother, who was two years older than us, got killed in a car crash with, like, five other seniors. They were all drunk and the driver, not her brother, was speeding on the curvy road that cut through Bloom's Woods. Slammed headfirst into an oak tree. You can still go see the five not-so-white-anymore crosses nailed to it. I said, "That was last year, right?"

"Thirteen months and nine days ago."

"So, wait, he's buried *here*?"

"His grave is over there near the north entrance. But it sucks over there. He likes this creek and these woods. His casket can't keep him up there. I get his vibe really strong right over there where I was standing. I hardly get it at all at his grave."

I could kind of understand that.

"It's kind of a coincidence that you're here." She took a breath and blinked her eyes and said, "You know what the last thing he ever said to me was? He said, 'You need to figure out what matters to you, sis.' Isn't that weird? That he would say that to me and then die?"

"It's pretty true, though. Right? I mean, for everybody. Not easy though."

"Not easy. There's something even weirder about that conversation, but I don't know if I should tell you. Just because it would freak you out." She looked at the water and said, "I was telling him about... never mind."

I was glad she didn't tell me.

"My name's Emma, by the way. You probably don't remember that. And yours is Blaise. I always loved that name. It fits you. Well, sometimes it does."

"Thanks," I said, though as soon as I said it I realized that maybe it wasn't a compliment. I mean, when did my name fit me and when did it not fit me? "I should go," I said. "My cousin's up there trying to catch a crow and put it in a cage so we can show it to this, you know, this messed up — I mean, like, *challenged* — girl. She loves crows."

"They call it special needs."

"Right. Well, this girl's got a lot of special needs."

"I think everybody's needs are special, but some people have to deal with more than others."

I nodded.

Emma said, "I don't know how I feel about catching crows, like, morally. But if it's for this girl, maybe it's okay. I hope he doesn't hurt the crow when he gets it."

"Don't worry about it. We're not going to be able to catch a crow. It's a stupid idea. It was sort of my idea, except I was kidding."

"I can try to put some energy into it for you if you want."

Wait. What?

She sighed. "Okay, so I have a little gift with energy. Sometimes. My grandmother has it, too. So did her grandmother, actually. Sort of like ESP, but not exactly. It's complicated. I can get at certain things. It doesn't always work when I want it to, but I definitely have it."

"That's interesting." I turned and looked back up the hill at where the graves were. "Okay, well, guess I better — "

"Don't go yet," she said and she shut her eyes. Her hands started to move in this flowy way, like she was scooping little pockets of air and shaping them into something.

She opened her eyes and smiled a tiny smile and said, "Worth a try, right?" Then she looked down at the water. "Do you still play in that band Last Minute?"

"You heard of us?"

"I went to a party at the beach that you guys played at the summer after freshman year. You didn't notice me. That girl Candy who was in our math class was there. I think you were going out with her at the time."

"You mean Carly."

"Carly then."

Something about the way she said Carly's name bothered me. "I quit last year," I said. "I never really liked that kind of music anyway." I thought about telling her that I was into rap now, but then I thought, why bother? She was definitely not the rap type.

Her head tipped like somebody behind her was saying something to her. "Music is so important," she said. "I think we need a whole new kind of music. Something nobody's ever thought of yet."

I must have stared for too long, because she asked me if I was still there.

Good question. That's when I realized that I was right up at the edge of the water, and that I was dipping the toe of my sneaker in. "Oh," I stammered. "Yeah, I'm here. But I better go."

"Okay. Bye, Blaise. I hope the special girl gets her crow. You never know, right?"

My legs were wobbly as I climbed up the slope, and my eyes wouldn't stop blinking. When I walked back out into the cemetery it was gloomier than ever, still drizzling, but the rain was mixed with even more ice now, ticking against the gravestones.

But no sign of Connor.

I called his name. Nothing.

Oh, shit, I thought, *he didn't... No, no way. No way.*

"Connor!" I screamed. What was the last thing I said to him? Was it "Fuck you"? Oh, no, no. "*Connor!*"

I started trotting toward the stone wall, thinking, hoping, that he realized what a stupid idea the whole thing was and just decided to go home. He would definitely do that, leave without telling me. He would totally do that.

But the harder, worse question was, would he actually kill himself? Could he be *that* depressed? Could he be *that* stupid?

No.

I spotted him, way down the other end of the tunnel of willows, carrying the cage out ahead of him with the tarp draped over it.

"Connor," I called. "Hold up."

He didn't.

I finally caught up to him at the corner. "You got something in there?"

He lifted the tarp for me to see. A fat, shiny crow, calm as can be.

"How did you do that?"

He was breathing hard from carrying the cage. I could tell he didn't want to stop, but he put it down on the sidewalk to rest his arms. "Dude," he huffed, "it was unbelievable. I put the cage next to that hamburger and waited. So the fucking crow took a piece of meat, looks around, then hops straight in. I just had to walk over and shut the door."

"Are you telling me he just hopped into the cage on his own?"

"Dude, it's like he was down with the plan."

I don't know what I expected to see, but I turned and looked back at the cemetery. Just icy drizzle blowing around in ghost gray sheets.

$\bullet \quad \bullet \quad \bullet$

We were four houses from Petunia's when the patrol car came cruising up the street, slow. Trouble slow.

"Keep walking," Connor whispered.

The car was barely moving now, and real close, but we acted like we didn't even notice it. Out of the side of his mouth Connor said to me, "Go tell Petunia's old man to bring her out to the porch. He'll do it. Go."

I shrugged, walked ahead of Connor as casually as I could, walked up the path to Petunia's house, rang the bell. The cop stopped the car and rolled down the window and said to Connor, "What you got under that tarp? Gold bars?"

Connor kept walking.

"Hey, son. Stop right where you are please." Connor stopped. The cop pulled up beside him and shut off the engine. He took his time getting out.

I rang the bell again. When Petunia's father came to the door, I said to him, "Do you think you can let Patricia come out on the porch for a second? Connor caught a crow for her to see. Except that cop's probably gonna make him turn it loose, so if you want her to see it, you better hurry."

He looked at me, then at the cop and Connor down on the street. There was no expression on his sad, thin face. He turned and went back inside.

"It's just a crow," Connor was saying to the cop. The tarp was still over the cage. "I just wanted to show it to my neighbor. She likes crows. Swear I'm not going to hurt it or anything."

"You're breaking the law, son."

"There's a crow law?"

"It's illegal to entrap a wild animal or bird."

We heard a door opening behind us. Petunia's dad wheeled her onto the porch. She was bundled under two or three wool blankets.

"Can I just show that girl up there the bird for one minute?" Connor said. "It'll make her really happy. You don't mind making a girl with a lot of problems happy for one minute, do you officer? That's not against the law, is it?"

The cop reached down and pulled away the tarp like a matador. "Release the bird. Now."

"Okay, okay," Connor said. He leaned down like he was going to open the latch, but instead he picked up the cage and ran up the walkway onto Petunia's porch. "Look at the crow, Petunia. Look real close. Good luck! Good luck for you, Petunia." He lifted up the cage and held it a few feet from her face, and when her eyes locked on it, I swear she let out this squeal of pure joy. But her head kept moving around every which way, so Connor kept moving the cage so her eyes could stay on the crow.

The cop leaped up onto the porch. "Sir," he said to Petunia's father, "I'm sorry, but I can't allow this." He grabbed the cage out of Connor's hand and walked down to the front lawn with it. Petunia wailed this high-pitched, tortured sound.

The cop put the cage on the grass and opened it, but the bird stayed where it was. So he rattled it, but the crow only raised its wings and cawed. Finally he lifted one end way up and the bird sort of tumbled out. It got itself up on its legs right away, but then just stood on the grass and looked around like this kind of thing happened to it every day. At last, it flapped its big black wings and flew up into a tree.

The cop asked Connor to step off the porch, which he did. Petunia's dad hesitated for a second before he started to wheel her back inside. Petunia moaned this eerie moan, like the music you might hear on a dead star, and then they were inside the house.

"You defied me, son," the cop said to Connor. "I ought to bring you in and make you spend a night in a cell. Might teach you a lesson about basic respect for authority."

"Actually, officer, it's too late to teach me anything."

"Is it? You know what, let's find out. You're under arrest." He grabbed Connor by the shoulders and made him lean against the squad car and put his hands behind his back. Then he cuffed him.

"Hey, wait up," I said to the cop. "This was my idea, man. We just wanted to give the girl a little thrill. You don't really have to arrest him, do you?"

"Don't worry about it, Blaise," Connor said. "I always wanted to go to jail before I died. But, tell me something, dude, do you think she liked it? You think she got a good look at it?"

"Definitely. Did you see her face, man? She was thrilled. It was sick. I'm glad we did it."

The cop opened the door and pushed Connor's head down and shoved him into the back seat. I just stood there like an idiot and watched. Right before they pulled away, Connor looked at me and smiled and pointed with his chin to the cage that separated the back seat from the front. He flapped his shoulders like wings. Then the cop car sped off.

Up in the tree, the crow cawed. I watched it as it lifted off the branch and flew, low to the ground, all the way up the street. I watched it land on the curb near the corner. A few feet away from it, standing there like some orphan in the icy drizzle, was the girl from the graveyard. She was staring at me.

YOU CALL ME UGLY?

YANSHUO ZHANG

It all happened that evening, during the girls' night out. One friend accidentally called another ugly, when she was only teasing her. This ugly incident allowed them to share the deepest secrets in life and discover what is truly ugly in human nature: an indifferent, selfish heart.

Mei Ling Cheung and Algae Lo had been planning a fancy outing since fall break. They are both seniors in college — while Mei Ling is from China, Algae is a Vietnamese immigrant. Every time Mei Ling passed by the college bookstore where Algae worked, the two would propose their night out.

"Algae, how come we never have been to the bar when we've both passed twenty-one?" Standing in front of the cashier's table, Mei Ling would question Algae while playfully stroking her fingers through the earrings hanging on the shelf on the table. In this women's college, bookstores also sell jewelry and accessories.

But Algae ignored her question. She suggested to her friend, instead, "Don't buy these earrings — they're fragile."

AMERICAN FICTION

Hearing that, Mei Ling raised her head. That day, Algae wore a short, tight gray jacket — even though it looked stylish, this was obviously an old piece of clothing with white washed spots.

If only girls as delicate and pretty as Algae could afford fashion! Mei Ling was struck by an amorphous pity for her friend.

Mei Ling finally let go of the earrings she was playing with. "I already have too many earrings anyway," she said. Meanwhile, she caught a glimpse of the label with fading ink: Genuine Sterling Silver. *How can you tell the genuine from the fake?* Mei Ling was lost in her thoughts. But she soon woke up: "Do we want to ask Lily, too? She can drive." Lily Vang was their common friend who always kindly offered a ride for their adventures.

Algae shook her head: "Call her if you want. Lily always pisses me off." Mei Ling later learned that, according to Algae, Lily always changed her mind at the last minute.

"I will still call her." Mei Ling didn't seem to be bothered. "Bars are for adults! Aren't you excited?"

The three girls finally made it happen. Going out was such a big deal for these students whose lives are a linear progression from one day to another — these young women had always settled their minds in studying. Maybe things were a little different for Lily, who got to know many people through her nursing career, an interactive job. But for Mei Ling, a student from China with her typical "Asian diligence," despite her comfortable life as the only child of a middle-class family, she never dared to indulge in the American revelry of party and night life. The same was true for Algae. As the daughter of a Vietnamese couple who moved to America in the early 1990s, twenty years after the Vietnam War, Algae had tasted the bitterness of newcomers estranged in an alien culture. When she first came over, her classmates stared at this only Asian girl in class with long black hair, curious big brown eyes. Algae was one of the five siblings who grew up on her mum's thin salary, and she understood the cruelty of life after her parents tragically split up. Therefore, like Mei Ling,

YOU CALL ME UGLY?

Algae — "a simple nonflowering plant of a large group that includes seaweeds" according to English dictionaries — only aspired to be a good daughter away from the seductions in life. Were the girls doomed to be humble, quiet weeds and grass in this colorful world?

No. They had their own glorious dreams of beauty. "We should dress up like celebrities!" Algae not only accepted the invitation from Mei Ling and Lily later, but also proposed something crazy. "Hairdo, heels, fancy dresses...I'm too carried away by this." When Mei Ling read this message on Facebook, she could see Algae's eyes shining behind the screen. She was also excited. Mei Ling herself only dressed up a couple of times a year, for the most special occasions.

The girls indeed turned out to be like stars. It was a very cold night in early January. In the frozen air of minus ten degrees where their every breath got eaten by the darkness, the three girls had to hold each other tight to get to the bar from the car. Three pairs of bare legs with thin black stockings, flowery dresses that hardly went over the knees, high heels that hit the ground with sharp noises...The girls never felt closer to vanity.

"This is the price of beauty," Mei Ling murmured, "We're *way* cool." Algae and Lily laughed with chattering teeth. Their lips, too, were trembling with elegant pink and red gloss.

When the girls finally settled down in their own booth in the bar-restaurant, Mei Ling and Lily both took out their cameras. After a couple of photos, Algae became a little sullen: "My face looks so round. Mei Ling, can I delete the pictures?" Algae reached out for Mei Ling's hand.

Mei Ling dodged her and laughed: "Come on, they're just photos. What's wrong with round faces? Love thyself!" Jokingly throwing out these words, Mei Ling moved to the other side of the booth to be close to Lily so they could take more photos together. She hardly noticed that she was getting on the nerves of Algae. At that time, the waiter happened to have come back to take their order.

"Want a group picture?" He put down his notepad. Lily and Mei Ling handed him their cameras. When the flash shone, Algae covered her face with her hands. The waiter complained that he didn't get "the girl in the corner."

"That's okay, as long as they look fine." Algae seemed to have lost the last pinch of patience. She dropped her head and started to carelessly stir her cocktail with the giant straw.

"Algae, what's the matter? Are you afraid that I'll show these photos around and people would say, 'What an ugly friend you have'?" Mei Ling exaggerated her tone to sound funny, hoping that Algae would laugh too. She didn't.

"That's what you think?" Algae was infuriated. But she tamed her anger so well that Mei Ling, the girl most virginal in her thoughts, thought Algae just didn't get the joke.

"No, but I thought *you* might think that way…" Mei Ling stopped. Algae became red as an apple fully ripened, and her eyes were sparkling with a wild fire. She said nothing more and only continued to stir her cocktail while occasionally sniffing disdainfully at the topic Mei Ling and Lily brought up: Men.

"Men, what's so interesting about these creatures? All the crows under heaven are the same black. Ugly." The pink liquid in front of Algae was dancing frantically in the transparent glass as Algae quickened her fingers to stir the cocktail. Her face became redder and redder, when Mei Ling realized too late that tears started to rim her eyes.

Even though Algae seemed to distain the topic of her friends, she was the first to pick up the topic: "I don't know what's interesting about men; I don't trust any of them."

Hearing that, both Mei Ling and Lily opened their eyes curiously with concerns. Algae felt encouraged and became bolder: "Even my father doesn't deserve to be trusted. My father is not a man. When I was young, I don't remember how many times he came home too drunk to walk, so he woke up all the jars and boxes while stumbling through the living room, and he woke

YOU CALL ME UGLY?

us all up too.

"At first, Mum chose to tolerate it. It was 1992, after they brought the entire family to this country from Vietnam. Mum was tired of working on the farm like a man since the war ended in late 1970s, and America sounded like a fresh dream. She had been the major helper of my grandpa's field in South Vietnam after the war, which forced the family to hide in the countryside — my grandpa was a Vietcong solider who helped America to fight against the Communists; America was defeated. Mum resented the arranged marriage with my father. She had never given him her heart since they married at nineteen.

"But Mum chose to swallow the bitterness and planned a new life for the family. She believed that America would change her husband, since people here are all ambitious. Life was hard for both of them in the new country, but Mum was brave. During our first five years here, she bounced back and forth between a Vietnamese-American sewing company, Big Fruit, and night classes for English. Six dollars an hour, sixty hours a week, can you imagine? She made beef soup pho and rice every morning before leaving for work, and would shout us children out of the bed. At first she had mercy for my father — she wanted him to sleep longer in the morning so didn't wake him up whenever she left at seven. 'Wait until you all eat before you wake up your father,' that's what Mum often told big sister. Then she would take down the plastic bag hanging on the back of our front door, put her lunch box in the bag, tie her hair in a bun, and close the shrieking door behind her.

"At the end of the day, after putting us all to bed, Mum would still be busy: She always sat at the wooden table, doing her night lesson of practicing English and her patience for an alcoholic husband. She would open her English book and a greasy notepad, uttering funny-sounding words, and sometimes scribble the grocery list for the next day, while waiting for my father, who was away, drinking. 'This man, him!' Sometimes when I went to the bathroom in the middle of the night, I saw Mum hitting her forehead in great agony. Even though I was only ten, I started to hate my father. I wondered, 'Why can't he ever come home early and sober?'

"Finally, something horrible happened and Mum decided to end it all. Those days, I heard my parents shouting a lot about money, job, alcohol, and failure. Mum was supporting the seven of us when my father lived like a parasite: He sucked the blood of my mother! He would come home calling her 'yellow-faced witch' when every bottle of his alcohol was bought with my mum's money earned in a sweatshop. One night, it must have been really late when we heard the familiar heavy steps on the doorway. Mum turned on the lamp, pushed us back to bed, threw on her bathrobe, and sneaked out. The lamp started to shake as the lace of her robe touched it. I was scared by my own shadow; it appeared big and monstrous in the empty room. But I didn't forget to pat my baby sister when all of a sudden my father started to throw away his boots while cursing around.

"'Look at the clock, what time is it?' Mum's voice was obscure behind the heavy wooden door. 'Even if you had a job, your boss would kick out such a drunkard right away!'

"'Get out of th...the way, woman.' Father finally started to shout back. 'If you're not h...happy in this country, go back to Vie...Vietnam tomorrow!' He was roaring, sounding like a retard. I almost laughed.

"Then Mum must have started to search Father's jacket when she found out that his purse was lost. She demanded, in a frightened voice: 'Where's your money, the money I gave you yesterday? Where? Your ragged purse is gone!'

"'Shout, shout, you ignorant woman. Gone, then wh...what? Tomorrow I'll earn you a gold mountain, haha, hahahaha...' Father started to laugh so hysterically that I became afraid. I seized the corner of my blanket while cradling my sister to make sure that she wouldn't be woken up.

"That night, Mum never went back to bed. I finally fell asleep again in their endless shouting and arguing. But the next morning when I woke up, my father was gone. Mum had kicked him out. She dared that he wouldn't be able to live without her, a woman. My father was so provoked he left. Two weeks later,

Mum told us to forget about our bastard father — they divorced. But you know why I can never consider him as a man? Like Mum expected, he didn't even have the dignity to start his own life. He came back to beg Mum to shelter him. Mum refused.

"So when I grew up, I was never loved by my father. This is what I learned about men — even my own father is an ugly figure."

As she finished her story, Algae's shoulders started to shake, and her voice cracked. She turned her head to the side and covered her face with her hand, so Mei Ling and Lily could not see the big, hot tears rolling down her face like pearls broken from a necklace. The three of them were quiet.

Mei Ling was lost in her thoughts as Algae's words were still haunting. Contrary to Algae, she had the best father in the world who protected her from the cruelties of the world with his wholehearted devotion and the most enduring generosity. As a little girl, how many times did Mei Ling enjoy being pricked by Dad's beard when he kissed her? How she liked riding her father's shoulders to peek at the fresh, big world? While in high school, whenever she brought home a bad grade, how gentle was Dad's rebuke that she would swear to be number one in class the next time? And when she left home for America four years ago, how Dad's hair turned gray overnight when she failed to report to home that she had landed safely? Father was so caring and loving to his little princess that Mei Ling grew up as a carefree girl never troubled by the ugly side of life — nothing had ever cast a shadow to her sunny heart, until recently when even Father could not wipe her tears for a boy, the first man who had crushed her heart.

"I am really naïve. After all, what can a kiss promise?" Mei Ling would still blush whenever she talked about her first romantic encounter at twenty-one, like the belated spring after the endless dreary winter in Minnesota.

"I was lonely. I craved something new. I had been alone in America for three years, bearing every bit of life by myself, bitter or sweet. When JJ and I first became close, I read from his eyes that he liked me. The subtle sparkling behind his glasses touched me. He and his friend would come over to our school to visit my friends and me. Actually, it was through one of my friends that I got to know both of them. One night, when we settled on the bench in front of the library, he took off his jacket and asked me to sit on it. I was too shy to do that. But when he turned to me to speak, I almost felt his breath and thought he would kiss me. He hadn't yet.

"When all of us gathered near a table and chatted, I started to murmur to him: 'It's so late in the night; will you be okay on your way home?'

"He murmured back in Chinese, so gently that it melted my heart, 'We'll be fine. Are you worried? Thank you for worrying about me.'

"My friends teased us, 'Mei Ling and JJ, what secrets are you exchanging that you don't want us to know?'

"Unexpectedly, JJ answered, 'What if we do have something to say to each other?' He already felt like someone special to me.

"That night, JJ became a dream so sweet that I was filled with honey. 'Will I begin something new?' I questioned myself with a tender hope. If only I had known how bitter the fruit of this love would turn out to be.

"Soon, summer came, and we parted. We promised to get back together when we were both back at school. When we did in the fall, he took my hand for the first time. It was during an outdoor movie night at our school. We sat next to each other while leaning back on our hands. At first, I only felt his fingertips touching the back of my hand. All of a sudden, he covered my hand with his hand so firmly that I could not escape.

"I was both excited and afraid. I had never known how it felt to be in someone else's hand. How tender and sweet! Love was magic. But I could not allow myself to indulge in it — it would be my last year in college, and I had been prepared for a frantic life while figuring out my future — graduate school applications, grades, and internships. I finally took out my hand, so slowly that I wished he would grab it again. He never did. For the rest of the night, my hand felt empty on the damp grass full of the night dew of September.

"But that was not the end of the story. Even though we were both quiet, the attraction was so strong that we could not cut it off. We started to see each other again. How many times JJ tried to be close to me: He put his hands on my waist; he rested his head on my shoulder like a vulnerable baby...I had to push him away. Maybe I was too much an abstainer to take even a sip of love's sweetness.

"Finally, the battle against myself became so hard that I gave up. I longed for him. I could not deny it anymore. For twenty-one years, I had cornered myself in my safe shell, never allowing any intruder to disturb my peace. I thought love was troublesome and would only distract myself from the serious business of life, like my study. I was used to the tranquility of staying at a women's college as a good student faithful to my academic commitment, a promise I had made to my parents before leaving China four years before.

"JJ changed it all. He brought life back to me. We strolled down the campus in the magnificent colors of autumn; we listened to his iPod with each side of the earphone while humming the same melodies. Finally, in November, he gave me my first kiss. That night, in the wind, while still in his hand, I tasted another human being. The juice of life moistened my heart of a desert. It was unforgettable. We talked all night. I rested on his chest and felt the fresh blood running through my body. I was renewed.

"When he finally left, our hands joined each other so naturally we were like a new couple, even though we had agreed that we would never become lovers. With my grad school deadlines one month ahead, I could not compromise my future, even for the most beautiful reason of love. JJ took off his coat to put on me. That time, I did not refuse. It warmed me up immediately with his warmth. Seeing his eyes sparkling with crystal shine once again and feeling his white shirt flying next to me, I was touched. I would never forget this evening. Before he disappeared in the dark, he kissed me again on the cheek, and I kissed him back. We were standing on the hill near my dorm. The darkness was pure and tranquil.

"That was the end of the sweet part. After that night, JJ never sent me a word or called me at all. I was too busy to reach my deadlines and compiling ten thousand pieces of documents together for grad schools to heed him too — even though I missed him. I never questioned his indifference. After everything was settled in January, I decided to reach him again. He agreed, a little hesitantly, to meet with me for the Chinese New Year celebration at his university. His messages already sounded dull and distant. I should have realized earlier what that meant.

"On that night, he finally showed up — with another girl. When the girl appeared from his back like a shy little bird, her hands still lingering at the corner of his coat, my heart broke. How could he betray me like that? I felt a rush of blood to the head, but tamed my anger. Yes, we had agreed to only be friends. But how could he crush my heart so abruptly, knowing about my vulnerability and attachment to him?

"I took the two of them to the ballroom where the event was going on, pretending nothing was unusual. In the karaoke section, JJ wanted to sing his favorite song, 'Fairy Tale,' but it wasn't in the program. He had to sing it without background music. 'Please believe that we'll have a happy ending together, like in a fairy tale . . .' As the familiar melody started, I joined him. He had sung it to me so many times when we were together. But now, he didn't even dare to look at me. Seeing him drop his head and the familiar brown hair in front of me, I could only chagrin. The song ended, and they had to leave. As I saw his shadow disappearing from the room, with his back turned to me, I realized how badly indifference could hurt."

As Mei Ling finished her story, she was trembling. Algae had sucked the last drop of pink liquid from her glass, while Lily was sitting still, trying to ruminate on the drama.

"A selfish heart," Algae started slowly, "is what's ugly. Everyone is afraid to be hurt, but sometimes we are too ignorant and careless about other people that we become hurtful ourselves." She took a quick look at Mei Ling. Mei

Ling dropped her head. After all, Mei Ling had called her friend ugly just half an hour ago. Algae continued, "The true ugliness of humans is a careless and insensitive heart. Look at what my father and your boyfriend have done. If people only care about their own needs and pleasures, many hearts will break." Magically, Algae sounded like a preacher with her hoarse voice.

At that time, the waiter happened to be at the table again, distributing the cheesecakes the girls had ordered. Mei Ling received a slice coated in smooth chocolate, and Lily was happy about the shining red cherries on her piece. When the waiter handed Algae's vanilla cake to her, surprisingly, a stick of candle was flickering above the cake.

"Happy birthday!" the waiter gave them a generous smile and put down the plate.

They were all confused. "We didn't order a birthday cake..."

He must have made a mistake. But it was Mei Ling who first realized that Algae's birthday was ten days away anyway.

"Algae, happy birthday!" Now that they had all finished their drinks, Mei Ling started to toast with her ice water.

Lily raised her glass too, but Algae still seemed a little hesitant and sullen for what her friend had just called her a while ago.

"Oh, I happen to have a small thing that could be a present for you." Mei Ling put down her glass and fumbled in her purse. She took out a very delicate traditional Chinese peach wood comb. "Take it, Algae. My father brought this for me from China. It's for good luck."

Algae was tentatively reaching out her hand to the comb. Before she could take it, Mei Ling grabbed the comb back again: "Algae, what beautiful black hair you have! This comb will work perfectly for you." She started to playfully comb Algae's hair with the pretty little comb, and twisted her hair to make flowers. Algae no longer cringed. Finally, Algae's hair was turned into a flowery bun shining against the dim light in the bar-restaurant.

"A gift from Father, for love, for beauty, for the friendship that helps us melt down the coldness of life. Algae, I'm sorry for what has happened. You have taught me a lot." Mei Ling stroked her fingers gently through Algae's hair to finish the styling. She could feel the slight trembling of her friend.

Without saying a word, Algae raised her glass. The two other girls raised theirs. With the clear sound of the glasses touching each other, the three of them smile from the bottom of their hearts. Finally, Mei Ling answered the question she had asked herself in the bookstore: There is one way to tell true friendship, the genuine from the fake: sincere friends forgive each other and embrace the imperfections of one another.

Who says that algae, the humblest kind of seaweed, could never blossom into pretty flowers? Mei ling, the beautiful jade, is also shining through the harsh carvings and rubbings in life.

BRUSH STROKES
MADELINE WISE

Late at night at Bentwood House, I turned my wheelchair around and rolled down the corridor again into the dim light of her room. Minutes passed before I managed to climb into bed and straighten out beside Juanita. *If she turns toward me, I'll feel her breath on my cheek.* My fingers touched her soft nightgown. It was good to know she was under the covers next to me. My eyes felt heavy, my body spent.

   This is good. This is enough. This is good enough.

● ● ●

Six weeks after my stroke, my doctor at the rehab center near Boston meted out enough information to keep me hopeful. "To the extent that you can, Jerry," he said, "you'll chart your own future." I was sixty-three.

   When I was learning to stand up and walk again, my wife, Inez, gave me the news. One evening at rehab she stood over my bed buttoning her coat, about to plant her departing kiss, and said, "I had to make a decision for you, Jerry."

I'd lost my speech so I nodded and waited. She leaned toward me and spoke louder than she needed. "I'm sorry, but I broke the rental agreement for your studio. We'll rent the room again when you start painting."

My heart lurched, my breath quickened. I could not pull my thoughts together. I raised my good hand, thumb down, and let it drop. The dream of walking to my studio in the Artists' Co-op kept me trying. With a few words, Inez banished it.

Why?

I always thought of Inez as a neat, dollars-and-cents kind of woman, which was in part what I found admirable about her, perhaps because I didn't find those qualities in myself. Portraiture had been my specialty, but landscapes sold, which is why Inez half-jokingly called me a "motel painter." I guess it figured that she wouldn't keep an unused studio.

Given a choice at the rehab center I would have sulked in bed, but the upbeat staff kept me to a schedule. After several weeks, my doctor arranged a meeting with Inez and myself and announced my impending discharge.

I shot a glance at Inez who sat with her hands folded, ankles crossed. Inez's doctor once said she handled everything with her nerves.

"My husband can't speak yet," she said. "He's begun to walk — thank God for the therapist — but he's still in a wheelchair." Gesturing toward me, she said, "Look at his arm, still propped on the arm-board. How can this…this discharging him possibly work?"

"He'll have more therapy," the doctor said, "and he'll have health aides and homemakers."

When I got home I found that Inez had moved out of our bedroom. Our room, now mine, had been transformed by devices, gadgets, and an electric bed. Inez said she'd sleep better in the spare room next door. I wanted her close and I hoped it was temporary. For the past several years — since she'd been working in a school office, our relationship had shifted in a way that seemed to please Inez, but was disappointing to me. Granted, the job made her life more predictable (my income fluctuated) and brought money of her own, but I missed her touch.

• • •

More health workers than I cared to meet came into our house, and some sense of a new life was taking effect. Inez came home at lunchtime and when she left for work again, I wheeled to the kitchen window and watched for my neighbor, Jeanette. She lived two blocks up, on Common Street. Inez hired her to fill the gaps between homemakers and health aides, until the agency found permanent help.

Jeanette was a piano student in her senior year at the conservatory. At first, she visited daily. She talked and pointed and I nodded, grunted, "Ehhh-ehh." Her face would be easy to caricature: a narrow forehead and wide jaw, a straight lower lip that seemed to underline what she said. Her watchful eyes were too close together and revealed a certain kind of energy, an intuitive way of understanding.

Until a ramp could be built for me, my kitchen window framed my view of the world. As weeks passed I became eager for Jeanette's visits. She brought what she called her "spunky classical" music tapes. While she taught me to play checkers, we listened to *The Rite of Spring*, and she told me about her classes. She was studying Mussorgsky, she said, who wrote a piece she wanted me to hear.

One afternoon, Jeanette popped a tape into her tape recorder. "This is especially for you — *Pictures at an Exhibition*."

I seldom listened to classical music, heard some strange sounds in it, but I tried to look pleased.

Jeanette set the dial of her metronome. "I want you to tap the rhythm with me," she said, handing me a pencil. "I'll nod on the downbeat and you follow." I bobbed my head for a couple minutes.

"Now close your eyes and pick up your imaginary brush. Be like Mussorgsky and throw away the rules."

I closed my eyes.

"Now, listen to this picture and paint your own."

I rapped my pencil against the table. The volume increased and I tapped my shoe on the wheelchair's pedal.

"Listen for the theme," she said, "the promenade that connects the pictures."

To signal the return of the promenade, Jeanette put her hand on mine and with our eyes closed we walked from picture to picture. When I knew each picture was finished, I raised my thumb. Jeanette said, "Sonorous splendor, right Jerry?"

I nodded, raised my thumb higher than my head.

"You're a beautiful man making a beautiful recovery," she said.

• • •

My new ramp lay like a giant plywood tongue from the front door of my house halfway to the street. For several weeks, I had walked inside the house with assistance. Now, in early autumn, I was ready for my first step onto the ramp. Standing by my limp arm, the therapist urged me ahead. I inched my braced leg down the ramp and back. Smiling my crooked smile and quivering inside, I forgot to think about falling. Later, when I sat at the kitchen table, I tried to write a note telling Inez but I couldn't direct my left hand, and threw the pencil down.

Another month passed before I was able to show my therapist that I could clomp two blocks to Common Street. Common was busy with commuter traffic, but the sidewalks were even and Jeanette lived there. Although I only walked on mild days, my face felt blown and bleached from concentrating. On my left, I planted my cane; then in my mind, I shouted at my right leg and swung it through. My leg was never so stubborn that I couldn't order it to move. Yet, I sensed that my thoughts were not always within my grasp. I judged from others' responses — my therapist's puzzled expression, Inez's disbelieving look — that my memory was sometimes clouded, my thinking confused.

Now, on the sidewalk along Common Street, I felt like a tortoise passing Jeanette's house and wondered if she was in class. Jeanette knocked on her picture window, waved, moved her fingers like she was practicing. Each time my braced shoe cleared the sidewalk, I looked up and thought Jeanette might be holding her breath. She mouthed, "Go Jerry!"

That night, I lay in bed with my eyes open. *Dark against dark is nothing. Dark is only to make the light show.* Imagining that I could still paint, I added a strip of yellow ochre to a brass mail slot, outlined knots on a white birch and threw a shadow underneath it. Then I dabbed in two green parrots. *Have a little fun. Paint anything you want. It's all illusions.*

Jeanette made a point to visit on rainy days, and insisted that we page through my book of Fauve landscapes, for their vibrant color. "Splashy colors on gray days," Jeanette said. "Matisse, Derain — they're always cheerful." She often read to me and once she chose to read about a long, slow Balinese dance that needed time to unfold, like a flower. Then she told me to be patient with myself.

One morning during our routine game of checkers, Jeanette tested me — waited to see if I would crown her red checker. Mindlessly, she began to hum. The rocking rhythm of a folk tune caught in my mind; then the tune became a song. First the tune, then the song, and then...I slapped my checker down and a hoarse, thin buzz started in my throat, then a strange growling sound. I cleared my throat. Slowly, tentatively, I began to sing. "Bring back, bring back, bring back my Bonnie..."

Jeanette pushed her chair away, stood up. I kept singing "...bring back my

Bonnie to me." My heart went wild.

"Speak, Jerry, speak. Your speech!" Jeanette shouted. She shook my shoulders. "Can you speak?"

"Ehhrrrhagh." I felt my face fold into a weeping grimace, dropped my chin.

With tears welling in her eyes, Jeanette lifted my damp cheeks. "Let's sing, then — what else can you sing?"

I closed my eyes, shook my head.

"C'mon, don't clam up," she said. "Think of another song."

I coughed, cleared my throat again. The words that rolled, "She'll be coming round the mountain..." touched off more folksongs sung by two oddly mismatched voices.

That evening, I surprised Inez with my singing, heard her laugh for the first time in weeks and like old times, she sang with me a bit, too.

If I can sing, why can't I speak? I wondered. The speech therapist told me that singing and painting came from the right side, but it was the left side, speech, that was hit. I couldn't eat for a time and I didn't sleep much either. I felt like a blank space on my own canvas — an impression of form suggested by brush strokes. During the night, after my mind had painted itself out, the idea came to me to sing. From the bed next door, Inez tapped on the wall. Then I heard her get up and take a pill.

• • •

It was safe now, the doctor said, for me to be left alone for a few hours. Inez fastened a call box around my neck. "It's for my peace of mind," she said. I didn't want to wear a chain around my neck — *Good ol' Jerry, good dog.* I didn't need to be connected to the hospital.

Days later, I sat near the window, waiting for the homemaker who would fix my lunch and walk me. I heard only the sound of my own breathing. Gradually I became aware of a slight weight on my chest — the emergency box. I slid my thumb onto the red button, pressed it. Shortly, the phone rang and I didn't answer. Soon, the doorbell rang and at eight-minutes-seventeen-seconds, I heard someone put a key in the lock and a stranger (who said he was a neighbor) walked in. The first time — well, who wouldn't think it was an accident? Over the next two weeks, three neighbors clocked in, and each one reduced the time until it was under five minutes. Then Inez took the emergency box away. "After all I've done for you," she said, waving the box, "and you use this for entertainment."

One day, after my one-o'clock homemaker dropped the mail onto the table, I spotted an announcement about a new day-care program across town. After phoning the director, Inez said it sounded like a program with a lot of stimulation. They accepted nonspeaking clients but to qualify, I had to be ambulatory and continent. So Inez charted in a second daily walk and I hung the urinal on my wheelchair, used it by the clock, got accurate.

When I qualified two months later, Inez said, "Our appointment's on Thursday at one o'clock. I'm going to visit the day-care center myself, Jerry. I'll approve it for you."

I nodded. Then I scribbled, *me.*

"You want to see it, Jerry?" Inez asked.

I made a fist and thumped my chest.

"It will take less time if I ask questions."

After Inez returned from the day-care center she pulled a chair close to mine and began to tell me about it. "It's kind of silly," she said, "watching half-walking clients trying to dance with their therapists."

Dancing. I'd like to try dancing again. I'd like to see how the half-walking people do it. I can imagine a therapist's fingertips pressing my shoulder. If I had a partner instead of a cane, I could balance. Step-step-together, step-step-together. It would have to be a waltz, and a slow one at that.

"Jerry, Jerry," Inez said. Her face was close to mine now, but it was not the Inez I had danced with. "They sing 'Happy Birthday' and blow out candles like children."

Make it a devil's food cake, but could I blow out candles? Maybe I'll practice blowing on my coffee, my soup. I'd have helpers there, friends. Old friends seldom visited now—too many awkward silences.

"They teach computers at the day-care center," Inez said, "but you're intuitive, Jerry, you've never liked machines. You're a painter."

Funny that you picked now to call me a painter. They teach computers? The tip of my finger would fit on one of those keys. I could poke out words and maybe use an iPad, too, like Jeanette. High-tech could be a new art form.

Inez squinted through her bifocals, then raised her eyes, shook her head. "You're not a mixer, Jerry. It's true that others can speak to you, but I can't imagine you fitting in."

Prickles swept my neck. *You don't understand that I've changed. How would you know whether I'd like it?*

Inez crossed her legs, dangled her wedged slipper and said, "I'm sorry, Jerry, really sorry."

Funny thing. By the look on her face, I think she meant it.

● ● ●

As spring came and magnolias bloomed in my neighbor's yard, the days grew unbearably long. I heard the mail carrier's footsteps around eleven and my homemaker came at lunchtime. Jeanette visited occasionally, and accompanied me for a block or two. She was practicing for her senior recital and looked fatigued.

Late one morning, I sat alone by the window. *So this is it. All of my engines aren't going to fire. I've got losses, yes, but I've got feelings, too. I've got passion.* I thought about what I'd wished for over the past months. I stared at the wall clock, watched a black hand move. Eight minutes past one. *Where is she? Maybe the homemaker missed her bus.*

Minutes later, clutching the rail, I wondered if I had closed the front door. With my limp-tromping gait, I started down the ramp that would take me to Common Street where the din of the street — horns, brakes, the whish of wheels now faint in my ears — meant people were moving. *Got a full head of steam now, you tough old bastard. Go!*

I heard a mail slot clank, saw a mail carrier turn from Jeanette's door. The drapes flew open and Jeanette stood near her picture window, head down, shuffling envelopes. *If she spots me, she'll let me pass because she'll see I'm doing all right. Like a hovercraft, I'm moving two feet off the ground. That's the stuff, Jerry, get going! I've earned a part of me back. Oh Jesus, Jesus, I'm moving!*

Moist air began to reach me from the pond not far away. I knew the pond well, having painted it in all seasons. In a way, the pond had provided my living. In my mind's eye, I began to smear paint as I pulled myself along. I noted house numbers, chimney smoke, and shadows on grass. With cars shrieking past in a whirr of colors, I became a little reckless with the pallet knife. Even the acrid smell of exhaust was a nostalgic reminder of paint thinner. Where was I headed? The pond? My studio? Did it matter?

● ● ●

With difficulty, two policemen stuffed me into the back seat of their patrol car. I saw that they weren't used to working with a dangling arm, a braced and half-dead leg. But I gave them no trouble — how could I? Caged in the backseat I began to feel chauffeured. *I must have covered two-and-a-half miles — a marathon, my personal best!* A dozen helium balloons seemed to swell my head and press the ceiling. When I began to shake, and tears rolled, I understood that the officers thought I was crying with relief. They assured me that I was almost home. I had wanted to see the precinct headquarters, but the patrol car was on Common Street, traveling in the direction of my house.

The cops seemed to know where I lived — someone had squealed. Maybe the homemaker showed up.

• • •

In bed that night, I heard Inez talking on the phone in the next room. I caught, "Can't have it — not knowing where he is…place him."

Place me, there you're talking. Pack me up. I raised my head and heard, "…tell him tomorrow."

Tomorrow. I slipped my hand onto my chest as if to quiet my pounding heart.

• • •

Sundays around one, I counted on hearing Inez's voice at the Bentwood House desk, her footsteps in the corridor. Once a week, she clocked into my new life. Inez brought ground round from home, cooked well-done, and usually talked about her job while I ate. She was often complimentary, saying something like, "Looks like your face is filling out."

I kept a pencil in my shirt pocket for the times she didn't understand my gestures. I might have rolled my wheelchair to a computer and typed answers to her questions, as my friends Ross and Percy taught me to do. I might have asked some questions of my own but like the memories she brought, Inez began to slip into the past.

In mid-June Jeanette breezed into my room and when she bent to kiss my forehead, her hair smelled like summer. She'd sent four applications for teaching jobs, and she'd visited with Inez. She brought my art books in her backpack. *When the residents see me leafing through my books, they'll understand that I'm a painter. They'll hear Jeanette ask questions and realize I can think. When they see how quickly I scribble an answer, they might speak to me more often. And with a friend like Jeanette, well, a man like that still has some stuffing.* Before Jeanette left that day, I walked with her to the photo board and pointed to a snapshot of myself with Juanita. On my first field trip to the arboretum, Juanita sat beside me in the van. "You're in a good place, Jerry," Jeanette said.

One Sunday a month later, Jeanette arranged my painting demonstration, "an in-house demo," she called it. Visitors and staff gathered in the visitors' lounge. The rug had been rolled against the wall and newspapers covered the floor. Jeanette put a huge piece of poster-board down. "Think of Jerry as your new resident painter," she said. She dripped pink paint onto the white board, then gave a tube of yellow to me and said, "Squeeze it, Jerry, you've nothing to lose."

I glanced at the expectant faces around the room. The little crowd cheered. *"Nothing to lose," so why stop now?* I rolled my wheelchair across the board. Ross, Eddie, Juanita, and the rest of my audience hooted and clapped. I rolled again, this time stopping mid-board, turning. I rolled and turned, until my hand and the wheels were wet and varicolored. *Got 'em laughing now. Why, even old Percy sitting over in the corner, can't keep a straight face.* I dropped my heel, slid it through the paint and stamped the board with my cane. Finally, I tossed my pencil down.

When I was finished, Jeanette cleaned paint from the wheels and a few hours later, the poster-board was dry. I pointed to the better sections, Jeanette cut them out and assembled a mural on the wall near my bed.

● ● ●

Often before drifting off to sleep, I gazed at my new art and thought how lucky I was. I needed so little: a few clothes, pencils and paper, some snapshots, and art books. Yet, I could scarcely imagine a more comfortable life. As fall turned to winter, I stopped wondering what I might be doing if I hadn't had a stroke, if I were not at Bentwood House. Once in a while, some feelings surfaced that I couldn't account for.

One night, I awakened feeling restless, fearful. I checked my clock frequently, was afraid it had stopped. I feared that this new good life might not last and I feared the night itself. My bedtime sleeping tablet seemed to have worn off and the idea came to me to move about. Pushing away the covers, I got myself onto the side of the bed. In the dim light, I fumbled with my robe, and found that I couldn't manage my leg-brace alone, so I set out in my wheelchair. I waved to the nurse who looked up as I passed her desk. "Jerry, dear," she said, "you need another sleeping pill?" I shook my head and rolled down the hall into Juanita's room.

At the foot of her bed, I slipped my hand beneath the covers and touched her ankle. She moved and groaned, then opened her eyes. "What is it, Jerry?"

I nodded my head.

"Go to bed now, love," she said, "I'll dance with you tomorrow." She turned her back to me.

I recognized the round freckled face of the Irish woman in the next bed, but I couldn't remember her name. I stroked her pale fingers until she smiled and opened her eyes. She patted my hand and reached for the rosary on her bedspread.

I made my way to Ross's room. Ross didn't awaken when I rubbed his toes. I stretched to reach Ross's penlight, clipped to the neck of his pajamas, and shined it in his face.

"Chocolate milk you lookin' for?" Ross said, pointing to the little carton beside his bed. "Help yourself. Straw's in it."

When I didn't move, Ross said, "Hey, you in a mood, again? Here," he said, "take my hand. We'll talk tomorrow on the computer." I took Ross's hand for a moment.

Old Percy lay in the next bed and he'd also had a stroke. Percy could speak a little if he chose, but I didn't disturb him. I sat near Percy for a short while, noticed his cassette, music tapes, and headset. Then I wheeled away.

On a night like this, when I was restless, I wondered why I found myself at my friends' bedsides.

I rolled back to Juanita's room and sat for several minutes before reaching under the covers for her soft foot. Gently, I pressed my thumb into the pads of her toes. With her back to me, Juanita raised her head slightly.

"That you again, Jerry?" she said, her voice thick with sleep. "What is it now?"

I locked my wheelchair and struggled to my feet. I grasped an edge of the covers and folded them back a little.

"It's okay, Jerry," Juanita murmured. "Okay."

It's okay, Jerry. Okay. Juanita's words were not an invitation, nor were they a protest. They seemed welcoming to me, as if it were natural to want to be close. As if wanting to be near her was not a bold and unusual move. As if it were an everyday thing.

Wanting to be near her. An everyday thing.

WIDE OPEN

THE HUMAN NATURE
MARGUERITE DEL GIUDICE

When I lived on Loveland I used to let that stupid fat thing next door put all her garbage and ashes on the side of my house. Rachel. For one thing they had coal heat and I had oil, and she would put the basket of ashes at my side of the house, and when I opened my window naturally all the ashes would fly in and stick to the furniture. And no matter what they did to their house — lumber, linoleum, wallpaper — the mess ended up on my side of the house, and meanwhile they're keeping their house looking nice.

My sister Vivian used to say, "You know, Ceil, you shouldn't let her get away with that, because if your landlord comes by he'll say, 'Hey, you're making my house look like a dump.'" But I'd say, "Oh, Viv, it really doesn't show, it's on the side of the house. Who's gonna see it?"

I mean, *Who wants to argue with a neighbor?* So I never said anything.

So what happens. One day your brother Anthony comes in and says, "Mommy, Rachel's putting up a little fence."

"A little fence?" I says. "Where?"

He says, "Over here, on the side of the house."

My bathroom on Loveland overlooked the behind of her house, remember that? So I lifted up the window and I says, "Ra." I says, "What are you doing that for?"

This fence, it was just the width of the driveway, you know?

And she says, "Well, we don't want your papers to go in our yard."

Imagine.

So I says, "My papers! There's a store down the street, and the papers blow everywhere. How about when you put your garbage next to my house? I never said anything to you about that."

"Well," she says, "we don't do it anymore."

So what am I going to do, fight with her? My mother always said, "Never fight with people, especially on the street or out your window." So I says to Rachel, "Okay," and I closed the window, and I didn't talk to her anymore.

A few weeks go by and she calls me up.

"Hello, this is Rachel," she says.

"Yeah?" I says. "Rachel who?"

"Rachel next door," she says.

"Yes?" I says.

"Well," she says, "your clothesline. You better put it down on Friday around twelve, because if it isn't down around twelve, we're gonna cut it down."

The Cervones had put it up, the Cervones around the corner who we rented from. They had the hook on our house, the pole was in the Molitos' yard, and there was nothing in Rachel's yard but the overhang. For thirteen years it was that way and they never said a word.

I says, "Well, thank you, Rachel," and I hung up and went and told Mister Cervone the whole thing. He says, "You leave that clothesline right there." He had a little accent, like. So I forgot about it, and come Friday, like always, I washed and hung my clothes, a lot of them because I had three young kids. It must've been twenty yards of wet clothes, sheets, pajamas, housedresses, and your diapers. I didn't even know it had happened until Nancy Prudenti came over.

"Cecilia!" she says. "Your neighbor is cutting down your clothesline!"

I says, "Do me a favor, Nancy. I don't want to put a foot on that property. Go pick them up for me, will you?"

So I'm watching from the window, her and Elsie from down the street picking up my wet clothes from that jackass's yard, and my first reaction is to call a cop, which I did. Marty Cooper, who used to live next door to us when we lived on Niles Avenue. He came right away.

"I've been on the police force for twenty years and I never heard of a thing like this!" he says to me.

But what could he do, really, so I sent him home and called up Mister Cervone. Daddy and I actually went to see him. And afterwards Cervone went directly to the jackass's house.

He says to her, "You think you spited Cecilia? You spited me. That was *my* property, Rachel. Any problem, you should have come to me for. I could've lost a tenant because of you, because of you aggravating them. And shame on you. Are you proud of what you did? A woman with three children and you have the nerve to cut her clothesline down with all the wet clothes on it? You couldn't cut it without the clothes on it?"

She started to cry, but she never said boo to us. And the next day, maybe it was two days, she actually went up to my landlady on the street, Mrs. Cervone, with her hand on her hip like this and says, "Do you know what I did to Cecilia?" She got joy out of it, *after* she cried.

Now what her problem was, you tell me.

Cervone said to us, "We'll take care of it. We'll put another clothesline." So him and his son put another clothesline where you had your bedroom — you and Frances, remember? From that window it went to a pole by the birch trees, and I never talked to Rachel again. I never said a bad word about her, and I never fought with her. But I could never talk to her again. And then she moved away, I don't know where, and I didn't even have to go out of my way to ignore her anymore. But years after I still really hated her. If I saw her, God forgive me, if I saw her dying on the street I would have walked right by.

So today, thirty-five years later, what happens — just to show that God doesn't forget. He's like an artist. What do you call it, that phrase for when things come out perfect like this. Yes — poetic justice. Like God had His hand in it.

This morning I'm driving up Prospect in your father's Oldsmobile because he took the Caddy to go help your brother Anthony at the market. The Caddy will start up early in the morning when it's cold, and the Olds you have to wait for the sun to thaw the engine. So I'm in the Olds, nobody recognizes me when I'm in the Olds, and I come up to the intersection by that little diner where your Uncle Buzzie found the old lady frozen in the alley that time. And the car in front of me, it goes right through the intersection and smashes a car going across Main Street. Naturally I pull over, see what's what, and who comes up to my window but the cop. Marty Cooper's son it was — what's his name? You went once with him to a prom, or was it Frances? They call him Sonny. He says, "Hello, Mrs. Bonelli," and I says, "I'm fine, Sonny, and how are you, and how's your father and mother. Did you see what happened?"

Just then one of the drivers gets out, the one who was driving in front of me, and who is it but that jackass Rachel who by then I hadn't seen since she threw herself on your godfather Rocky's grave when he died — when was it, twenty years ago? She actually got into the ground and Korr the undertaker had to go in after her. She just doesn't know how to act.

She says to Sonny, "He ran the light, my side was green," and meanwhile the other man is running up, shaking his head, waving his fingers. Sonny's just nodding at the two of them — he's a lot like his father in the face. Then she sees me: "Cecilia!" She has this face on like we're old friends, which right away burns me up.

"Hello, Rachel," I says.

She says, "Cecilia, it's been years and years. When was the last time?"

"Rocky's funeral," I says and her face falls down, like it should. I almost felt sorry for her, thin the way she was.

Sonny says to me, "Mrs. Bonelli, did you see what happened?"

How do you like this, I'm thinking. The son's gonna do for me in 1988 what the father Marty couldn't do in 1953 when you were one.

I says, "Yes, officer, I saw it," and I says to Rachel, "Were you in that car?"

"Yes, I was," she says.

"Well, then you were right in front of me," I says.

She's smiling, like this home-free smile. That's when I did it. I don't know where I got the nerve. I says to Sonny, "The light was red, officer. I was right behind Mrs. Condurso and I had already applied my own brake because I saw it coming." I just shrugged at her. I says, "I have to tell the truth, Rachel. You wouldn't want me to lie to the police, would you?"

Well, the look on her face? I felt like I had won the lottery! Sonny goes to appraise the dents and I says to her, "You like it, Rachel?"

"The light was green, Cecilia," she says. "I know the light was green."

Now to tell the truth I don't know what color the light was. I wasn't paying attention. All I know is, when I saw Rachel Condurso, all I saw was red.

"What can I say, Ra?" I says. "What looks green to you looks red to me." If they called me to the witness stand, I would have to say red — that's what I told her.

Sonny puts it all down, takes my number. I get in the Olds, roll down the window.

"What goes around comes around, Rachel," I says and I leave her in the street with her open mouth.

Forgive and forget? Baloney, I say.

I used to console myself by thinking up excuses for her. But now I realize something about people that I didn't at the time Rachel cut my clothesline. Then, I was young, and I loved everyone. Now I know God makes some of them rotten, and they'll just turn on you, like it's part of the human nature.

EVERYTHING SHINING
LEIGH CAMACHO ROURKS

Teenie leaned against the back door, shoulder to glass, and considered the fat, black water moccasin lazing on the slab outside. He didn't see the orange tom that'd been coming around lately, the too lean cat with only one eye and a ragged bit missing from both ears. Most evenings, it would sweetly pluck scraps of steak and catfish from his fingers, and Teenie'd gotten used to him. He figured the tom was probably somewhere cooler than his usual spot on the stained slab, snoozing under one of the camellias or his mama's roses, thank God, what with the moccasin fatter around than probably all four of the tom's thin legs put together—the snake's a winner in that fight, for sure.

Teenie considered the shotgun in the closet, but grabbed a sharp-edged shovel out of the garage instead. He hated to kill the snake, but he knew the tom wouldn't survive a bite. Hell, he might not survive one either, not with the Ford blowing black smoke and his cell service turned off. Teenie sighed, stepped out the back door, and swung the shovel twice, hard.

The clang of metal to concrete still ringing in his ears, Teenie lifted the snake's head with the shovel, squinting as he carried it back to the coulee, filled with water after the recent rains. The summer sun seemed extra bright these days — the light kicking off the pile of copper his cousin Ray'd dumped in the back. The UV index was off the charts, the weather channel said. Wear sun block, it advised. Teenie didn't have any, but Ida, Ray's wife, was forever talking about how they were all going to burn up; Teenie was never quite sure if she meant that hell or UV would be the cause.

Teenie took his time moving across his half acre. He was a long-legged man who strolled with a lazy, rolling limp ever since he took a tumble on a rig, but still sweat pricked at his shaved scalp and stung his cracked lips, and he figured he should buy some sun block, just in case.

He didn't like how Ray's scrap metal pile was growing, the copper wire a twisted mess in his yard, like a strange nest or even a mass of shining, curling snakes. About ten hastily cut pipes and a parking meter pregnant with quarters topped off Ray's ever-expanding haul.

"I'm not your fucking bank, Ray," he'd said, last time that his cousin dropped some off.

"You're not much fucking else, Teenie," Ray had said back, tossing a Miller at him. Ray's wife just shrugged her skinny shoulders when Teenie looked to her for help. He wondered sometimes if Ray didn't feed Ida, keeping her hungry like a fighting dog or something.

As he took the snake's body to join its head at the coulee, Teenie watched the sun play against the scales, the black not absorbing the light like you'd think, but slinging it out like polished metal. Everything in his yard shined like that these days.

"All this glittering, you'd think we were rich," he said to no one at all as he watched the snake float away.

●   ●   ●

Later he told the tom about it. "You be careful, don't get bit by one of those black bastards," he said, offering the back of his hand for the cat to butt up against. A car's engine caught his attention, and he scratched at the base of one of the cat's ruined ears. "And stay clear of Ray's truck when he pulls up. The sumbitch drives too fast, won't even see you."

Pretty much no one but Ray and Ida drove down Teenie's road. It was a pot-holed dead end the parish had let his daddy name a million years ago: Whiskey Lane, as if he was a bootlegger instead of just a crippled dreamer with a half-built radiator still. Teenie's mama had huffed every time she pulled past the sign, sick of her husband's schemes. Both of them dead now, but Teenie imagined them still bickering over that sign every time he hit the end of his road.

Ray thought the name was hilarious, still chuckling over it; Teenie's daddy was some kind of comic-god to him.

The sound of the engine drew closer, and Teenie went inside and pulled out some sandwich stuff. The front door slammed open and Teenie cursed.

"Hey, cuz?" Ray called into the house.

Teenie didn't bother playing out the fight he saw coming, instead saying, "Last time. I mean it," to his cousin, then, after a pause, "and don't hit my goddamn cat when you're pulling around."

The door closed in answer.

Ida wandered into the kitchen, sashaying in her short denim skirt, like she was still in high school. "You got a cat?" she asked, her voice somehow husky and girlish all at once.

Teenie shrugged, handed her a sandwich, watching her carefully to see if she'd take a bite. Her pale legs were just knees and angles, spotted by a bruise or two. She spent her evenings helping Ray get the copper wire out of new construction and was always covered in the marks of their "business." Ray said she could climb as good as a monkey, scrambling over just about anything. His helpful girl.

"Lucky. Ray won't let me keep anything alive around." She looked at the sandwich, one of her limp, brown curls sliding into the mustard as she lowered her head to inspect it. "I don't eat meat. It's bad for your colon."

Teenie nodded. Ida was constantly going on about colons. "Don't think there's much meat in that bologna. I can make you one with just cheese, I guess."

Ida shrugged and took a bite of the one he'd already made, mustard still in her hair. "It's bad for the environment too, meat eating. And ungodly. I read that…"

Teenie stopped listening, continued nodding as he washed the mayonnaise off the knife, put away the bread, the bologna. He liked the sound of her voice filling the nooks of his kitchen, but figured most of what she said was as good as white noise.

"You and Ray gonna have to sell that stuff soon," he said when there was a lull.

"That's all him." She grinned, and Teenie searched for anger or sarcasm or irony in her voice when she added, "He says that I'm too pretty to worry about it, anyway." He didn't find any.

Teenie nodded, and the back door opened. Ray was younger by two years, but he out-bulked and out-stood Teenie by a good fifty pounds and four inches. "Don't be so impatient, cuz," Ray said, using his dirty t-shirt to wipe sweat from his face. "You're going to get a nice chunk of rent money for the lawn space soon enough."

"I'd rather have my yard back."

"The shit you would. That truck of yours needs new rings." Ray poked him, square in the middle of his work shirt, finger thudding. "And it ain't like you're getting any calls to go out these days." Then came the crooked smile, teeth covered like Ray'd never done when they were kids. Back then that smile was what he called gold for pussy. "You need me and my rent, cuz, and I need you." Ray didn't stop poking.

Teenie pulled away from the finger, thinking of how he'd got canned after slipping on the rig. Not following procedure, they'd said, making the fall his fault. An OSHA violation was the last thing he needed following him around. The rigs might not seem to take safety seriously, but they certainly took the possibility of being noticed by OSHA and MMS serious enough, especially since the big spill. And now no one in oil would hire him. He was blacklisted, not even the shallow-water death traps called him back, lax as they were. And his back was as bad off as his truck these days, so what could he do? But then, maybe he wasn't too bad off to take a swing at Ray if the sumbitch kept poking.

Then Ray was saying, "Aww, come on. Look, I brought you a gift. Good shit," sweeping his arm out at Ida, all grand like. "Rack 'em, girl."

She pulled a fifth of drugstore tequila from her bag and lined up some paper cups from the cabinet. Ray stood there, arm still out, grinning like an asshole, like he fucking invented tequila, like he expected Teenie to start clapping.

They tossed back the shots, and Ray told Teenie all about a nearby substation he was pretty sure wasn't guarded too good. Teenie told him not to shit where they all ate. He had enough fucking copper he didn't know how to sell. They put back another round, and then another, and Ida said, "Teenie says I can name his cat." Teenie nodded as if he'd told this girl he'd loved way back in high school any such thing.

• • •

The sound of someone banging around in his bathroom woke Teenie, and from his place on the carpet he could see that Ray was still passed out on the couch. There was a clanging crash, a bright noise he worried was the back of the toilet tank slipping, cracking as Ida searched for his back pills. He'd just started hiding them, tired of there never being one when he needed it. But he had no interest now in listening to Ida search and no will to confront her. So he pushed himself up, found the bag of cat food, what was left of last night's tequila, and his book, and turned the knob of the back door with his elbow, wishing she'd at least be quiet about it, that she'd sneak around, pretend that she didn't know that he knew she was stealing from him.

Teenie stepped into the night air, wet and heavy and hard to breathe. Bullfrogs sounding like ducks, their voices so big out here, called to each other. The moon seemed barely a sliver, the rest of its fullness behind clouds, but the soft, blue haze of city lights that never left the horizon anymore made it easy enough for Teenie to see. After spilling some food on the concrete for the tom, he settled into the cypress rocker his mother made when he was about sixteen. "No use letting the tools rust," she'd said out in the shop, showing him how to sand the gray wood, how to measure the curve of the runners so they'd fall smooth and flat. That day, thanks to his mother, his father's plan to sell driftwood he'd stolen off state land — any of his father's great plans, really — finally resulted in something Teenie could actually see, something he could touch.

All the while they were out there sweating over the cypress, Ray and his dad sat inside smoking and laughing. Dreaming bigger, they called it.

Setting the tequila bottle between his thighs and the book on his lap, Teenie thought about his dream, not so big, maybe. He'd figured on working offshore for a few years, ten or so, and putting enough money away to start a real business. Not some back of the yard, piece of shit scam, but a hardware store or a gas station. Maybe a little bar. He clicked his tongue, a quiet call, and the tom was there, ignoring the food to push at his hand, rubbing the sides of his teeth across Teenie's knuckles, his purring a heavy vibration against Teenie's skin. There were no savings though. The first little bit went to bury his mother in the family plot, and what he'd saved all these years since was now gone too, swallowed up by hospital bills and the time out of work.

The door made a noise and Ida was standing there with them, grinning wide, her teeth black in the shadows. "You can't read in the dark," she said, and Teenie thought she might be shaking a bit, then thought maybe it was just the tremor of his own hangover.

"Got a flashlight," he said, gesturing under the chair, and she was reaching between his thighs for the bottle, yanking on it in a way that told Teenie his pills were still under his mattress. The cat wandered to the spilled food.

"You always were a book guy," she said, settling to the concrete, her lips staying close to the mouth of the bottle. "Even in high school."

Teenie watched the tom and thought of Ida back then, always smoking by the Dumpster, Ray's hand at the small of her back, his fingers down in the gap her jeans made there. Thought of the three of them riding around in Ray's truck, never anywhere to go but the levee, their stolen beers and pot making it almost interesting out there. Her face was rounder then, the skin pink at the edges instead of the hollow yellow-gray it had become. Wherever they went, Teenie ended up in a book, mostly so he didn't have to watch her make-out with Ray. Then later, when Ray passed out, he'd put the book down and watch her fiddle with her cigarettes or the pulled wrapper from a beer bottle, the two of them sometimes talking about their lives in that golden time after Ray was out.

"We could name him after that guy in that book they made us read," she said, and Teenie almost said "Who?" but then caught up with her. The tom.

"Name him what you like," he said, still unsure of the book.

"Higgen?" She ran her hand across his leg. "Holden?" Teenie thought of how he'd hated *The Catcher in the Rye*, how he'd hated selfish, snide Holden Caulfield, how everyone else had loved him.

"Sure," he said, brushing her bony fingers from his thigh and then imagining them still there. Knowing he was betraying the tom, he said, "Holden's good."

The next night when the lights popped, there was no lightning in the sky, no rain or heavy winds, no reason but his own empty bank account to be sweating in the dark. Teenie cursed himself for forgetting to pay the bill. He slipped outside and tried to do the math in his head, pacing the backyard with Holden following him, both of them stopping and staring at Ray's pile of copper, that sort of "one day" treasure no good for paying a reconnect fee.

He could hear Holden purring, could hear the bullfrogs extra loud, and then he realized he didn't hear anything else, not even the one buzzing street light. Everything was dark. He moved to the side of the lot, trying to remember if he could usually see the house down the way, trying to remember if he could always hear the crickets so loud.

Then there was the angry sound of a gunned engine and of tires spitting gravel and Holden was high-tailing it to the back. Teenie turned and watched the cat even as he heard Ray's truck hit the driveway. He could hear a pounding from the front door and finally he looked back and Ray was standing there, just another shadow in the dark. But the pounding was too hard and the shadow was too erect, weirdly stiff and lacking Ray's easy slump. And it was alone.

Ray was alone.

Ida was not there. The taste of metal suddenly filled the back of Teenie's throat. The date flicked into his head, and he realized it was too early in the month for a disconnect.

Ida always followed Ray. For fifteen years, Ida was always in his footsteps. Always.

Ida was not there now.

And then Teenie knew why the lights were out. Copper.

His feet shifted in the slick mud as if waiting for a command, and then he was running, his boots fighting for traction. When he got to the front, he shoved Ray hard. "Where is she? Where the fuck, Ray?"

And Ray was shaking his head. "She wasn't even touching anything."

"You didn't leave her? Jesus."

Ray still shaking his head, "I put her out. There was a flash. She wasn't even touching anything and then this flash and . . . " Ray finally stopped shaking his head and looked at his cousin, "Jesus, Teenie, she was on fire."

Teenie stared at Ray. "You didn't leave her there." His voice was matter of fact, and he went over to the truck, looked in the cab, in the bed, screaming at

Ray now, "You didn't fucking leave her." And then he was back at the front door where Ray was standing and then inside and then getting his daddy's wheelchair out of the spare room and then back at the truck putting the wheelchair in the bed. "Get in the fucking truck, Ray," he said.

And Ray just staring at him, mouth open so even in the dark Teenie could see his ruined teeth, the bulk of them eaten away, leaving them sharp and crooked like fangs. "You fucking shortcut-taking junkie. Get in the truck or I'm getting the shotgun and shooting your ass where you stand." Teenie felt himself panting.

"It's not my — " and Teenie knew Ray was about to say "fault."

"Electricity jumps when it's hot, Ray. Arcing. It's fucking called arcing, and for what? Just to steal a thousand dollars worth of scrap metal you can't even sell? For that, you took her someplace really hot?" Teenie looked at his dark house, the dark street lamp. "Really fucking hot?"

Ray started shaking his head again, but he moved finally, and Teenie could hear the soles of Ray's shoes scraping the driveway as he slinked over to the truck. The sound of it way too loud.

The substation was small, surprisingly small, as if it would hold only a little electricity. It was barely a shotgun patch of land where not much at all could have ever lived, where not even a bootlegger would bother to squat. As they pulled up, something seemed familiar. The smell. It reminded Teenie of a *cochon de lait*, and even as he thought of those pig roasts his father would throw when a scheme went well, he realized what he smelled now was no pig. A cloud moved a fraction and the light from the full summer moon, huge and orange, suddenly hit the edge of her hand, glittering against the sheen of her blackened fingernails. Teenie threw up in the truck.

At least his stomach was empty when he saw the rest of Ida.

Getting at her was not easy, even after they'd cut out a chunk of the fence, and Teenie could hardly bear any of it, not the walking to her, not the picking her up, not the carrying her like she was just one of his father's pigs. There was a quarter-sized patch on her forehead that somehow was still her sweet pale skin in a sea of thin black meat. Teenie set his eyes on a freckle there in the middle of it, one she'd had as long as he'd known her, and kept the mantra of her name rolling over and over his tongue as they walked.

Neither man knew how or where to hold this cracked and blackened version of Ray's helpful girl, so Teenie just tried to be gentle, but the skin of her left arm, crackling like tin foil, tried to slough as they moved her, and she was still so very hot to the touch even through the blanket Ray'd thrown on her to put out the fire. The blanket he'd left when he'd left her. Even with that shroud protecting their hands, the heat bit at them.

Her face was bloated and broken, the skin around her left eye especially swollen, creating a crack that threatened to split near the orb. He wondered if that was where the current had entered or exited, unsure of where the damage would be the worst, but he could still see her in there, in that freckle, that small patch of clear skin, and he would not look away.

They moved her to the wheelchair, her body small enough so that Teenie's back barely complained. Then he realized they'd have to take her out again to get her in the truck, the bed the only place that made sense, but he still thought maybe she could sit in the cab. Wanted to put her there, sitting up like she was still alive.

All the while he tried to imagine this was some other thing they were holding, some other thing they were out to do. But he couldn't. It was Ida.

"Hurry," Ray said, and Teenie tried to not hear him. "With lights out everywhere, someone will be out here soon to check." Ray now composed, Teenie the one just shaking his head.

The drive back was short, Teenie thinking of the huge pile of stolen copper at the back of his yard instead of the dead woman in the bed of Ray's truck.

• • •

Their grandfather had owned acres and acres of sugarcane fields once, but Teenie's father hadn't been interested in farming, and then, after the wheelchair, wasn't able to do the work, even if he'd been willing. So he'd sold the fields off a parcel at a time, the money from each piece of family land never enough to do more than buy whiskey and dreams and disappointment. But there was one parcel no one ever bought, the little family cemetery started for Teenie's four stillborn aunts and uncles and later filled up with his grandparents, then Ray's daddy (shot while his son was still in the crib), a drowned cousin, and finally Teenie's parents. All of them in tombs like small stone beds, hard and flat and gray, everyone above ground here.

"She should be with the family," Teenie'd said in the truck.

And so the two men ended up behind someone else's fields, straining to pry open Teenie's mother's little tomb with a couple of crowbars from the big metal tool box next to Ida's head. Her grave was small, but it was the biggest one in the plot, Teenie spending all that he could when she died. The smell of dusty rot filled the air when the top slid sideways, and they pushed until the space was big enough. Grunting, they lowered Ida's curled body, wrapped in her rough shroud, into the stone bed, laying it so it was bowed around his mother's corpse. Teenie imagined the painted stone cherubs on the babies' graves watching them with their chipped blue eyes.

Then Ray moved to the truck too quickly, uttering no words over his wife's grave even, and Teenie watched him and, for just a minute, imagined splitting Ray's skull. Then, thinking of his mama shifting his cousin, just a squalling baby then, into his lap at Ray's father's funeral, thinking of her voice stiff and quiet as she explained that him and Ray'd be like brothers now, Teenie felt guilty.

"The police are bound to end up at your place soon enough," he said to Ray, and then under his breath to Ida and his mother, "and then mine."

Ray nodded, his hand on the door handle, and Teenie understood that Ray would slither away, leaving him with all that tangled, shiny evidence in his yard, too broke to pay the bail he was sure to need soon enough. He looked down at the flat gray tomb, closed again, and thought of his mother at the end, scrubbing other people's floors despite the cancer, his father's debts their only inheritance.

Ray and his father, the same man, really.

"A drink, maybe," Teenie said, knowing Ray would not turn him down.

• • •

When he went to pour the vodka, Teenie left his pills on the table, saying, "It's been a long night," as if he'd understand if Ray needed one or two, as if he was happy to share, and when he handed Ray a cup, he noticed the bottle'd moved, skidded to the left like it too was ready to run.

Teenie'd thought Ray would pass out fast, that maybe he'd call the cops once his cousin was snoring, but Ray was jumpy, talking a thousand words a minute, saying, "Maybe California. Maybe Vermont," going on about pot farming, already on to the next scheme. Ida's name never even coming up.

"What about the mess back there?" Teenie finally said, knocking on the glass of the back door in case Ray wasn't sure where he meant. Without any light shining on it, the treasure was just a gray lump.

Ray shrugged. "Don't think I got the time to find a buyer," he said. "I'll have to do without that cash."

Teenie looked at his reflection in the glass, saw his father's face outlined by the pile in the backyard. He jerked his head away and looked over at Ray. "You'll have to... What the fuck is wrong with you?"

And Ray was saying, "Aw, come on, cuz. Be cool."

The shovel was still propped against the back door where he'd left it the morning before. "She loved you," Teenie said, his hand finding the handle, just meaning to lean on it like a cane, his back hurting so bad now.

Then Ray shrugged again, and Teenie sort of limped towards him, the head of the shovel a dull thump on the bare floor.

"You can't leave me with this mess," he said, and Ray turned and smiled at him, raised the paper cup in some sort of toast, like he was trying to charm him or something, like Teenie hadn't seen that smile pointed at a thousand chumps and lays over the years, like Teenie didn't know what it meant.

That smile exhausted him and he leaned deep into the shovel's handle, the wood so very smooth from years of use. "She loved you," he said again, the wonder of it flattening his voice.

And for a moment it looked like Ray got it, a tiny nod of his head, a shift of his eyes, but then he was talk-talking like always, some bullshit about love and loss, his tongue a rattler buzzing in Teenie's skull.

And Teenie thought of the tom, imagined putting him in the cabin of Ray's truck, saying, "It's okay, Holden," or something like that, before turning Ray's keys in the ignition. Before driving away, maybe leaving the amazing heat of a house on fire behind them.

The shovel's handle was smooth, almost silky against his fingers, and Teenie thought of the beautiful ache that would live in his shoulders if he swung. He stood up, pulling his heft off the soft, worked wood, and felt the weight of the shovel in every part of his tired back. And he held it up like that despite the pain, the head hovering just a little off the ground, his back straight as it would get, his tired body paralyzed by the thought of Ida, burnt up like leaves in a trash pile, curled in his mother's grave.

GREEN HILLS
TERRY RUUD

"Yonder's Miss Minnie Pearl's house," Fred said, pointing — with his face — toward the driver's side window. I peered around him, across the cab of the furniture delivery truck. Through the thick jade foliage and the early-morning Nashville fog, I could barely distinguish the white colonial house. "She treated me real good, Miss Minnie. I brought a china cabinet over there last summer. Nice lady. Yes, indeed."

He whistled a few aimless notes and pulled thoughtfully at his graying mustache. "Col', this mornin'. Where you say you was from? Minnesota? Real col' up there." He paused, to turn onto the bypass on the south side of Music City. "Them blizzards and shit up there ain't for me. I like it here, warm. How you stand it up there?"

I shivered, and as Fred passed his thermos cup of steaming coffee to me, the black and white reflection of our hands shone blurry and distorted on the shiny side of it.

"It's not that bad. You get used to it," I said.

"Different kind of col', though, huh?" he asked, turning up the heat. "Wet kind of col', down here."

"Umm-hmm," I replied through a mouthful of coffee, and passed the cup back.

"Miss Quarles say you play music? You ain't alone, in *this* town! I gotta hand it to you, movin' clear down here like that. Me? I can't carry a tune in a bucket. Look there!"

The sun was burning basketball-orange through the mist.

"That's nice. No sir, you can't beat Tennessee for sights like that. I love the South. I was born and raised right here. Family's here — wife and kids. I pay my bills. A man can't ask for no more. I got everythin' I need. The Lord's good to me." He seconded his opinion with a deep "Umm-hmm."

We turned south onto Hillsboro Road, back toward Quarles's Furniture. I watched the Green Hills Mall roll by my window. Fred stopped for the light. A group of white teenagers in blue and white school uniforms were playing hackey-sack under an oak tree on the Hillsboro Academy High School lawn. The light changed. He waved his fingers over the steering wheel to encourage the Mercedes in front of us, then eased the truck along behind it.

"Bluebird," he said, gesturing as we drove by the Bluebird Cafe. "You ever play there?"

"Last Sunday — for the amateur writers' night."

"You must be pretty good, then. Ever'body that wants to make it big plays the Bluebird. I've never been — I don't come into Green Hills too much — but that's the place, for songwriters." He offered the cup again. "Have some more. You col'. How'd it go?"

The comfort of the coffee went clear to my bones. I held my hands over the cup to warm them, then handed it back to Fred. "Okay. I was nervous. My voice was shaky, and so were my hands. I could barely play my guitar. But the owner of the place walked in while I was playing, and she grinned and gave me a thumbs-up sign. That made me feel good."

Fred shook his head. "I could never do that! You must do all right, Mister Minnesota," he grinned. "Any record people there? Anybody worth knowin'?"

"A publisher invited me down to Music Row Monday afternoon to play him some songs, so I went. But he said that he didn't know of any country artists looking for songs like mine — my style — right now. My songs aren't really Top 40 country radio. I write a lot of story songs — about farming, about country, about Minnesota, the Midwest."

"But there ain't no *country* up there, is there? I mean, when I hear Minnesota, all I think is Minneapolis and Prince and shit." Fred drained the last of the coffee, then handed the cup back to me, nodding at the thermos for me to refill it.

"I grew up way north of Minneapolis, up by the Canadian border, on a farm outside of a town of twenty-four people. We had to drive forty-five miles to see a movie."

"Twenty-four people! Whoa, man, that's *country*! I didn't know there was that kind of country up *there*. Up by Canada? That's real col'."

"Well, the winters get cold — sometimes a hundred below, with windchill. You just have to dress for it." I held the coffee cup between my knees, and pulled my jacket collar closer to my neck.

Fred thought awhile. "So — here's you, a Yankee, down here, tryin' to make it in music, humpin' furniture for Miss Quarles wit' me?"

"I'm working for a temp agency to pay the bills until I get a music gig. I told them I grew up on a farm, so they send me out on a lot of manual labor jobs. They called me at 5:30 this morning, said you needed help, right here in Green Hills, and my apartment is just across 440, in Hillsboro Village."

The Mercedes driver, talking on his cell-phone, weaved slightly into the oncoming traffic. A lady in a gold Jaguar honked her horn. Fred hit the brakes. "Whoa, there!" he hollered. I grabbed the coffee so it wouldn't spill. The Mercedes moved back in front of us, the driver still holding the phone to his ear.

"That's reasonable. That's reasonable," Fred continued without batting an eye. "But the music business, from what folks say, is tough. It's ol' money.

Real southern, *good* ol' boy money. All them folks at the Opry, and Opryland, and Gaylord, all these record companies 'round here, the whole country music business — they're *good* ol' boys, through and through. Country music's *for* southern folks. Always been that way. That ain't gonna change. *They ain't* gonna change." He shook his head.

"I'm starting to see that. I've already dealt with some of that 'Yankee' shit, playing in little dives out in the hills around here on the weekends — Lebanon, Murfreesboro." I deliberately left out the middle syllables of each town name, imitating the locals.

"Leb'non." Fred repeated after me. "Murf's'borah." He laughed, and slapped his knee. "You got it *down*, man!" Quarles's Furniture appeared, a block ahead.

"I almost got in a fight, last weekend." I drew a last bit of heat from the coffee cup, and passed it back. "Hole-in-the-wall bar in Leb'non. They had the World Series on the big screen. I was wearing my Minnesota Twins shirt. Some redneck started in about how the Braves were gonna kick the Twins' asses. He yelled, 'The South is gonna rise again!' I said, into the microphone, 'Yeah, like so much bread dough.' You'd think it was the Civil War, all over again! He came up on-stage after me, but some old guy grabbed him by the belt loops. The old guy calmed him down, and then came up on the stage. He grabbed my mic and said, 'I don't give a shit where this boy is from, he can play the goddamned *gi*-tar, so set your asses down and shut up.' That was the end of it."

"You gotta watch yourself," Fred replied. "Be smart. You have talent, but be careful. Ain't nothin' worth all that. Don't let nothin' bad happen to you. I wish you all the luck on God's green earth. Umm-hmm. Hold this." He handed me the coffee as we pulled into Quarles's and backed the truck up to the loading dock behind the store.

• • •

The door to the loading dock opened at the same time the back of the truck reached the dock, and Miss Betty Quarles — Barbie-blonde hair sprayed into a perfect, beauty-parlor dome — stamped out from behind it.

"Fred! Where have you boys been?" she squawked, with a Tammy Wynette tone and twang. "I thought maybe you was in a wreck! I expected y'all back forty-five minutes ago!"

"That was a big armoire, Miss Quarles," Fred mumbled. "Nice piece. Fussy people. Fancy house. We didn't want to wreck nothing, so we took our time. South Brentwood. Almost to Franklin."

Fred and I walked up the cement steps to where Miss Quarles stood. She waited for Fred to punch a number on the security lock and open the door for her, then — jabbering, not looking back — she led us through the furniture in the loading area.

"Now Fred, you've just got to finish things up around here this morning," she said. "That bedroom suite has to be in Belle Meade by 10:00. Then we've got a truck-load of oriental rugs coming in for the sale this afternoon at 1:30. We need to get this place in order before then, so let's get on it."

"Yes, ma'am," Fred said, adjusting a packing blanket draped over an antique roll-top desk as he walked by.

"Thank the good Lord we've got Dwight to help out around here. We need it. How are you liking Tennessee, Dwight?"

"Just fine," I said. "Nice people. I appreciate the work."

"You'll never find better people than right here," she said. "Good, God-fearing, genu-wine people. And there's a bunch coming in this afternoon, so we need to get this place presentable. Dwight, I need you to go out and change the letters on the marquee. Fred, bless his heart, can't spell so good. There's a long rod with a suction cup on the end you can use. It's in here," she said, pointing at a closet door.

"Okay," I answered.

"When you get done with that, come back inside and vacuum. It's chilly this morning, but later on it'll get too hot to be out in that parking lot. Fred, show Dwight where the vacuum cleaner is, then pick up the cigarette butts in the lot, and do something with those packing crates and boxes out back by the garbage."

"Yes, ma'am," Fred replied, as he handed me the pail full of plastic letters and the telescoping rod. "Vacuum cleaner's here, too," he said to me, pointing into the closet. He grabbed the garbage poker for himself and then ambled out the back door. Miss Quarles waited for the door to close.

"Dwight, how do you like working with Fred?"

"Great. He's a nice guy. He's teaching me a lot."

"Yeah, he's a pretty good worker, for a *black*." She whispered the word "black," looking around as if someone besides me could hear her. "You've got to keep on 'em, all the time. Some would just dawdle the whole day away, if you let 'em. I swear, Fred would stretch an hour-long job into a month of Sundays, with nobody watching over him. You make sure and keep him working, while you're here, okay?"

"He seems really on the ball to me. He's organized, and careful—"

Miss Quarles shushed me with a finger to her lips. "Trust me," she said, motioning with her unmoving hair toward the main showroom, "I'll show you what to do."

● ● ●

After I had hung "Oriental Rug Sale Today" on the marquee, I headed back inside. The sun was beginning to bake, and thermals were dancing on the parking lot. I opened the door to a blast of air-conditioning. I shivered as I put the letters and suction-cup rod back in the closet, pulled out the vacuum, and headed to the nearest electrical outlet.

The vacuum cleaner roared to life, its headlight paving a yellow path across the white carpet. The motor kept gaining momentum, whining louder and higher. I kept a tight grip on the handle until my entire body rattled with the din. I stepped on the off switch. Nothing happened. Smoke began billowing from the chassis. I stomped on the off switch. Sparks and then flames spewed black, sticky soot and ash all over the thick, pile rug. I ran for the plug and freed it, just as Miss Quarles came running.

"Lord!" she said. "Are you okay?"

"Yes, ma'am," I said, remembering Fred's deference earlier. "I'm so sorry."

"Oh, don't worry about that. We sure are lucky you got that put out as quick as you did, or we'd've had a real mess on our hands." She leaned over to examine the scars in the carpet with the toe of her shoe and one finger. "That's not so serious. I'll get Fred to look at it, and if there's no quick fix we'll just throw a rug over it. None of the customers this afternoon'll know any different. I need you to clean the windows in the showroom till Fred gets back."

I sprayed Windex across the inside of the storefront windows and scrubbed them with paper towels until they squeaked. I could see Fred outside. Sweat was pouring off his face and soaking his shirt as he man-handled, by himself, furniture crates twice his size onto the back of the flatbed truck and drove load after load away, pausing only occasionally to mop his brow with a handkerchief. Miss Quarles' voice, directly behind me, startled me back to my task. "You about done here?"

"Yes, ma'am. This is the last little bit, right here," I said, dabbing at a smudge with a towel.

"You did a real nice job with these. The place is looking good. Now run out and tell Fred that you boys have about thirty minutes to get that bedroom suite delivered."

I put the supplies away and headed out the back door, into a thick, humid heat. Fred was still breaking up crates and loading them onto the truck as I approached. He smiled. "Man! Grapevines say you burned up the vacuum."

I hung my head. "Word gets around fast."

"Aw, don't worry 'bout it. That machine's been like that for years. Only works at low speed; switch don't work at all. I'm the only one who uses it. I knew that would happen as soon as she told you to do it." He made sure I was looking him in the eye. "She's too tight to buy a new one, and she'd blame me if I burnt it up. A new one's long been overdue." He slapped me on the back and laughed. "Let's me and you go load up that bedroom suite."

● ● ●

"Show you how the other half lives," Fred said as we pulled onto Hillsboro Road. "Goin' to Belle Meade. You bring them directions?"

I produced a small map from my shirt pocket. He held a brown magic marker out to me. "You might need this later, too."

The hectic city gave way to lazy, rolling land and stands of trees, immaculately emerald pastures, horses arching their shining, golden-brown necks, long driveways — some red dirt, some cobblestone, some paved — stark and uniform against the deep, immeasurable green. We rumbled down the road, winding over and through the gentle hills.

"Check that out," Fred said, breaking the serenity. "That guy ships in sod to keep his lawn green all winter. Guys that work for him, that's all they do — change out the sod so he can have green grass all year-round."

I stared at the palace-sized house, the fountain in front sending rainbows of water as high as the gables, and the whorled designs of the black wrought-iron fence surrounding it all. The wind at our open windows wafted a potpourri of freshly-mown grass, mulch, and horses. I closed my eyes and leaned my face into it. "Smells like summer!"

"Smells like money," Fred said. A jungle of underbrush alongside the road seemed to suddenly swallow the whole scene.

He turned the truck onto an asphalt driveway leading up to an immense, brick mansion with four towering, white pillars. Red and yellow rose-beds suffocated the walls on either side of the porch. An elderly couple — he in a straw hat, polo shirt, suspenders, and slacks, with a cane propped between his legs, she in a crisp floral-print sundress and a white bonnet decorated with a red and a yellow rose — were seated beneath a patio umbrella, at a table that held a pitcher of sun-tea with lemons, two empty high-ball glasses, and a vase full of more roses. A Confederate flag hung heavily on a pole at the corner of the house. Fred wiped the sweat from his forehead, and gave me a nudge with his elbow. A hound started baying. We got out of the truck.

"Now, Blue! You stop that!" the lady drawled.

"Y'all order a bedroom suite?" Fred asked.

"Yep," the man said.

"Well, sir, we come to the right place then," Fred replied.

"Shore did," the lady confirmed. "It's a hot one, today. Want some tea before y'all git after it?"

"Ah, no thank you, ma'am. We got a lot of work to — " Fred caught himself on her glare.

"You mind your manners! I was not talkin' to *you*." Her scowl at Fred turned instantly into a sweet smile for me. "Would you like some tea?"

"No thank you, ma'am," I answered. "We do have to get back to the store. Miss Quarles has got a big Oriental rug sale this afternoon that we need to get ready for."

"Well, ain't you ambitious," the lady laughed. "And your accent tells me you ain't got the sense to take a break from the heat. You wouldn't get so sunburned if you did."

She and the old man chuckled good-naturedly. I smiled. "Come here, Yankee, I'll show you where I want the furniture." Fred followed, without a word.

Across a broad expanse of flawless hardwood floor rose a staircase winding into the upper reaches of the house. The lady stopped every three or four steps to catch her breath and to tell a story, always deliberately directing the conversation at only me. Whenever I looked back, Fred was scanning everything in the room, taking make-shift measurements of tight turns, railings, and doorways with his hands and arms against his approximations of the bedroom suite.

"After you get it up here," she droned, "I want you to bring it back over here, and it looks like you'll have to angle it through that doorway there and put it in that room. It won't be an easy job."

"Don't worry, ma'am," I assured her. "We'll have it done in no time."

As Fred and I lifted the packing blankets off the furniture in the back of the truck, he whispered, "You're doin' great. Keep doin' the talkin'."

"Damn!" I said, "We have to carry all this heavy shit up all those stairs, around all those corners, in *that* ritzy house, with *her* watching us?"

"Shhh. We don't want customers hearin' us and complainin' to Miss Quarles. This one's the type that would, too. Don't worry. This'll be all over, before you know it."

We took the bed up first, because it was disassembled. We would save the assembly for last. Then we each carried a matching night-stand up the stairs, around the corner at the top, then back along the railing at a tight angle to the bedroom. The sweat stains were soaking through the waists of our jeans. Fred threw me a towel he had hung from his belt.

We mopped off, got on either end of the vanity, hefted it across the lawn and held it as steady as we could while we tried to open the door. The lady stood beside Fred, smiling, but being careful not to help. He got his edge of the vanity past the edge of the door, and the weight of the piece propelled us into the house.

"Hold it there, Dwight. Go easy." Fred slowed us down, and started up the stairs.

Sweat poured out of my hair and into my eyes. I blinked and shook my head. "You doin' all right?"

"I'm okay." I shifted the weight of the vanity and changed my grip. We climbed the stairs, one step at a time, to the top. The lady followed us, step for step, keeping a close eye on our progress.

"Wait," Fred said, "We're gonna have to turn it around back over our heads, and rest it on the railing. You'll have to hold it, while I get around it and up on the top level, on the floor. Then, when I'm able to lift it up, you come on up after me. You think you can hold it that long?"

"Yeah, I'm doing fine."

"All right then, jis' let me know if you need to rest. Okay, now, up, up — a little more, jis' a little more, a little higher. There! We're over the railing. Now hold it there till I get around here and get ahold of it from the top."

I was standing close to the top of the stairs, my arms fully extended straight up, holding the full weight of the vanity. I was blinking constantly, to be able to see and to keep the sweat out of my eyes. The lady stood just below me, staring at me. "I'll bet you wish you had taken me up on that tea *now*, don't you?" she asked.

"Okay," Fred's voice drifted to me from somewhere up above. "I got this end now. Bring it on up and it'll go right in the room."

Fred carried his end toward the room as I came up. When I reached the top of the stairs, I rested the vanity on the railing as I went around to gain a good grip on it. As soon as I lifted it up, the lady came over and rubbed her finger across the railing where it had been sitting. "I would rather you didn't do *that* again." Fred and I continued on with the vanity, into the bedroom. We held it, looking around at the floor.

"Where you want it, ma'am?" Fred asked.

"Oh, right over here by the window will be fine, for now," she said to me. Fred and I mopped off again, so we wouldn't sweat all over the floor. Then the three of us marched down the stairs and out to the truck for the last item — a ten thousand dollar armoire. We removed the packing quilts, and the lady went over to chat with her husband.

"You still got that marker I gave you?" Fred whispered.

"Yup."

"I don't know if you'll need it or not, but if you see any scratches on the armoire, give me a look. I'll distract the lady, and you color over the scratches with the marker."

"Okay."

The piece was heavy, and both Fred and I were panting by the time we got to the door. The lady was even kind or impatient enough to hold the door. "That's such a beautiful armoire!" she said. "I just love it!" As we came through, I stumbled over the doorsill, and caught myself.

"Hold on for a second, Fred. Let me catch my breath." We stood, holding the armoire, for a moment. "Okay."

We crossed the polished floor to the foot of the stairs, where we paused again before we began the ascent. The side of the armoire clicked against the iron railing. Fred raised his head over the armoire and pointed at a noticeable scratch in the finish. I nodded.

"That couldn't have been good," the lady said.

Fred answered before I could say anything. "My tape measure jis' caught. That's all."

We reached the top of the stairs, and Fred put his end over the railing. My arms were shaking from the strain. "Hold it there, partner," he said. "It'll take me a little while to get up there. Ain't no room for me to squeeze by, so I have to climb the railing and get over the top."

The lady frowned up beyond the armoire, at Fred's voice. I could feel sweat running down my hands, arms, and legs. I concentrated on my breathing, to distract myself.

"Go ahead," I said. "I've got it."

When Fred grabbed his end of the armoire, the weight shifted slightly. It slipped across my hands, but I regained control and was just redirecting its momentum when it banged loudly into the railing.

"That's a one-of-a-kind piece," I heard the lady say from a few steps below me. "If I have to send that one back, I believe I'll also have the two of you fired."

"My fault, ma'am," Fred said. "It hit on the back here, where there's a protective piece attached. No harm done, as far as I can tell." He lifted the armoire slightly higher so she couldn't see him, and peeked around the corner of it at me, pointing to a nick in the front of the cabinet. As we moved it into the room, Fred set his end down and hurried to the top of the stairs.

"I'm awfully sorry, ma'am, but I'm sweatin' so much I don't dare lay a finger on any any of this nice furniture unless I wash up first. Do you have a hose, or some water outside? Dwight, you start unpacking the bags of nails and screws for the bed."

Fred gave me a thumbs up and off they went, down the stairway and out the door. I pulled the brown marker from my pocket and carefully marked over a couple of fresh scars in the wood until even I couldn't tell they were there.

When I heard them coming back, I slipped the marker back into my pocket and emptied the bags of screws onto the floor. Fred escorted the woman right up to the armoire and said, "See ma'am? Ain't a scratch on it!"

She scrutinized it for what seemed an eternity. "There is a little scuff right here," she said, pointing at a vintage blemish, "but I guess you boys got lucky, this time. You do pretty good work. Would you like a cold drink now?"

As we guzzled our tea outside in the yard, the old man hobbled over and motioned for me to listen. "For your trouble," he whispered. He slipped something into my hand. I looked at it. A hundred dollar bill. "Keep it," he said with a wink.

Fred drove the truck down the driveway. I pulled the money out of my pocket, and showed it to him. "When we get back to town, I'll split it for us."

"Oh no," he said. "Miss Quarles don't allow me to take tips, but *you* can — you jis' a temp. You keep it."

We had the windows rolled down, and the breeze, even though it was hot, was soothing. "Feel that sun," Fred said. "Love that *warm*."

I watched the Confederate flag get smaller in the rearview mirror as we drove away and then turned onto the main road. "There's a different kind of cold, down here," I said. Fred raised an eyebrow and glanced at me. "How do you stand it, Fred?"

Just then, a cardinal flashed brilliant crimson against the deep green of the trees. Fred slapped the dash. "Did you see that? It's gonna be a *good* day! I jis' seen a red bird!"

HIGH LIFE
TIMOTHY ZILA

My brother moved back to New Mexico after his divorce, the first week of June, while the wind was carrying smoke from the forest fires in Arizona. He moved back the same week our grandparents died alone in their bedroom, from carbon monoxide poisoning that leaked from the gas water heater in the hallway adjoining their bedroom. The neighbors found them three days later, their bodies pale green and bloated.

Thomas, my brother, hadn't been to the house in years. When we arrived after the funeral, he walked through it like one might walk through a place that exists only in memory, shocked to discover that it was all — all of it — real.

"It's been a long time," he said, sticking his neck in and out of different rooms. Thomas had put the FOR SALE sign up as soon as we'd gotten back from the funeral, hammering the stake into the ground with the resigned air of someone done with life, finished.

The house was a ranch-style adobe, built in the sixties, when my dad, the oldest of four children (three brothers and one sister) was born, and my grandparents had moved from Nebraska to New Mexico, where Paw was a pastor until his church split. In New Mexico, he made a new life — as a butcher, a budding veterinarian, an insurance agent, and a handyman. Memaw was always a housewife and a mother, which sounds reductive, but it is what it is.

The last time I had seen Paw was earlier that year when he, my dad, and I went to the Bosque del Apache wildlife refuge in February and watched sandhill cranes rise from the blue water, the sun stained orange in the background against the plateaus and mesas. Later that day Mom called to say that Thomas was getting divorced. That summer, the largest wildfire in Arizona state history began, the smoke blowing westward across New Mexico as our grandparents were laid six feet under the ground, and Thomas moped around because his divorce had been finalized. Who knows why things happen in the way and order they do? I sure don't.

Thomas said the house was just as he remembered — the living room a hodgepodge of recliners and love seats from the sixties, seventies, and eighties; the garage a cluttered maze of sawhorses with plywood piled on top to form tables and shelves full of jars and boxes of shotgun shells.

Thomas picked up a box, sneezing as he pulled it close to read the faded red lettering.

"What are you doing?" I asked.

"Nothing," he said as he put the box down. "I don't know. You were always the one into hunting. But I like the typography," he added, running his hands over those old red letters.

The basement, filled with boxes and unused exercise equipment, smelled of mildew. I found a banker box full of Aunt Sally's old Barbies, over thirty years old.

Finally, we settled in the kitchen, sitting at the wooden table we had eaten at as children, which seemed a long time ago. I asked Thomas how things were, but he ignored me and pointed to a shelf in the living room where a piranha was framed on a plaque. The piranha stared at us as it always had, with its vacant, bulbous eyes, teeth gleaming. It could be smiling almost, despite being dead.

"How are you handling everything?" I asked Thomas. "I mean, it's a lot…the divorce, the funeral."

"I'm fine," he said, rubbing his palms against the unfinished kitchen table.

But I knew that he wasn't.

My brother was born in California in 1986. By the time I was born, five years later, our family had moved back to New Mexico. There we met our grandparents for the first time. Our parents had been on uneasy terms with them since shortly after the wedding, largely because of my mother, who had made distance a condition of the marriage.

Moving had been another condition. My mother wanted to forget that she had come from Nuevo Mexico, had grown up as a white child in the North Valley, that her husband was the son of a butcher and a handyman. That their river, the Rio Grande (which means Big River in Spanish) was a pathetic, shallow thing. Hell, even we couldn't help but laugh at it. No longer the river the conquistadores were afraid to cross, littered with plastic bags and aluminum cans, it was a river that made the news because environmentalists wanted to save an endangered species of four-inch minnow that no one could remember the name of.

This, certainly, has been my brother's perception: That we had grown up in the laughingstock of the Southwest. A place dominated by kitschy Georgia O'Keefe paintings and fake Native American jewelry sold by actual Native Americans, where the most exciting event of the year was the Balloon Fiesta, the stereotypical image of which, imprinted on patches and pamphlets and postcards, is of a lone yellow balloon floating against a pale blue sky.

Mom, a realtor, had a phrase: "Location is destiny." Her bitter twist on the "location, location, location" slogan. Thomas thought he knew what that meant so he fell in love with someone who hated New Mexico even more than he.

Thomas wasn't enough for Lenore, though. He couldn't be. It wasn't in his constitution or his background. After the divorce, he was forced to move back.

Location is destiny.

• • •

Uncle Ford arrived in his tan Mazda pick-up, a thirty pack of beer in hand. The first thing he asked when he walked into the house was, "What's up, bros?" The second thing he did was ask for a high-five. "You've gotta give your uncle a high-five."

"We're not ten anymore," Thomas said while he sat in the living room, flipping through an old issue of *Life*.

"You're not?" Uncle Ford feigned incredulity. Thomas didn't look up, but if he had he would have seen Uncle Ford smile so wide he looked stupid. "You're not ten? I'm sincerely sorry. Really, I am. I mean, I just didn't know. I was unaware. You've grown up so quickly... and, well, I've done a lot of drinking, you know? A lot of drugs and such back in the day." He smiled even wider. "You wouldn't know anything about that, would you?"

Uncle Ford stepped across the living room and approached Thomas, who looked up for the first time. "You wouldn't know anything about that, would you, sir?" Uncle Ford placed his right hand on his imaginary holster. He lowered his voice. "Sir, I need you to come with me." He grabbed Thomas's shoulder.

Then he stepped back, smiled again. "So, are we going to get this party started or what?" Uncle Ford asked, looking around the house. "It's been too long since this house has seen a real party... back since I was in high school and they left the house every once and a while. I mean, they never left the house. You had to do a lot to get them to split. Hotel reservations," he smirked. "Restaurant reservations. We tried to get them to do dancing lessons once, even." He looked up at the ceiling and smiled.

"I can't picture them, dancing. It hurts to even try. But if I had to, if I had to, then I see my dad. Tall, obviously. Stiff as a flamingo. Trying to get his legs to move in a fluid motion, like a wooden marionette. Mom, a full two feet shorter than him, squat like a penguin." Uncle Ford knelt down. "Taking all these little stubby steps for one of Paw's big ones."

"Are you stoned?" Thomas asked, his voice harsh.

Uncle Ford stared at him, started at him for too long. "Stoned?" he asked, repeating the word aloud. "Stoned, stoned, stoned." Then he sat down in the middle of the rug and started to laugh.

● ● ●

Later that afternoon, while Uncle Ford was sorting through our grandparents' stuff, Thomas and I took a walk behind the house, following a drainage ditch that led, eventually, to the Rio Grande.

The funeral had been windy and the smoke from the Arizona fire had moved east as the clouds inched their way across the sky, the ghost of their shadow slowly spreading over everything. While our grandparents were lowered into the earth, Uncle Ford paced back and forth behind us, kicking up the dirt with his dress shoes. He paced like a man going somewhere, and as he did he shook his long blonde hair back and forth. Then he stopped suddenly and blew Memaw and Paw a final kiss, a gesture that seemed at once sincere and mocking.

Then he strode away, his shoulders bouncing as if no weight in the world could keep him down.

"You remember when we used to come down here and fish?" I asked, smiling.

"Yeah," Thomas said. "I never liked fishing, though. I got bored too easily."

"I know."

"And I didn't care whether I caught anything either. If anything, I probably would have *preferred* not to catch anything. I would have never gutted the thing anyway."

"Of course you wouldn't have," I said, laughing.

When we reached the bridge I stopped and placed my hand on Thomas's shoulder. "You know," I said. "I've always loved you. You're my brother, after all."

Thomas stared back at me. "That sounds like the kind of statement that's followed by a but."

"No but," I said. I threw a rock over the railing, watched it float in the air, almost majestically, before it disappeared into the water. Whatever disturbance it caused was impossible to see. It was as if it had never existed at all, as if I had never thrown the rock, as if Thomas and I had never walked alongside the ditch that night at all. I looked at my brother, smiled mischievously. "*But*," I said and we laughed together.

As we smoked, Thomas leaned against the railing, looking out at the river. "Do you remember when I caught that bullfrog?" he asked.

"I don't think so."

"After the rain? It must have been in the summer, during monsoon season. I caught it in front of the house, in the driveway, under the halogen lights."

"No, I don't remember. That makes me think of something else, though," I said, as we walked back to the house alongside the ditch, kicking dirt as we did, the sun setting against our backs, the last bit of warmth leaving us. The summer was oddly cool, considering the smoke that surrounded us, enveloping our grandparents' death, Thomas's return. "Do you remember when we went hunting with Dad and Grandpa? You spent the whole time at the campsite, zipped up in a tent by yourself, playing Gameboy?"

Thomas admitted that he didn't.

"Then we're even," I said, rubbing out my cigarette in the dirt. I remembered exploring, hiking, going out. I wanted Thomas to come with me but, of course, he wouldn't. I was young, maybe seven, and without my brother, I was lost. One evening, while exploring the area around our camp, I lost my way. The night grew darker, my heartbeat accelerated, and the sense that maybe things *weren't* going to be okay lengthened with the shadows. Finally, I turned around and realized I had only been walking the wrong way. That was it. That was all. Sometimes life can be like that. When I returned no one had even noticed that I had been missing in the first place. No one had shared in my terror. Thomas certainly hadn't. He was sitting next to Paw, roasting marshmallows. "I can't believe you don't remember that," I said, as much to myself as to my brother.

"Well, *I* can't believe you don't remember the bullfrog."

"Like I said, we're *even*."

Later that night, while Uncle Ford made dinner and I helped, I watched my brother through the wire mesh of the screen door. He was sitting on the porch, carving a piece of wood, looking, maybe, past the neighbor's lawn and tire swing and stucco roof out to the sky — out there somewhere, untouchable.

Thomas had never belonged here, never fit with any of our family members. As a kid, he spoke only of travel. Of San Diego, Seattle, New York, Chicago, even Columbus. Anywhere but Albuquerque. He only stayed for his scholarship. Thomas believed he could be happier anywhere else. That was the claim he staked his marriage on. And he was wrong. Because, for all the effort Thomas had put in to be different — different than our parents, our grandparents, and even New Mexico — he was ultimately just like all of them. He was of those things, like the stone and the earth, like the acrid smell of water hitting dry dirt, or hands and lips chapped from dryness. If he was divorced and disillusioned, he still held himself with some sense of pride, sitting out on the porch, staring at the sky, wishing he could be somewhere, anywhere else.

That was why Thomas returned to New Mexico after the divorce. Technically, he could have gone anywhere — Paris, Peru, Japan. But secretly, in his heart, he knew where he belonged: He belonged here, at home. Thomas told me something once. He told me that the only thing he liked about New Mexico was the sky. "It's like the entire world is set before you. Like a stage."

I didn't know what he meant until later.

• • •

Sitting around the fire pit in the backyard, Uncle Ford asked about our lives. "What have you been doing, Brandon," he said, holding his spit with the marshmallows down by the coals.

"Oh, I've been working at an apartment complex," I said. "As a maintenance man."

"You mean a maintenance *tech*," Thomas added.

"Shut up man," I said. "You don't know what you're talking about. What have *you* been doing, Thomas?"

"We're not talking about me."

"Oh, really? We're talking about it now, aren't we? So I pose the question again, what have you been doing?"

Thomas kept silent.

"Does divorce ring a bell?" I asked.

Thomas stood up, looked like he was about to say something, but Uncle Ford shot both of us a warning.

"Hey, I'm sorry," I said as he walked away. "I didn't mean it."

"Really?" Thomas asked, his eyes fixated on me. "Because I think you did."

Later that night, when we had nearly depleted the thirty pack of High Life, Uncle Ford talked about our grandparents. "Dad was so tall," he said, half talking into his can of High Life, leaning toward the fire for warmth. "Tall and stern. Though he was so skinny, he just couldn't be blown down. He was from Nebraska, of course, and I can just picture him in his tan overalls...his flannel shirt, the one with the duck pattern. I can see him standing in a field, somewhere, hunting. Sturdy, that's the way he was." Uncle Ford paused, like he didn't know what else there was to add.

"And what about Memaw?" I asked. I wanted to hear him talk. That was all there was, his voice. I wanted Uncle Ford to talk until nothing else mattered.

• • •

"Mom was different. She stayed inside and worked. She always had to work. If she wanted to take a nap in the daytime, she'd have to *sneak* it. She wanted everyone to know that she was working. That she worked like hell. If Paw could sit down and just read the paper or watch basketball, if we could blow off our chores and ride bikes or go fishing, she couldn't. She had to be working. It was the thing she hated most, work. It was also the thing she needed. The thing she couldn't live without."

Thomas had collapsed in the dirt, hadn't bothered to sit in a chair. He didn't have any energy when he drank. "Her hands," Thomas said. "I remember Memaw told me that her parents used to run this little inn and she had to do the dishes. With scalding hot water."

Thomas stretched his hands out over the fire, like he was warming them. Warming them or showing us his scars. And I thought, maybe New Mexico is the thing Thomas hates, the thing he can't live without.

That night, Uncle Ford seemed profound, waving his blonde mane. He looked majestic, in the light of the fire, in his territory, in *their* backyard, telling us about his parents. "At the funeral today," Uncle Ford said. "Just watching them go into the ground. Their bodies suspended in coffins, about to go under." He made a motion with his hands, almost like a submarine diving. "Like an elevator, almost. A coffin's not that different than an elevator when you think about it." Uncle Ford paused after that, like he had said something profound.

• • •

Once, when Thomas and I were little, we helped rake up some old lady's house just down the street from our grandparents. Her yard was little more than dirt and weeds, but Dad set fire to the side-yard to get rid of the weeds. Somewhere between all the raking and pulling we found a toad, a spadefoot toad. These things live in the desert, lie dormant there for years, waiting till there's enough rain for them to reproduce. And then they burst from the earth. Maybe that's us, I thought.

"I just don't know where they went," Uncle Ford said, sort of vaguely looking at me, like he wanted help with something. There was something he couldn't say, or something that couldn't be put into words at all, but he wanted to try. He had to try.

"They didn't go anywhere," Thomas said quietly, his face splotchy and raw in the red light. He was kneeling, picking up clumps of dirt and dropping them onto his shoes.

"What are you doing?" I asked him.

Thomas lifted his head and looked at me wearily. "What are *you* doing?" he returned the question. Getting onto his knees, Thomas stretched his hands out like a magician or a witch, about to chant an incantation or brew a potion. He let the dirt slip between his fingers and into the fire. As he did, logs shifted and crackled and the smoke blew toward Thomas, kneeling before the fire, the last vestiges of dirt stuck to his hands, sweat lacing his forehead.

"What are you doing, Brandon?" he asked again, standing up and brushing the dirt off himself. "Working at an apartment complex with a bunch of high-school dropouts who can't even write their name legibly? Is that what you're doing?"

"That's where I'm *working*," I said. "But that's not what I'm doing. I mean, fuck you, man. At least I know my place and I'm okay with it. I'm not someone else. This is where I grew up, in New Mexico. I'm proud of it. I can't *marry* out of it. And I'm okay with that. I'm okay with who I am. Why can't you be okay too?"

Thomas held his hands out again, like he was cooking his own flesh, or at least considering it. He might prefer it, after all. I thought that my grandparents were dead, and my brother was back in New Mexico and divorced, and though

I couldn't in that moment recall what exactly had happened in the years between Thomas' marriage and his return, or the things I had done and what those things might have meant, if they had meant anything at all…I was okay with things not working out. Thomas wasn't.

"Why can't you be okay?" I asked.

I closed my eyes and felt Thomas place his hands on my shoulder. "You know why they died in that house?" he said in response. "They died because of everything they couldn't give up. Because of all the junk. Because it was more important to them than anything. It was only right that they died that way, like hoarders. Fucking peasant pharaohs. They died. And I don't want to be like that."

When I opened my eyes Thomas had collapsed into the dirt, his body shaking, visible even in the night.

"But you *are* that way," I said. "Look at everything you can't give up." The words sounded stupid as they left my mouth. But the stupidity was washed away by Thomas's sobbing, by the sight of Uncle Ford kneeling in front of my brother, his hands on Thomas's shoulders, like he was saying a prayer or appointing a minister.

Thomas shrugged at first, fought whatever Uncle Ford was doing, but he was persistent, his arms wrapped around my brother like a blood pressure cuff that would not stop squeezing, would not stop reminding you that this is your heartbeat, this is your grandparents' yard, this is who you are when everything else is gone.

"I get it," I said. "Why do you want to be better than everyone else? Because you're not," I said. "You're not better than me." I looked at the house, the ditch, the river, the old speedboat rotting in the side-yard, not going anywhere, ever.

And Thomas didn't say that we are not drainage ditches and tan Mazda trucks and chicken wire and toads that come bursting from this dead earth when it rains. He did not say that because, in the night, by the fire, the day of their funeral, with all of us staring at the world through the prism of High Life, he knew that we were. He sat on the ground and dropped dirt on his shoes and the double lines on his forehead spoke of things lost to the smoke and the fire and time.

A BLIND HORSE

ROBIN MULLET

Wiley's coming. Who else would be driving down this god-forsaken road like it's a NASCAR track, spewing dust and dirt? *Only my crazy ex-husband, that's who*, Jo Lynn thought. *He's coming for his precious collection of guns and video games.* She kept rocking on the porch, sipping lemonade, determined to keep him from ruining her one day off in the last two weeks.

The blood-red '69 Impala came to an abrupt stop at the edge of Jo Lynn's front lawn, if you can call a bunch of dried crabgrass and chickweed that hadn't seen a lick of rain in months a lawn. Jake, her old blue heeler, sat up on his haunches, the merle-hued fur on the back of his neck standing straight up, and stared at the car.

"Stay, Jake," she murmured. He lay back down, but his hair didn't.

A tall, gangly man in a backwards ball cap and tight jeans popped out of the driver's seat, a dagger tattoo showing just below the sleeve of his t-shirt. Easy on the eyes if you didn't look too close, too close being anything less than the next county in Jo Lynn's opinion. He sidled up the porch steps.

"Hey, sweet cheeks," he grinned, showing the slight gap in his front teeth that Jo Lynn used to think was adorable. Now she thought it made him look like a damn redneck — the stupid kind, not the country music singer kind.

"Wiley, I am not in the mood for bullshit. Just get what you came to get, then get gone."

"That any way to talk to the man who was once the love of your life?" Wiley kicked a stone off the porch. Jake rose to his haunches again. "'Course you was never in the mood for a lotta things, as I recall."

Jo Lynn refused the bait. "Your stuff's in those boxes in the living room. Don't go snooping all over." She thrust her chin at the car. "She gonna help you?"

A young woman leaned back in the passenger seat, drinking a beer, one sandaled foot on the dash. She was making a concerted effort not to look their way, waving her hand at a fly and cooling the back of her neck with the beer bottle.

"Naw, those boxes are heavy. I wouldn't want her straining those pretty little shoulders of hers."

Wiley drew his hand across the back of Jo Lynn's neck as he passed her to go inside. She shrugged him off. He cackled and leaned down to pet Jake. The heeler growled and moved closer to Jo Lynn.

"Asshole dog," Wiley muttered, and slammed the screen door.

His touch made her a little sick, or maybe it was just the heat. She took another sip of lemonade and looked out at the passenger in the Impala. *Got to be hot in that convertible in this sun*, she thought.

"You hot?" she called out to the girl. The girl didn't turn but shrugged. "He might be awhile. Probably snooping through my mail. S'cooler on the porch. Your call — no skin off my back."

The girl sat for a minute, let out an exaggerated sigh, opened the car door and swung out long legs. Taking a swig of her beer, she shut the door with her hip and sashayed up the walk, ponytail swinging. Cleavage-proud, she had on a white beater shirt, probably Wiley's. It was tucked into some Daisy Duke cutoffs. She would have turned the head of any straight man, maybe even a few that weren't, and she knew it. *I looked like that once*, Jo Lynn thought. *Still could, if I gave a shit.*

The girl plopped herself in the other rocking chair. Flinging one leg over the armrest, she positioned herself sideways to avoid the missing board in the back of the chair. Her manicured toenails and fingernails matched the red of the Impala. Wiley emerged, carrying a big box of VCR tapes and video games, covered with his old high school letter jacket.

"Hey Jo Lynn, you remember when I caught that pass against Rockcastle? They all thought they was big stuff, state champs and all . . . hey, babe, what are you doing out of the car?" He turned to the girl.

"It was too hot to wait in there, Wiley. I was meltin' away," she whined. "Can you bring me another beer?"

"Sure thing, baby. You just sit there and cool off. And don't you let Jo Lynn get you upset, now."

Jo Lynn waved him off. "I ain't said a thing to her, except that it was cooler here on the porch. My porch," she added just for spite.

Wiley frowned at her and took the box to the car. He grabbed a beer for the girl and one for himself and stomped back up to the porch.

"Where's the horses?" he asked as he popped the cap off the girl's brew and handed it to her like a real gentleman. Jo Lynn rolled her eyes. "You got 'em in the barn on a hot day like this, Jo Lynn? That ain't smart."

"There are no horses, Wiley. I can't afford hay on a waitress's paycheck. The pasture dried up and the property tax was due, so I sold them. All but Starr. Her blind like that, nobody wanted her. She's out back in the shade. Neighbors gave me some oats for her."

"Sold 'em? And never said crap to me about it? How much? Maybe I wanted 'em."

He glared at her with his fist clenched around his unopened beer bottle.

"Wiley, you hated the horses; thought they were too much work, remember? Besides, I didn't have to tell you anything. This is my home place. My parents built it and took care of it long before you were a speck in your mama's eye. I bought those horses. They're mine to sell, not yours. Not anymore. You closed that gate."

"You just had to throw that in my face, didn't you." As Wiley stepped toward her, the girl piped up.

"Wiley, it ain't worth it, honey. Let's get out of here and get some supper. I'm starved."

Wiley flashed a crooked, mean sort of grin at Jo Lynn, leaned down and kissed the girl's cheek. He twisted off his bottle cap and threw it at Jo Lynn's feet, making Jake yip. Jo Lynn laid her hand on the dog's head to settle him.

"Sure, baby, I got just a couple more things."

Wiley made two more trips to the car while the women sat in an uneasy silence, looking out at the hills beyond the highway. Lush and covered with wildflowers earlier this spring, like Jo Lynn's lawn they were now the color of dirt. When the screen door slammed behind Wiley one more time, Jo Lynn inhaled and turned to the girl.

"I got to say it. Can't you see what you are getting into here, Amy? He's a dangerous man. And by the way, drinkin' age in this state is twenty-one."

The girl propped her sunglasses on the top of her head and leaned toward Jo Lynn.

"You just bring out the worst in him, always arguing and contradicting him," the girl retorted, ignoring the drinking remark. "He's a pussycat with me. I know how to treat a man."

Jo Lynn stood up. "That is no man, little girl. That is a woman beater, a coward who can't deal with his going-nowhere-fast loser life. Blames everybody else for it. He blamed me, and he will get around to blaming you too. He's the lowest of the low. You have to..."

"Shut up, Jo Lynn," Wiley's voice broke in, an odd, steely sound to it.

Jo Lynn turned around. Wiley had his favorite hunting rifle in his hand and it was pointed right at her. Jake growled low in his throat.

"You tell that dog to stand down, or I'll shoot his ass."

Jo Lynn put her hand on Jake's head. "Quiet, Jake."

"Wiley," the girl cajoled. "Don't you pay Jo Lynn no mind, she…"

"You stay out of this, girl," Wiley put his hand up towards her. "This is between me and this bitch of an ex-wife."

The girl's eyes widened. She sat very still, except for the slight shake of the beer bottle in her hand.

"What you going to do, Wiley? Shoot me in front of a witness? Even if you get a shot off, Jake will be on your throat in two seconds, and he won't let go. Don't be stupid. Look, you got all your stuff now. After today, you'll never have to see me again. Hardly worth throwing your life away for an assault charge."

Jo Lynn's chest felt wrapped in iron. She hoped Wiley couldn't see her fear. Jake stayed crouched down but never took his dark eyes off Wiley and neither did Jo Lynn. She knew that she had stored away the gun unloaded, but Wiley had had plenty of time to reload it while he was in the house. Seconds ticked away. Nobody moved.

Suddenly, Wiley laughed a small, hollow laugh and pointed the gun down to the porch.

"I just wanted to scare ya, Jo Lynn. You know, a little going away present for all the good times," he snorted. "You shoulda seen your mug!"

He turned to the girl who sat white-faced, staring at the both of them. "Come on, baby. Let's get the hell out of here and go get a sandwich. Adios, Jo Lynn, been good to know you — not." He shouldered the rifle and swaggered down the steps to the Impala. Jo Lynn let out the breath she didn't even know she'd been holding.

As the girl rose to follow him, Jo Lynn touched her arm.

"Amy honey, you be careful. Make sure he stores those guns unloaded.

You've seen my bruises, baby girl. I'm going to say it again; he's a dangerous man."

The girl just shook her head, headed down the steps. Jo Lynn called after her.

"I'll be here if you need me. No matter what, this is your home too. You've always got a place here if it gets bad. For God's sake, you're my sister. I still love you."

The girl hesitated for a second but didn't turn around. Speaking so low Jo Lynn could barely hear her, she said, "You take good care of Starr now; she was always my favorite."

When she got into the car, Wiley pulled her over close to him, flipped Jo Lynn the bird, and peeled out down the drive, gravel flying. Jo Lynn watched the dust plume of the car fade away. She turned back to her rocker, Jake settling at her feet. She sat there for a long while, watching the hills swallow the day. Jake nosed her hand.

"No worries, boy, he won't be back. Maybe she will." She closed her eyes for a split second prayer. "God please, maybe she'll make it back." She sat rocking for a long time after that, listening, just listening. From the backyard, Starr whinnied softly in the twilight.

FINDING HOME

CIRCUS
JULIA LICHTBLAU

After the Tbilisi circus school closed, Shukhia looked for work until the night her father brought home a graying bus driver who'd worked in a Mercedes plant in Germany. "Meet your rich husband," he said. They drank *araki* and toasted the advantages of a seventeen-year-old wife, while she and her mother served lamb and pilaf.

"To ten sons!" the bus driver said, tipping his chair.

"Ten sons!" her father roared.

How young would he die? she thought, and the bowl of hot pilaf slipped from her greasy fingers onto his lap. His round, red face looked devastated, like a baby whose mama has bitten its finger too hard in play. She felt elated and almost laughed. Her mother brushed the steaming grains off his thighs. "Sorry, sorry," she cried.

The man left early. Her father came into her dark room, belt in hand. Shukhia pulled the blankets over her head. Her mother took his arm. "Buka, it was an accident. Invite him back!"

Her father hit her through the blankets only three times, a concession. "I'm sending you to the country. My brothers will find you a husband, since you're too good for this one." The next morning, she called the number on a flyer advertising for models in France and met a Serb in a café. He took her upstairs to an empty room and locked the door.

"Take everything off," he said, like a doctor. She left her underpants on because she had her period. He didn't insist, which helped her trust him, despite his cold eyes. *Models must do what the director says*, she thought. *He's weeding out spoiled girls.*

He looked her up and down, told her to walk, turn. "You're like a guy, no tits, no hips, all muscle," he said. "They want blonds and redheads."

"Look," Shukhia said. Taking foot in hand, she extended her leg, then did a backbend, a walkover, and the splits.

The man looked. "Come back tomorrow. I might have something."

That night, she dyed her light-brown hair red while her parents slept and left before they woke, wearing a scarf.

A French circus needed a girl, the Serb said. Unfortunately, she couldn't get work papers because E.U. countries resented the beauty and talent in the East. She'd have to come in "the back door." But, once she got there, she'd get a "kartdesezhour," a residence card, in a French name. His fee was 6,000 euros.

"I have one hundred," she said.

He pinched his forehead, as if weighing many variables: "You can work off the rest." He gave her a bus ticket to Trabzon and said to find his friend D. in the Russian Market. "Don't bring a suitcase," he said.

Kartdesezhour. She repeated the word until it rolled off her tongue.

No one was home. She put her makeup kit, a compact her mother had given her, and two changes of clothes in a shopping bag and went to the bus station.

The bus to Trabzon took all night. The drive to Slovenia, two days. Near the border, D. pulled off the road, opened the trunk and unbolted a steel plate under the spare tire, revealing a well. D. told her to get in and make herself small. As he tightened the bolts, she thought about rumors of Russian girls who ended up as "Natashas." Russian girls would do anything. D. hadn't bothered her, except at the beginning when he kept touching her leg, and she'd threatened to run away. After that he left her alone.

D. left her in Marseille at a high-rise. A charred car sat in the parking lot. From the window, she watched black-shrouded Arab women herd their children. The women in the apartment came from Russia, Moldova, Africa. Men appeared and led them away. She asked two Moldovan girls where they planned to work. "We'll be hostesses or dancers in a club," one said. "And you?"

"A circus," Shukhia said.

"How did you land that?" one said.

"I'm a trapeze artist," Shukhia said smugly.

The girls smirked.

• • •

On the second afternoon, a man with skinny hips and slick black hair showed up. He handed the man who ran the apartment an envelope.

He called her over: "You." He pointed to the skinny man. "Benoît."

Shukhia picked up her bag and followed him to a truck. He argued on his cell phone in French. She couldn't understand, but worried he'd get angry when he saw how out of shape she was. He was an angry person. As they drove, she wondered if the circus would have an elephant.

They met the others at a tourist campground. Three campers and two trailers, a man and two women drinking wine. The man, Charlot, was younger than Benoît, and plump; Madame Nina was leathery and had burgundy hair like a costume-party gypsy; Marilyne, who looked Shukhia's age, was thin and blonde.

Charlot shook Shukhia's hand. Marilyne turned to Madame Nina. "Why do we need her?"

"*Ce sera notre pain quotidien*," Madame Nina answered. Our daily bread.

Jealous bitches, Shukhia thought.

Benoît took her into his trailer, which had a double bed, a refrigerator, sink, toilet, a TV. He opened a cupboard and tossed her bag in. She asked to use the bathroom. He pointed. When she came out, he'd left and locked her in.

That night, she lay under him and swore to never let him see her feelings.

The next night, he drove her to a truck stop and handed her a bag and a piece of paper with numbers on it. The bag held a sheer nylon top, a bra, red satin shorts, spike heels, a package of wipes, and condoms. The bathroom was full of women. She stood at the mirror, watching them in corsets, garter-belts, half-naked. She showed a Russian girl the paper. "What do the numbers mean?"

"One hundred euros a fuck, fifty for a blow job."

She looked at Shukhia's white face and said, "Are you doing this for anyone, honey?"

"Only myself."

"I feel sorry for you then," the girl said.

At 4:00 a.m., Benoît picked her up. She could barely walk. When she handed him the money, he said, "I expect twice this." She was crying so hard, she couldn't answer.

That was a year ago.

They do six shows a week, a different town each day. After dark, he drops her at a truck stop or a parking lot.

●　●　●

Charlot talks to her. He knows some Russian. Once, he tried to explain what Cirque Grimaldi was like in the old days, when his and Benoît's great-grandfather was alive. "*Bolshoi tzirk*," he said, and opened his arms. Big Circus. "*Mnogo lyudey*." Many people. "*Khorosho!*" Good! Then he made a sad clown face. *"Tepyer nye mnogo lyudey. Plokho!"* Now not many people. Bad!

He and Benoît are cousins. Madame Nina's his mother, Marilyne his girlfriend.

Benoît is the ringmaster, Charlot, the clown; Madame Nina tells fortunes and takes tickets; Marilyne walks a tightrope. Shukhia does a routine with hoops and a little trapeze act. They never work on their acts or replace their costumes. Benoît won't buy her new fishnets when her stockings run. He hates stores. The police watch them, he says.

• • •

Mondays, when they're dark, he goes off on "business," locking her in. She cleans the trailer to get rid of his smell, a mix of cigarettes, his sweat, and *pastis*. Mentally, she practices her old tricks: the bird's-nest, timing the twist, the catch, the release. The bus driver loses weight, grows younger, handsomer. Poor man. He looked so hurt when she dropped the pilaf on him. How do her parents explain her disappearance? That her village husband keeps her in a cave with a stone in front like Ali Baba's? She wishes she could tell them she's alive, but her cell phone died before she reached Trabzon.

• • •

Two weeks ago, Benoît had a round of deliveries. Marilyne and Madame Nina went shopping. Charlot let himself in with his own key. Benoît trusts him like a brother. He found her in bed.

"Benoît *pas là*," Shukhia said. Not here.

He sat next to her on the bed. "I can't take my eyes off you."

"Benoît come soon," she said.

"Not for a few hours," Charlot said. "I asked."

He kissed her. His tongue was gentle and searching, not hard and stabbing like Benoît's. Instead of pushing him away, she let him enter her. By the time she came to her senses, it was too late.

"Benoît kill me," she said.

"I'll save you," Charlot said.

She poked his stomach. "He kill you, too."

He looked insulted.

"I sorry," she said. "How you meet Marilyne?"

"I found her in a park. She was like you — *une pute*." He shrugged. A slut.

"You love her?"

"Not much."

He wanted to make love again. She pushed him off her. "No time."

After he left, Shukhia scrubbed herself with dish detergent in the tiny camper sink and dried the wet spot with the hair dryer. She couldn't get his smell out of her nose.

When Benoît came back, he turned on the soccer game and sprawled on the bed. She opened her compact. Could he tell from her face what she had done? She sniffed. Charlot's smell filled the air.

The French goalie let a Turkish penalty shot through. Benoît grabbed the compact from her hand and threw it against the wall.

"Mine!"

"You belong to me. You owe me 6,000 euros. "

"I pay you ten, hundred, thousand times!"

She heard Charlot's low voice in the dark. "*Pomogitye mne*!" Help me!

"He can't help you," Benoît said. But he released her.

● ● ●

They drive into a town over an ancient, arched bridge, and pitch the blue plastic Cirque Grimaldi tent in the field set aside for gypsies.

The audience consists mostly of parents with young children.

Charlot, wearing a green and white polka-dotted clown suit and floppy shoes, stands next to a beam across two saw-horses, a set of hula hoops on his arm.

Shukhia, wearing laddered black fishnets, a red leotard, and red ballet slippers, runs into the ring.

Charlot gives her a hand up. He hands the hoops to her one at a time.

She cranks her hips to get the hoops going, then starts across the beam, red-slippered toes feeling the way. How does she do it? Charlot eggs on the audience: Clap! She does a pirouette. Bravo! Another. A few more feet. She pirouettes again, only this time, her arms windmill. The hoops drop. The audience laughs. She lands on her back, hoops splayed out around her.

Her head hit something hard in the dirt. She can't lift her head.

Charlot flops over in his clown shoes, kneels, and brushes the dirt off her face.

She mouths, "Merci."

A child says in a worried voice, "*Elle a mal, la dame?*" The lady, is she hurt? "*Chût,*" his mother says. "*Je ne sais pas*" Shh, I don't know.

A man in the audience stands. "I'm a doctor. Let me look at her."

"We'll call you if she needs someone," Benoît says.

Charlot helps Shukhia up, and she limps out.

At intermission, Charlot brings her ice from his trailer. She sits on a folding chair outside the tent, head between her knees. The doctor comes over. "I advise you to go to the hospital."

"We heard you," Benoit says, and the doctor returns to his family.

Shukhia gets up and goes to the truck, where they keep the merchandise they sell at intermission. Shukhia and Marilyne bring out big plastic bags full of pink and blue stuffed bears. They circle the ring, hawking the bears. Marilyne smiles constantly.

Shukhia bumps Marilyne with her bag. "Pute," she whispers.

"*Et toi?*" And you? Shukhia answers. Marilyne looks surprised. Shukhia never talks to her.

AMERICAN FICTION

• • •

She gets through her trapeze act somehow.

Benoît drives Shukhia to a truck stop. She sidles between the semis, knocking on cab doors. The fumes and the flashing headlights make her sick to her stomach. She goes behind a bush. When she finishes, she sits down on a curb, head on her knees. A Senegalese girl in a gold bikini takes two oxycontins from her purse."*Prends ça, ma chère.*" Take this my dear. The pounding subsides, and she falls asleep. The Senegalese girl shakes her. "Get up. You don't want him to catch you like this."

"You right," she says. Shukhia means light in Georgian. Headlights swim in front of her eyes like errant constellations.

One man pushes her out of his cab. "*Je veux pas de paumées.*" I don't want a druggie.

Another girl helps her up. "You're making trouble for the rest of us," she said. "Pull yourself together."

When Benoît drives up, Shukhia hands him the money and curls up in the seat.

"You fucked up on purpose this morning," he says.

"*Non.*" She holds her head. "How?"

He counts the thin wad of euros. "Where's the rest?"

"*Je suis malade.*" I am sick.

He pulls her toward him.

"Benoît, *je te jure.*" I swear.

He raises his right hand, the one with the silver and turquoise ring, and cracks her across the cheekbone.

Monday again, Charlot lets himself in while she is cleaning the bathroom. She squirts the cream-colored, lavender-scented scouring liquid into the bowl. Charlot wraps his arms around her, a spider preparing to devour a fly.

"*Tu es belle,*" he says. You are pretty.

"Non." She points to the bruise on her cheek.

He kisses it and carries her to the bed. She lets him pull her shorts off, but doesn't respond to his caresses.

"What's wrong? You don't like me anymore?"

"You tell Marilyne."

"That's a lie."

She goes to the cupboard and pulls out a bottle of olive oil and mimes slipping.

"You women are animals. She must have smelled you on me," he says.

Charlot twirls the hair on his belly. Cirque Grimaldi is the only place he's worked, not counting his year of military service. "We'll run away together."

She looks at his plump white body and feels the same revulsion she did from the bus driver before dropping the hot bowl.

"My kartedesezhour," she says.

Her fake *carte de séjour*, residence permit, says "Sylvie Grimaldi." When the police come around looking for illegal Roms, Madame Nina gives it to Shukhia. When they leave, she takes it back.

"It's in her jewelry box."

"Please get it."

"I'll do my best," he said.

All week, she watches to see if he visits his mother's camper. He seems to be avoiding her.

The highway winds along a deep gorge, a silver river at the bottom. Vacation traffic is heavy. Benoît drives too fast. More than once, she thinks they'll go flying on a tight curve. If she dies at the bottom of a ravine in France, her parents will never know what became of her. She ran away, willful girl.

"Smile. You look like you're at a fucking funeral. This is a circus," Benoît says.

"Maybe for me is funeral." She knows better than to talk back, but the temptation is so great now that she's leaving.

AMERICAN FICTION

He holds up his hand, the one with the heavy turquoise and silver ring. *"T'en veux une autre?"* Do you want another one?

"Non, merci." She shakes her head.

• • •

The road turns away from the river, past lavender and wheat fields and vineyards. They enter a village built of gray stone. It has a castle, a church, three cafés. Today is market day. People crowd around stands of vegetables, wine, cheese, sausage, bras, t-shirts. Charlot's voice comes through a loudspeaker, *"Venez au cirque, messieurs dames. Cet après-midi à trois. Venez au cirque."* Come to the circus, ladies and gentlemen, this afternoon at three. Come to the circus. Hearing his voice so loud makes her nervous.

They park in a dusty field below the town. Shukhia and Marilyne get out of their vehicles at the same moment. Marilyne shoots her such a poisonous look that Shukhia almost says out loud, *I don't want your Charlot. You can have him back when I'm done.*

Benoît and Charlot carry the frame, guy ropes, and the rolled-up tent to the middle of the field. They toss rocks away and start setting up. Marilyne and Madame Nina back the pony out of its trailer and tether it in a grassy spot under a tree. They go into their campers to change. Shukhia unloads the hoops, props, the trapeze, and ropes. Passing Charlot, she keeps her eyes on the ground.

The men have the tent up and move inside to set up the trapeze. She goes to dress. What if she married Charlot? Would that be so bad? He could drive a bus. She laughs to herself.

• • •

Madame Nina sells tickets. Marilyne minds the entrance. Shukhia makes sure no one sits in the front row without paying two euros extra. No one sits in front. No one wants to pay extra.

Benoît steps into the ring, microphone in hand. *"Messieurs — dames! Bienvenue au Cirque Grimaldi!"* Ladies and gentlemen! Welcome to the Grimaldi Circus!

Shukhia does her hoop act. Marilyne walks a tightrope a meter off the ground. In Tbilisi, tightrope walkers worked ten meters up in the air. They rode bicycles. They did entire clown acts while the audience sat, mouths open, heads back, like baby birds awaiting a worm.

Marilyne loses her balance and jumps down midway, laughing. She doesn't care. The children clap anyway. They like to make noise. She runs out through the tent flap as Charlot goes in to take down the tightrope. She catches his arm. "Kiss me," she says.

He pushes her away. *"Ça va pas?"* Are you okay?

"You think I'm blind? Stupid?"

She runs to her camper and slams its tinny door, startling the pony, who stops cropping grass and whinnies.

Benoît announces intermission. Normally, Shukhia and Marilyne go to the truck now to retrieve their plastic bags of pink and blue stuffed bears. Marilyne is still sulking. Shukhia sells alone.

No one wants to buy stuffed animals on such a hot afternoon. She lugs the bags back to the truck while Charlot, Benoît, and Madame Nina stand under the tree, smoking. Madame Nina has changed into her shimmery green fortune-teller's dress. The smoke from their cigarettes rises straight up like chalk lines in the still air.

Shukhia climbs into the truck container and drops the bag. The truck smells of diesel. She lies back on the squashy bag and closes her eyes. The church bell clangs the hour. She doesn't move. She thinks she heard someone shouting her name. Not her real name, Shukhia. Sylvie, the name they call her on the rare occasions when they call her anything but *"tu"* — you. Sound carries strangely in the truck. The walls mute sound, but when people pass the open door, their voices suddenly amplify.

She goes to the open door and sees all backs turned the same way, like at a street fair when a card-shark has people emptying their wallets. Benoît shoves Charlot, who trips in his big clown shoes, falls, kicks back. Madame Nina, hobbled by her tight dress, grabs Benoît. "Boys, that's enough!" she screeches.

Benoît lunges for Charlot's neck: "You always want what's mine."

Shukhia's trapeze teacher in Tbilisi used to say, "To go fast, slow down." This has always worked.

She climbs down from the truck and walks toward the campers. She keeps walking until she gets to Madame Nina's and tries the door. It opens, waking Madame Nina's black and white cat, who jumps off the bed and tries to nuzzle her legs. She kicks him away. The camper smells of cheap perfume and old tuna. Madame Nina's costumes are strewn on the bed. Bras and panties spill from her drawers. She looks out. Marilyne has her arms around Charlot, holding him back.

Madame Nina's jewelry box sits on the counter, in plain sight. She parts the beads, and her own face looks out from a plastic rectangle. She slides the card into her bra, smoothes the beads, and exits.

Shukhia walks toward the crowd. "Excusez-moi, excusez-moi," she says, in her thick accent. She pushes through to the others. They stop fighting and stare.

"Time for show," Shukhia says. For the first time, they obey her. Everyone goes to their places. The audience returns to their seats.

Charlot starts the music. Benoît comes out. "*Et le spectacle continue!*" And the show continues. He waves his arm as if nothing had happened out there, as if he doesn't have dirt on his pants.

Shukhia climbs the ladder to the platform. She raises her arms, like in the big top in Tbilisi. She smiles, grabs the bar and pushes off. Her feet leave the platform. She soars over the ring. At the farthest point of her swing, she kicks her legs up. There's a snap, a lurch. The bar dangles by one rope. An electric charge goes through her as it slides through her fingers. Her ears roar as if she were falling from outer space.

Thank God, no one sat in the chairs, she thinks as hard plastic punches through her ribs. "Help me," someone screams in Georgian. She tastes metal, sees a blinding flash.

●　●　●

She comes to in the emergency room strapped to a board.

"Ne bougez pas," the nurse says. Don't move. "If you feel pain, you're not paralyzed. The doctor's waiting for the x-rays. A little longer."

●　●　●

Shukhia floats up toward the light, as if from the bottom of a pond. A man in white stands over her. "We put a rod in your back. Broken ribs, a damaged kidney. No more trapeze. But you'll walk."

The next day, two policemen stop by. They hand her the carte de séjour. "We know you're not Sylvie Grimaldi. Come clean."

She tells them everything she knows about Benoît down to the color of his underwear.

She tells them about the apartment in Marseille and the women, about Benoît's Monday "business" and the truck stops, about Marilyne and the greased balance beam, about the fight and the fall.

When she's finished, she begs them not to send her back to Georgia. "My father kill me."

"We'll speak to our *chief.* Maybe he can pull a string or two," one policeman says.

The other nods. "A clear humanitarian case."

• • •

The police catch Madame Nina, then Charlot and Marilyne. They find Benoît in the Pyrenées. Madame Nina gave him away, hoping for a break for Charlot.

French TV and newspapers pick up the story. They love the circus angle. **Trapeze Artist Survives Murder Attempt In Love Triangle, Prostitution-Immigration Scam!**

The day of the verdict, she walks up the gray stone steps of the *Palais de Justice* in Nîmes slowly, painfully, but without a cane. A women's organization bought her a *tailleur*, suit, to wear to court. The red dye has grown out of her hair. The judge and lawyers wear long black robes and white stocks. The chamber is wood-panelled. Her French is still not good enough to follow court proceedings, so she testifies in Georgian through an interpreter. Her own voice sounds foreign to her now.

Benoît sits across the court room, knitting his thin lips as she speaks. He's like a plastic bag in which something has rotted. The stench never goes away.

Marilyne gets off on the attempted murder charge, though Charlot testified that she was jealous of Shukhia. No one saw Marilyne cut the rope. Benoît gets seven years and a 150,000-euro fine for human trafficking, plus another five years for drug dealing. Charlot gets five for drug dealing and a 200,000-euro fine. Madame Nina gets five and 75,000 euros for non-assistance to a person in danger.

The Interior Ministry issues Shukhia a carte de séjour in her real name: Shukhia Khutsishvili.

A TV journalist interviews her in front of the Palais de Justice after the verdict. "There is an expression about life in France. *Heureux comme Dieu en France.* Happy as God in France. After what happened to you here, are you happy? Was it worth it?" he asks, extending the microphone.

She smiles. She has seen herself on TV several times by now, so she knows the camera likes her high cheekbones. "Since a young child, I dreamed to live in France. So, yes, I can say honestly. Like God, I am happy."

THE STORY OF CHA CHA MCGEE

BETH MAYER

You may hear that it came to no good when Cha Cha McGee moved to town, but I will tell you otherwise. I still reside in the same narrow place, and though it's been close to thirty years since I last saw Cha Cha, I still remember the first time she invited me inside. My aunt had sent me over with a blueberry pie. Cha Cha came to the door in bare feet and a yellow baby-doll negligee, two perfect round peaches where I kept my secret raisins. Her family was new, and she was one grade ahead of me in school. I had seen her there a few times, but I had no idea what Cha Cha McGee was made of yet. She just stood there, looking at me through the screen door.

"It's Janie Jameson," I told her.

"Hey," she said.

"My Aunt Sarah made this for you," I held up the pie.

"Who the hell's that?" Cha Cha asked me.

I wasn't used to girls swearing. And I wasn't used to explaining anything about my family. I don't think I ever had cause to tell anyone the story, not before Cha Cha McGee.

Everyone already knew that the day before I turned eleven my parents and brother had driven off the high bridge by mistake. Cha Cha listened, and I ended with the fact that now I had to live with my aunt, Sarah Jameson.

"Oh," she said, "well, that makes sense." It was such a strange response, and she was still just standing there looking at me. I thought maybe she was slow.

"The pie's a welcoming gift," I said, "for your family." I was raised to have good manners, brought up to be kind. For so many years, even later as a woman and a lover, I thought that being kind meant doing things I didn't want to do so as not to hurt someone else's feelings. I wanted Cha Cha to take that pie from me so that I could go home, but she had already decided that I should stay.

"Well, Janie Jameson," she said, except it sounded like an accusation, "are you coming in or not?" I stepped into the McGee's dark kitchen, stood there until Cha Cha said, "Sit down, why don't you?"

She placed the pie on top of my Aunt Sarah's good cotton dishtowel, in the middle of the kitchen table. Cha Cha hadn't even said anything about the pie yet. Not thank you, or it looks wonderful, or how nice. I wanted a witness. For someone with good sense and authority to see that pie. I wanted to teach Cha Cha something about how we did things. "Are Mr. and Mrs. McGee around?" I asked.

"Mama's asleep and so are the twin babies. And Mr. McGee?" she laughed at this, "He's already down at Reuben's. Can you believe that?" Cha Cha laughed again, I assumed it was about mothers who slept the afternoon away, and fathers drinking hard before supper.

The year before I might have laughed right along with her.

I used to laugh like a regular girl. But at that time I was still sad and too young and hadn't made any sense of losing my family. I could have pretended to laugh. I had learned how to do that. From the start, something about Cha Cha McGee made me want to tell the truth. So I told her that I wasn't that particular anymore, that even a lazy mother and a drunken father sounded pretty good to me.

For the first time of many, Cha Cha McGee gave me something unexpected and completely necessary. "Listen," she leaned in, whispering, "he's not my real daddy, you know. He's not even married to my mama. And he's not her first boyfriend like that, either. He only talks to me when he wants something. The twin boys are his own, but not me."

"Oh," I said. I was both uncertain and grateful regarding what I would later come to understand as her peculiar brand of kindness. Then she put on some coffee for us, which I didn't care for yet. But I was beginning to like her company.

"Make mine with milk and sugar," I told her. And Cha Cha McGee laughed at this. Oh, her laugh was a singular sound.

"Why bother? I always take mine black. Say! Blueberry pie's always better when it's fresh, don't you think?" Cha Cha said. I could feel how clever she was, where this was going. I wasn't sure I wanted to stay anymore, but I wanted to see what Cha Cha would do next.

"Yes," I told her.

"We'll have some of this pie to go with our coffee, then." She got up to get a knife. I was worried that no one in charge had seen the pie yet, not knowing that most of the time, Cha Cha McGee was the one in charge.

"We should wait," I said, "because it's supposed to be for all of you." She was already cutting the first piece. "That's why my aunt sent it over!"

"Nice of her," Cha Cha said. She placed the piece of blueberry pie on a chipped saucer rimmed with tiny pink flowers and tiny green leaves, and then she pushed it across the table at me, "Company first."

From that moment, I knew that it would never be easy to say no to Cha Cha McGee. We ate those first pieces of pie quickly, without talking. She crossed her legs at her ankles, the way my Aunt Sarah said a lady should while wearing a dress. And even though Cha Cha was in a nightie, and I was wearing blue jeans and my Peter Pan blouse, I crossed my ankles, too. Then we sipped our coffee and talked for a while like this was our common way.

When her piece was gone, Cha Cha said, "You be sure to tell your aunt that the McGees enjoyed her blueberry pie." She was running her index finger across flowers and leaves, sucking off the blue.

"I will," I said and stood up to go. But Cha Cha wasn't through with me yet.

"Janie Jameson, didn't your folks ever teach you any manners before they passed?" That stopped me. Here she was, speaking of my dead parents so easy, when no one else would say a word. At the time, I didn't know the value of candor, the varying shades of integrity, or why Cha Cha's way could feel so much better than anything I had ever known before.

And after a while, Cha Cha said, "I don't suppose anyone will miss this." She lifted out another piece of blueberry pie and put it in front of me. "And I'll have another myself." This time, she tipped the whole pie plate toward her and pulled almost a quarter of it out onto her own saucer.

"Cha Cha McGee," I whispered, but I was impressed. "There'll be none of it left!"

"You're right, Janie!" she feigned surprise. She was a fine actress, already. "Well then, we may as well send this plate home with you clean!" Then she gave me a wink. "More coffee?"

I knew right then that Cha Cha McGee was what people would call trouble. And I knew that I wanted to be her friend.

"Just a little," I said.

• • •

Looking back, I don't suppose I've ever loved anyone as much as I loved Cha Cha McGee. She was my first real friend and together we crossed the perilous bridge that spans being a girl and being a woman. Who can travel this alone? No one should have to. It is the most dangerous terrain. Cha Cha loved anything sweet and so almost every day after school we would walk to the store at the edge of town, just to get Cha Cha some candy. We always got two lollypops for the baby boys, too. Cha Cha said she didn't care that the twins were half Mr. McGee's — they couldn't help that. She would make damn sure that they grew up to be good anyway. On our walks to the Candy Pantry, Cha Cha taught me many things: how to pull the bottom of my shirt up and through my collar, halter-style, so that my soft belly showed; how to swing my hips side-to-side, just enough, as I moved. I pretended to be brave, and for a time I was. Now I know that I was simply lucky. Too many girls never get a chance to try their womanhood on, like a costume. Too few can claim their own season of such recklessness.

Another favorite pastime of Cha Cha McGee's involved standing in front of Lady Pearson's house and imagining what went on inside. I did a lot of following Cha Cha around back then but I couldn't see what she found so fascinating about Lady Pearson. I looked at the jars of colored water that Lady Pearson had arranged on the old picnic table in her front yard. Most of us were afraid of Lady Pearson. There were plenty of rumors about her. Depending on who you asked, she decorated the jars with rare wild flowers, or blood and guts.

One afternoon, standing there with Cha Cha looking at the jars, I was surprised by a memory of my mother. My mother had been sitting on the bathroom floor with a tiny dead baby in a white handkerchief on her lap. I was sorry for her, but to me it looked disposable — the bony, bloody slick of a hen's egg. (This had happened in the spring, before the high bridge.) My brother and I would have been seven and ten, respectively. After that, our mother couldn't seem to stop talking about the three other dead babies she had back when she was still a young wife. We could look them all up in the town hall, she told us. It was a matter of public record. Aunt Sarah started coming over most evenings to make us dinner, and when our mother remembered to tuck us in and kiss us goodnight, she would sing an odd song about meeting up one precious day with all her lost little souls.

I am thankful that as a child the possibility, the likelihood, never came to me in any concrete way: Perhaps my mother meant to drive off the high bridge that day. And my father and brother happened to be, most unfortunately, along for the ride. But the recollection of my mother, there on the bathroom floor, was one seed of truth. I began to recognize the nature of my mother's irrevocable, terminal sadness. So in that first moment of remembering with Cha Cha, I'm sure that I missed my mother. But even more I was confused and inexplicably angry. I wanted to scare my friend. I wanted to mar something she admired, to shake her the way I so often felt shaken.

"You know," I told her, "they say that Lady Pearson's got body parts in those jars."

Cha Cha looked at me hard. Then she turned to the jars. "That's a load of crap," she said. "They're pretty."

How I had wanted to take it back, to tell Cha Cha I already knew that. I knew it long before her. The first beautiful thing I ever saw were Lady Pearson's jars of colored water.

• • •

There came a time when Cha Cha grew to know Lady Pearson very well, and so I knew her, too. Some of the worst stories about town weren't true after all, but Lady Pearson kept a better secret of her own. Cha Cha and I had not yet heard the real story from anyone. (And I never did hear it, directly, from anyone but her.) To speak it: To say that Lady Pearson had once been the local whore, was also to say that there had been patrons in our town. Who would they be? Our banker, our doctor, our mayor. (Our fathers, our husbands!) Who else? Lady Pearson told us that she knew exactly which men had fallen over the years. She kept a journal. But she did not name names. She did say that these were the men of our town, where she herself had been born and most certainly would die. Sometimes she liked to imagine them all back, she told us, long ago, when they were just still boys and girls just like Cha Cha and me.

THE STORY OF CHA CHA MCGEE

I imagine the scene, too. There they sat, hands scrubbed, around the dinner table waiting for Daddy. The buttered potatoes congealed and Mother nipped at the drink she had prepared for her husband, a taste she might soon acquire for herself. In walked Daddy, rumpled and flushed, forty-five minutes past due. Famished and reeking of her. If those boys and girls, most of them grown-up now into husbands and wives themselves, had witnessed the exchange of looks, words, accusations, denials — most had forgotten, as children conveniently do. They preferred to remember their fathers as providers and righteous men. Those who could not avoid recalling their fathers' indiscretions simply created other reasons to hate Lady Pearson.

A smart woman who knows her own pleasure in a town full of foolish men and frigid women is necessarily under great suspicion. Such a woman is thought either a witch or a bitch, and Lady Pearson was frequently called both. Lady Pearson didn't often seem lonely, though, as she enjoyed the latest crevices of her own mind, and the company of fine music followed by conversation. She said that she relished the quiet as well, for it never seemed empty to her.

And I must agree with her there. The longer I remain unmarried though seldom alone — and when alone seldom unhappy — the more it seems that I risk a fate like that of Lady Pearson. And the older I become, the better that sounds to me.

●　●　●

When I was a girl, my Aunt Sarah and I attended services at the First Methodist Church of the Way. The McGee family never went to church, but Cha Cha used to warn me about some of us who did. The social hour that followed our church services is as close to the fires of hell as I ever hope to get. I remember smallish boys and self-conscious girls from my seventh grade class standing around long brown tables eating cookies, drinking watered down apple juice, and having nothing worthwhile to say.

213

Cha Cha had told me to watch out for my classmate Nancy Carpenter in particular. That was easy enough, as I had never really liked Nancy. She seemed too perfect, or was trying to be. I suspected that Nancy Carpenter hated Cha Cha because the boys preferred her to Nancy now. Cha Cha was never shy about how pretty she was, and she was smart, too.

I suppose Cha Cha was what so many boastful parents now like to call "gifted," although Cha Cha actually was. I never saw her study, though she loved to read anything and remembered every word. Our schoolwork was not rigorous in any way. The parents in our town were content with their children learning whatever academics, religion, and civics they had learned, and anything more would have been suspect. I was smart enough, but memorizing facts had always seemed challenge enough for me. Cha Cha was an inherently curious person, though, which was frowned upon in our school. She made no pretense of anything but the boredom and frustration she felt every day. There is such a thing, I'm sure, as a good teacher who fosters thinking and welcomes dissent, and perhaps even one who might be thrilled with (instead of threatened by) a student like Cha Cha McGee.

But we had none of these.

I pointed out to Cha Cha that before she came to town, Nancy Carpenter had been the best student in school. How Cha Cha had quickly surprised everyone, including me, when she showed what she could do. Such as never missing a spelling word. Ever. Cha Cha said, even so, she needed to be careful, too. She said that Nancy was full of spite, and claimed she could smell it on her.

So I couldn't wait to tell Cha Cha, when one Sunday Nancy proved her right, once again. Nancy Carpenter was loud, showy, an excellent liar.

"Janie, my mama says it's real charitable, the way your aunt is looking after them McGee's," Nancy said. She knew that I had to smile and take it with all the witnesses. "Mama said you all been bringing them pies and what not, and if that isn't real good of you." I know plenty of women who once were girls like Nancy. They grow up to be the women who run things in order to gossip, and the ones who desperately work and spend in order to remain young for their husbands.

"Well, my Aunt Sarah's a real Christian after all," I told her.

"Mama thinks a good girl like you ought to watch herself though, Janie, running with that kind." Nancy's mother was the laziest teacher at our school and a terrible snoop.

"So what?" I said, and for emphasis took a bite of my peanut butter blossom cookie.

"That's just fine by me, Janie," Nancy said, easing herself into a gray folding chair. "But you know what they say? Birds of a feather."

Later I told Cha Cha that I didn't care to be classed in the same genus or species as Nancy Carpenter because I saw for myself what kind of creature she really was.

• • •

Sometimes, on our trips to the Candy Pantry, Cha Cha and I would climb over the chain link fence in the field behind school, and one Monday Cha Cha stopped.

"There's no park."

"What?"

"It's a stupid name for our school, Janie," Cha Cha told me. "Parkview." She was waiting for me to catch up in my mind. We both knew by now that Cha Cha McGee was faster than me, in every respect. "Get it? There's no park."

And she was right again, of course. Cha Cha always noticed things like that. When I told her how after Dutch Elm came through, the Education Board had run out of money for new trees, she laughed for almost half a minute. Cha Cha said I was hilarious. She said that a lot but I was hardly ever joking. We were already halfway to the Candy Pantry when Bart Benson pulled up next to us in his truck.

"Hello Mr. Benson," I said, looking into the cab. The girls at school thought Bart Benson looked just like Burt Reynolds and he always seemed to have a brand new truck. He was driving along slowly with us as we walked.

"Hey Janie," he said quickly, and then looked at Cha Cha. I was used to this. I didn't get much attention whenever Cha Cha was around. "You young ladies need a ride someplace? It's no trouble, you're both on my way."

Cha Cha stopped and so did the truck. She turned to meet Bart Benson eye-to-eye. Cha Cha McGee looked everyone in the eye when she talked, and as a girl I admired her for it. It's a skill I'm still working on. I remember the way Bart Benson smiled at Cha Cha as he reached over to open the door. I had known him all my life, but I had never seen that kind of smile before. I took a step forward, but Cha Cha put her arm out, blocking me.

"You can drive your truck straight to hell," Cha Cha said to him. Then she took my hand and marched me away from the street. We were headed into someone's yard.

We could hear Bart Benson calling after us, "That's funny. You really think you're somebody special, don't you Cha Cha McGee? You really think you're somebody?"

"What are we doing?" I asked. Cha Cha was walking too fast, and her legs were much longer than mine.

"Short cut," she said.

"I'd rather get a ride!" I looked back. Bart Benson had laid on his horn once, and now was watching us go.

Cha Cha didn't turn around and she didn't slow down. "Janie, you don't know anything."

"Yes I do!" I said. She was only a year older than me, and I was growing tired of her acting so much wiser. "I know plenty."

"Not about assholes like Bart Benson," she said, her strides still rhythmic.

I thought I had her now.

"Well, I know him a lot better than you. Mr. Benson goes to my church." That just made her laugh.

"I don't care what that asshole does with himself on Sundays, Janie," she said. Then she stopped walking and looked at me softly, sad, like she was about to tell me something that might finally break my heart. "It's not the first time he's offered me a ride, okay? And I've gone with him, too."

"So?" I said. She sat down in the grass. I sat down next to her and we didn't say anything for a while. I had no idea what we were waiting for.

"We kissed a couple of times," she told me, "and other stuff." I didn't understand.

"But Cha Cha," I said, "Mr. Benson is a grown-up. And he's married."

"Janie, you're such a good girl." Cha Cha was a girl, too, and my friend. "Listen, he wouldn't take no for an answer. He's a bad man, Janie. And we have to stay away from him. Both of us." I thought she might be making it up. I wanted her to be making it up. I didn't know what to say. "Come on, it's time to go get ourselves something sweet."

Then Cha Cha stood up, and pulled me up with her. Cha Cha was only thirteen, but she seemed far older to me, now. I wasn't jealous anymore. And I was afraid for my friend. But I was too young and fortunate to fully understand precisely what was at stake for Cha Cha McGee.

Why does a man like Bart Benson, or any such man, lust after a young girl? I often wonder still, though it is not pleasant to consider. Maybe such a man did not mature past his boyish sticky dreams and acts of self-gratification. Maybe he was poked and stuck himself, as a boy, electing to forget in his mind, unable to do so in his groin, with his hands. The boy grows up, becomes a man, has children of his own, and should know better. He does know better. Isn't it nice to imagine castration would do the trick? I used to think so. It seems to me now, though, that this really is the least of it. Once such a man has been made, he would find a way.

AMERICAN FICTION

• • •

Every night at ten, like clockwork, my Aunt Sarah fell asleep in the front room with a book across her chest. On clear nights when there was a moon, I snuck out through the back door and went to see Cha Cha McGee.

It was one of those nights, a Sunday, when everything changed. We sat on the roof like we always did, and Cha Cha told me about the way she had woken up in a quiet house. She poured a bowl of cereal, made herself some coffee, and sat down in the stillness. Around lunch, she got a bad feeling. The last thing she wanted to do was wake Mr. McGee while he was sleeping it off but the bad feeling was so strong she went upstairs anyway. And as soon as she opened the door to the room he and her mother shared, Cha Cha knew that they all had gone. Her mother had left the window wide open, Cha Cha said. This was just careless. She would never forgive her mother for that.

I remember thinking first about those sweet little boys with no more lollies and no more Cha Cha McGee to love them up. Then I thought of my friend, standing there alone and cold, at the top of the stairs.

"We need to build a bonfire," I said. Cha Cha looked at me in a brand new way. We took what was left of her mother, some fancy clothes Cha Cha never even saw her wear, a box of letters from old boyfriends, and some cologne. Cha Cha said she did not want to touch anything belonging to Mr. McGee, so I handled whatever he had left behind. We hauled everything out to the dirt driveway, poured her mother's cologne on top of the pile, and I lit a match.

"Jasmine," Cha Cha said, when the smoke reached up to us, and I agreed.

The fire burned too quick and hot. But it was beautiful, and Cha Cha and I had made it together, and I didn't want it to die. I threw on paper and trash, some sticks, anything I could find in the yard.

When the fire was low Cha Cha said, "Let's go in."

We sat down in the hall and Cha Cha pulled open a box with a few little shirts and pairs of pajamas. She was crying, but I knew that she would not want me to mention it, now or ever. She held up a baby shirt, "Don't worry, the twins won't need these. They barely even fit anymore."

"Can I keep something?" I said. She told me to have my pick.

Then we folded every tiny thing, dirty or fresh, all into nice tidy squares and placed them in the best drawer in the house.

Cha Cha said she'd had the whole day to think. She already had a plan and before she would tell me she made me sign in blood that I wouldn't tell a soul. Cha Cha McGee wasn't going anywhere. She was going to stay and raise herself alone, which we both acknowledged really wouldn't be such a change.

Cha Cha kept house and I kept my word, but after a while people started to notice. Cha Cha had always been thin, but she was starting to run out of food. The McGee's never had much in their pantry, and even though I gave Cha Cha everything I could, we didn't have much to spare at my house, either. Cha Cha's favorite little dress wasn't tight any more.

"Cha Cha McGee," Nancy Carpenter said in a whisper, loud though, so the rest of us could hear, "you wore that thing twice last week. What are you, some kind a prisoner-of-war? Are your people too poor to make gravy?"

"It's alright," Cha Cha whispered back, louder yet, "your asshole boyfriend likes me just fine." And it was true. All the boys liked whatever she wore. Especially that blue flowered sundress with straps as thin as sewing thread.

My Aunt Sarah worked at our school. She pulled the tables and chairs out for lunch, cleaned up, and put everything away again after. She watched me give my lunch to Cha Cha every day. She watched my friend fading away.

"Are her folks really that bad off?" she asked me, more than once. I would only shrug, my secret kept, and my loyalty to Cha Cha tested. But I couldn't save Cha Cha McGee in the way we had planned. After Aunt Sarah told the principal and the teachers that the McGee's must really be in trouble, some of them went over before church one Sunday morning to find Cha Cha home alone. Yes, it was true. Her family had been gone for months and she didn't know where. Only one remarked on her fortitude, several on her lies, and a few more on the filth. Aunt Sarah told me that Cha Cha McGee would have to become a ward of the state now.

"Cha Cha won't have to become a ward of the state," I said, "because she'll become my sister, instead. She's going to come and live with us." I suppose that I had convinced myself, with my young logic, that if I posed my greatest hope as a declaration rather than a question, my aunt would be unable to tell me "no."

"I was afraid of this, Janie," Aunt Sarah said, and I started to cry. "I'm so sorry." She tried to pull me close, but I wouldn't let her. "I know how fond you are of the girl, but we just can't."

"She's not just a girl," I said. "She's Cha Cha McGee. And she's my friend."

"I know, I know. I'm afraid Cha Cha McGee is too much of a handful for me."

I was offended now. It seemed to me that everyone, even my own aunt, thought Cha Cha McGee possessed something remarkable, extraordinary, that I couldn't identify and apparently lacked. "I'm a handful, too, and you took me in."

My aunt laughed at this notion, a quick release, "Oh, Janie. You're a very good girl. And you're my flesh and blood."

That night, I didn't bother with the moon and I didn't care if my Aunt Sarah heard me go out. I found Cha Cha up on her roof, waiting for me.

"They told me to be ready first thing in the morning. Damn it, Janie! I would have been fine, except for the food."

"I asked if you could come and live with us." I was ashamed of my aunt. "But she said no! I hate her. How could she say no?"

"It's not her, Janie," Cha Cha said. "It's everyone." And by this, even then, I knew exactly what she meant. It was awful, the way that the people and parts of our town, together, added up to something ugly.

"I'll just come with you, then," I told Cha Cha. "Wherever you go. We'll be like sisters."

"You can't, Janie," she said. In truth, I was both relieved and stricken. At that moment, Cha Cha McGee was more real to me than anyone. Just being near her made me real, too.

"The fools can tell me I'm off to the Children's Home, but they are quite mistaken."

"What do you mean?" I asked. I didn't want to lose my friend. I was selfish, really, and didn't think about her fate. I was naïve enough to believe that Cha Cha McGee would be fine wherever she went. And I wanted to know exactly where to find her, "Please, don't run away."

"Janie, it's only called running away if you don't know where you're going." She had a bag already packed full of her things. She told me Lady Pearson's house was just under two miles away. That night Cha Cha McGee would knock on Lady Pearson's door and ask for the woman to take her in. I wouldn't let Cha Cha go there alone.

We were cutting through yards and dark streets, the way we knew how, when we saw the headlights of Bart Benson's truck pointing at us. He spotted us, stopped, and got out. He was standing there in front of us, like a cowboy. He told us, "Now settle down girls." He said they had figured Cha Cha might try to run tonight, and he had volunteered to go and get her. I turned to Cha Cha for our next move, but she was just standing there, looking at Bart Benson.

He smiled and took a few steps forward. I remember wondering what was wrong with Cha Cha. Where was my friend with all her choice words?

"Cha Cha!" I shouted at her, to try and wake her up. We had to get away and she wasn't doing anything. I had no occasion as a reference point. Now, of course, I see how fortunate I was, that circumstance had given me no reason to understand how Cha Cha McGee must have felt at that moment as a girl, just a girl, facing off in the dark with a man like Bart Benson.

"That's good," he said to Cha Cha. He was getting closer, looking at her skinny wrist, like he was sizing up whatever fight was left in her bones. "That's good," he told her. He said not to worry, that he knew the Director of the Children's Home quite well. The man was very fond of wayward tramps, like herself. Cha Cha McGee would never be lonely. "And you're cooperating. See? That's very good."

I felt an unprecedented surge of rage toward Bart Benson, a new and useful kind of hatred. Cha Cha McGee was there in the flesh, but the rest of her was going, going, gone. I have known times like this myself by now, of course, times of grief and shock. But that night I witnessed my friend's actual departure. I saw Cha Cha McGee's frightened spirit fly and leave her there, empty, to fend for her earthly self.

How could I have known that a girl who has been trained up, a girl who has nowhere else to go, will crawl in (again and again) next to the likes of Bart Benson? But I believe something in me must have understood the threat, even then. Something in me knew where Cha Cha McGee would be forced to land when she was ready to come back to her body.

I have never been bad, not really. And though I still couldn't bring myself to tell Bart Benson to go to hell, I was ready to do my best to send him there. I looked at his truck: the driver's side door left open, the keys in the ignition, the engine running. We all knew how to drive back then. I didn't even close the door before I shifted into forward. Bart Benson turned his head just in time to see me hit him square in the face with the grill of his truck. The headlights were glaring at him, curling up in the road, gurgling his fury.

I shouted at Cha Cha, "Get in here!" And just like that, she was back. Cha Cha climbed over me, into the passenger seat, as I put the truck into reverse.

"Holy shit, holy shit! Look at what you did, Janie. Holy shit, look at what you did!"

"Cha Cha!" I said. I'm sure I reasoned that we had enough sins against us at that moment without unnecessary cursing.

"Janie, are you kidding me? You just hit Bart Benson with his truck, and you're after me about my language?" Now she was laughing. "You are so funny, you are so damn funny." My friend Cha Cha McGee was laughing, my favorite sound, and she couldn't stop and I started laughing, too. I turned left, heading toward Lady Pearson's house. Cha Cha was craning her neck back, trying to make something out through the cab window.

"Janie, he's barely moving. That's not good."

"Well, that's your opinion," I said. We were quiet then. I delivered Cha Cha to the curb in front of Lady Pearson's house. We saw her standing in her doorway, waving, like she had been expecting us.

Cha Cha told me, "You really should come in. I bet she'll know what we should do."

No, I said. It was time to give Bart Benson back his truck.

How I imagined and did what came next is still a mystery to me. And it's been a secret that Cha Cha McGee and I have both kept all these years.

The road was nice and dark when I parked the truck right next to Bart Benson's body. I found a flashlight, a rag, and a screwdriver in a toolbox in the back of the truck. The flashlight caught some blood on the shiny bumper, so I wiped it clean with the rag. Then I put the flashlight and the wrench near Bart's right hand. I took the screwdriver and punctured the tire closest to his body. He wasn't making sounds anymore, and I took that as a good sign.

I stood over Bart Benson then, trying to feel something acceptable. But I wasn't sorry Bart Benson was dead, or that I had been the one to make him so.

All this took me less than five minutes. I threw the screwdriver and rag into the woods on my way home.

That night I tried to fall asleep, but kept throwing up. I imagined this was my punishment and now there would be nothing left in me but secrets. I was getting a cold drink of water at the kitchen sink when my Aunt Sarah caught me and asked what I was doing awake at that hour.

"Just cleaning up," I said, rinsing out my glass.

"The dishes are done, Janie," she said. Then she saw my face, and asked me, "Are you sick?"

I said I didn't know, because I had never felt better or worse in my life.

She came to my side.

"Are you hot at all?" She touched my forehead, "Oh, Janie. You are burning up!" Then Aunt Sarah put her cheek against mine, and that did me in.

She smelled just like pink soap, and my mother. I put my arms around her neck. Aunt Sarah knew about Cha Cha McGee without anywhere good to go, but I couldn't tell her about Lady Pearson or Bart Benson, probably dead in the road. I couldn't tell her any of this. I couldn't...

"What are all those birds doing in here?"

"I'm calling the doctor right now," she said. And then I was out.

I still remember my fever dreams. I started on the head of a pin, flew down the front hall stairs, and out the screen door. I saw the whole town, all of it, and everyone. There was Parkview School and some boys smoking in the bare yard by the fence. There was Nancy Carpenter letting her boyfriend put his left hand up her shirt. Aunt Sarah was reading a book, Bart Benson was trying to start his truck, and five dead babies were stuffed into a gray filing cabinet at the town hall. And then those babies were floating in Lady Pearson's jars of colored water. I could see each one of them, each with a jar of purple or red or blue. Because where else can you go when you are just a baby with a little fishy spine and all that original sin to carry around on your back? It was one last chance to be something beautiful.

I ran hot for three nights. After, everyone was still talking about Cha Cha McGee running away and poor Bart Benson killed, hit and run, while he was trying to change his tire. That all sounded close enough to me. For two weeks, I waited everyday after school in front of Lady Pearson's place, hoping for some sign of Cha Cha. I missed her, but I was careful not to give anything away. Finally I saw Cha Cha coming out to the front yard, holding a metal watering can.

"Cha Cha McGee!" I called out, "There you are. Are you okay?"

"Of course I am. I just had to lie low until things passed, what do you think? I'm eating goat cheese and learning Latin. We're listening to Chopin."

I didn't know Chopin then, and I didn't know what to say to my friend.

"But what are you doing with that watering can?" I shouted again. She began filling a jar with fresh purple.

"Quit yelling, will you?" she yelled back at me. Then, in the steady voice that I knew so well, "I can hear you fine, Janie. Lady Pearson told me this water turns sour after a while, so I'm changing it." Cha Cha gave me a smile, a wink, and went back inside.

Sometimes I wonder about that moment still, what might have happened if I had followed Cha Cha McGee into that house. Would we have become like sisters? When it was my time, would I have found something extraordinary in me? Would I have gone away, like my friend — on to university, to Europe and back, to the city, and a life I can only just imagine?

Cha Cha McGee showed up at Parkview School the next morning in a brand new red silk dress. The get-up, as the teachers called it, was completely inappropriate. Lady Pearson sent Cha Cha with a typed letter officially declaring that Cha Cha McGee was her legal ward now. They had acquired all the necessary documentation from the state, and it was all a matter of public record.

"Cha Cha McPearson," Nancy Carpenter tried to rename her, but Cha Cha was already leaving us behind.

We all just looked on and on at Cha Cha McGee in that red silk dress, becoming as she was.

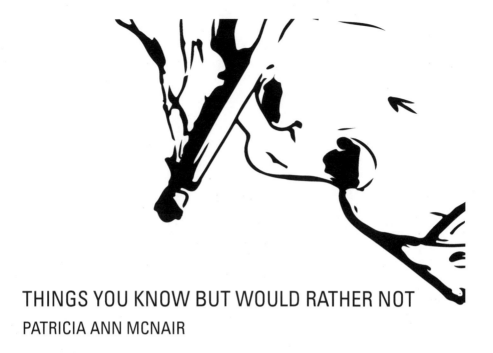

THINGS YOU KNOW BUT WOULD RATHER NOT
PATRICIA ANN MCNAIR

She knew she was dying. No one could tell her anything different. When Mary Alice woke up in the morning she could feel it in her bones, in her heart, the slight ache and rattle, the slow chug that felt like an engine unwilling to start. She'd work to extricate herself from the pile of things that blanketed her during the night: her three cats, Jax, Jill, and Eddie; the books she'd been reading (*The Outsiders, Jane Eyre, Go Ask Alice, Algebra I, Symptoms and Early Warning Signs*); the wrappers from the SuzyQs she'd bought at the hot dog stand on her way home from school and had stashed in her bedside table for that moment when she would wake with a start in the deep dark and feel the ravaging hunger like teeth in her belly; the orange and green afghan her grandmother (dead before she was born) had made for her father (out of the picture before she was two except for his monthly checks in the mail); the mimeographed pages of her homework assignments that still smelled of glue; a scattering of pens and her journal where, before she'd fallen asleep, she had practiced writing swear words in first cursive, then thick block letters. Her favorite, she'd concluded, was **shit**.

Her mother was hardly ever up when Mary Alice got out of bed in the morning, didn't matter if it was a school day or like today, a Saturday. Mary Alice could hear the radio alarm going down the hall, a tinny whine of static and voices and the Saturday morning countdown that was never quite enough to push through the deep sleep of her mother, Sam. (Her name was Sally, really, but she liked to be called Sam, a man's name.) Mary Alice made her own bed, pulling the corners tight and tucking her pillow under the afghan; she built neat piles of books and papers on her bedside tables; she pet the cats and swept crumbs from the bed and up from the floor, and went to her mother's room to shake her awake. Then she would go make the coffee, the Tang and the toast, get the day started. These were no easy tasks for a girl who knew she was dying. And besides, she was only thirteen. Why did she have to do everything?

"Can you get me my ciggies, hon?" Sam asked before her eyes were fully open. Mary Alice breathed in the ashy smell of her mother's room, the stale smoke of it. It smelled, too, like the chemicals Sam used in her darkroom: gummy, sharp. And there was something else — Mary Alice tried to breathe through her mouth, to swallow the smell before it lodged in her nose, in her forehead — something sour and yeasty. A pair of socks that were far too big for her mother's tiny feet ("These puppies haven't grown a bit since I was twelve," she liked to brag when she and Mary Alice went shoe shopping, which they had to do every six months with Mary Alice's big and getting-bigger-all-the-time dogs) were stretched out on the plush white rug at Sam's bedside. They looked sinister there, Mary Alice thought, long and snake-like.

She went to the table under the window, the little round thing her mother kept covered with a velvet cloth that was marked now with cigarette burns and mug stains. Two packs of cigarettes were there, a red and white box and her mother's Camels. A glass with something brown and the doused butts of last night's smokes, another with lipstick on its edges. Sam pushed herself up in the bed, her shoulders knobby beneath the straps of her undershirt. Her hair fell to her biceps, her boobs jiggled. She had raccoon-y mascara circles under her eyes and she looked like a picture, but not just any old picture, she looked like a painting, like something in a museum. Sam looked — Mary Alice could never quite get over this — gorgeous. Her mother was gorgeous.

The smoke clouded in the space between them, and her mother inhaled hard, thirsty for it. Mary Alice thought it might be the smoke that was killing her. The way the house reeked of it, the way it filled her own lungs when Sam gulped at it like this. Yes, maybe it was the smoke.

Or perhaps it was that she simply could never get enough sleep. Mary Alice had read somewhere that teenagers needed more sleep than adults do, maybe as much as babies even. They were still growing, their brains still forming. But there was too much noise, sometimes, and too much quiet other times, and Mary Alice would wake up in the middle of the night to the noise or the quiet, her bedside light — left on from her reading herself into sleep — shining like a headlight through her dreams. Mary Alice admired the way her cats were able to sleep all the time no matter the circumstances, getting up long enough to eat, maybe drink, jump to a windowsill to chitter at a bird in a nearby tree, then back to sleep in tight circles, or on hot days, long stretched-out things. Like these socks, the ones on her mother's rug.

Mary Alice kicked them under the bed.

"Late night?" she asked.

"Hmmm?" Sam said, distracted as always, plucking tobacco off her tongue with her manicured nails, sharp and purple. Didn't most people smoke cigarettes with filters these days?

If she squinted just right, the smoke and the shiny silvery sheets her mother slept on made things look not like a painting as Mary Alice had thought, but like one of those photographs Sam would take. Black and white and all sorts of shades of gray. Like the ones in the galleries. They looked dirty to Mary Alice, those photos. Dirty and beautiful. Except, of course, the ones of her.

• • •

Things she hated:

1. Having her picture taken.

2. Dogs.

3. School (not the classes, really, the learning part — but the other stuff. The kids, none of them her friends. The teachers. The low-slung building that too many students crammed into and so her grade, grade seven, had to go out back to the mobiles for class, those tin box trailers that dipped and sprang when you climbed up into them, that rattled when the winds came, when the spring rains started.)

4. The war. She didn't know much about this one, but she was sure it was wrong. There were protests. Kids got shot at a college in Ohio because of it. Or something like that.

5. Tang.

6. Her mother. (Not really.)

7. The way her boobs were starting to bounce when she walked. That she was going to need a bra soon.

8. Lists.

9. The creepy guy next door who was old but played basketball in the driveway after it got dark.

10. Being something that wasn't really a kid, but wasn't an adult, either.

You'd think Mary Alice would hate that she was dying, too, but she didn't. She liked it. It gave her something to focus on. Something all her own to look forward to.

Her mother kept on smoking and Mary Alice went to make the coffee, to prepare the Tang. To check the fridge for food she was pretty certain wasn't there except for butter maybe, or margarine. And grape jelly. She passed through the den with its soft leather furniture, its paneled walls, its red shag rug. Mary Alice tried not to look at the photos over the couch, the ones of her when she was little, pretty, blonde and big-eyed, naked and sitting on the beach in one, on a tree stump in another. The one, too, of her crying, her face so red you could even tell in the black and white of the photo, a deep crimson-like gray. Her little arms wrapped around her chest, hugging herself — like if she let go, she'd fly away. And somewhere in the way back background, a station wagon with wood panels, a wooden fence, a tiny house. She didn't know where they were, the picture was years and years old, in the olden days it could've been, because she was wearing something weird, puffy and gauzy and scalloped with ribbons everywhere. Wherever they were, though, when this picture was taken, Mary Alice was pretty sure her dad was there, too.

But she didn't pay attention to those photos; they were a landscape she was so familiar with she didn't see it anymore. Like the sound of the heavy ticking of the grandfather clock on the bookcase also in the den, a sound that Mary Alice forgot about because it was always there. So when she actually heard it lifting out of the other sounds of the house (refrigerator hum, murmur of her mother's radio, tick of the baseboard heaters on cold mornings) it startled her.

"Jaques the croc, swallowed the clock," she said to the clock like she did every morning. It had been her grandfather's, Mary Alice was pretty certain. Or perhaps her grandmother's — she thought maybe she believed it was her grandfather's because it was a grandfather clock. She could be like that, she knew. Literal. She didn't actually know her grandparents. None of them. They all died young, she suspected. She wasn't sure. It probably was like that in her family. Dying young.

Mary Alice started with the Tang, dumping tablespoons of the powder into a small pitcher. The dust of it flew into her nose and she sneezed; its sweetness coated her sinuses and made her gag. Later, her mother would pour two glasses and Mary Alice would drink hers down quick trying not to breathe, to smell it, to taste it. And Sam would pour a little something in her own, a pick-me-up she'd call it, a day-starter.

The refrigerator smelled like metal inside, cold and sharp. Jars of things rattled in the door: mustard, ketchup, horseradish, herring in cream sauce that was so old Mary Alice had never not seen it there. Boxes of film filled the crisper. Nothing edible. She could make a shopping list, but she didn't want to, she hated lists. Instead Mary Alice filled the coffee pot with water and scooped in the coffee, and it occurred to her that she was unable to swallow. *Dying*, she thought. *I'm dying.* And she tried and tried to swallow, the back of her tongue still tasting of Tang. She lifted her chin up, ducked her head, but it wouldn't work. Jax, the marmalade cat of her trio jumped up on the counter next to the range, pushed her head against Mary Alice's soft stomach. Cats always knew.

"Swallow," Mary Alice commanded herself, and Jax mewled, which gave Mary Alice the idea to rub her fingers up and down her own throat, like they did with the cats when they had to pill them. She rubbed and rubbed, and yes! To her great and frantic relief, Mary Alice swallowed. She gulped. She did it twice more just to show that she could — gulp, gulp. Loud swallows like a bad actress. Jax jumped off the counter.

● ● ●

To Do:

(This was why Mary Alice hated lists. Her mother was a list-maker. She had them all over the house, like this one here on the fridge held by a magnet that looked like a carrot. One of her usuals, the list of Saturday chores for Mary Alice.)

1. Laundry. (And this one had a sublist, in case Mary Alice might forget.)
   a. Collect
   b. Wash
   c. Fold
   d. Put Away
2. Cat litter.
3. Dusting.

THINGS YOU KNOW BUT WOULD RATHER NOT

4. Homework.

5. Change Sheets.

6. Pose.

Shit. Shit, shit. It had been months since Mary Alice had to pose for her mother. Sam was onto something different for a while, taking her camera to the parking lot at the HiLo, sitting there in her Volkswagen, smoking, watching. She had a show coming up soon, and she'd been shooting for days, developing deep into nights. She'd tried a few rolls of color film, too, making photos that Mary Alice saw hanging from the line in the darkroom next to the kitchen and off the garage. Bright things that looked like images out of the movies: shining cars and people talking, close-ups of cans of beans, watermelons, shopping carts, sales signs (done in a way you couldn't read the words, but could see a letter or two, or a curving line with the blur of a head or something passing in front of it.) Mary Alice loved these photos. Loved loved loved them. She loved, too, that when her mother took pictures in the grocery store like this, she actually bought things, and there would be food in the house, things to make into real meals. But then one night, while she sat up reading in bed with Jax on her lap and Jill (the tabby) and Eddie (the gray) at her ankles, Mary Alice heard her mother down in the darkroom, throwing things, yelling, crying. Then she heard noises in the kitchen, water running, ice trays cracking, cabinets slamming. And her mother muttering, talking like someone was there, but there wasn't, Mary Alice was pretty certain. Not this time.

In the morning Mary Alice slept late and came to thickly, her engine slow but not yet dead, and the house smelled like bacon and Sam was already up and cooking, stirring the Tang, the kitchen sparkling clean around her, the door to her darkroom open, everything in place, nothing hanging on the line to dry. Later, when Mary Alice changed the litter box, she found the color photographs in shreds in the garbage can at the edge of the driveway.

• • •

AMERICAN FICTION

Things she loved:

  1. Her cats. (All cats, really. Cats. Cats were good.)

  2. Shit. (The word. She really loved it.)

  3. Sleep.

  4. Her mother. (Mostly.)

  5. Making things clean.

  6. That life could not possibly be long. Life was short. Everyone said so. And wasn't this something to look forward to?

She poured the coffee for her mother, black and strong, and one for herself with Coffeemate and sugar, lots of it, and wiped the sticky drink powder from the counter, rinsed the dishrag, hung it over the neck of the faucet. Mary Alice carried the mugs back to her mother's room, where Sam had moved from the bed to the table by the window, list-making and smoking and studying contact sheets with a magnifier that looked like a shot glass. She patted her knee for Mary Alice to sit, which she did, but hated. (11. Sitting on her mother's knee.) Sam's legs were bony and hard, and Mary Alice was fat, she knew it, bigger than her mom, and she had to balance on her mother's knee while holding her weight off her sort-of, and she could feel her own legs, plump, white limbs that stuck out from under her nightgown, shake with the effort. Sam swept Mary Alice's hair to one side and said, "Know what the back of little girls' necks are for?" before she kissed her daughter's neck. It was swift and sweet, and something she'd done pretty much every morning for as long as Mary Alice could remember. She could feel her mother's breath warm on her skin; the kiss both embarrassed and delighted her.

"Not really a little girl anymore," Mary Alice said and stood up from her mother's knee. She pulled another chair close to the table and sat. She brushed ashes into her palm. Rubbed them away on the hem of her nightgown.

"You'll always be my little girl," Sam answered on cue. She was back at her writing now, making her list and reciting her part of the script like a poem they said by heart together, alternating lines.

"Even when I die?"

"Even when you die."

When had Mary Alice added that line, *even when I die?* She thought it must have been ages ago, she couldn't remember not saying it. Had she always known she was dying? Jax and Jill and Eddie were rolling over one another in the hallway just outside her mother's doorway. Jax landed on Jill's back and Eddie crashed into them. They made noises in their throats and hissed, just playing. Every now and then one or another of them would stop and lick a paw, turn away from his buddies, stare at Mary Alice at the table. They rarely came into Sam's room.

"Did you see the list?" Sam asked, her head still over the notepad in front of her. She was drawing little asterisks down the margin. Sometimes it was asterisks, stars, sometimes it was numbers. Today looked like a star day for lists.

"Umm hmm." Mary Alice swallowed the sugary, beige coffee, looked out the window but there was nothing to see. The basketball in the strip of grass between their driveway and the neighbor's. The street. The houses. All kind of like theirs, long and sleek with flat lawns and bushes shaped like walls and boulders. She knew they were called ranch houses, but she didn't know why. They were miles away from horses, states away maybe.

"Let's get started, then," Sam said and stubbed out her cigarette. She sipped at her coffee and tucked the notepad into the waistband of the shorts she slept in. "The light is good, I think. We don't have a lot of time."

"We don't," Mary Alice agreed.

● ● ●

Her mother's last show was at a gallery in the city, in a neighborhood of high rises and small, expensive shops and restaurants. Mary Alice counted the number of men in uniforms and caps, standing just outside entrances, at the ready to pull open car doors and ring buzzers. Some had whistles. The doormen nodded at them while they passed, and Sam gave the men her asterisk smile, the one that glinted in her lipsticked mouth, that shined like something neon, or like a flash from her camera. Mary Alice, in new purple velvet bellbottoms and a flowering silk blouse, trotted along at her mother's side, trying to match her walk that was both brisk and slinky. *Like the cats*, she thought, *the way their bodies moved in long, curving lines when they hurried down the hall to the kitchen at dinnertime.* Sam wore an ankle-length leather coat the color of cream, and a fuzzy golden tam. It was autumn and Mary Alice's mother was beautiful.

The gallery was already full of bodies and chatter when they arrived, its wide windows cloudy with warmth and breath. Men in jackets and turtleneck sweaters, women in long skirts or wide-legged pantsuits gathered in groups of three and four, smoking, lifting glasses, eating crackers topped with swirls of cheese and tiny pickles. Some huddled in the middle of the room glancing over their shoulders, while others moved along its edges, studying the photos, dozens and dozens of them like a gray border half-way up the stark white walls. They were small, and so you had to lean in close to get a good look.

• • •

How to behave at an opening when you are only thirteen:
  * Smile.
  * Don't eat too many crackers with cheese.
  * Say please and thank you.
  * Come when your mother calls, but don't cling.
  * Don't let people know you are eavesdropping even if they say things like: "That poor dear" or "what kind of mother" or "shh, she's right there."
  * Don't look at your reflection in the glass frames over the pictures from

when you were little and beautiful. Because you are neither of these things anymore.

•   •   •

It was here at the gallery on this opening night that Mary Alice figured she must be dying. She bent toward a photo of her legs in a pair of her mother's white patent boots in the doorway of the garage, the cats at her ankles. She liked this one. A man in a brown shining suit and a woman in a tin-colored blouse with silver beads that jingled as she lifted her glass stood close by in front of a different photograph. When they spoke, Mary Alice pretended not to hear.

"Is she ill?"

"Oh no, I don't think so."

"Her face looks so sad."

"Those eyes."

"Those pudgy little legs."

"Those big feet."

When they turned and saw her there they smiled, but more like grimaces than grins, and moved on to the next photo, the breeze of their escape lifting Mary Alice's bangs from her forehead. She felt hot, dizzy. She pressed the cool glass of club soda against her face. She stepped closer to the photo they'd been looking at, one her mother took on a recent morning before Mary Alice had gotten out of bed. Her hair was everywhere on the pillow; she was tangled in sheets and books and cats. You could see the bruises on her shins, the ones from the everyday use of her legs, her big feet. There was a shadow at the tops of her legs, just under the sheet, something black and mysterious. She looked closer. It was true what they said; her eyes were foggy, not right. Was she ill? She couldn't remember now. All she knew for certain was that she was hideous. People could see her like this. She wanted to die. She felt something rumbling inside her. She gulped soda and wanted more, needed more. She was thirsty like a cat in the desert. She was hot, so hot. She was, Mary Alice hoped — no, was sure — dying.

• • •

The Saturday morning shoot started out okay, fun even, with Sam in one of her high, good moods, running from place to place in the shopping center, working her light meter, swinging her camera on its leather strap around her neck. She laughed and Mary Alice laughed, too, because why not? There were so many other times to be sad, to be dying, she thought today she might try something else. Living, maybe. And why was that? The warm spring sun that shone on them as they drove in the Volkswagen with its top down, the way boys looked at her mother and then Mary Alice and nodded hello. She was beautiful in Sam's light, Mary Alice was pretty certain, in the clothes her mother had chosen for her from her own closet: a long camel-colored vest that swept in circles around her knees, a silk scarf with squares and rectangles of green, of orange, of pink. Flowing pants that were almost a skirt. And at Loehmann's Sam bought Mary Alice a floppy hat, like something from an ad, that one on the billboards for women's cigarettes, maybe, or a Pepsi commercial. The brim dipped low over Mary Alice's eyes that her mother had made big with mascara, a bit of shadow. Sam was scrubbed clean and looked trim and efficient in cowboy boots and jeans, a turtleneck shell with no sleeves that showed the balls of muscles in her arms, the freckles on her shoulders. They stopped in front of a toy store, the sort of place Mary Alice had never shopped, she was never much for toys, and Sam asked her to bend forward and look at a train on a track, had her frown. Inside the store, Mary Alice gathered up armloads of Barbies and hugged them all to her chest — as Sam instructed — and looked up towards the ceiling. Sam clicked and laughed, clicked and laughed. People stopped and watched as the shoot went on. Some asked questions.

"Is this for a catalog?" from a woman with a sheer scarf tied under her chin and bobby pins holding curls near her ears. Mary Alice loved that she might be mistaken for a catalog model.

"What kind of camera is that?" a man in a windbreaker asked. He held a little girl's hand and a dog on a leash. He smiled at Sam. The nosy dog sniffed Mary Alice's knees.

"Are you famous?" The little girl asked. She wore a yellow tutu and a sparkling plastic tiara.

"Yes," Mary Alice said.

Late in the afternoon Mary Alice and Sam stopped for an Orange Nehi and a plate of french fries at the cafeteria in Woolworths. They sat in a booth surrounded by dozens of shoppers at rest. Mary Alice poured ketchup onto the plate with the fries, a pool for dipping. She ate one fry, then another. She was famished, starving. Hours had passed since she'd toasted the last heel of bread and spread it with margarine and grape jelly.

It smelled like tuna salad and hot grease at Woolworths, Mary Alice always thought so. And like wet wood chips, like sawdust. Close by were the cages of small animals and birds, she could see the pink noses of things from where she sat, and hear the tiny living sounds they made. She pushed the plate of fries toward her mother over the sticky table. Mary Alice wished she had remembered to bring her wet'n'dries so she could clean things up a little. Sam nibbled a fry and lit a cigarette. She read from her list.

Possible backdrops:

* Toy Store. ("Check," Mary Alice said, and sucked the orange drink through her straw, swallowed easily.)

* Travel Agency. ("Check," Mary Alice said even though they hadn't actually gone into the place, but instead she was instructed to look longingly in the window at the posters of Paris, of Yellowstone.)

* Hardware Store. ("Check," Mary Alice said. She loved the oily smell of that place, a smell that made her think of men, of fathers.)

* Housewares. (And here Sam shook her head and drew a line through the word.)

Mary Alice leaned forward to see the other places on the list, and the floppy brim of her hat knocked her mother's glass over on the table. Ice and soda splashed everywhere, soaking the fries and turning the ketchup into soup, filling the plastic ashtray and dousing the freshly-lit cigarette. An expanding river of orange ran toward her mother's camera.

"You little...!" Sam hissed, and grabbed the camera up and away from danger. A waterfall of orange spilled over the edge of the table onto Sam's bluejeaned knees. The glass hit the floor and shattered.

"Shit!" Mary Alice whispered, something she'd never said before in the company of another person, and quick as that her mother slapped her across the mouth — something she'd never done before. Ever.

At the tables close by, people stopped their conversations and stared at the mother and daughter. Mary Alice felt her eyes burn and fill. She felt her chest seize. She tried to swallow, but couldn't. Tears leaked down her cheeks. She needed to swallow. She slid out from the booth, banging her shin on the table leg on the way.

"Oh damn, hon. Oh damn. Bad me. Bad Mama." And Sam reached toward her daughter, but Mary Alice spun and walked away. She wanted to run, but people already were watching, and what was the huge drama anyway? A girl fighting with her mother. No big deal. Look away now, look away. Mary Alice pulled the brim of the hat further over her face and tried desperately to swallow while she navigated the maze of aisles between tables and booths and animals in their cages and hurried toward the bathroom.

Her blouse was spattered with Orange Nehi and ketchup, and of course that would not do. Mary Alice made sure the bathroom was empty and pulled off the vest, unwound the scarf, unbuttoned the blouse. Goosebumps. Her boobs were low, pink hills over the naked roundness of her belly that bounced as she swallowed finally, swallowed and swallowed air, gulping down the crying that was right there in her eyes, in her chest, in her throat. She could see it all in the mirror. She turned the water to cold — cold was best for food stains, she knew — and held the blouse under the tap. Behind her, the door opened and in the mirror Mary Alice could see her mother standing there, camera around her neck, the knees of her jeans dark and wet-looking.

"Oh, honey," she said. Mary Alice thought her mother looked really sad, really sorry, and if she didn't have to get her blouse cleaned right in that instant, Mary Alice might even have gone to her, hugged her, forgiven her. Her hands went red and cold under the sink's spray. She swallowed because she could; she dipped her head and the brim of the hat fell over her forehead. Mary Alice studied the disappearing orange stain under water.

When she looked up again, the stain was pretty much gone, but her mother wasn't. There stood Sam, camera to her eye, the lens focused on Mary Alice in the mirror.

● ● ●

They took a long way home, detouring through the city where Sam parked the Volkswagen in front of a fire hydrant and asked one of the uniformed doormen to watch the car, to watch Mary Alice while she popped for just a second into the gallery. Mary Alice stared at the sun (you weren't supposed to do this, you could go blind) as it sank over the tops of the buildings. She blinked and saw stars in her eyelids, and saw shadows in the sky. Her blouse was wet under her mother's vest; she was cold and hungry and wanted the doorman to stop watching her. It was ages before her mother returned, excited and chatty. Mary Alice pretended to listen but didn't; instead, she played with the hamster her mother had bought her at Woolworths after she'd shot a roll of film in the bathroom. She tickled its nose through the skinny bars of its cage. She felt the pins of its little teeth on the tip of her pinky.

It was full dark when they pulled up to the house and the old guy was out dribbling the ball in his driveway. He waved at Sam and Mary Alice, and Sam waved back. Mary Alice carried the hamster to her room; Jax and Jill and Eddie followed her, howling and hungry and onto the scent from the cage.

• • •

Things You Know But Would Rather Not:

1. That the only food in the house is for pets, not people.

2. That when your mother closes the darkroom door behind her, you are on your own.

3. That care and feeding is up to you. And that you are still only thirteen.

4. That creamed herring does go bad, no matter what your mother told you. And that Tang can be eaten for a meal if necessary, straight out of the jar by the spoonful, swallowed down until you can't swallow anymore. And then you won't be hungry.

5. What the top of your mother's head looks like in the dark when you watch her from your bedroom window cross the grassy patch between your house and the neighbor's and he drops his basketball and puts his hands on your mother, on her butt, under her shell.

6. That you should not let a hamster out of its cage when there are cats in your bedroom.

7. That your mother loves you best when you are ugly.

8. What dying sounds like. And that cats don't like the taste of spleen.

9. That when you wake in the dark to another sound, someone yelling, crying maybe, but moaning you figure — Jesus. God. Jesus God — you think it could be your own dying finally. But there you are, under the blankets with the cats in circles at your ankles and on the pillow. And you hear it again, from the

room down the hall: Jesus. God. And still, damnit, you are alive.

    10. Shit. You are alive.

THE POLISH GIRL
MOLLY POWER

Mr. Araki, the owner and manager of Chef Sukura's Japanese Cuisine, at the bottom of Newbury Street in Boston, asks the Polish girl, "You legal?"

The Polish girl takes off her blue mittens and places them on the bar in front of her. She bobs her head. "Sure, legal."

He stands on a raised floor behind the bar; she stands in front of him, her white fingers and short red nails on the smooth gray bar top, watching his face. He has smooth, cream-colored skin, round steel-rimmed glasses, tinted gray. Everything about him is narrow — narrow head, shoulders, and long, narrow hands.

She thinks: *What is this bar made of? It feels like a floor — yes, the concrete floor in Denmark.* (She lived there with a German boy, Deter, before coming to the United States. He turned out to be a bad person, just like her girlfriend, Karen, said. He took money from her purse while she slept, then disappeared.) But could a bar top be made of such a material? She wants to run her hands over the surface, check it out, but she stands quietly by a bar stool, her hands ready to push her application closer to Mr. Araki.

As though it isn't really important to him, he slowly reaches for her application and turns it around to look at it. He pins it down with two fingers. Now she tilts her head back to look at his face, daring to smile.

"You are available days?" He speaks quietly, with no inflection.

"Yes, yes, days. All days."

Mr. Araki — with his high cheekbones and small, hairless chin, his thin lips, his clipped gray-white hair — asks, "Nights?"

"Sure, all nights."

Mr. Araki lights a cigarette. He inhales, glancing up at the black ceiling with its hundreds of tiny pin lights then lets the smoke ripple out of his mouth in a ribbon that flows wider, flatter, and transparent as it heads for the pin lights above. "Cigarette?" He picks up the pack and shakes it.

"Thank you, Mr. Araki." He lights hers with his silver lighter.

Helena wants to direct her smoke away from Mr. Araki but finds it difficult. Now she wishes she hadn't taken the cigarette; she can't enjoy it. She wants to put it out in the ashtray on the bar but decides that will seem rude and ungrateful. Instead, she smokes quickly, blowing smoke downward toward her feet and a band of blue neon that glows beneath the bar's countertop. Mr. Araki enjoys his cigarette with a meditative air.

"So. You are living with your aunt and uncle." Those are her only references.

"Yes." She thinks of the cot she sleeps on in their crowded living room. In the daytime she folds it up and puts it behind the sofa. Her Uncle Don (not really her uncle, but her aunt's American boyfriend) told her she would be better off going home, back to Warsaw. He warned her, more than once, "You'll see, this country isn't all it's cracked up to be. Promises are made — oh sure — but then what?" He made the number O with his thumb and forefinger.

"Mr. Araki. I am a hard worker."

"Yes, no doubt." He is silent. Then, after a long moment, "I can use you, one lunch shift — Tuesday. And Sunday, too. We see what you can do."

"Sure!" She stubs out her cigarette and begins to button her patent leather jacket. "This you will not regret, Mr. Araki."

He steps down from the raised floor and comes around the bar to stand by her. "Good. No smoking on the job. Not in the bathroom, either. Smoking in the alley behind the kitchen."

"I don't have the tobacco habit, Mr. Araki."

"We have a high-quality clientele. Big shots — bankers, lobbyists, accountants; the politicians." He leans over to point to the right out the front window. "The State House. They all come to Chef Sukura's."

"Yes, Mr. Araki. I will work hard."

"Must be discreet. No matter what you hear, what you see."

She doesn't know the word *discreet* but agrees. Now he leads her through the kitchen to the alley, then shakes her hand. Helena hurries down the street to the corner, thinking he might still be standing at the doorway, watching her, but when she turns slightly to see, he isn't there.

She holds her chin up as she moves quickly — only looking for six days and now employed at Chef Sukura's Japanese Cuisine! She hesitates now and again, at some of the windows as she walks along, imagining she might buy something with her new money.

Something small. It is important to send her mother money. Clothes, too. In Warsaw Helena knew people who got great clothes from the United States — blue jeans, angora sweaters, platform shoes, slouch shoulder bags. She stares at two winter coats in a window — one red and one black. Her mother, with her yellow hair, would look great in the red one. It is a long coat, with a belt and gold buttons. Helena walks on — there is no price tag showing so she knows it must be expensive. This is how it happened that the Polish girl came to work in Chef Sukura's Japanese Cuisine.

Helena's aunt lends her money to buy her uniform: She buys two white shirts and a long black skirt at the Dress Barn. Every night she washes one of the shirts in the kitchen sink, then hangs it up on a wire hanger suspended from one of the window locks in the living room. In the morning, after Don leaves for work, she irons it on a folded towel on the kitchen table. The skirt was a mistake. The material is scratchy and causes red marks on her thighs. She will have to buy another.

"Mr. Kusada will teach you all the need to know," Mr. Araki tells her. "Listen. Learn." Mr. Kusada is the manager of Chef Sukura's.

On the first Tuesday, Mr. Kusada shows her where to put her things in the back hallway then how to tie the cherry-red apron around her waist, pulling the strings from back to front, and tying the long sash smartly on the left side with a bow. He gives her a small pad and pencil, which she is to keep in the pocket of her apron until ready to take an order. He wears black pants with a ribbon down the side of each leg, a short black jacket over a white shirt, and black shiny shoes with pointed toes.

When the first Tuesday's shift is over, Mr. Kusada tells her the business they experienced that day is typical.

"This is why no one wants Tuesday lunch: Too slow. Not much in tips. Students eating bowls of noodles, the usual old Japanese retirees, you can see, taking all day over their tea. And the old grandfather at table fifteen — that is his table on Tuesdays, unless he is in Georgia, visiting his daughter."

Helena had assumed the gloomy November weather contributed to the slow business but no, Mr. Kusada assures her, even Tuesdays in the summer are the same. The first Tuesday Mr. Kusada gives her two tables, but things are so slow on the second Tuesday that he gives her four. Mr. Araki, wearing his daytime gray cashmere sweater and charcoal-colored pants, opens the restaurant at eleven-thirty, but slips away after that and does not reappear. She wonders where he goes.

While there he talks unhurriedly, quietly, into the telephone behind the bar, all the while smoking, keeping his cigarette in an ashtray below the bar. Helena can see he has the tobacco habit; she has never seen him without a cigarette for more than a few minutes. She doubts that he knows the dangers of smoking.

The kitchen staff is light on her shifts — a Japanese cook who apparently speaks no English and his helper, a very old woman, who doubles as the dishwasher. Mr. Kusada, a middle-aged man with a round face and a broad chest, is quiet and serious, like Mr. Araki. He tells her he has been at Chef Sukura's Japanese Cuisine from the beginning. Helena admires his correctness. She can't imagine Mr. Kusada — or Mr. Araki — ever raising their voices, or showing any emotion beyond the quietest sort of amusement.

She considers these men, comparing them to her own father, a drunk who careens from maudlin self-pity to bellicose anger before passing out, and Don, her aunt's boyfriend, who is worse. Helena feels badly for her aunt. He belittles her in front of other people and takes money from her.

● ● ●

At three o'clock, with the door locked and her shift over, Helena tosses her apron in a basket, and walks through the kitchen to the alley, nodding to the chef and his helper. The chef pays no attention to her but the old woman smiles, showing her nut-brown gums and a gold tooth.

"So long, Polish," she says, hiding her mouth behind her hand. Helena doesn't know how she knows she is Polish but she assumes Mr. Kusada must have said something.

Sundays, from eleven to three, are a little better: these students have credit cards and girlfriends to impress; large cheerful Japanese families come in to celebrate birthdays or promotions; cheerful gay couples wander up from the South End with plenty of money for a leisurely lunch.

After six weeks, Mr. Araki tells her to come in on Friday nights as well as her day shifts. Friday night — the best shift! Everyone who comes in is in a celebratory mood, ready to spend plenty of money, drink plenty from the top shelf, and give generous tips.

"Fast learner," Mr. Araki says, tapping the side of his head with a finger. "I could see that right away."

"Is that why you hired me, Mr. Araki?"

"Yes, in part." He stands, as usual, on the raised floor behind the bar, his face wreathed in smoke. His lips turn up slightly. Everything Mr. Araki does he does slowly, gradually, as though he considers his move first.

"In part?" She smiles.

"I liked your nose." He opens his mouth wide and laughs, watching her look of amazement. "Oh, a joke! No, I know what it is to leave your country, to travel so far from home. So much left behind, eh? It is not easy."

Helena turns away with a tray full of drinks, walking in what she thinks of as a Japanese way; slightly pigeon-toed and silent because of the soft cotton slippers she recently bought. Also, now, she bends from the waist to listen to customers, especially men, looking into their faces with all her attention, as though she is prepared to hear something of the utmost importance.

On Friday nights a bald Japanese bartender named Jake moves smoothly back and forth on the raised floor; mixing, shaking and pouring drinks with flair. Helena can see he has a following—young men in suspenders sit at the bar, drinking Jake's original drink: The Belvedere-Wasabi Martini adorned with a sliver of Daicon radish. It is the most expensive cocktail on the menu.

The two Japanese sisters, May and Janet, have the best tables—they have been at Chef Sukura's for more than ten years.

On Helena's first Friday night, May says, "Hey, Polish girl. Come. Let me show you."

Helena follows May to the back hall. They stand beneath a row of coat hooks.

May picks up Helena's coat and holds it out in front of her, pinching it with two long gold fingernails.

"You put your coat on my hook, honey. See? The first hook is my hook. The second hook? Is Janet's hook." Her mouth pulls back, showing her white, even teeth.

Helena takes her coat from her. She smiles. "No one told me. Which one is my hook?"

"Last hook — closest to the toilet — that's your special hook."

Helena flings her coat onto the designated hook. She tells May, looking sincere, "I was hoping you'd say that — that's my favorite hook!"

"You talk funny English. Must be hard for our clientele to understand what you saying." May says.

"People are kind, May," Helena answers. They look at each other with arched eyebrows until May shakes her head slightly before she turns and walks away.

On Friday nights two chefs work in the kitchen. They hate each other. The red-faced one who works weekdays is jealous of the long-faced one and glances at everything he puts out with distain. The old woman chops vegetables and washes the dishes with a teenage boy to help her; *perhaps a grandson*, Helena assumes. But she sees him grab the old woman around the neck, trying to kiss her passionately. The old woman hopped away from him, hissing, saying, "Hey, crazy! Not here!"

Most nights after work, the restaurant workers hurry off, Helena, too. One Friday before they open, Mr. Araki tells her his regular staff is invited to share a drink or two after work on an occasional Friday night, in fact, this night.

"You should stay, join us," Mr. Araki says. "You will get to know some of the others."

After midnight the last customers leave, a noisy party who came back for a cashmere scarf that no one finds. Mr. Kusada escorts them back to the front door with good humor and locks the door behind them.

The employees line up at the bar — first the sisters, May and Janet, then Helena, then Mr. Kusada, who has removed his well-fitting black waiter's jacket. The two chefs sit at the far end of the bar, side-by-side but not talking. Apparently the helper and the dishwasher are not invited to come to the front room with the others. Jake, the bartender, carries five Kirin beers into the kitchen and returns to sit on a stool next to the chefs. Looking down the bar,

Helena sees the obvious hierarchy. She hopes she is sitting in the right place.

Mr. Araki pours each of them sake, a generic brand. It is so quiet they can hear muffled voices and clattering in the kitchen.

"Excellent week. Thank you." Mr. Araki gives his staff a little bow, and refills everyone's green porcelain cups.

Everyone nods and loosens up; their tips are great tonight. The sisters begin to talk rapidly to each other in Japanese, their voices low. They nod to Mr. Araki when he fills their cups a third time. Mr. Kusada holds his cup up and looks at Helena.

"We must welcome our newcomer," he says loudly enough for everyone to hear.

Helena smiles and he taps her cup before he drinks his sake down. He says, "You are doing well."

Jake holds up his cup. "Hey, Helena, you're good for my business, I can tell you."

Helena beams at him and holds up her own cup to recognize his kindness.

Mr. Araki empties the bottle. He stops in front of Helena. "There is an opening for another shift. You feel ready?"

May and Janet abruptly fall silent and turn on their stools sharply to look at her. They half-close their eyes and suck in their cheeks. Janet crosses her legs, May puts her large gold purse on the bar in front of her and snaps it shut with a sharp click.

"Yes, Mr. Araki," Helena says quietly. The mood at the bar is changed. She wished Mr. Araki would talk about her new shift at another time. Mr. Kusada leans toward her in a friendly way, beginning an amusing story about a stuffy customer while the sisters writhe about on their stools.

Janet, the younger one stands up, saying, "I need to point out, perhaps, that I been here a long time. Excellent work record. Faithful to Chef Sukura's always. Never — I mean nev-er, ev-er — call in with fake sickness or any funny stuff like that."

May snorts. "You? Hey, what's wrong with your head? I been here six months more than you. I have more regulars for sure." Now she stands up and pulls her coat belt tight. Janet does the same; they wear matching red raincoats.

Mr. Kusada lights a cigarette. He watches everyone in the mirror behind the bar, but says nothing. He looks relaxed, almost languid; Helena thinks he looks like a movie star. The two chefs are silent, smoking also, and seem not to register the sisters' outburst, or perhaps they don't care. Jake fiddles with a book of matches, trying out a trick.

Mr. Araki glances down at the sisters' empty cups. He says, forcing heartiness, "Oh, you two leaving now? Goodnight, then."

The older one blasts out rapid-fire Japanese and spit hits the bar counter. Mr. Araki wipes the counter with a white cloth. The other one, Janet, wheels around and stamps toward the locked front door, but turns back and stands in the middle of the tables and chairs, speaking sternly in Mr. Araki's direction.

He puts out his cigarette. He shakes his head slowly. "It is rude to speak Japanese with Helena here, having her goodnight sake with us. So unkind."

May throws her arms out. "Too bad we don't know Polish, huh?"

Janet nods vigorously, calling out, "Ha! She mispronounce English so much we don't get her. She sound like Daffy Duck or something."

No one says anything to this. The sisters take a last defiant look at Helena before they walk one behind the other to the door, jerk it open and pull it closed behind them. Helena can understand their frustration but what can she do about it? Mr. Araki is the owner. Mr. Araki can do as he pleases. Soon the chefs and Jake leave also, through the kitchen.

Helena stands up. "It's late, Mr. Araki. Thank you for the sake. It is delicious."

"Sit, sit. Let me teach you about sake." He reaches for a bottle from the top shelf. "Ah, it is Mr. Kusada who is the real expert, he will help."

She suppresses a sigh and sits back down. Mr. Kusada reaches behind him to a chair for his jacket and black overcoat, but put them down again. "I cannot stay long. My wife is not well."

"Her ulcer again?" Mr. Araki asks.

"Yes, again."

There is a long silence and then the old woman calls out from the kitchen that they are leaving. The little window in the kitchen door goes dark.

Helena gives Mr. Araki a thin smile. He opens a cupboard door and takes out three lacquered sake cups. He says, "Mr. Kusada has been fortunate enough to attend the huge sake competition — Zenkoku Shinshu Kampyo kai — more than once."

Mr. Kusada nods "Two times. I have tasted the best sakes."

"Now. This sake — Kamoshibito Kuheji — this is special." Mr. Araki pours directly from the bottle. "Wonderful rice aroma. Smell."

Mr. Kusada nods. "Not the very best, but very special." He drinks with relish.

Mr. Araki's cheeks show two pink, round dots. Helena wonders what her face looks like. She puts her hands on her cheeks — her skin feels rubbery, loose. Mr. Kusada puts down his little cup and puts on his coat.

"That's it for me, I'm afraid. I must go home to Irene." He gives Helena a little pat on her shoulder.

She says, "Oh, yes, I should go home now." She thinks to watch Mr. Kusada leave, but is afraid to turn on her stool. She feels unsteady.

Mr. Araki says, "Yes, I will order a cab for you. You're tired. Oh — let me introduce just this one more. This is super-premium, the very best category of sakes. Jyokigen. Very special." Mr. Araki quickly pours them each a cupful, puddling some onto the bar. "Uh oh," he says.

Helena takes a sip. Mr. Araki pours them a small amount more, to bring the sake to the top of their cups again.

They fell silent while they drink. When he picks up the bottle again, Helena puts her hand over her cup. "Oh, Mr. Araki, I can't drink anymore." Now the room spins so fast she has to lower her face to the counter, wanting the coolness of the smooth concrete on her cheek.

She whispers, "Warsaw. Beautiful, beautiful Warsaw." She is suddenly homesick. She imagines walking along the street where she lived; she can see the old trees, the way they were in summer, immense, casting their almost round, dark shadows on the pavement; then the front steps to their apartment building with its heavy iron railing, and at the top, the large black door with the old door knocker in the center; and finally, most precious, she imagines running up the stairs to their flat on the third floor, carrying her book bag, which she hasn't thought of since grade school. She imagines seeing her mother's old felt slippers by the door, and her own — smaller, plaid on the top, and maroon. "Warsaw. So beautiful." Tears splash onto the bar, making her cheek wet.

"Oh dear. Helena. My fault. Now look."

"Boston? Old? Ha." She raises her head to wag it back and forth, but stops because of the room's movement. "Boston is not old. Boston? Nothing."

Mr. Araki puts the bottle away and places the little lacquered cups in the sink. He is talking but she can't follow what he says. She suspects he was quite drunk, too; she noticed him lurch slightly to one side when he moved to put away the sake and the cups. He has become very deliberate in his movements. He says, "So, Boston is nothing compared to Warsaw."

"Yes, you know? You have seen my Warsaw?" She wipes her nose on her sleeve and he hands her a bar napkin.

"No. I know of it, of course. A very old, fine city. One of the capitals of Europe. No, I have no chance to travel. I can't leave Chef Sukura's. Sometimes it occurs to me I am a prisoner of my own making." Mr. Araki's lips turn down. He comes around the bar and peers at Helena's face, which is once again lying on the bar, now with closed eyes. Her fingers hold tight to the bar-top's edge. Very gently he picks up strands of her hair that lie over her face and tucks them behind her ear, but they slip across her face again.

She swats at his hand. "Oh God," she murmurs. She starts to cry again, this time because she has made the mistake of getting drunk at the place where she works. She is ashamed.

"Poor Helena. You are too sleepy to go home." Mr. Araki steadies himself on a bar stool.

She raises her head and he attempts to wipe her nose with his white handkerchief.

"My fault. Lean on me. You need to lie down now. Rest." He puts an arm around her waist, and attempts to lift her off the bar stool. She continues to cry sleepily, clutching at his jacket and falling in his direction. She says, "I just want to go home."

"Poor girl," he says, half-carrying her across the restaurant. "I, too, know this feeling. So far from home."

She flings her arms around his neck and drops her head on his chest, quiet except for an occasional deep, shuddering intake of breath. Helena's shoes make a hissing sound as Mr. Araki pulls her across the carpet toward the foyer. He holds her tighter around the waist while he inserts a plastic card into a slot that opens an elevator door.

"Up we go."

She tries to stand up in the elevator while he supports her, then allows him to pull her off and through a small entryway, on through a sitting room and into a darkened bedroom.

Helena sinks onto the bed with her feet hanging to the floor. She opens her eyes and says, "I have plans, Mr. Araki! Good plans. I'm not always going to be a Japanese waitress, you know."

"Of course not, you are young, ambitious. You have dreams." He watches her fumbling to get her shoes off and reaches down to pull them off for her.

Helena flops back and turns over to crawl up the bed, wanting to reach the pillows. "This is a lovely bed," she mumbles, letting her head fall onto the pillow.

She watches him take off his shoes and socks, then look down at his pants before he pulls his shirt tails out and walks to the far side of the bed. He lies down on the top of the covers. He turns on his side facing away from her.

She moans and throws her arm out over his pillow; her fingers touch his neck. Mr. Araki reaches up and puts his hand over hers, stroking her wrist with his thumb.

"Warm," she mutters. "Can I hold you a little, Mr. Araki?"

He pushes back closer to her. She wraps her arm around his middle, bunching his shirt material in her hand, brushing his skin under it.

"It has been many years since anyone has held me so," he tells her. His voice is shaking. "You smell of almonds."

Helena chuckles. "What? Almonds?"

He doesn't answer. She takes her hand from his shirt and touches his cheeks. They are wet. She puts her hand back under his arm, onto his belly and clutches his shirt again.

"Mr. Araki?"

"Yes."

She pushes close enough to him that she can whisper into his ear. "Will you talk to me a little?"

He turns over onto his back, and turns his face to her. She picks up his hand and he squeezes her fingers and holds onto to them. "Let me sing to you."

In a barely audible voice, he sings a Japanese lullaby, one his grandmother sang to him and his sister when he was a boy.

SPIRITUAL CLOSURE

FALLING THROUGH CHAIRS

CAROL COOLEY

Daddy's stroke happened almost a year ago and was no surprise to anyone. He lived his whole life on bacon, cheese, and butter beans drenched in pork fat. The doctor told him for years to stop jamming up his arteries, but Daddy'd say, "Hell, I ain't living without my simple pleasures." One time I asked him, "Daddy, do all simple pleasures have to wreak havoc on our bodies?" He said, "Only the good ones, Ruby-girl." We laughed hard as I sipped Budweiser out of a long neck and Daddy spit snuff juice into an old coffee can.

Unable to eat, talk, or even sit up, Daddy spent his days in a hospital bed Mama got set up for him. She broke her back turning him over to clean the mess off his scrotum and legs. And with all that, the thing she worried about most was getting him baptized. Mama tried her whole life to get Daddy to cave in to Jesus. He'd drive her to church every Sunday, take her to Bible study, and even let the preacher hit him up with reasons why he needed to be saved by the Lord. Daddy'd make some joke like, "Hell, why don't I go down to the pond so me and Jesus can take a good skinny-dip together." Mama would storm out, mumbling something about Daddy's crotch catching on fire.

One time Mama was at the sink cleaning up supper while me and Daddy were leafing through newspapers at the kitchen table. She ran over to him, kneeled on the floor, and grabbed his legs. Mama looked up into his hazel eyes and pleaded, "Please go on and get baptized for me — if you love me, you'll do it for me." Daddy didn't have a joke for that one and looked ready to cry. I thought he was going to agree to it before saying, "Sadie, stand up and find yourself somewhere in all this," like he was talking to a small child. Mama was leaning on him with tears flowing into her mouth. She stood up, walked back to the sink, and finished scraping meatloaf and hard ketchup off the dishes. Daddy went outside.

● ● ●

The doorbell rang. It was Preacher Gray T. coming for his weekly visit to pray over Daddy. No matter how many times I greeted him at the door I couldn't get used to his blonde buzz cut and hard-tipped shoes. Gray T. and me went to high school together and it was no secret in our small town that we'd had a thing for each other. We'd leave school, head down to the creek, and park our backs up against an old oak tree. He used to tell me that after high school he wanted to grow his hair long and study philosophy. I had no idea what I wanted to do, but I was fine with that. Swapping our future plans usually got us rolling around in the grass. His wet tongue in my mouth was the closest to heaven I'd ever been. When I was underneath him I would open my eyes and see the sun finding its way through the branches and leaves, like it was shining on everything pure in the world. He'd pull his lips slowly off mine and I'd say, "I swear, your blue eyes have electricity running through them."

After a year or so, Gray T.'s grip around my waist started to feel less urgent. He was talking more about the Lord and that his plans were changing to go to seminary school. I asked him why he was leaving the things that made him happy and he chopped back that people can change their minds. As hurt as I was, I let him go without a fight. I knew Gray T. had both his parents shoving the Lord in his mouth, and one thing was for sure — the more he swallowed the less he wanted to kiss and fondle me under that old tree.

I opened the door. Gray T. scanned the skinny foyer.

"Are you behaving yourself, Ruby?" he asked.

"Not by your standards," I said. His eyes were a muted blue now and I could only guess that he was calling me a heathen somewhere in his mind.

"Alright now, how's your daddy?" Gray T. asked.

"He's no better than the last time you came and prayed over him." Preacher finally met my eyes. He drew in a long deep breath as I felt my skin heat up.

"I know you're upset, Ruby," he said. "Is your mama here?"

"She's back there waiting for a miracle," I told him.

Gray T. turned sideways and slid past me. His exhale timed just right with my inhale. I wasn't sure if he was giving himself to me with that breath or if I was taking him in. I watched him walk down the hallway to the bedroom. He had broad shoulders under his buttoned collar shirts and beefy thighs. When I couldn't see him anymore I turned and looked in the hallway mirror. What did Gray T. see when he looked at me? Someone lost? Auburn curls framed my plump, pale skin. The freckles on my nose that used to punch out in the summer were now barely noticeable, and my hazel eyes, Daddy's eyes, seemed to have lost their unique specks. I was fading like the red stripes on a piece of peppermint candy.

I picked up my cigarettes from the kitchen table and headed for the back patio. There were twelve or thirteen old aluminum chairs scattered around and each one had ripped or weak straps on the seat, some worse than others. Being out of the house for twenty years, I had no idea which one would hold my hip-heavy body and keep me from shooting through to the cement like some circus act. I pushed down on the chair closest to me. I had a feeling it wasn't the right one, but sat down anyway. With Marlboro in tow, I sank straight to the ground — stuck in a big transparent pail for all to see. I sat squished in there for a good minute as smoke from my cigarette swirled around me like a sinner's halo. With no way out I decided to dump myself sideways.

When I stood up I noticed my hand print in the spring pollen on the porch. I thought about all the hand prints I made my mama growing up — how excited she used to get when I brought one home from school so she could pin it up on the refrigerator. This one, though, felt as empty of innocent spirit as her chronic need to lecture me about the Bible. I threw my cigarette on the ground, stepped on it, and twisted my foot until the fire was squelched. Then I did the same to my handprint just before Mama pulled the sliding door open.

"Ruby, you have green dust all over your clothes." Mama started wiping me down like a filthy window.

"Don't worry about it," I told her.

"You've got to take better care of yourself," she said. "All this smoking and leaning up against messy things aren't good for you."

"Sometime I'd like to talk about what's good for you."

"What's good for me is having your daddy baptized." Mama held her petite frame erect. Her dirty blonde hair was fine, like dandelion fur, and she had puffy skin under her eyes from too many restless nights.

"I know you believe that," I said. Mama crossed her arms, sighed, and moved back towards the house. She had no business keeping Daddy alive — tugging on Preacher's shirttails to baptize him every time he came over. I felt on fire watching those two manipulate the end of Daddy's life, knowing full well that all he wanted was to settle in the dust.

"Is Preacher still here?" I asked.

"Yes, he's back there praying with your daddy," she said.

"You mean praying *to* Daddy." Mama turned and faced me.

"Just because your daddy had a stroke doesn't mean he can't understand." I knew she was under enough stress without the flame from my cigarette lighter challenging her faith, so I kept quiet.

"You come on in when you're ready," she said, "and you know I appreciate you moving back in to see after things."

"Well, maybe it was God's perfection that I got laid off right after Daddy's stroke," I told her. Living back at home in my mid-forties made being jobless ten times worse.

"Stop being smart about the Lord, Ruby. He doesn't like that."

I pressed my lips together and watched her slide the heavy rusted door. I couldn't help but laugh out loud — she was no more than a hundred pounds soaking wet and made moving that door look like it was riding on lard. When I opened it, I had to yank on it three or four times, and not without making a muscle ache. There was hidden strength in that woman, no doubt in my mind.

A few minutes later, I went into the kitchen. Dishes with egg crumbs sat in the sink and the counters were covered with unopened mail, empty milk bottles, and piles of newspapers. Preacher Gray T. was sitting at the table with Mama. He looked down at the pack of smokes I was holding, then into my eyes.

"Preacher, we all commit so-called crimes against the self," I said.

"I'm not judging you, Ruby."

"People who don't judge have no need to say they're not judging," I told him.

"Ruby, now simmer down," Mama said. I turned my back towards both of them and walked down the hall to visit Daddy.

I stalled at the doorway and pumped up my lungs with extra air. Seeing Daddy helpless felt like my insides were running through a meat grinder. His powerful arms used to build sheds, hold rifles in a marine platoon, and lift me into the air on a breezy day. I couldn't stand seeing him curled up, crapping all over the place, with only a tube in his stomach keeping him alive — all so Mama could have more time to get him baptized.

I sat in a chair next to the hospital bed and scanned the room. It was supposed to be Mama and Daddy's bedroom, but when I looked at the cross over the bed and the huge rectangular painting of *The Last Supper* Mama got at the flea market, it seemed like her room. Daddy was on his side with his eyes closed and mouth open. A short tube hung out of the space between the buttons on his cotton pajama shirt — capped shut until the next feeding. His dry, flaky scalp had a few pieces of thin black hair standing straight up. All four limbs were loose skin and bones, and his unruly eyebrows were pointing left and right.

"Here Daddy," I said, "let me trim up those eyebrows." I walked into the bathroom and grabbed the cuticle scissors. I dabbed my eyes with a tissue, went back to the bed, and started clipping. Like he cares, I thought to myself. I could just see him saying, "Hell Roo, let the little bastards find their own way."

I pulled down the cold bed railing and rested my hand in his. "Daddy, tell me what to do. I know you want to die right now more than Mama wants to dunk you in holy water." I looked for something — an eye twitch, a squint — something telling me I should go ahead and end it for him. Just then, Mama walked in.

"Did he smile for you today?" she asked.

"No, Mama, he doesn't smile."

"Well, let's roll him over and get him cleaned up," she said.

We turned Daddy on his back, pulled off his pajama bottoms, and loosened the tabs on his diaper. I turned towards the wall when Mama stripped off the pad. I acted like I couldn't take the rising stench, but the truth was I didn't want to see Daddy's privates. I knew they had to look as frail and shriveled up as his forearms.

"Mama, how long is this going to continue?"

"What do you mean?" Mama put on a pair of rubber gloves.

"This — this keeping Daddy dependent — you know he wouldn't want this."

"We're close, Ruby," she snapped. "Don't start."

"Close to what?"

"Preacher said he would try to work something out with the baptism."

"Like what?"

"He said he'd think about trying something different." Daddy grunted as

Mama scrubbed his skin.

"I thought you said he couldn't baptize Daddy because it was too risky — that Preacher wasn't comfortable with an immersion?"

"Well, I'm pleading with him now, Ruby," she said, "so please don't start."

"Mama, I need to go — can you finish this okay?" She nodded.

I got in my car and drove like the devil's lightning to catch up with Gray T. His command over Mama's peace of mind and Daddy's passing was sending me over the edge. As I passed the church I saw his car sitting alone in the parking lot. I turned around, pulled in next to him, and hung my arms over the steering wheel. I looked at the bigger than thou glass front and had no idea how talking in tongues and Christmas decorations were so good at distracting God's children from accepting their own shadows and simple pleasures. I took a deep breath, got out, and walked inside the greeting area. There were tables with donation baskets, pamphlets on divorce support, and sign-up sheets for the next Bible study potluck. I opened the doors to the sanctuary. Gray T. was sitting in the front pew with his head down.

"Howdy, Preacher," I said.

"Ruby?" Preacher's eyes opened wide. He shifted side to side as I sat down next to him. I stared at the side of his face as he looked straight ahead at the crucifix.

"Why won't you baptize my father?" Gray T. turned and looked at me.

"It's not that simple, Ruby."

"Well, make it that simple," I said. Gray T. squeezed his thumbs into fists and turned back towards Jesus.

"Ruby, someone like you could never understand the sacredness of this event." My throat tensed up like cement hardening on a fence post. *Someone like me*, I thought. *A heathen like me who was good enough to love him, but not good enough for his God.* I couldn't help but wonder — what was the real reason Gray T. kept coming over to see Daddy?

"Like you can't understand the control you and your God have on my mama?"

I said. He held his head down and sighed. I wanted to grab his hand and bring the two of us back to our nature under the old oak, but dragging him there would've been like Mama trying to baptize Daddy. I stood up.

"Baptize my father so he can die, Preacher." I turned around and walked towards the exit. "Dammit, Ruby" was all I could hear until I flung the door open and the fresh air hit my face.

● ● ●

The house was quiet for a few days afterwards. Preacher Gray T. hadn't been around, Mama ran to the phone every time it rang, and Daddy kept soiling himself. A week or so later, Mama finally got the call—Preacher would baptize Daddy at home on Sunday after service. As soon as she told me I smacked out a cigarette, went outside, and sat down on the brick patio. I lit my smoke and stared at the varicose veins on my legs. *Great*, I thought, *simple pleasures*.

Mama followed a minute later. She pulled weeds and straightened things up, knowing we'd have a house full of people on Sunday. A second later I couldn't stand the image of myself pulling smoke into my lungs so I tossed the cigarette on the ground. Mama came running over.

"I'll get it Mama," I said.

"But Sunday, I—"

"Mama, I'll get it—just grab my hands and pull me up." She took a hold of my forearms and yanked me upright—as easily as she opened the sliding door. I looked at the ground and closed my eyes.

"What is it, Ruby?" she asked.

"Nothing, Mama, your strength intimidates me sometimes."

"It's my faith, Ruby—that's what you see." She put her arms around my waist, sank her head into my chest, and gave me a squeeze. That day was the closest I'd ever been to believing her faith was any good.

FALLING THROUGH CHAIRS

• • •

Sunday morning finally came and Mama asked me if I would help her get Daddy in the new brown slacks and white shirt she bought for him.

"Mama, do you really think he would want this?"

"Yes I do," she said, straightening his collar. "I think he'd be real pleased we're finally going to do this."

"No, I mean the outfit. Daddy would never wear these clothes."

"It's important, Ruby. Let me do this." I helped her pull the pants over Daddy's diaper and put the stomach tube through an open space on his shirt. Daddy was flat—not resisting, not aware. It hit me right then he had been gone since the day they drilled the hole in his belly, and if Mama was ever going to have her wish it would be like this.

The front bell rang. Preacher Gray T. was in a crisp white shirt gripping a red leather Bible. He had a young man with him, an assistant, who was holding a galvanized bucket.

"Preacher, come on in—Mama's in the bedroom." Gray T. stumbled inside without looking at me and went down the hall.

I could see Mama's sisters and cousins getting out of their cars and walking towards the house. Everyone was in their Sunday best: spring floral skirts, violet hats, and strapped ivory shoes cutting into swollen ankles. The men were dressed in navy suits and thick ties. They formed a circle in the driveway until they had to come in, probably swapping comments about "poor Brock Carlyle getting baptized against his own damn will."

Mama asked everyone to wait in the living room except me, Preacher Gray T., and his assistant. We turned Daddy on his right side and pulled him towards the edge of the bed. Preacher went to fill the bucket with water while Mama brought down the bed railing and put a chair next to Daddy. Preacher came back and set the bucket on the chair. Mama stood at the head of the bed, while me and Gray T. faced Daddy.

"What's your plan, Preacher?" I asked.

"We're going to roll up his sleeve and put his left arm in the water." Daddy's left was the side that went limp from the stroke. I had no time to figure out if that was good or bad. I took a quick look into his eyes — they were as lifeless as dried worms on a summer sidewalk, so I kept quiet and rolled up Daddy's shirt.

"Ready, Preacher," I said.

Gray T. opened his Bible and flipped through the pages — front to back, back to front. The sweat beads on his forehead looked like rain on a windshield. He finally slapped the book shut and rested it next to the pillow. He turned sideways, faced me and the bucket, and picked up Daddy's naked forearm. Daddy's hand flopped down like flowers that stayed in a vase too long. Preacher stretched his own arm up towards the ceiling and started the baptism.

"Brock Carlyle, do you accept the Lord Jesus Christ as your personal savior?"

"Preacher, he can't talk," I said.

"Hush, Ruby," Mama said. "Preacher knows he can't talk."

"Brock — ah, Mr. Carlyle — do you receive Jesus as your savior and do you want to follow him for the rest of your life?"

"He does," Mama said. She started sniffling and my breathing picked up. Preacher looked at Mama instead of Daddy for his next question.

"Mr. Carlyle, when did you receive Christ as your personal savior?"

"About a year ago," she said. "Just after my stroke is when the Lord saved me." Preacher closed his eyes and started praying, his right hand hanging above me.

"Father, we thank you for coming into Mr. Carlyle's heart as his personal savior and by his testimony, we — "

"Her testimony," I interrupted. Preacher didn't open his eyes and Mama missed what I said under her sobbing. Gray T. continued.

"Lord, we pray that you continue to minister to Mr. Carlyle and touch his heart and help him grow. Mr. Carlyle, because of your...of *the* testimony...that you love the Lord and are now born again, I baptize you in the name of the Father, the Son, and the Holy Spirit, Amen."

As Preacher guided Daddy's limp hand towards the bucket I felt a rush looking at his muscular shoulders and tight jaw line. Daddy's fingers were just covered in water when I snatched Preacher's high hand and laid it on my left breast. Mama was in a full bawl when she screamed, "Ruby, yes! Take Jesus into your heart!" I pushed deeper and deeper on Gray T.'s hand until I felt a tingle run down my front. When I let go, he stayed on my breast as he lured Daddy's arm into the lukewarm water. When Daddy's hand hit the bottom of the bucket Gray T.'s hand fell from my chest. He raised the dead limb back into the air as the assistant rushed over with a towel.

"It's over now," Gray T. said, using his sleeve to wipe the sweat off his face.

"Praise Jesus," Mama followed with both hands stretched above her.

"Let's get him on his back," I said. "He looks uncomfortable."

Mama and her family finished out the day eating peach pie with Cool Whip dollops and shared stories about flat hair from summer humidity. Preacher stayed for only thirty minutes, pretending he couldn't talk because cubed cheese filled up his mouth. I changed Daddy back into his old pajamas and stayed in the room with him. I cried myself to sleep that night, not knowing what's true and wanting to be okay with everything I don't know.

• • •

A couple of weeks went by before I brought up the subject of making some decisions about Daddy. Mama was scrubbing dishes at the sink, singing and humming like Snow White. I was sitting at the table flipping through newspapers.

"Are you ready to talk about what's next?" I asked her.

"What do you mean, Ruby?"

"The feeding tube and letting what needs to happen next happen." She stopped humming.

"Well, I suppose you wanted to make those decisions, right?" she said. I walked over to her and leaned against the counter. I lowered my head under hers to try and get our eyes to meet, but she kept focused on the suds in the sink.

"Are you saying that's what you want — you want me to decide?" I asked.

"I think maybe you'd be better about all that," she said, "if you want."

"Are you sure?" Staring at murky dishwater, Mama reminded me of the strongest hatchling in the brood who just couldn't seem to fledge.

"If you don't mind, Ruby," she said, "you go ahead when you want."

"It will be soon," I told her. She nodded and went back to humming.

I called the doctor the next day and let him know we were ready to remove the tube. He sent out some nurses and they told us what to expect. Two weeks later, with just me and Mama hanging onto him, Daddy took his last breath.

Preacher Gray T. didn't look at me during the funeral. No doubt his shame over caressing me during a baptism felt like God was raking brown weeds out of his heart. Had I held his hand down the whole time I might have cared, but I knew he was the one who had to deal with wanting to find comfort on my breast.

After service, Mama and her family went out to eat and I went back to the empty house. I moved straight through the foyer to the back patio and pulled out a cigarette. I took a good look at all the chairs scattered around, resting there like choices in my life. I wondered which one would hold me or even belonged to me. I walked up toward the trees near two chairs — both had frayed and weather chewed straps on the seat. I stood in between them and sat on the grass.

The earth underneath me was rugged and muscular — steady with no need to be perfect. My two fingers held an unlit cigarette as I laid back and looked up at the sky. Without my exhale fogging up the clear air, I saw a color blue that was calm and untroubled. Lying there and not fighting anyone for it, I was sure of what my Daddy always knew — that no chair in the world would ever hold me as safe and secure as the dirty ground.

THE FATHER
MATHIEU CAILLER

Father Dyer stood at the lectern, then paced in front of the crucifix, the hot lights burning through his thick alb. He stared at the sea of white faces that begged him for guidance, examined the desperation in their expressions, and knew that they needed his one-hour Mass to make sense of the six days prior.

"Good morning." His deep voice bellowed through the pews. "I would like to invite all here to take a moment trusting in the Lord to ask for forgiveness of our sins."

Many priests bowed their heads, but only counted to five or ten. That was what Father Dyer had been told in seminary — repent on your own time, in Mass, just one one-thousand, two one-thousand . . . But today, on a sunny Easter Sunday, Father Dyer folded his hands and closed his eyes. "I have sinned," he said, under his breath. "It was a long time ago, but I have sinned. Please guide me."

When Father Dyer brought his head up, many parishioners were already looking quizzically at him, even turning their heads from side to side, tacitly confirming with one another that this portion had gone on for longer than the so-called "moment."

He cleared his throat and led the Confiteor: "I confess almighty God, and to you, my brothers and sisters, that I have sinned…"

• • •

Two days prior, on Good Friday, Father Dyer sat in his office revising his sermon. He was to head the 10:00 a.m. Easter Mass, only the eighth time he'd lead the congregation in his year and a half at St. John the Baptist Parish.

It wasn't customary for parochial vicars to lead Easter Mass, but Monsignor Broussard was eager to see what the young priest could do. According to Monsignor, Father Dyer "had a way about him, a wonderful blend of wisdom and compassion."

Father Dyer sat in his office chair and listened to a gust of wind push a tree branch against his office window. The branch reminded him of a Bible verse: "All the tithe of the land, whether of the seed of the land or of the fruit of the tree, is the Lord's: it is holy unto the Lord." Sunshine then streamed through the window and exaggerated the amber hues of his desk and wooden floors.

Footsteps neared, stopping outside his office. Father Dyer stared at the thin strip of light between the floor and the door. "Come in," he said. No movement. "Please come in," he said again. He watched the brass knob turn, the polished metal glinting in the soft sunlight.

Before Father Dyer had a chance to identify the person, she said, "Patrick …Oh, my God! Oh, sorry, can you say 'God' in a place like this?"

"Beth!" he said, pushing out his office chair. He laughed. "Yes, yes, of course. He understands."

Beth wore a fashionable navy skirt with a white blouse that was unbuttoned enough to see her prominent collarbones. Her blue eyes, like always, were surrounded by a heavy coat of eyeliner, and clusters of freckles — now more prominent than before — dotted her soft cheeks.

Father Dyer got up and hugged her. Ringlets of black hair flooded his face — and he drew in the scents of coconut and vanilla. He held her tightly. The warmth of her body felt as good as he remembered.

"Look at you," she said.

He smiled. "How long's it been?"

"Forever," she said.

"Have a seat. Would you like some tea?"

"Sure," Beth said, smoothing out her skirt as she took the chair he offered.

Father Dyer plugged in his electric kettle then sat back down. "Seriously, though, how long's it been? I can't believe you're here ... just can't believe it."

"It'll be seven years in June."

"That long," he said. "Yes ... I guess it has been. Are you back in LA?"

"I'm in Ojai, with my parents."

"I'll always remember those nights at your parents' house — the Sunday dinners, your dad's jazz music, your mom's meatloaf ... shiny with ketchup. How are they?" Father Dyer said.

"Fine," Beth said.

They held each other's gaze for a few moments without speaking.

While Beth looked the same as ever, Father Dyer believed her to be different inside. Back then, she was always fast with a smile, but now she seemed distant, wearing an eyes-on-the-floor expression that suggested that life had brought her responsibilities worthy of her age rather than an ability to cope with them.

"Is everything okay?" he asked.

"Yes, very good," she said. Beth stood up and walked around the office. She brushed Father Dyer's white Easter alb that hung on the back of his door, and twirled her fingers around his matching stole. Her nail polish was Pentecost red, quite different from the French manicures she used to give herself as an undergrad. "It's so good to see you, Patrick, especially so ... so in your element." She tucked a ringlet of hair behind her ear.

The kettle's water began to boil. Father Dyer perked up to the rumble, poured the scalding liquid into two mugs, and opened a flat wooden box containing assorted teas (a Christmas gift from a parishioner — he'd received four such boxes). Beth selected Earl Gray, while Father Dyer picked a raspberry blend. He preferred the former but nobody ever chose fruit teas, so it fell to him to drink them. He lifted the bag in and out of his cup, allowing it to shed its red ribbons.

Beth blew across the surface of her tea.

"What have you been up to?" Father Dyer asked.

"Well," said Beth, playing with a turquoise ring on her index finger, "a lot's been going on, actually, but not all good."

"That's what we're used to in the church. No one comes here unless something's gone wrong; it's how we've survived for as long as we have. Other people's tough luck is our good fortune."

She drew a deep breath and cracked a polite smile. Father Dyer thought about apologizing for saying such a thing, but he knew her — she always had a good sense of humor, so he leaned back and sipped. He was used to spending time in the confessional, hearing these clipped statements, the foreshocks of trouble.

"My husband and I haven't been getting along. We, Mark and I that is, have been arguing a lot the last few months... I won't bore you with such a thing, and then, about a month ago, he left."

"Oh, I didn't know you'd gotten married."

"Yes."

Father Dyer nodded.

"We married quick," Beth said, as if justifying it, "only a few months after you and me, actually."

"Oh, wow." Father Dyer took a sip and burned the roof of his mouth. "I didn't — "

"I thought of telling you."

"If you want there's an excellent marriage counselor."

"It's just..." Beth said, taking another deep breath. "Patrick, do you remember that weekend we spent together, before you went to seminary?"

"Of course," Father Dyer said. He got up from his chair, went over to the door, opened it, and looked around—no one was there save for the image of Beth undressing in that dim New York hotel room, resting one hand on the nightstand while the other flipped off her heels. He envisioned her tan lines, heard her breath, felt her moisturized skin. Color flushed his face and his palms grew moist. He closed the door and returned to his desk.

"Anyway," Beth said, "that weekend, I got pregnant." Her voice dropped off at the end.

Father Dyer didn't respond. Strands of sunlight sliced through the window. He'd always thought he'd escaped unscathed and been absolved of his sin through continuous commitment and prayer.

Beth continued, "I didn't tell you because you'd just gone to seminary and then I met Mark. I let him think the baby was his. When Sam was born, Mark just thought he was premature. I never told him otherwise. You and Sam really look alike—floppy hair, thin lips, and hazel eyes. There's—"

"Why are you telling me this now? What the hell am I supposed to do?" Blood beat in his ears and his mouth went dry. He closed his eyes. "Why tell me?" he said softly.

"Nobody knows," Beth said.

"*I* know!"

"I'm..." Beth said. She pulled a tissue from her purse and dabbed her eyes. "I'm desperate, Patrick. Sam needs a man in his life, and I don't know a better one than you. He just hasn't been the same since Mark left. He doesn't draw or play anymore. He's just quiet... and too sad for a boy to be."

Father Dyer rested his head in his hands. He knew that in time Beth would get up and leave, but that the problem wouldn't, and that he'd replay that weekend in his head and wonder how he could have been so selfish. In the past, he justified it by saying to himself that it was before seminary, before he'd taken his vow. He even thought that it would make him a better priest, one that was *really* able to identify with carnal sin. Then he pictured his boy, Sam, crawling, standing, walking, and talking.

Beth uncrossed her legs and stood. "Good-bye, Patrick. I thought that maybe you'd...That's all, that maybe..." she said.

Father Dyer didn't budge, his eyes fixed on slats of hardwood. Beth draped her purse over her shoulder, slowly, as if she was allowing him time to get his thoughts together and possibly say something. When she realized he wasn't going to, she turned the brass knob, and escaped down the hall, her high heels tapping the wood. He listened to her stride for as long as he could.

Minutes later, Father Dyer ran across the hall to the bathroom and threw up. He splashed some water on his face and inspected himself in the mirror. Cool beads of water slid over his skin, and he shut his eyes and listened to the hum of the air vent. For a minute or two, he tried not to breathe.

● ● ●

Later that evening, Father Dyer sat in the rectory watching his thirteen-inch black-and-white TV that he'd picked up at last month's rummage sale. While the buttons were worn and the picture was a touch fuzzy, he liked how people looked in black-and-white better than in living color. He thought they looked more noble and polished, rather than real people undergoing real lives.

The Dodgers game was on, and in between pitches, batters, and innings, Father Dyer's mind wandered. He thought of Beth. In college, they'd both decided to study philosophy and Patrick had often invited Beth to study with him. They'd grown close — Patrick's rigidity and Beth's blithe freedom an interesting mixture. He remembered her torn jeans, dream-catcher earrings, laughing till his gut hurt, and her generous family. Thinking of her parents made him think of his. Even as a boy, he remembered discerning that they weren't right for one another. They were a cold couple with a big house, uncomfortable furniture, and shiny silverware — a house where laughter and smiles only escaped from the TV set. Only once did Father Dyer remember seeing his parents kiss; they'd probably kissed more often, but he was certain he'd seen it only one time: his junior year of high school, after he'd awakened in the hospital from a car accident. They stood together under the fluorescent lighting, the beep of the heart monitor in the background. Father Dyer had found his calling, but not as quickly as other priests, and while his love for the church was steadfast, his parents' life made him fearful of his ability to be a husband and father.

Even though Father Dyer had spent years burying the memories of that weekend with Beth, they breathed quite easily. He pictured the meal at the Italian restaurant where she'd ordered linguine with clams, the used bookstore where she scoured for collectible copies of anything André Gide, and the fancy boutiques where even window-shopping seemed expensive.

That weekend, he'd made love to Beth four times. He recalled the smoothness of her calves, the saltiness of her neck, and the way she whispered his name with humid breath. After they were finished, she always placed her head on his chest and told him how strongly his heart beat. But as much as he cared for her, celibacy was a sacrifice he was willing to make to pursue his calling. He even felt exalted in having done so. Few knew that long ago the church allowed its priests to marry, but Father Dyer wholeheartedly supported the ways of the recent doctrine, believing that it was only possible to walk one path.

What he loved so much about priesthood was that he couldn't hurt anyone. In front of the tabernacle, behind the altar, underneath the crucifix, in the sanctuary, life felt right. He was serving Him, and in a time where every Catholic story seemed to be about the less than savory news about priests and their hellish transgressions, he'd worked extra hard to restore the name of the church.

At St. John the Baptist Parish, Father Dyer was safe and respected. The way people looked at him was new and exciting, and while he reminded himself of Matthew's words, "Call no man Father," he was proud of what he'd become. He wasn't sure what would happen if St. John the Baptist Parish found out about his son; he figured that he'd be assigned to teach religion at the school. They'd place him as far in the background as possible — send him to raise funds and run bingo games. No longer would he stand on the steps. No longer would he lead Mass. He'd lose his pride and his calling.

He made himself an early dinner — a couple of scrambled eggs, a piece of dry toast, and a glass of water. He ate standing up, over the sink, looking out the window, watching the clouds change positions and brighten and darken the day, sorry for the way he'd spoken to Beth. She'd been selfless, deceiving her son and husband and stuffing this secret for years so that he could live unburdened. It was hard to believe that he and Sam had lived separate lives under the same sky for so long. In the stillness, his mind continued to roam, and he didn't get in the way. *What kind of books does Sam like?* he thought. *Does he have many friends? Is he afraid of the dark? And then, could I be a good father?*

● ● ●

The pews were full. Easter Sunday brought in the "twice-a-yearers," as priests called them. Father Dyer stared over the paschal candles at the stained-glass window at the narthex of the church — a portrayal of Jesus, Mary, and Joseph. They looked peaceful, like the perfect nuclear family.

Father Dyer descended the steps and stood in front of the parishioners. "My friends," he said, "today I'd like to talk to you about sacrifice. Jesus died for our sins. He gave his life. The ultimate sacrifice. I ask you — have we returned this sacrifice? Returned it to one another? If we wanted to repay His gift, we'd sacrifice more. We'd part with what is wanted and do what is right. There are many battles in Catholicism: right and wrong, sin and promise, receiving and giving, selfishness and sacrifice, death and resurrection."

Light poured through the Noah's ark stained-glass window on the gospel side of the church and tinted some of the parishioners' faces blue. Father Dyer dried a few beads of sweat from his upper lip with a handkerchief. A baby began to cry, and the baby's mother picked him up, headed towards the back, and bounced the kid's troubles away. Normally, Father Dyer tried his best to ignore crying babies, but now, the cry occupied his mind. It was easier to be a priest when he hadn't been so close to the life of a layperson.

"To me," Father Dyer said, "it's almost blasphemous to use the word 'sacrifice' to describe what He did. That's because in today's world, we've diluted the word's puissance. We use it to describe much less. Just the other day, I read in the paper that an athlete was *sacrificing* by deciding to take two million dollars less per year. Something that doesn't hurt you — hurt you seriously, doesn't affect your life in a great way, is not *sacrifice*. Sure, it may be kind and generous, but it doesn't warrant being called *sacrifice*."

The mother with the crying boy continued to move back and forth, nuzzling and lifting the boy, pointing at the votive candles lined up before Mary. Father Dyer always liked the way the flames danced inside the red glass holders, and he often imagined for whom the wicks had been lit: a dying father, a couple in the midst of a rough divorce, an estranged husband, someone who needed the courage to sacrifice?

Father Dyer continued, "Many people ask me why the symbol of our church is a pelican. The pelican is the perfect representation of Jesus. I believe *vuln* is the word. When adult pelicans are unable to find food for their young, they vuln themselves, or rip flesh from their own bodies to feed their young. *That's* sacrifice," Father Dyer said, walking the polished floor. He felt warmed by the parishioners' gazes.

"I grew up going to church. Most of the children didn't like it — they doodled on the missal envelopes and closed their eyes, like many of you are doing now...but I was always drawn to religion, uplifted, and I always dressed up.

One day at Mass, a priest, Father McClintock, came up to me while I was tugging at my shirt and tie. He asked me if I was comfortable. 'No,' I said. 'Good,' he answered. The priest took a long look at me and said, 'Grace is never comfortable.' And I think the same thing of sacrifice. It's not effortless; it's not easy; it's *never* comfortable. Are there people out there who are deeply satisfied by such discomfort? I don't know. We need to try to be."

The congregation was quiet as Father Dyer took a long pause and let his words ring. "Remember Romans 12: Give Him your bodies as a living sacrifice, consecrated by Him, acceptable by Him. Prove in practice that the plan of God for you is good and move towards the goal of maturity."

After the sermon, Father Dyer walked to the altar and offered the body and blood of Christ: "This is my body, which will be given up for you." The altar boy rang the sanctus bells, while Father Dyer placed the Host delicately atop his tongue and took a sip of sweet wine. He bowed his head. Usually his prayers were short and crisp, but today they wobbled, as he thought of Beth and Sam, and how he didn't want to go through life seeing children and knowing how he'd abandoned his, and how he thought he'd be more needed as Sam's father than as God's servant.

When Mass concluded, Father Dyer exited the church and shook hands, greeted parishioners and wished everyone a joyous Easter. There was a fountain out front and every so often a gust of wind would blow a few droplets onto Father Dyer's face.

"Thank you for a beautiful Mass," a woman said. Her lips were shiny and a few curls spilled onto her forehead. She held a camera in her hand and a man and two girls stood in front of the fountain, waiting for her to snap away.

"Would you like me to take the photo...so you can join in?" Father Dyer offered.

"Oh," she said, "I was just going to ask another parishioner."

"It's not a problem. I'm just like everybody else," he said, bringing his eye to the viewfinder and lining up the family of four. Father Dyer took his time, making sure the light was right and there weren't any stray parishioners in the background, counted to three, and snapped the picture.

He continued to mingle, meet people from out of town, and thank families for coming.

Soon after, back in the rectory, he carefully removed his alb and put on his traditional black-and-white garb. He gazed out the window, sipping a glass of tap water, and watched family after family get in their cars and leave the lot. The once loud sidewalk was quiet; only the wind made noise.

The sun was high and Father Dyer stared directly at it. He closed his eyes and watched yellow dots float around the inside of his eyelids. Sam, he thought, was around seven years old, an age when, research had shown, the most important person in the family was the same-sex parent. It was his path: God had brought Beth to him; God needed him to be a father, to spend time with his boy, to live out the words of sacrifice he so proudly preached. After a few glasses of water, he walked out to the empty lot, got in his car, and drove off.

Traffic was fluid and Father Dyer made good time. The ocean to his left, the dunes to his right. The windows were up, the radio off, and the cross that hung from the rearview mirror swayed. As the tires hummed on the asphalt, his mind drifted, and he thought of a Bible verse from Samuel: "Moreover, as for me, far be it from me to sin against the Lord by ceasing to pray for you, but I will instruct you in the good and right way." Verses regarding fatherhood came to his mind, too: "He accepts the responsibility that comes with being a father." "The father of one who is right with God will have much joy; he who has a wise son will be glad in him." "The righteous who walks in His integrity, blessed are his children after him."

A long time had passed since Father Dyer had been to Beth's parents' house in Ojai, but it was just as he remembered, with poppies blanketing soft hills, avocado trees standing in soldier-like rows, and the scent of rosemary and sweet dirt hanging in the air. Beth usually sat next to him, though, her window down, her right hand making aerodynamic shapes in the air. He turned down the gravel road without even needing to think about it. Pebbles crunched under his tires and clouds of dust grew behind his car, just as they always had years before.

The two-story white rambler sat in the shade of a fortress of cypresses, a car and a truck in the driveway. He recalled the way Beth's dad always played Ellington records, and the way Beth's mother kissed him on both cheeks, as though she were French. He always sat across from Beth. He loved that whenever she smiled, she placed her tongue between her teeth, and he remembered that she always laughed at his bad jokes and told her own about Professor Neblett, the philosophy chair, and his watching-paint-dry class.

Father Dyer parked a little ways from the house and opened his window enough to let a breeze whisper across his forehead. He relished the sounds of the country: the chirp of a bird, the sigh of rustling leaves, and the hiss of industrial sprinklers.

A basketball hoop with a frayed net and worn backboard was nailed to an oak. He smiled when he thought of Sam shooting. A tree stump stood not far from the basket, and Father Dyer wondered if Sam had ever attempted a shot while standing atop it.

He got out of his car, exhaled long and steady, and headed towards the home. The pickup in the driveway was cooling down and making little ticking noises.

The front door was a Dutch door with the top half open. Father Dyer wasn't sure whether he should knock or just call hello.

Just then, he heard a little boy's laugh coming from inside.

Father Dyer stood still, frightened, rehearsing "Hi, Sam" over and over. The boy laughed again. His giggle sounded a lot like Beth's — high and lingering. A gentle burn spread in his limbs, and he felt a welling in his chest. He imagined his boy sitting on the floor, wearing a white t-shirt and navy shorts. Maybe a shoelace untied.

He kept quiet, trying his best to absorb Sam's voice. He thought he could detect the enthusiastic rubbing of pencil on paper.

"You're turning into Picasso over there," a man said. His voice was gravelly. "Let's see what you got." The man cracked open a can.

"One second," Sam said. Pencils dropped to the floor and rolled along the hardwood. "Okay, Dad, I'm ready."

Father Dyer felt a bright pain in his neck.

"You'll be better on my lap," the man said, followed by a grunting sound and a "there we are."

"Remember that day at the beach?" Sam said. His voice was soft and Father Dyer savored his words.

"Of course," the man said. "What a picnic."

On the wall opposite the door, atop a varnished table, was a photo: Beth, Sam, and Mark. They were all wearing jean shirts and loud smiles.

"That's what I've been drawing," Sam said. "Look!" There was a crinkle of paper and then an explanation from Sam: "That's me, right there, with the striped shirt and basketball shoes. And there, that's Mom. She has on her high heels and sunglasses, and there, that's you, with the hat."

Father Dyer drew a deep breath and shut his eyes.

"I don't wear those kinds of hats," the man said. "I look like Lincoln!"

Sam giggled. "I know, I messed up and tried to fix it."

As Sam continued to talk about that day at the beach with seagulls, sand, and sun, Father Dyer peeled open his eyes and scanned the foyer. He stared at the smattering of photos, the vase full of tired gardenias, and a pile of different-sized shoes strewn next to the hallway closet. He swallowed hard and walked back to his car, stepping only where his feet wouldn't make any noise.

287

THE HAND OF GOD
LIBBY CUDMORE

Sitting in the second-to-back pew with her mom and her dad, Lila Ann Albany
fanned herself with her church bulletin and stared into the abyss of fuzzy black
hair on the back of the head of the teenage boy sitting in the third pew, next
to Ms. Artemis Keys. The early September sunlight filtered lazily through the
stained glass windows and Reverend Marcus McKinnon drawled through his
sermon in his soft, sleepy timbre. If it wasn't for the mysterious boy in the
third pew, Lila might have drifted off to sleep.

For the women of Harmon, Alabama, church wasn't about religion, or faith,
or God. It was purely a social arrangement, a bridge club, a way to organize
themselves so they knew who it was safe to talk to. The Methodists were the
wealthiest ones, in the big church on Main Street with the green slate roof and
the privilege of ringing the bells at noon. The black Baptist women wore bright
colors and held picnics that they invited everyone to, while the white Baptists
stood off to the side and hollered about damnation. All the really good-looking
boys were Catholic, and no one talked to the Born-Agains. Born-Agains drank

too much and beat their children; rumor had it that their pastor laid hands upon women's breasts and claimed to be an exorcist.

Lila's parents were well-established middle class, with a three-generation Harmon lineage, which made them Presbyterians. Her father was an elder and her mother served as the director of Christian education. This meant Lila was stuck teaching Vacation Bible School for a week every July and had only recently got the insipid sing-along songs out of her head.

When Rev. McKinnon asked the congregation for Joys and Concerns, Ms. Artemis Keys stood up and waddled on thick legs to the podium. She wore a wide-brimmed red hat and a loud floral housedress with a tangle of lace and faux pearl beads down the bodice. "I just want to tell ya'll that my nephew, Owen Atwood, is staying with me while his daddy, the Reverend Raymond Atwood, is on a mission trip across the country. Owen, honey, why don't you stand up and introduce yourself?"

The boy slowly arched to his feet, standing in one fluid motion as though guided up by a string. Now facing forward, Lila saw that he was about her age, dressed in a black suit with his white shirt open at the top button, exposing his pale collarbone. His soft black hair was already high on his wide forehead, and made his eyes look infinitely darker, like orbs containing all of space. Lila thought he was the most beautiful boy she'd ever seen, and spent the rest of the service imagining what that wispy black hair would feel like between her fingers.

• • •

On Monday at school, Lila sat in homeroom with her fingers crossed underneath her desk, praying to a God she mostly ignored that Owen would be in at least one class, his desk alphabetically next to hers. She'd eschewed her usual jeans and t-shirt for the white eyelet sundress she kept in her closet for church picnics and backyard parties the families in her neighborhood took turns hosting. The minutes ticked by on the clock and sweat formed along the sides of her breasts. The announcements came low and stern over the loudspeaker; she stood and mumbled the pledge. The bell rang and no sign of Owen. She wondered if he was home schooled or if she'd misjudged his age entirely.

At lunch she went outside with the rest of the juniors and sat on a wooden bench, eating her lunch and watching the other girls — in their tight denim skirts and their thin cotton camisoles — laugh loud in small clusters with the other boys. Her friend Michelle and Michelle's boyfriend Mike waved from the other side of the field, but all Lila did was wave back. She wanted to wait for Owen, just in case he showed up.

She wadded up her lunch wrappings and stood to throw them in the garbage can by the gym and there was Owen, his back against the brick of the school, clutching a hardback Bible. The pebbly fake leather was flexible in the corners and creased in places, the cheap gold lettering faded and flaking from the detailing on the spine. He didn't react when the football players pushed him. His lips moved without sound. Lila stared. Her instinct put words to breath, made noise of his silence. *Our Father, who art in Heaven, hallowed be Thy name....*

God was on Owen's side. The boys couldn't shove him too hard; his back was against the wall and there were too many witnesses for them to pile on top of him and beat the new kid bloody. They wanted to, though. Lila knew that look in her cousin Lyle's eyes.

She and Lyle had only been born a week apart, when her mother was convinced she was having a boy and her sister, April, was sure she was having a girl. When the opposite held true for both women, they switched baby names. They'd grown up down the street from each other and played together every day but Sundays — April married a Methodist man and they had dinner with his parents after church. Wrestling with Lyle brought Lila up tough and strong. He'd shown her how to throw a punch and skip stones, how to toss a baseball, and how a football player tackled an opponent. She wasn't scared of him, or his friend Gary Ackerman, the captain, with his dark, mean face, or either of the two boys whose names she didn't know.

She grabbed a fistful of Lyle's t-shirt and yanked back hard. "You leave him alone!" she shouted.

Lyle's posse turned from Owen and surrounded her in one step. Owen didn't make his escape or cry for help, he just stood there, clutching his Bible to his skinny chest. Lila set her jaw and balled her fists. Lyle may have been a running back, but she'd kicked his ass in more than one childhood brawl.

"Back off, Gary," Lyle said, his voice heavy. "She's family."

"She ain't my family," Gary snarled.

"But she's mine, and if I stood back and let you wail on her, you know my daddy and her daddy would beat me so hard Coach would be using me as a towel."

Neither of their daddies had ever raised a hand against them, but Gary backed off her anyways, and the two other thugs with them relaxed their shoulders in synchronicity. Lyle shuffled them all down the field, and Lila turned back to Owen. "You okay?" she asked.

He nodded and looked up at her from under long lashes. "I'll pray for you," he murmured.

Lila clutched her hands by her side. "I'd like that," she replied.

●　●　●

Lila waited for Owen on the low brick wall outside of the school, staring at the cracks in the sidewalk and the scattered arrangements of cigarette butts left by the seniors on their lunch hour. Lyle and Gary trotted down the stairs on their way to practice; Lyle made a point of not looking at her and Gary glared hard until they rounded the corner.

Owen came out after the buses had left and Lila leapt to her feet. "I didn't get to introduce myself," she said, aware that her words were coming almost too fast to be understood. "I'm Lila Ann Albany, I saw you in church on Sunday. Your aunt and my aunt play bridge together on Tuesdays."

"It's nice to meet you, Lila," he said, bowing his head slightly. She was convinced that if he'd been wearing a hat, he would have tipped the brim to her. "Do you need a ride someplace? The buses have all left."

She lived right down the street, but she lowered her eyes and nodded. "That would be great, thanks."

She followed him out to the school parking lot. Only the cheerleaders and the football players' cars remained: Katy Benson's red convertible and the shiny black pick-up truck that Lila heard belching down her street every morning to pick up Lyle. She suspected the two enormous tail pipes were substitutions for what Gary wasn't blessed with at birth.

On the corner of the lot was a beat up truck that was redder with rust than it was blue with paint. The bench seat was sticky with remnants of duct tape, and a St. Christopher on a knotted blue ribbon dangled from the rearview mirror.

She hauled herself up into the cab and fumbled for what to say to him next. "Your daddy's a missionary?" she asked.

"My daddy's a preacher," he corrected. "My aunt doesn't like to tell people that because she gets ashamed when he starts going off about sinners and salvation when they're trying to eat at a restaurant or take a walk through town. She's a Presbyterian by name, but my daddy's a Jesus man — he doesn't need a building or a set of elders or anyone to tell him what God's law is." Owen got quiet for a minute. "I just kind of wished he'd taken me with him. I want to preach the word of the Lord, too." He turned to her and his face brightened. "You want to see my church?"

"I've been to your church," Lila repeated. "I sit in the back pew with my parents."

"That's my aunt's church," he said. "I'm starting my own church. You want to see it?"

In Harmon there was an unspoken law about the discussion of religion — it was not something to be done outside of your own kind. Catholics could talk faith with other Catholics and Presbyterians could talk faith with other Presbyterians, but to try and preach one's faith to outsiders was all but forbidden. It showed a lack of social grace and a strange betrayal, as though each faith wanted to keep the secrets of their salvation hidden from those they didn't want to meet in heaven.

For Lila, church on Sundays was a formality, a place she went with her parents, a way to pad out her college applications with volunteer hours and stints at the soup kitchen. She'd never given much thought to Jesus or Salvation; she just assumed that she would end up in heaven because she hadn't murdered anyone or stolen anything. But sitting next to Owen, his hardback Bible on the seat between them, she found herself longing to remember her baptism, that moment of purity when the cool water drizzled over her soft baby head. She longed to see candles lit in tall glass jars and feel a wooden cross worn soft beneath her fingertips. She wanted to feel that divine love deep inside her, she wanted to know what it felt like to love someone as purely as Owen loved his God — a love so deep that he openly risked a beating.

A beating that his faith delivered him from.

Lila nodded and smiled at him. "I would love to see your church," she said.

Owen grinned at her and her heart began pounding against her rib cage. She realized she hadn't seen him smile up until that point, his black eyes glittering like polished onyx, his heavy teeth white as new paper. He started the engine and turned out of the parking lot just in time to see Gary and Lyle jog past in full uniform.

• • •

When they had driven ten miles without seeing a building, Owen stopped the car. He looked down at Lila's feet, in little black polka-dot slippers, and asked, "You gonna be okay to walk in those?"

"How far are we walking?" she asked.

He pointed up a small incline to a cluster of willow trees and pink dogwoods, already beginning to turn to their red fall foliage. "Just up there," he said. "It's not far, but the trail is rocky." He grinned. "Sort of like the path to heaven."

"I'll be all right."

She left her backpack in the car and followed him up the narrow path, sidestepping rocks and gnarled roots twisting out of the dust. Sweat soaked into the polyester lining of her dress and pebbles rolled under the soles of her shoes, but she ignored both and kept climbing.

At the top of the hill, the cluster of trees formed a closed circle, inside of which Owen had set up a wooden crate and two empty silver candlesticks streaked with black tarnish. The floor had been swept down to the packed dry earth and the tops of the trees came together to form a stained-glass steeple, letting in only tendrils of light from the bright afternoon sky. "This is my church," he said. "And you're the first member of my new congregation."

Lila wasn't sure what to say, but Owen filled the silence. "Too many people think that just going to church, reciting the Lord's Prayer, or lighting candles will get you into heaven. Too many other people think that God's love is something only they can possess, or worse, that only they can judge whose worthy of learning the Bible's lessons. Not this church." He positioned himself behind his makeshift pulpit and spread his arms wide. "Everyone's welcomed in this church — atheists, homosexuals, even non-Christian religions. There's only one sin in my faith and that sin is to not love your neighbor. They say that pride is the worst sin, but pride is nothing compared to the hatred people lay on each other every day. That hatred is the devil's gift, and we must not accept it no matter how beautifully wrapped the package is.

"These days, we're more concerned about how big and flashy our church is than we are about what's being preached inside. They keep getting bigger and bigger, like the Tower of Babel — and we all know how that turned out." He laughed to himself and continued his impromptu sermon as though he was all but oblivious to her presence. She didn't mind. She liked watching his mouth move, they way his eyes fixed on her. "That's why my daddy preaches across the country, in tents and storefronts. It's not about filling all three balconies of a mega-church or giving a sermon in front of big-screen monitors wearing a headset and an Armani suit. Our preachers are more concerned with selling books of so-called Biblical dieting tips than offering salvation, and that, Lila, is taking the Lord's name in vain. It's vulgar and it misses the whole point of Jesus's message. All the love has been drained out of Christianity, and this church is going to put it all back in."

He set his Bible down and came back over to her, taking her hands. "That's the simple version of it. But today, when those boys were all gathered around, about to inflict violence upon me, I closed my eyes and I prayed for the strength to love each of them." He scrunched his eyes, closed hard, and opened them after a minute, smiling serenely. "And the Lord not only provided me with that love, he did me one better — he sent someone to protect me."

• • •

Climbing out of Owen's truck in front of her house on Orchid Street, Lila could already see her aunt's tall platinum hairpiece through the sitting room window. Lila pulled her cell phone out of the front pocket of her backpack. Five missed calls, all from her mother. She was late for dinner, and worse, she'd forgotten that Lyle and his parents were joining them.

Her mother met her in the hallway with a scowl, closing the French doors to the sitting room behind her. "Where have you been?" she hissed. "We're out of appetizers and dinner is getting cold."

"I'm sorry," she stammered. "I was studying with Michelle, I lost track of time."

Lila's mom looked down at Lila's dusty ankles, but just shook her head. "Wash up," she said. "We'll all be in the dining room."

Lila trudged upstairs to the bathroom and wet a washcloth in the sink. There was no one on earth she wanted to see less at that moment. She put on a clean pair of sandals and trudged back downstairs. From the way Lyle fidgeted in his stiff, high-backed dining-room chair, he felt the same way.

Lila picked at her fried okra and the strips of London broil on her plate, not looking at Lyle, thinking about Owen. "Anybody takin' you to the homecoming dance, Lila?" Her aunt interrupted her thoughts in her loud, shrill voice.

Lila looked up from her plate and quickly back down. "No," she murmured. "No one's asked me."

Her aunt pursed her lips. "Well," she said with polite curtness. "Maybe Lyle can ask Gary to take you. He's a very nice boy, and so handsome, and such a good ball player."

Lyle took a long sip of his Coke and from the way his eyes met Lila's, she knew he was thinking the same thing. They resumed dinner in silence, the chatter of the adults drifting over their heads, their parents oblivious to the tensions between them.

After dinner, their parents shuffled them outside, as though they were kids again. The backyard, once an oasis of childhood, had fallen trap to suburban polish. The swing set had long been dismantled, the turtle-shaped sandbox taken to the dump, the kiddy pool long drained and deflated. Her mother's Pink Double-Knockout Roses were beginning to drop their petals, like confetti after a parade.

The only remaining piece of their childhood was a tire swing dangling from a tree tucked into a back corner the neighbors couldn't see. Lila sat on the swing, pushing off with her feet half-heartedly. The memories of playing out here with Lyle were starting to soften with time but lacked the nostalgia or bittersweet longing present in seemingly everyone else's childhood recollections. When they'd turned to teenagers, things had changed so dramatically that any images from that past seemed dream-like, only half-remembered, and lacking sense or context. In seventh grade, Lyle joined the football team and suddenly he wasn't interested in playing tag with his girl cousin and the kids on Orchid Street. He teased and tormented the same kids he'd played kickball with every summer afternoon since he could walk; he shoved the weaker boys into lockers and strutted through the halls as though his football helmet was a king's crown.

Lyle tossed his football back and forth between his hands. "How do you know that new kid?" he asked.

"His name is Owen," Lila said. "He goes to my church."

"Seems like too much of a Jesus-freak for First Pres," Lyle joked. "Clutching that Bible and all."

"His dad's a preacher," she said. "And if I ever catch you picking on him again, I'll take on both you and Gary."

Lyle sighed and mocked a pass, shaking his head. "I'm sorry about that."

Lila stared at her mother's wilting roses and didn't respond. Lyle sighed and shoved his hands in the pockets of his khakis. "Gary's just that type, you know? A big dumb jock. What could I say; I just had to go with it. I was glad you showed up — you gave me an out before I did something I would have regretted."

"You're almost a grown man," Lila spat. "You shouldn't need a girl to come to your rescue."

He leaned against the tree and pushed the tire swing a bit. "You're right," he said. He grinned and changed the subject. "Maybe you should ask Owen to Homecoming," he suggested. "My dad's letting me take the car, I'll even give you a ride." He held out the football and she opened her hands for the pass. When the ball was firm in her hands, he winked and added, "But Cindy gets to sit up front, and there's no guarantee I'll be giving you a ride home."

"That's all right," Lila said, passing the ball back to him. "Owen's got his own wheels."

He tossed the football again. "It's a double date then?"

"Let me get a date first," she said. "But sure, I'd like that."

• • •

Lila and Owen had been lying on the floor of the Green Cathedral for the better part of an hour before Lila got up the courage to speak. "The Homecoming Dance is coming up," she said, staring up through the trees. "You think you'll go?"

Owen rolled his head so he was facing her and shrugged. "I don't know," he said. "I've never been to one."

"Really?" Lila said. In Harmon, not going to the Homecoming Dance was an admittance of outcast status, the high school equivalent of not belonging to a church. Even girls without dates went to the Homecoming Dance.

"The last high school I attended, back in North Carolina, was a Born-Again High School that outlawed dancing," he said. "And the year before that, I was part of a class of five hundred students in Northern Florida, so no one noticed me enough to ask. And the year before that I was in Memphis and, well, I don't even remember why I didn't go."

"How many high schools have you been to?" she asked.

"This is my third," he said. "My daddy takes off every August to go on the circuit, so he just leaves me with a different family each time. I was in eighth grade in North Carolina, it was his cousin Heather and her husband; in Florida, my Godparents and their four kids; and in Memphis, my grandmother, but she died that January and although he came back for the funeral, I was on my own for the rest of the year."

"Do you think you'll stay here when he gets back?"

Owen folded his hands behind his head and returned his gaze to the heavens. "I hope so," he said. "This is the first place that's ever felt like home."

• • •

Every weekday morning, Owen picked Lila up for school. They got coffee and donuts at The Donut Hut and he gave her a little sermon on the drive to school. They waited in the parking lot until the bell chimed eight exactly and, with much reluctance, went to their separate classes. The fifty-minute hours between the morning and lunchtime dragged by, and at lunch they staked their claim against a willow tree on the far edge of the field. Sometimes Owen would read his Bible aloud, and other times they would just talk about whatever came to mind.

The Thursday before Homecoming, they went to their usual spot to find Gary sitting there with his posse and an enormous "gotcha" grin on his face. "Gary, move," Lila demanded. "That's our spot."

"I don't see your name on it," he said.

Lila was about to snarl something back, but Owen took her hand. "Come on, darlin', we can sit on the bleachers. No need to be way out here; we're not lepers, after all."

Lila was impressed. Gary was insulted. He jumped to his feet and his friends repeated the gesture. He grabbed Lila's shoulder, but before she could shove off his hand, Owen brought his hardback Bible down on Gary's wrist. Gary spat out a torrent of blue words and gripped his forearm. "I have to play tomorrow, you Jesus-spouting jackass!"

"You touch her again and the hand of God will make sure you never play anything with more contact than tic-tac-toe," Owen spat back. "Come on, Lila. Lunch is almost over and I'm starving."

He guided Lila to turn her back and they began walking toward the bleachers, but Gary called after them. When they turned back, she saw that he and his two friends were pissing on their tree, laughing.

Owen shook his head and tried to continue moving forward, but Lila jerked back. "If I were you I wouldn't whip it out in public," she taunted. "You wouldn't want anyone staring at what you're practically missing."

If he hadn't been mid-stream, Gary probably would have come after her, but by the time he got his flow stopped and his pants zipped, Lila and Owen were almost to the bleachers. Neither of them could stifle their laughter.

•   •   •

They never made it to the Homecoming Dance. Instead they lay on a fleece blanket spread out on the floor of Green Cathedral, legs entwined, tongues gingerly exploring between wet lips, the skirt of her purple taffeta dress bunched up around her waist, exposing the French-panty cut of her nylons.

Lila had never given much thought to her virginity. For some girls, it was like a game of Hot Potato, something they wanted to give away quickly so they could move past the stigma. For others, it was a prized possession, something not to be surrendered until absolutely necessary. For Lila, it was like her appendix or her tonsils. It was a part of her, but not one that she needed or thought about. There were no plans for rose petals on white silk sheets, no fear of pain or blood. She understood sex as a concept; Harmon High School's abstinence-only education did little to cool the blood of teenagers and left most of them resorting to the internet, or worse, red-faced parents. She knew where to get birth control and condoms; she knew, in theory, all the moves from the back pages of a hundred *Cosmopolitan* magazines read at every pre-teen sleepover. But sex held no real appeal to her until she was lying on her back with Owen on top of her, hard through his suit pants, her panties damp, staring up at the stars and feeling more love, from Owen and his God, than she'd ever known in her life.

He rolled off her and sucked in a long, deep breath. "Have you ever read the 'Song of Songs' in the Old Testament?" he asked. She shook her head and he continued. "Smack dab in the middle of the Bible is this love poem between a man and a woman — 'my darling, I am yours and you are mine. Turn away your eyes, they make me melt...' Some scholars say that the man and the woman stand for Christ and the Church, but I like to think that it's just a love song." He folded his hands under his head. "Jesus just wanted us to love each other, every single one of us. Too many Christians are too concerned with abstinence and homosexuality and making pleasure seem like a sin worse than all seven deadlies combined. But they always forget about the 'Song of Songs,' this celebration of love and marriage and sex. 'Your breasts are perfect, they are like twin deer feeding among lilies, I will hasten to those hills'?" Come on, it's pure pornography. The Bible's filled with that sort of stuff, but people usually forget that in favor of the judgment and damnation."

And in that moment, Lila knew who she was giving her virginity to.

● ● ●

Studying history was boring enough, but studying when she wanted to be out with Owen was like lugging bricks to the top of the pyramids. Michelle always tried to make it like a slumber party, with BBQ chips and Dr Pepper and nail polish while they quizzed each other with flashcards, but there weren't enough distractions in the world to silence the slow chime of each passing hour on the grandfather clock in Michelle's living room.

Michelle offered her a ride home, but the evening was still warm and Lila liked staring at the stars, reflecting on the heaven Owen told her about every afternoon. She would text Owen and he would meet her in the high school parking lot so they could go up to the Green Cathedral and make love under the stars. She even had a blanket in her bag.

She packed up her bags and thanked Michelle's mother. Passing by Michelle's bedroom window, she could already hear Michelle on the phone to Mike, making plans for later that night. Lila smiled and took out her phone. *Meet me in 10.* Her texts were always grammatically correct; she hated shorthand and the vowel-less jumble of consonants that passed for her generation's language. Tower of Babel indeed.

She took the dirt path up through the tree line and across the backfield. She heard traffic on the street below, the thick sound of exhaust and revved engines. A vehicle pulled into the parking lot in front of the school. Lila picked up her pace.

Boots crunched on the dry ground behind her and before she could turn to see who it was, a wide fist clocked her across the jaw. She stumbled and saw Gary out of the corner of one watering eye. He grabbed her wrist and shoved her back against a willow tree, pressing his barrel chest against hers. His beery breath was hot in her face and she tried to turn her head away, but he grabbed her chin and squeezed until she was sure her back molars would pop out. "I could fuck you," he hissed, releasing her jaw. "But I don't stick my dick in livestock."

Lila spat blood into the dust. "That's not what your mama tells me."

He slugged her and she crumpled to the ground. He kicked her in the stomach and she clenched her eyes shut, determined not to let any tears spill out. He might kill her if she cried. He struck her in the shoulder twice and through the fight to stay conscious, she heard another set of footsteps. He'd brought the rest of his posse. Maybe he wasn't going to fuck her, but there was no guarantee that his friends wouldn't. She just hoped Lyle wasn't there with them, too drunk to recognize the girl face down on the ground as his own flesh and blood.

A hard thud sounded next to her and she opened one eye to see Gary lying there beside her. She rolled away and climbed up against the tree, wondering if he'd passed out. She tried to catch her breath, tried to focus her blurry eyes, tried to get her footing enough to run away. She felt her way around the tree's thick trunk, and then she saw Owen.

He was straddling Gary's lifeless body, lifting his hardback Bible and bringing the spine down hard on the back of Gary's neck. Blood oozed into the dirt. Gary moaned and Owen's breath came in great ragged gasps. Lila turned back around the tree so that he wouldn't see her when she retched.

When Gary was finally silent, Owen rose to his feet. He and Lila stumbled towards each other and she fell into his arms, his heart echoing hard and fast in his rib cage. She wasn't sure if the blood on his blue shirt was from her face or from Gary.

She was surprised he still had strength enough to pick her up, but she let him, her body too sore and limp to insist she could walk. He popped opened the truck door with his elbow and draped her over the seat. The seconds it took him to get in the driver's side felt like slow, half-slept hours. He started the car and she inched up so that her head was on his lap.

"What do we do now?" she moaned.

He stroked her hair and through her swelling eyes she saw him smile down at her. "The Lord will provide," he said, turning onto the highway, away from Harmon. "Don't you worry about a thing."

CONTRIBUTORS
AMERICAN FICTION VOL. 13

EDITOR

Bruce Pratt's novel, *The Serpents of Blissfull*, was published by Mountain State Press in April 2011. His 2007 poetry collection, Boreal, is available from Antrim House Books, and his short fiction, poetry, and drama have won numerous awards and have appeared in dozens of journals in the United States, Canada, and Europe. Pratt teaches creative writing at the University of Maine, and is past director of The Northern Writes New Works Project at Penobscot Theatre Company in Bangor. He lives with his wife, Janet, in Eddington, Maine.

FINALIST JUDGE

Michael White is the author of six novels: *Soul Catcher*, which was a *Booksense* and *Historical Novels Review* selection, as well as a finalist for the

Connecticut Book Award; *A Brother's Blood*, which was a New York Times Book Review Notable Book and a Barnes and Noble Discover Great New Writers nominee; *The Blind Side of the Heart*, *A Dream of Wolves*, and *The Garden of Martyrs*, also a Connecticut Book Award finalist and recently made into an opera. His latest novel, *Beautiful Assassin*, won the 2011 Connecticut Book Award for Fiction. A collection of his short stories, *Marked Men*, was published by the University of Missouri Press. White has also published more than fifty short stories in national magazines and journals, and he has won the Advocate Newspapers Fiction Award. He was the founding editor of the yearly fiction anthology, *American Fiction*, as well as *Dogwood*. White is the founder and director of Fairfield University's MFA Creative Writing Program.

AUTHORS

Jill Birdsall enjoys inspiration for writing at the lovely Shrewsbury River in New Jersey. Her short stories can be read in *Alaska Quarterly Review*, *Ascent*, *Chicago Quarterly Review*, *Crazyhorse*, *Doctor T.J. Eckleburg Review*, *Emerson Review*, *Gargoyle*, *Iowa Review*, *Painted Bride Quarterly Review*, *Potomac Review*, *Southern Humanities Review*, and *Story Quarterly*. An MFA graduate of Columbia University's School of the Arts, her recent awards include Eckleburg's Gertrude Stein Award and Potomac Review's Short Fiction Award. To read other stories written by Jill, please visit www. jillbirdsall.com.

Mathieu Cailler is the author of *Clotheslines* (Red Bird Press) and *Loss Angeles* (Short Story America Press). A graduate of Vermont College of Fine Arts, his work has been published in numerous national and international literary journals. He has been named a finalist for the Glimmer Train New Writers Award, and he won the Short Story America Prize for Short Fiction and the Shakespeare Award for Poetry. He lives in Los Angeles.

Carol Cooley is an essayist and short story writer. Her writing has appeared in numerous anthologies and magazines, including collections by Creative Nonfiction, SMU Press, and SUNY Press. She has received Honorable

Mentions from the North Carolina Literary Review and Glimmer Train Press, and is a contributing author to a CNF blog. She lives in Wake Forest, North Carolina where she writes, works as a healthcare professional, and leads writing workshops for adults and teenagers. She is currently working on a short story collection.

Libby Cudmore's stories and essays have appeared in *Big Lucks*, *The Big Click*, *Chamber Four*, *The Vestal Review*, *Pank*, *The Citron Review*, *Kneejerk*, *Connotation Press*, *Postcard Press*, *Umbrella Factory*, *The MacGuffin*, *The Yalobusha Review*, and *The Chaffey Review*, as well as *The Writer*, *Mixitini Matrix*, and *ARCANE II* (with Matthew Quinn Martin).

Marguerite Del Giudice is currently editing books and writing fiction from her home outside Philadelphia. She has been a national-award-winning newspaperwoman and Pulitzer Prize nominee for *The Boston Globe* and *The Philadelphia Inquirer,* and she's taught magazine writing at Temple University. Her work, which over the years has explored subjects ranging from the Mafia to UFOs to the meaning of life, has appeared in national publications and been translated worldwide, including cover stories for *The New York Times Magazine* and *National Geographic*. She also practices and teaches aikido, a Japanese martial art, in which she holds the rank of *sandan*, or third-degree black belt. "The Human Nature" is her first published work of fiction.

Lee Hope is the recipient of the Theodore Goodman Award for Fiction, a Pennsylvania Council on the Arts Fellowship, and a Maine Arts Commission Fellowship for Fiction. She has published stories in numerous literary magazines, such as *Witness*, *The New Virginia Review*, *The North American Review*, *Beloit Fiction Journal*, and *Epiphany*. She founded the Stonecoast low-residency MFA program, played an instrumental role in the creation of Pine Manor's MFA program, and was the director of a national writers' conference. She has taught creative writing at various universities. She is president of the Solstice Writers' Institute, a nonprofit organization in the service of creative writers. Lately, she teaches for Changing Lives Through Literature, an organization that brings literature to people on probation and parole.

Julia Lichtblau's writing has been published in *Narrative Magazine*, *The Florida Review*, *Best Paris Stories*, *Temenos*, *Ploughshares* Blog, and elsewhere. She was a finalist in the Narrative Winter 2013 Story Contest, won the 2011 Paris Short Story Contest, and 2nd Prize in *The Florida Review*'s Jeanne Leiby Chapbook Contest. She is Book Review Editor for *The Common*, was a journalist at *BusinessWeek* and Dow Jones in New York and Paris and has an MFA from Bennington College.

Beth Mayer's short fiction has appeared in *The Threepenny Review*, *The Sun Magazine*, and elsewhere. Her story "The Way to Mercy," was anthologized in *New Stories from the Midwest 2011* and was named among "Other Distinguished Stories" by Best American Mystery Stories 2010. Red Bird Chapbooks features a limited hand-bound edition of *Niagara Falls*, a story with footnotes. Mayer holds an MFA from Hamline University and teaches English at Century College. She lives with her husband, two teenagers, and their little dog in Lakeville, Minnesota.

Patricia Ann McNair's short story collection, *The Temple of Air* won the Chicago Writers Association Book of the Year in Traditional Fiction, the Devil's Kitchen Literary Festival Reading Award in Prose, and the Society of Midland Authors Finalist Award in Adult Fiction. The title story of that collection was named finalist in *American Fiction: Volume 10*. Her work has been published widely and has received numerous Illinois Arts Council Awards and Pushcart Prize nominations. McNair teaches in the Department of Creative Writing at Columbia College Chicago and is at work on a novel and a new collection of stories. Her work can be seen at www.PatriciaAnnMcNair.

Robin Mullet, a former CPA, realized the stories of her clients were more interesting than their budgets, so she turned to writing. She writes short fiction, poetry, and non-fiction articles. A member of the Ohio State Poetry Association, Academy of American Poets, and SCBWI, she is most proud to be one of the Pentapoets, five women writers who are each other's biggest cheerleaders and most productive critics. Short fiction and poetry are her favorite forms because they provide a snapshot of the seminal moments of our lives. She lives on the edge of Appalachia with her husband and their deaf dog, who has taught her resiliency.

Steven Ostrowski is a fiction writer, poet, playwright, and songwriter. His work has been published widely. His first novel, *The Last Big Break*, will be published by LVCA in 2014. He teaches at Central Connecticut State University.

Molly Power writes short stories and poems on her farm in Vermont, where she is easily distracted by her dogs, horses, goats, and comical chickens.

Leigh Camacho Rourks teaches at Southeastern Louisiana University, where she is also the assistant editor of *Louisiana Literature*. She was a finalist for the 2012 Tennessee Williams Fiction Prize, and her work has appeared or is forthcoming in *Split Infinitive*, *Kenyon Review*, and *Prairie Schooner*. She is currently finishing her first novel.

Terry Ruud was raised on a tiny farm outside of Gatzke, Minnesota (population 24), but soon uprooted himself and wandered off in search of Bohemia. He toured North America for years with various musical groups and lived a while in Nashville before returning to the Midwest and to Minnesota State University Moorhead, where he was paper trained in English Education and Creative Writing. He: writes poetry, prose, and songs; teaches English/ Humanities at M-State, Fergus Falls; plays acoustic-eclectic folk music with the Cat Sank Trio; lives in Dilworth, Minnesota, with his wife, daughter, and two dogs; and is happy enough.

Lynn Sloan has a master's degree in photography and her photographs have been widely exhibited. Her stories have appeared in *American Literary Review*, *Inkwell*, *The Literary Review*, *Puerto del Sol*, and *Sou'wester*, among other journals. Her work can be found at www.LynnSloan.com.

Madeline Wise grew up in Washington State and graduated from the University of Washington with a BS in nursing. She has attended writing workshops with Tom Jenks and Carol Edgarian. "Brush Strokes" is an old story. At the suggestion of writers in a recent critique group, she changed the voice from third person to first, and felt the protagonist come to life. Her stories have appeared in *Bryant Literary Review*, *North Atlantic Review*, *Palo Alto Review*, *Pleiades*, *Chaminade*, *The Storyteller*, *AIM*, *Caprice*, *Mobius*, *Windhover*, and other small magazines.

Dallas Woodburn, a 2013-14 Steinbeck Fellow in Creative Writing at San Jose State University, has published work in *The Nashville Review*, *The Los Angeles Times*, *Monkeybicycle*, *Family Circle*, *Ayris*, and *Louisiana Literature*, among others. Her short story manuscript was a finalist for the Flannery O'Connor Award for Short Fiction and her plays have been produced in Los Angeles and New York City. She has also been honored with the Glass Woman Prize, the Brian Mexicott Playwriting Award, a scholarship to attend the Key West Literary Seminar, and a nomination for the Pushcart Prize.

John Zdrazil spent half of his life in the Minneapolis suburbs and the other half teaching in a small town. Two of his stories, "Delegation" and "Notices," appeared in *The Lake Region Review*, and he won the inaugural Lake Region Arts Council Six-Word Novel Contest ("Kenny Rogers ruined my life — *again*"). He treats his novel-in-progress, *Age, Wisdom or Something Worse*, like a car that's fun to tinker with, though he has no intention of putting it on the road. He believes in graph paper, Flair pens, and good coffee and has earned degrees in Creative Writing *and* Mortuary Science, which explains a lot.

Yanshuo Zhang is a PhD student in East Asian Languages and Cultures at Stanford University. Born in Chengdu, China' in 1988, she came to the United States at the age of eighteen for college and has been pursuing higher education here ever since. Zhang has published two collections of literary writings in China and her English works have also been published in the United States. Her genre ranges from fiction to essays to poetry. Zhang is also an artist and her paintings have been exhibited at Stanford. She strives to be a creative and compassionate intellectual to help make this world a better place.

Timothy Zila was born and raised in Albuquerque, New Mexico, where he was homeschooled before attending the University of New Mexico and earning degrees in English and history. While there, he worked on a thesis comprised of six stories set in New Mexico, of which "High Life" is the eponymous piece. He spent his summer painting, observing the progress of an in-construction IMAX, and writing. He's preoccupied with memory, philosophy, and the writing of Flannery O'Connor and Pinckney Benedict. Zila is currently working on a collection of stories and a novel.

ABOUT NEW RIVERS PRESS

New Rivers Press emerged from a drafty Massachusetts shed in winter 1968. Intent on publishing work by new and emerging poets, founder C. W. "Bill" Truesdale labored for weeks over an old Chandler & Price letterpress to publish three hundred fifty copies of Margaret Randall's collection, *So Many Rooms Has a House But One Roof*.

Nearly four hundred titles later, New Rivers, a non-profit and now teaching press based since 2001 at Minnesota State University Moorhead, has remained true to Bill's goal of publishing the best new literature — poetry and prose — from new, emerging, and established writers.

New Rivers Press authors range in age from twenty to eighty-nine. They include a silversmith, a carpenter, a geneticist, a monk, a tree-trimmer, and a rock musician. They hail from cities such as Christchurch, Honolulu, New Orleans, New York City, Northfield (Minnesota), and Prague.

Charles Baxter, one of the first authors with New Rivers, calls the press "the hidden backbone of the American literary tradition." Continuing this tradition, in 1981 New Rivers began to sponsor the Minnesota Voices Project — now called Many Voices Project — competition. It is one of the oldest literary competitions in the United States, bringing recognition and attention to emerging writers. Other New Rivers publications include the American Fiction Series, the American Poetry Series, New Rivers Abroad, and the Electronic Book Series.

We invite you to visit our website, newriverspress.com, for more information.